UNCAGED

THE UNSPOKEN TRILOGY
BOOK TWO

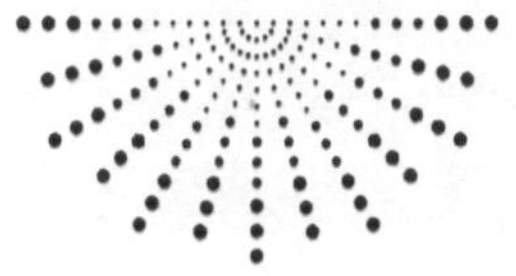

CELIA MCMAHON

CHAPTER ONE

Come closer. Let me look upon you. Oh, yes, I know you. Word has reached my ears. You are a legend. The princess who became a wolf. Now tell me, what could possess you to do such a thing? Oh, is he standing right behind you? Come closer. Let me look upon your face.

Light pierced through my eyelids as I stirred awake. I groaned and turned, shaking the dream-voice from my head. The smell of the fire from the night before burned my nostrils, igniting the remainder of my senses. The whistle of the wind. The taste of rabbit on my tongue. The battering of my panicked heart against my ribs.

I sat up as the slow steady rise of the sun lit the forest. My blanket froze overnight, so I shook it out and laid it over a nearby tree branch. I should go and find food, but my muscles ached and my head felt light. Instead, I sat against a tree in the snow, looking out at the mountains that encased me, and watched helplessly as a new day pulled me in.

We'd traveled for eight days through the Archway and into the mountains, leaving behind my old home of Stormwall, where, by now, Dal Paratheon and his son, Ashe, had taken the throne alongside the Voiceless Gwylis—cursed people of the Old Kingdom. Wolves. Where my mother fit into all of this remained to be seen. She had been alive when I last saw her, knocked unconscious by my own hand. My father died by my teeth. I never thought about him. I still didn't. But I did remember.

I wished I could forget them. When I'd gone to Wargrave—the skanky shop owner of the Barge—I'd hoped that when I became a wolf, my past would be erased. As if everything up until the moment Aquarius bit me would have been nothing but a bad dream. But just looking at my reflection made it impossible to push the memories aside. And the dreams got worse as the days went on.

It was always the same. I'm walking through a deep cave and there's a pool of water and the voice—the voice says the same thing over and over again, and I can't make it stop. I see shadows lurking in the corners of my vision—quick and gone before I turn my head. Before my cousin Lulu died, she told me that she'd had the very same dream. Only it never finished for her. I wondered how long it would be before I heard everything the woman's voice had to say.

I swallowed, sniffed the air, and watched the sun rise. Despite my muscles' objections, I pushed to my feet and headed into the woods.

The snow was about knee-deep in some places and took a bit of effort to push through. I went slow. There were predators out there. Bears. Wildcats. Even wolves. But it didn't matter anymore. Back in my old life, it would matter, but now it was different. Now they were afraid of me.

"Lulu," I said into the frosty morning air. "Henry."

The names of my cousin and brother brought life when life was no longer there. I was afraid that if I didn't say it often enough, they would fade away, lost in time and memory.

Lulu. Henry.

I wished I could forget.

But I couldn't. Somewhere out in the Old Kingdom, Henry took his last breath, both as a human and a Gwylis. He may have showed me what our father had done, but I had to know how my brother had come to the decision of betraying his flesh and blood. There was so much I didn't know.

My boots crunched along the ground. Henry's old wrapped boots. I clutched the emerald necklace at my neck, letting the familiarity of my brother's gift calm my nerves. I walked until I came to a spot by a river that cut horizontally through the range of mountains. Fray was there, bent over our doused fire, watching the smoke rise into the trees. I noticed our horse was already packed and saddled. Fray looked tired. With my mind as scattered as it was, he'd done more than pull my weight alongside his own.

I took in the moment of Fray, unaware of my presence until I remembered what he was. His clear blue eyes locked onto mine, and I instantly drowned.

"Izzy," he said. Still a man of few words.

Fray Castor used to be a Voiceless, but because of Pyrus' cure, he'd regained his voice. Each and every day since, it still made my heart skip a beat. My name on his lips was like honey. When he looked at me, I was reminded of the tiny vials in my pack. One cured an affliction. One took a life.

I smiled, took his face in my hands, and pushed aside strands of hair from his eyes and the bridge of his nose. His hair had grown unruly—he refused to let me properly comb it out—and a shadow of stubble ran the length of his jawline and upper lip. I kissed him, and a warmth ran through my body. He pulled me closer, locking me in his arms. The tightness in my chest loosened. When I was with him, everything felt all right. He took away the voices, if only for a little while.

"How are you?" he asked when we pulled apart. His words were smoke in the chill air. He looked into my eyes, but I couldn't seem to meet his. "Dreams again?"

"I don't really understand it," I told him. I watched the river take an old log downstream and swallowed the lump building in my throat. I wished he'd never asked. "It's like it's trying to tell me something, but I don't get it." I shrugged. "That's it. I don't get it."

"Do you want to talk about it?"

I knew what he meant. It was more than a simple question with a simple answer. What he wanted to know was what I'd seen painted across his face the very moment I'd climbed the stage where he was to be executed. What he wanted to know was how I had created the barrier that surrounded us—that ultimately saved us from the barrage of arrows set to kill the man I loved.

I had used magic; I knew this well. But it was a magic that seemed to scare Fray and, in turn, scare me.

I pondered day after day how to talk about it, how to tell Fray about Aquarius and how I'd come to know the old wolf that Wargrave kept in his cellar. But that would mean I would have to talk about Wargrave, which led to my dear cousin Lulu and all the things that hurt my heart to remember. To speak of the life before we'd crossed through the Archway was speaking of a world that no longer existed. My life was stitched together with a hundred memories of things I wanted to forget. Though I knew the time would come, today was not that day.

Fray waited for me to answer as long as he could. Eventually he dropped his eyes, pressing his lips together like he was holding in something he wanted to say.

"I'm sorry," I whispered. Shame burned my cheeks. How many times had I done this—made Fray feel as though I was as fragile as glass so that he felt like he had to sidestep around my feelings? "I promise when we settle, I will tell you everything I know," I said, "and we can figure out the things I don't."

"Maybe when we get closer to my home, we can find out."

Closer to Fray's home meant cutting through some dangerous terrain, avoiding the main roads, some of which my father and his men had taken. Some of which may still be occupied by Mirosa's army. But traveling the woods was easy. I felt at home in them, more so now than ever before.

Somewhere deep in the mountains was Fray's old pack. They lived in a place Fray called the Den, which Fray described as an area that overlooked a large crystalline lake where everybody knew each other's names. I smiled at that last bit. It seemed like a good place to put down roots. He mentioned in passing how unreachable it was by human feet, especially during this time of year, when the snow piled on inches almost every day. The sun would melt it and more would come, and some days there wasn't any sun at all, leaving the ground high and frozen. Not at all treacherous for wolf paws, though I preferred to stay in my human form. I knew there were still Mirosian armies out there who hadn't yet heard of what happened. Better safe than sorry.

I wondered if Fray feared the Den was no longer standing. His reluctance to even answer direct questions about his home led to more silences than necessary. I wished I could take some of his burden and add it to my own, since it weighed me down anyway. The unknown path that lay ahead of me branched out a hundred different directions. One wrong choice, and I'd lose everything. But when I felt that tang of fear, I remembered that Henry had come through this land. If he could do it, so could I.

"Are you hungry?"

I shook my head and felt his arms wrap around my body. A soft voice in my ear said, "Liar. You're always hungry."

He had a point. I'd probably kill for some of the palace's baked delights, but as with all things, I forced myself to forget them. Maybe the Den would have bakers just as good, but for now, I would stick to eating campfire meat. Maybe as a wolf, I'd find the taste of undercooked meat a little more satiable. But I wasn't ready to try.

Fray held me tighter, and all thoughts of my former life vanished. "We're going to get through it," he said.

I held him to that.

THE RIVER WAS FREEZING, BUT I DIDN'T FEEL IT. I STRIPPED NAKED and bathed the best I could. After, I pulled on my riding pants, tunic, cloak, and lastly my braided leather boots—Ashe's boots from when Fray made him relinquish them so we could get away. They bore extra scuffs and some blood. I wondered whose blood it was. I couldn't be sure. It felt eons ago.

A sudden shiver rippled through me and turned my attention across the river's edge. Something moved: a disturbance of underbrush too heavy to be the wind, but I could not discern its origin from this distance. A deer or some other woodland creature that would or would not end up on a stick on our campfire? The scent of the animal replaced all others and filled my nostrils. I inhaled it into my lungs, tasting it on my tongue, and found it not to be prey. A strange warning crawled inside of me. Crouched down, I watched the figure come. It materialized like a ghost from the feathery, snow-packed branches and stopped just along the river's edge.

There stood a massive wolf, its fur black as my own, its tail longer than the length of my own body. There was snow crusted over the top of its head, forming a crown. There was gray on his chest.

The word caught in my throat. Gwylis.

Its eyes were bright yellow.

It was watching me.

I rose slowly, setting my shoulders back. Could it smell me? Did it know that I wasn't human?

It stared at me for a moment longer before its ears pricked, showing me that it was well aware of my presence. Then, without a sound, it turned and disappeared into the skeleton trees. Did it know that I was one of them?

Was it on our side?

I found Fray back at our camp, adjusting the saddle on our horse, his hood pulled over his head. He was hard at work pulling the straps tight when I came up beside him.

"I think we're being followed," I said.

He turned, the hood obstructing one half of his face. "I know. He's been tracking us since we left Stormwall."

I eyed Fray suspiciously. "He has? There's no way . . . why didn't you tell me?"

"Because he's not a threat. Honestly, I thought he'd die by now." He let out a quick laugh. "Must be hard hunting with one arm."

I stepped back, confused. "What?"

Fray turned his entire body to me and frowned. "Prince Paratheon." He narrowed his eyes. "Wait. You're not talking about him?"

"No." I shook my head, still confused. "No, Fray, I wasn't." I looked away, still shaking my head. My thoughts returned to this new revelation that Ashe was following us. How had he survived out here all alone? He should be dead, and I'd be glad for it.

I blew out a gust of air, exasperated. Despite all that, I wished he hadn't done such a foolish thing like following us through the Archway. For some reason, I wished he was safe. "A wolf," I finally said. "I saw a wolf on the river's edge."

Fray raised his eyebrows and nodded knowingly. "The pack," he says. "No need to worry. They probably sensed us long ago. It's a good sign."

"How so?"

He turned to me, squinting against the sun. "It means they're still alive."

That was one good thing, at least. "Well, what do we do about Ashe?"

Fray tightened the last of the straps and shook his head before putting one foot in the stirrup and swinging a long leg over the seat. He gripped his reins and gave a heavy sigh. "He's good as dead, Izzy. Especially if the Gwylis find him. Unless you want me to—"

"No," I said. He was right. If the Gwylis didn't kill him, then the elements would.

LATER THAT EVENING, AFTER WE'D BUILT A FIRE AND CAUGHT supper, I sat between Fray's legs, staring at the fire, drifting in and out with my head tucked in the space between his chest and shoulder. Fray said I'd get used to the sensitive hearing, but for now, every branch snapping and every rustle of leaves sounded as if they were right by my ears.

"You said you knew the wolf whose head was staked in front of the castle gates," I said. "What was his name?"

Fray shifted. "Why do you want to know that?"

"Because he was important to you, and I'd like to know his name."

"His name was Jonai," Fray said in a tight voice. He trembled a little, and I pretended not to notice.

"How long did you know him?"

"Only a year or two. He'd been living in Stormwall quite a while by then. He'd avoided the Voiceless poison by fleeing past the Archway during the war. He'd avoided much up until that point. But he was like many—torn between his two worlds. He liked the speed of the wolf and the feelings of being human."

"Never both at once?"

"Always both at once."

Fray was quiet for a while. I listened to the fire crackle and the wind make the branches tap against the trees. He locked his fingers into mine with tight strength. I'd been careless with his heart. I needed to be better.

"Will you tell me about your people?" I asked. He knew all about my own family, so it only seemed fair.

"What do you want to know?"

I turned so that I was facing him. I studied the lines of his face and planted a soft kiss to his lips, finally turning his near-constant frown upward. "Everything."

"I'd have to go pretty far back, but I'll keep it brief."

Fray was still familiarizing himself with talking. He did in small bursts, and only after much thought of how he'd form the words. Which is why I knew that when he spoke, it was from his heart. He never said anything just to say it. It all meant something to him. Maybe more than I would ever realize.

"Long ago," he began, "we were all children of the gods. They blessed us with their powers, entrusted us, and with them we built cities and ideas. We fashioned weapons for hunting, formidable and ever-lasting. We imbued them with magic. We mixed potions and healed. We could speak to the animals. It was a small magic, but it was good. It was safe.

"And then men grew to want more. The lust for power drove them through the mountains into the place you call the New Kingdom. There, they found new gods to worship, but their magic waned because the gods had warned against leaving the land of creation. For that, they took away their magic, leaving them to their own devices. After, they grew bitter at the gods and vowed to destroy magic altogether. Thus the wars that brought your people to mine.

My father hated magic. My grandfathers sought out to erase it from history. As generations passed, nobody would remember it. By the time it came to me, the thought was a mere fantastical story in a child's book. It did not exist. But it was the idea that some small part of it did. This was what drove him deeper and deeper into the Old Kingdom: to wipe out the existence of the ancient gods. And of the people we used to be."

I recalled the words of Farrell, the old librarian in The Barge. *Different than you and I. But once the same.*

"After the reign of Aquarius and the deal with the Uncanny," Fray continued, "the gods decided that we were lost and abandoned us too. We used to be able to heal each other, make the flowers grow, and create music and art. We traded our small magic for something far more destructive." Fray paused briefly. "We used to look at the moon and see magic. People like your father looked and saw power. We no longer have the abilities to better the world. Only ruin."

"Do you believe that?" I asked, repeating what I had asked Farrell. "Do you believe they truly sold their souls?"

Fray's eyebrows sank down low over his eyes. He looked at me as though nobody had ever asked the question before. Maybe they hadn't. "I think we all failed in the gods' eyes. New and old alike."

It wasn't the answer I wanted, but it was the one that made the most sense.

I remembered looking out my balcony window toward the mountains to a place as unknown as the meaning of a dream, yet I knew I belonged there. I thought it was so infinite that there must be room for me. I knew I'd been naïve. Was I still? To think that the world could be fixed with one choice, by one small person who looked at things from a different angle, who asked the right questions? Would things ever get better? Could the gods forgive us for what we'd done?

Could we still be saved?

Sudden fear spread through me. What would we find at the Den? I knew by looking at Fray that the Gwylis could not all be wicked. But I'd seen the shadows creeping in the dark corners of the world, slipping in and out of my vision. What if the Uncanny affected people differently? What if they took one look at me and killed me?

"Izzy?"

I realized I'd been so lost in thought that I forgot to blink. Or even breathe.

Fray framed my face with his hands and drew me closer. "Please, don't worry. You're worrying too much."

Was I? I smiled despite the doubt inside of me and kissed him until they melted away.

In my mind, I saw nothing but him, and I let my body sink into the warmth his touch brought me. I trained my ears to the rustle of leaves, to the sounds of animals in the underbrush . . . anything other than the thoughts in my head. With my eyes still shut, I brought his hard, calloused hand down from my cheeks to my waist. This the thing I was sure of. The thing I would never question.

He laid down, and I tucked myself against him, our bodies linked.

My sleep was surprisingly peaceful.

Until I woke to what sounded like a hundred wolves howling.

I felt Fray move out from beside me. His arm that once held me tight went for the sword that he'd lain beside us. A few heartbeats passed before the black of the woods was lit by hundreds of glowing eyes. I sat up slowly, taking a stance behind Fray, my hands on his waist.

"Care to wager a bet that whether or not this is your estranged family?" I whispered.

"Let me do the talking, Izzy," Fray replied.

"So, what are you wagering?"

"Izzy, please."

His answer did nothing to stop the panic from rising in my chest. I walked in step with Fray, keeping behind him like a shadow. My own dagger was in its sheath on the horse. With how unstable I was with my newfound magic, I wished I'd brought it for a sense of familiarity, if nothing else.

"I think you've come far enough," came a low grumble.

A Gwylis shed the darkness and came into view. It was the black wolf with the gray chest that I'd seen earlier that day. He was so much bigger up close. He stalked slowly to where we stood, sniffing the air. He made no threatening movements, yet he didn't seem overly comfortable in our presence. Snow fell, dotting the wolf with specks of white.

As it approached, I had to remind myself of who I was. *I am Isabelle Victoria Rowan and I will kill you if you try to kill us.*

With every beat that passed, I began to think about Stormwall. Though I'd been trying to will myself to be calm, anger began to simmer just under my skin. I remembered the way the Gwylis tore through my home, how they obeyed the commands of a foreign king. I felt the sting of the arrow they'd shot me with. The screams of the innocent. The sounds of gnashing teeth and thundering storm clouds.

I am a Gwylis now. But I will never forget.

"Brother," Fray said, lowering his sword. "I don't mean harm."

The wolf's chest quaked. "How do you speak?" he asked. "What magic is this? What devils did you conjure?"

"Not magic. Just a simple potion of—"

"You smell of death," the wolf said. His voice was so cold that I began to tremble. Good or bad? Good or bad?

"I've been through quite a lot," Fray said, simplifying his answer.

The wolf lowered his head. And then shifted his yellow eyes from Fray. His ruff bristled. Bent low, he uttered a growl from his open maw. Fray swung both hands behind his back, locking me in.

"She's with me," he said. He spread his legs apart and repeated it through gritted teeth. "She's with me."

The wolf growled, this time louder and fiercer. "She reeks of royalty," he snarled. "We do not allow her kind here. Wolf or not."

"She is my responsibility," Fray said. "And you can't make us go."

"What is her name?" a voice said.

"Yes, tell us your name, sweet thing," another voice chided.

Sweet thing? "I am Isabelle Victoria Rowan, and I am a Gwylis like you," I snapped. "Don't talk to me like a child, or I'll—"

"Stop!" The black wolf stepped forward, quicker this time, full of purpose. The wolves between the trees began to shuffle and growl. It sounded like a storm of teeth and rustling underbrush. I felt them move away. Recoiling from my name, no doubt. Would they kill me then? Hold me accountable for my father's actions? Was it just as I feared?

How naïve I was. I was in a world I could not control.

I found the black wolf staring straight at me. As hard as it was to glean any sort of expression from an animal, I could at least see that he was not snarling at me; instead, his look bordered more on curiosity than murder. I let Fray's hands drop from their grip, and I stepped out from behind him. It wasn't until the wolf broke contact with me that I realized Fray's whispers under his breath.

No.

Fray's transformation knocked me back. For the third time since we'd been together, he became an oversized brown wolf, broad and muscular and filled with power beyond my understanding. He was incredibly handsome despite the bloodthirsty snarls curling from his throat. A blue glow emanated from his paws as ice crystals collected on the ground with each step he took. He snapped at the other wolf and lunged, pinning him to the earth in a sudden flurry of fur and roars.

"Please, stop! Don't hurt him!" I screamed the words, not even sure who I directed them toward.

The other wolf threw Fray off and scrambled to his feet. He backed away toward the tree line, toward the advancing wolves behind him, his jaw dripping with saliva.

I stood back, my chest heaving, wondering whether I should change or let this unfold without me. It became clear the longer the two wolves stood facing off that neither was going to kill the other.

"You could never stay human for long, Castor," said the black wolf. "Always more wolf than human and not very well-mannered."

Fray's entire body seemed to tremble. The other wolf pawed the ground. Both turned away. Whatever passed between them was fleeting, but not so quick that I did not take notice that their relationship was storied and somehow dropping in contempt.

Fray shook his ruff, saliva flinging from his open maw. "Such are we all."

"We forbid what you've done, Castor," said the wolf. "She will look upon you for only a second before casting you away."

Fray bristled at this. "I did not bite her, Olio."

Olio, as he was called, raised his head, his body tense. "Who changed her?" His stare drifted from Fray to me and stayed there. "Who changed you, girl?"

Fray stared at me, agonizingly long. He didn't need to be human to read the look. *It's time to talk about it, Izzy.*

I stepped forward. "I was changed by a wolf called Aquarius," I said. "Back in Stormwall in a place called the Barge—"

A strange sound erupted from Olio's chest. A laugh? "Aquarius is long dead, girl. It won't do you good to lie to me." He cocked his large head. "First impressions and all."

Fray let out a puff of air. "That's impossible."

"I assure you, Aquarius is very much alive," I insisted. I thought of the great wolf's pathetic state in the cellar of Wargrave's Wears and lowered my gaze. "More or less."

"She lies!" a voice said through the darkness. A dozen more called out the same. Olio called for quiet, and for a moment there was nothing but the sound of our own breathing.

I shook my head, unsure of why everyone was reacting the way they were. I set my gaze on Olio. "I did what I had to do," I snarled, then looked into the woods at the wolves watching me from the shadows. "And you don't get to call me a liar. You don't know me at all!"

"Which is why we don't trust you," Olio said coolly.

Fray bristled. "I trust her."

Olio laughed. "But I don't trust you, Castor, so that doesn't hold up much, does it?"

My eyes danced between the two wolves. I'd been so selfish to not give a thought to whether or not Fray would be welcomed back home. I'd only thought of myself. Now, there was a chance we'd both be cast away for separate crimes. Why did we come here? We could leave now. There was still a chance . . .

After a tense minute of deciding which direction to run, Olio finally spoke up. "Come here," he demanded.

"I will not," I said, undeterred. "You cannot tell me what to do."

Olio seethed, his head sweeping up and down. "Can't I? You are on my land, need I remind you?"

I started to speak but thought better of it. I walked until I was beside Fray. He lowered his head so I could rest my hand on his muzzle.

"Is it true?" he asked, softly.

"Yes, but—"

Olio coughed. "I don't have all day."

I moved forward, conjuring all the courage I kept reserved for moments like this, and stopped inches from Olio, close enough to feel his breath on my skin. I stood, looking up at his massive height, and exhaled. I was exhausted, mind, body, and soul. I yearned for a soft place to sleep. Maybe this pack could give it to us.

"Is she telling the truth?" asked another wolf from the darkness.

Olio's upper lip twitched. "She can't be."

I held out my arms, inviting him closer. "Wrong. Try again."

A tense moment passed.

"Well, is she?" barked another.

Olio dipped his head, taking in my scent. When he met my eyes again, my heart stuttered. His ears suddenly stood stick-straight, and his muzzle wrinkled. Even before he spoke, the message was clear.

They were going to kill me.

CHAPTER TWO

"**Y**ou can't, and you know it."

Fray stepped between me and Olio, nudging me away with his great muzzle. This wasn't going well at all.

Olio peeled back his lips, revealing bone white teeth. "Castor, we don't need trouble," he said. "I'll give you a head-start. Think of it as a parting gift." Some of the other Gwylis huffed in laughter. "But if we catch you, we kill you."

I put distance between us, clumsy on my feet. A thousand heart-beats went by before anyone spoke again. Darkness slithered across my vision as I began my chant, my mind made up to fight or die—the most natural feeling for me now.

I stood, steeling myself, legs spread shoulder-width apart, hands balled into fists, my body suddenly hot as flames. "You touch him, and I will rip out your throat and swallow it whole," I said carefully, quietly, pausing my change, waiting for a reprieve. I didn't want to kill anyone, but I'd done so before and would again if it meant keeping Fray and myself safe. "It's not cake, but it'll do fine."

There was a burst of smoke in the cold air as Olio exhaled. "I like you," he said with a laugh. I wasn't sure if I believed him, but he took no threatening stance toward Fray or myself. I seemed to have impressed him somehow. The other wolves either hadn't heard his order or chose to disobey, because they stayed in the shadows. Some eyes flashed in and out. Were they cowering?

"If she is a daughter of Aquarius, the queen will never accept her," Olio stated.

"Why?" I asked boldly, the heat in my body still raging. "I'm just like you. Maybe a little better looking."

Olio uttered a husky laugh and sat back onto his haunches. He seemed to observe me with new eyes. I felt different suddenly, as if the promise of a fight sparked the old Izzy—the one who faced everything with snark.

Within a split second, Olio's wolf form evaporated, shrinking and melting away into a human—a completely naked one, lean and tall, a few years older than I with hair just as long as my own. "You are not like me," he said, knowing something I didn't, and turned away toward the trees. "You're not like any of us."

"What does that mean?" I asked. I turned to Fray, who was back in human form and dusting himself off.

"It means you've been bitten by one of the most powerful Gwylis to ever walk this land," he responded coolly. "The very first Gwylis, to be exact."

I met Fray's eyes with abject shock. "The first Gwylis?" I asked, my voice half surprised, half angry. "The very one who—"

"Made the deal with the Uncanny?" Olio finished, still out of sight. "The one and only."

Fray sighed. I prepared myself for a tongue-lashing. Gods, I deserved it. I let the Gwylis king bite me! The powers Aquarius must hold . . . the powers I now held that I still didn't know anything about— they could be depthless. My head began to spin.

But instead of anger, Fray chose understanding.

"Izzy didn't know, and if she did, I'm sure she'd do it all over again the very same way."

I smiled. Understanding and a little bit of snark.

"Castor?" Olio stepped back into view. He wore pants and nothing else. Small victories. "I don't have all night."

Fray furrowed his brow and nodded reassuringly. I went to my horse, but Olio cut in, saying "Leave the horse, you won't need it," so I retrieved my pack, my dagger, and my bow, and by the light of the moon, we followed the pack into the woods.

I clung to Fray's arm. For the first time since Fray had been captured, there was true fear gripping my heart. Never once had I thought that I'd be in danger amongst the Gwylis, but I still bore the Rowan name. How could I expect anything less than pure hatred at the sight of me?

Olio lingered behind the rest of the pack, close enough to see his outline but far enough away for me to whisper to Fray as we wound our way through the forest that carpeted the mountains running north. None of Henry or Fray's stories could have prepared me for such an uninhabited land. Though I hadn't been outside of Stormwall, I knew the New Kingdom spread out west in lush country of hills and snaking rivers. Deserts rolled out in the south, sand like a crawling ocean, and cities jutted out like mountain peaks, built up and up. Never would I have thought the snowcapped mountains that separated both kingdoms were as monstrous as they were. After eight days out here, I expected more. What did my father see in this place?

"Aquarius was exiled, wasn't he?" I asked Fray, who kept pace behind me.

"Not in the way you think," he replied. "He banished himself. You see, he thought what he was doing was good, but he changed his mind."

"How can you change your mind about such a thing?" To make sure an enormous choice for your own people and then turn your back on them was something I could not fathom doing. What had been going through Aquarius's mind?

"Because he was still human," said Olio.

Wolf hearing. Great.

"And because of that, we're susceptible to the weakness of the human race," Olio continued. He stopped so we could catch up to him. He was a lean man, all legs and torso. He had wild but clever dark eyes that locked onto me when I spoke, like he was actually listening, but liking him was very much up in the air at that point. He certainly did not look at me as if I were royalty. In his eyes, I was probably less than the dirt between his paws.

"Greed," he said. "Lust. Jealousy. Love. Regret."

"Love is not a weakness," I said.

"It is. Some mistake lust for love so often." He stopped and waited for my reaction. I gave none, but he reiterated anyway, "It is."

I rolled my eyes, unable to take anything Olio said to heart. He walked ahead again. "Okay, so Aquarius regretted the deal with the Uncanny. Did he need to isolate himself in the cellar of a crazy old man?"

Olio stopped walking again and looked at Fray. "You didn't tell her?" Olio asked him.

I loathed when people talk about me as if I weren't standing right there. "Tell me what?"

"I haven't exactly had my voice for very long," Fray said defensively. He gave Olio a pointed look.

"It's not my fault you sided with the wrong pack, Castor. You all wanted to fight that king so badly, and he poisoned your tails." He gave a look that said, *You more than deserved it.*

"I don't understand," I said.

"Tell her," Olio replied and walked ahead. "You've got your voice. Use words like a big boy."

I looked to Fray. "You don't want to tell me?"

Fray sighed. "Listen, here's the gist of it," he said tightly as we began walking again. "Two packs emerged after the deal with the Uncanny. One wanted to fight, and the other didn't. Olio is right. People change their minds all the time, and so it happened here."

All of this I knew, to an extent. The Gwylis had been fractured. Those who fought my father later bowed to him and soon integrated into life in the New Kingdom. Some even acted as palace servants.

I thought of Crim then, and my heart sank into my stomach. He had fought with Aquarius. All those who lost their voices had. That meant that the pack we were now headed to meet had avoided such a fate. There would be no Voiceless.

They would all be wolves.

Olio cleared his throat, bringing me back from my thoughts. Fray continued speaking: "The pack led by Aquarius was eventually poisoned by your father and lost their voices, rendering their power useless, so they gave in. The other pack fled, hidden away. That's the one we're going to, and it's led by my mother."

He stopped and took my arms as his words started to process, albeit slowly. I was almost certain that I imagined them.

"Your mother . . ." My voice caught and vanished. I mouthed the next words—*is Rixon?*

The fire woman.

I'd seen her once. She walked out of the old crone Abiyaya's fireplace, cloaked in flames as if she were created from it. She and the soothsayer had spoken more than once, I assumed, by the familiarity of their encounter. Her magic was strong. She was the queen.

"She's the one who turned you when you were a baby," I said, my words broken.

Fray came up close, putting his forehead to my own. His face was a heap of emotion, and my stomach sank at the thought of him feeling pain.

I didn't want to hate Rixon, but I did.

"Izzy."

I curled my hands into fists, then slowly relaxed them. "Fray, it's all right."

"I'm sorry that I didn't tell you." He ran a hand through his hair. Some of it fell into his eyes. "I'm unprepared for all of this."

"I know." I pressed my body close to his as the sound of Olio clearing his throat sounded from the shadows. *He's sorry for withholding information, but I've done the same.* "There's time for everything, isn't there?"

Fray nodded, his lips meeting my skin in the place between my neck and shoulder. "Yes, there's time."

WE WALKED FAR FROM OUR CAMP THROUGH THE MOUNTAIN PASSES toward a steep cliff overlooking a great lake. It was not the sea and its salty air, but I could still smell the crisp water—even under the layer of ice—just as well as I could smell the pine from beneath the snow-drenched trees.

When Aquarius had changed me into a Gwylis, I had no time to learn everything there was to know. Fray was still trying to remember his power for himself. I couldn't expect him to teach me. There were times when I'd forget that I was different. Until the smells or the sounds and the burning way my heart tugged me into the wild woods to stand atop a cliff and stare at the moon.

We descended the cliff, heading east, keeping the lake within my peripheral. I wondered what it was like in the summer months. I wondered what it would be like to swim in it as a wolf. But just like every other instance of wondering who I now was, I pushed it back into the furthest reaches of my mind. *One step at a time, Izzy.*

"Where are we going?" I asked.

"The Den," Olio replied, pointing off into the distance. "Just over that rise." He grinned, and added, "Princess."

He darted out of reach of Fray's flying fist, disappearing into the darkness ahead.

"I really don't like him," Fray said. "Never have."

The trail declined as we rounded a corner, further down the dark, rocky path. I caught a glimpse of our destination briefly as the path bent and turned. A tower in the distance, lit by torches, smoke rising into the night. And then the voices of the Gwylis who had gone ahead.

No, not voices. Howls.

A few minutes more of descending the winding path, and we came to it at last. The Den, a compound surrounded by a massive wall of stone, crowned the top of a slope with hundreds of burning torches all around it. Though small from this distance, I felt the imposing crush of this place. Watchtowers jutted up like spearheads from the walls, and I could make out figures moving atop them. The full moon rose overhead, a sentinel in the star-spattered sky.

I'd imagined what Fray's home would look like, but my imaginings were nothing like this. Compared to the visions I'd had of it, this was so much more exotic. I could feel the excitement warming Fray's skin and the jarring way he flinched his eyes. This was the first time he'd been home in years. Everything about it must have felt familiar. Yet not.

I looked back at the dark forest, jarred by its stillness and by what laid ahead.

Olio appeared at Fray's side. "Still want to go see Mommy?"

Fray shifted as if he were cracking his back and nodded, serious despite the humor in Olio's tone. He looked to me, his eyes smiling in a way that I knew was forced. He studied the sight for a moment longer before descending the slope.

There wasn't much space between the ridge and the entrance, so we all moved single file. Olio and his men became clearer as we approached the bright light of the torches. They were all shirtless, lean, and toned. It was their eyes that startled me. Clear and bright and wild. Just like Fray's.

They stop at the gate, where Olio pounded both fists rapidly against the wood as if he were playing drums. Soon, there were dozens on fists drumming back at him, a chorus paired with yelps and hollers.

"Open up, Kap!" Olio called out.

"Not until you yelp like a pup!"

The male's voice came from above, some fifty feet in the air. A face came into view, hanging upside-down. A child, but there was no telling how young.

"Who's that with you?" the boy asked. He twisted, peering down, and suddenly threw down what appeared to be a torch. The second it landed, it burst, flame and embers filling the space between me and the gate. I hopped back as the air erupted in a chorus of enthused yips. "We got a new girl and—" He hung down so far that I thought he was going to fall to his death, "—shit. Open the gates!"

"Welcome home," Olio said as he swept past us. The massive doors groaned as they opened, like a beast opening its mouth to swallow us whole.

From a distance, the Den seemed like a mystery. But once inside its walls, it was a different story.

We were led inward by Olio. As we took our first steps into the city, I could feel hundreds of eyes on me, like I was a horse at an auction. Small buildings lined the main road—homes by the look of them— dozens of cooking fires sending smoke into the night sky like diabolical ghosts. It was quiet save for the whispers that followed in our wake. I tried to block them out, but it was no use. They asked who we were. They wondered if we were a threat. I couldn't blame them for their suspicions. I'd be wary of a princess turned wolf, too.

As we moved inward, I caught the distant sound of music and a woman singing sweetly. The rhythm started slow and then quickened. The voice accompanying the song grew into a haunting keening that goose-pimpled my skin. She sounded broken. She sounded sad.

"This way," said Olio in a bored voice. He led up through the center of town to a looming structure with double towers that stretched into the night sky. I'd forgotten all about the music as I stared. A pair of iron-bound wooden doors caught my eyes as we passed. Was I expecting someone to come out and greet me? The building did look like a smaller version of the palace in Stormwall. Far be it to house its own royalty.

"That's where my mother lives," Fray said, glowering up at the structure. He blinked away a fleeting memory. "It's been a long time."

"She's not here." A brawny man moved from the shadows of the towers. A guard.

Olio scoffed and flicked his wrist. "Surprise, surprise. Where is she then?"

"Where do you think?"

I studied the guard, Olio, and Fray. They all seemed to know the answer to the question, but nobody offered it to me. Instead, Olio turned away and grunted.

"Go away, you scavengers," he snarled at the crowd of people forming around us. But they didn't. Some began asking who I was. Some even started to pull on my cloak and sniff me. I got the feeling that they could smell my anxiety as if it were blood.

More people slid from their homes, peeked through windows. Olio's men dispersed and we were left with just Olio to lead us. He snipped and snarled at the people that gathered. A slight woman rose from a bench and gawked for a moment before coming toward us. Her pace quickened almost to a jog before she stopped, impeding the path just in front of Fray. Something heated up between the two of them, and the world fell into a thick silence.

"How long's it been, Igosho?" the woman asked, her tone flat. Her dark eyes swept over Fray, and once they locked with his again, her mouth twisted in disgust. "Do you even know?"

Before Fray could answer, the woman pivoted her gaze to me as if just realizing that I was there. She was beautiful like a storm, thrumming with charged energy. Her demeanor demanded attention. And respect. Her blue-black hair braided and twisted in a way that reminded me of what my mother would do to my own. I was suddenly and painfully aware of how far from home I really was.

"Many years," said Fray, fighting the urge to say more to this woman. "She used to be a princess. Now she's one of us, and I'd like you stop looking like that, Sonia."

Sonia gaped looking from Fray to me and then back to Fray. There was a questioning look in her eyes, and I got the feeling it had nothing to do with me.

I held myself back from asking questions. I was stepping into Fray's world. Fray's past. I would need more than a night to determine how each and every person here fit into it. If they did at all. Sonia, I was quick to realize, had a history with Fray that extended deep. And it wasn't a good history, it seemed.

"A Rowan," she said, practically spitting the name, but before I could say a word, Olio stepped between them and held his hands up to Sonia.

"Play nice, now," he said, sticking his finger in her face. She swatted it away. "You know the law, Sonia. Gather the elders quickly so we can decide if they can stay for tonight at least. I don't know about you, but I'd like to get a nap before the sun comes up."

I remembered Olio's seemingly easy decision to have me killed. Could these elders make the same choice? If they didn't kill us, would they cast us out? Where would we go next? My vow of taking things one day at a time began weaken in favor of casting doubt on everything.

Sonia shook her head, a look of disgust on her face. "How is he speaking?" she snapped at Olio. She looked back to me, and my body tensed. "What do you have to say for yourself, *Princess*?"

A flash of heat warmed my cheeks. My hands balled into fists without me even realizing it, but before I could even conjure a retort, Olio interfered and pushed Sonia back. She bristled at this, baring her teeth.

"Your bitterness can wait a night," Olio said, gaining control of the situation. He noticed my shaking hands before I did and narrowed his eyes at me. "You don't want to fight this pup." I made a face, but he ignored it entirely. "Believe me, Sonia. This can wait."

Sonia stepped back, her wicked smile full of challenge. I felt her eyes boring into me as we passed, and it stung like a needle in my skin.

"Is she always like that?" I asked.

Fray laughed bitterly. "Always."

CHAPTER THREE

It was so crowded by the time we'd reached the meeting hall that we had to push our way through the front door. Once people started to notice us, they parted, allowing a clear path to the center of the large room. There was a thick heat from all the bodies, making the air humid.

The building was made of wood, and the floor was polished and slid like velvet under my boots. Along the walls hung tapestries stitched with vivid scenes that depicted everything from dancing to cooking. One even showed a woman giving birth with dozens of people surrounding her, waiting to help whatever way they could. It reminded me of what Fray had said about everyone knowing your name. There was a sense of family and a deep love in the images. There was a sense of the artistic abilities Fray once mentioned. They were certainly a far cry from the gaudy portraits of bored-looking royals in the halls of Stormwall Palace. The tapestries weaved more than threads. They told stories.

An old woman came to the center of the room. Her hair was snow-white and her eyes gray, almost silver, and her skin wrinkled as if it never had never been any way but.

She's a leader, I thought. I knew they were different here—the way they governed. Back home, there were councils and many, many boring meetings in order to get one thing done. Though one thing was similar:

my father never directly spoke to his people. There were always advisors for that. It'd been far too easy for him to avoid any contact whatsoever with the very people he ruled. He could not have been more separated.

But this woman was no ruddy advisor. I watched as she held out her hands and curled her fingers inward. The torches along the walls swayed as if a wind had blown through their flames. The old woman flicked her fingers out, and the gust of wind grew stronger. But the torches did not go out. They grew larger. An image crawled into my mind, unbidden: the Gwylis I'd seen huddled around the campfire back at Stormwall. One of them seemed to have an affinity for controlling the weather. Was this woman just the same?

Everyone in the room quieted at the show of magic. I found a vacant spot in the outer circle beside Fray and Olio and sat with my legs crossed. I swallowed hard. Being around so many Gwylis knotted my stomach. I scanned the crowd, wondering how many wanted to rip me apart. Fray sensed this, laced his fingers with mine, and said, "It's going to be all right."

Such simple words for such a tense moment.

I gave a tight mouthed smile as the old woman stepped forward, quieting the last of the crowd's murmurs. She was elderly, but she possessed a strength in her movements that painted her a worthy figure-head for the pack. She stood amongst them, a great oak tree in a forest of seedlings.

All eyes turned to her. For a moment, I found it easy to breathe without all the attention on me.

"It seems our numbers have grown this evening," she said, her voice harsh with age. "Step forward, young woman. We wish to speak to you."

My heart stopped beating. Nobody warned me that I was going to be interrogated. After a minute of sitting there in chafing silence, I felt Fray's grip tighten in a reassuring gesture.

"It's all right," the old woman said, beckoning me to stand. "We won't bite."

A few people laughed at this, which wasn't reassuring. Eyes. So many different colors on so many different faces in all different shades. Beautiful faces that looked down on me. All faces that I feared would cast me away.

Wolves, I thought. Big, nasty wolves.

I shook my head. *Yes, but so am I.* And that thought brought me to my feet. The old woman put a gentle hand to my waist and leaned into me, telling me that her name was Kester and to call her just that. "None of that 'ma'am' stuff, yes?" She smiled through her words.

I looked over the faces. Some were still and indifferent while others represented the parts of the pack that were untrusting—the ones that took a stand against their enemies. They were the ones inept at hiding their emotions. I wondered if they would find a kinship in me instead of looking as though they wanted to tear me shreds.

How many were there? Four, five hundred?

"It has come to my attention that this young woman here comes from beyond the Archway," Kester said. "Beyond the Archway" took on a whole new meaning now. "And to those who are not aware of her lineage, she is named Isabelle Victoria of the Rowan family."

Straight away, I was not the most popular girl in the room.

People started murmuring in shock and in anger. I couldn't help but see the way they looked at me, as if I'd been the one to invade their land. Several people stood up and left the hall altogether. I caught sight of Sonia, whose face was a blizzard of emotion, mostly disgust, and all directed at me. I looked to Fray to calm my nerves, but even he looked caught.

"The law," Kester said simply, and most of the crowd quieted down. *You know the law*, Olio had reminded Sonia. What law were they speaking of?

Kester cleared her throat. "One of the laws of our pack dictates that we must welcome any Gwylis who comes for sanctuary."

"She is no Gwylis." The voice came from deep in the crowd, bitter and poisonous. "What makes her so?"

Different answers came from all directions. I felt exposed, dizzy and anxious and wondering if the room would ever stop tilting so I wouldn't look like such a weakling.

"She was changed," came the voice of Olio. He stepped forward into the center of the circle. A savior still in just his pants and boots. He held up a staving hand to Fray, who had begun to stand, and motioned him to sit back down. "That makes her a Gwylis."

"That makes her stupid," came another voice. Murmurs of agreement filled the room. Olio took up position beside me. I could feel his warmth, and it calmed my nerves enough for me to raise my chin high. I supposed that me threatening to kill him really did make an impression. If only it were that easy for the rest of the pack.

Still, time was running out. If I didn't act now, my fate would be decided sooner rather than later.

"I know I wasn't born into your pack." I said with sudden courage. "I can't change that, but I'm a fast learner." My eyes roamed over the room. "I've been here for no more than an hour, and despite the less than warm welcome, I still feel like I belong. I've never felt that way before. I think maybe some part of me always knew."

"We've heard that before," a man growled as he got to his feet. Kester held up her hand in a stopping motion, and the man sank back down.

I barely heard the voices around me. I lowered my eyes briefly and thought of Stormwall. I made it a goal to learn everyone's name in the palace and the Voiceless camps I'd visited, but how well did I truly know them? Did I know their dreams and fears? Did I see past the outer shell of who they truly were? They knew me, sure, but maybe not as well as they wished, either.

"What is your name?" I asked the man who'd last spoken. It took a moment before he realized I was talking to him.

"My name is Gen," he said.

"Gen, I don't expect you to trust me right now, but maybe down the line we can learn to trust each other." I scanned the room, settling my eyes on every person I could. "I want to belong somewhere. I'd like to belong here."

Gen eyed me appraisingly. "We all need somewhere to belong."

We all need somewhere to belong. The words made my world shift like sand beneath my feet. That feeling that kept me awake at night . . . the one that made life hard to live. It was hollow, and it was dark. But here, it didn't feel so bad. Here, I felt a sliver of hope that I did not have to search for what my heart longed for. Maybe I could finally belong.

"What do you bring with you?" Kester asked. "You bring a trail of death, no doubt."

I thought of Lulu then, and my heart stuttered. Her passing was still too raw. Missing her was sometimes crippling. "I don't bring anything with me. I promise—"

A woman cackled. "I've never seen a royal beg!"

I gazed around, open-mouthed. Several people began to join in the laughter. My body threatened to shrink in on itself, but I jutted out my chin and stood tall. *I will not let myself be dragged down by a crowd.*

"What do you promise, wolf-princess?" Kester asked softly. Her breath was warm against my ear but still sent a shudder down my spine. "You look to be a mere shadow of what you used to be."

"I am not a shadow," I said forcefully, then loud enough for all to hear, "And I am in no one's shadow." Not my father's. Not even Henry's.

"I don't see the big deal," Gen said. "She is a Gwylis. Let her stay!"

The tone of the crowd began to shift, and it occurred to me how fleeting the mentality was when just one voice could stir their minds. Especially one so loud and clear.

"But there's something else you must know," said Olio. He paced the width of the room and found everyone's eyes. "Forgive me for not telling you before, Kester, but this girl—she was bitten by Aquarius of the Greatwolf Pack."

"We have nothing to do with that pack!" Sonia called out. "Aquarius should not have done what he has in cursing us this way. He deserves nothing less than a long and torturous death!"

"She's a liar!" someone else shouted.

There was a moment of tense silence before Kester moved to face me.

"Aquarius is dead," she said in a thin nervous voice. Something crossed over her eyes. Something that looked like fear. "That is not possible."

"Why would I lie?" I asked. "I have no reason to."

"Why would you forsake your kingdom?" asked a man. I couldn't see his face.

The room threatened to close in, but I lifted my chin against it. This was no longer going well at all. "I did what I had to do."

"Was lying one of those things?"

I looked around in disbelief. Kester was now facing me, her mouth slack, her eyes dark and probing. Olio was looking at me from under dark eyebrows pulled together as if in pain. I dared not look at the rest of the pack. I'd sooner run than meet the eyes of every person who doubted my own integrity.

"I am not lying to you," I stated, cool and calm. I may have lied about a lot of things in my life, one being that I'd been a dutiful daughter and future queen, but not about this.

"And just why would we even begin to believe you?" asked Sonia. She stood up, tall, her mouth down in the corners as if they were melting from her pretty face. She was a mere ten to fifteen feet away, but I could feel the heat of her gaze as it locked onto Fray. "You're with a traitor, after all."

I held her gaze and blinked away the spots of fury in my eyes. Her disdain for Fray and me was palpable and seemed to ripple the air between us. I imagined she'd lived a life of people bowing to her whim—she may have even been a pack leader for all I knew—and expected the same of me. I saw that she wanted me to tuck my tail and shrink away.

She expected less of me. So I had to be more.

But words died on my lips—words that never failed me—and instead of taking the high road and ignoring her, I felt the shadow of my anger fill me.

I lunged at her in a fury but couldn't get close to even the outer circle before Olio pulled me back. I caught eyes with Sonia, who looked both stunned and satisfied.

"That's not helping your cause, Rowan," he whispered harshly into my ear.

"I have no cause!" I blazed back at him. The words were a lie that soured in my mouth. Fray's eyes found me and, like a rabbit, he was on his feet and next to me. Everyone looked upon us, some confused and some stunned. Not all of them had seen Fray up until this point. They stared at him. They stared at me. I felt the heat rising within my chest.

"She is a Gwylis now," Fray said, his voice stony. This was met with wide eyes and gasps. A few even jumped to their feet in shock, but Fray didn't let a word get through. "I don't care what you all say and what you decide. Either way, she is what she is, and I am what I am, and you all are what you are. Nothing will change that. Ever. So, either suck it up and deal or cast us away, but do it quick. I will not put Izzy through this trial longer than necessary."

A chorus of yelling ensued. Fray intertwined his fingers in mine, letting Olio trade me off to him as if I were a firecracker about to explode. I leaned into Fray, grateful for his help but ashamed I needed it in the first place. None of this was going the way I imagined it. How *had* I imagined it, after all? Nothing in my life seemed to go right without some bit of conflict thrown in for good measure.

For the first time in over a week, I began to make plans. If we were cast away, we could move deeper into the Old Kingdom, find a home somewhere far away, just the two of us. It wouldn't be so bad. Would it?

But wolves needed a pack. I felt it in my bones, the burning need to stay amongst the people of the Den. If they didn't accept us, would we suffer like lone wolves of the wild? Would we scavenge and feel the press of loneliness each night? I would regret my choices and bear the scars for a long time to come, and it would transfer to Fray, who deserved more than just myself. He deserved a family. He deserved love and a sense of belonging. Something I may not be able to give to him wholly.

Our lives depended on this night.

When I came to from my thoughts, I took in the flurry in the room. Behind me, Kester paced and muttered to someone, though I couldn't hear what she said. Olio kept his feet planted near us. Sonia stared with a stone-cold gaze.

After a moment, a couple of sane voices broke through the shouts. One belonged to an old woman who stood slowly and turned a soft look toward Fray. "I remember you as a child, Fray Castor," she said. "You used to eat my flowers."

A laugh bubbled up into my throat. "You used to eat flowers?"

Several people laughed, and the tone of the crowd settled to a manageable level. The old woman's words seemed to cast a spell. They gave Fray humanity. They showed that he was once a part of their family and that he could be once again. I thanked her inwardly. She nodded to me like she'd heard.

A sudden debate rocked the room. Voices calling out and answering, one after another.

"She is a new wolf. She will need training."

I raised my eyebrows and nodded knowingly. Aquarius had said I needed a teacher. Maybe one of these angry Gwylis could take me on.

"It is the cusp of winter. You cannot cast her out."

"How did you regain your voice, Castor?"

Fray relaxed and even broke a smile. "She did it. There's a cure."

The crowd became so still. The effect somehow reminded me of a scene sewn into one of their tapestries of a single person commanding the attention of the mass in the foreground. I wasn't commanding, but I felt a sort of power over them nonetheless. Nobody spoke up for the first time since we'd arrived. Were they deciding if Fray was lying?

"Do you have this cure?" asked Olio.

I shook my head. "It's back at Stormwall with my friend Pyrus."

Olio grunted knowingly, seeing past my lie. "Back at Stormwall where the Greatwolf Pack has invaded with the Peek Islanders and your mother? Where the prince tried to force himself into her bed? He sounds like a treat, by the way. Isn't that what you told me, Castor?"

"Ashe didn't have anything to do with it," I declared. At least, not as much I hoped.

Fray snorted softly. I looked up at him, and he met my eyes. *Are you sure?* they said.

"It doesn't matter," Kester finally said, stepping forward once again. "Stormwall is nothing to us. Now, at least, it will stop the Rowan army from invading the land. Let us think about that."

I faced her, my words almost begging: "Do you believe that?"

Kester nodded and hushed the people when they started to protest. Sonia set her jaw as if she were about to pounce and devour me whole. I should have looked away, but I didn't. I said with my eyes what I shouldn't say with my mouth.

I am not afraid of you, angry wolf. But if you want a fight, I will bring it, sharpened and ready. I don't know half of what I'm capable of, but I'm happy to try it out on you.

Kester raised both hands, and the crowds silenced. "She will stay until we receive official word from the queen. Same with Castor. They will earn their keep together until then." She looked at both Fray and I, speaking slowly. "You will obey everyone here, not only the pack leaders. You will not fight. You will not venture outside of the Den or into any other home except your own. You will come at my beck and call any time of day. Is this all clear to you?"

Fray and I nodded in assent. Her rules sounded as though we were prisoners, but there was no use fighting it. They were letting us stay for the time being. That was enough for me.

This concluded the meeting. I deflated the moment people began to leave the hall. My bones stopped shaking and my heart felt set in its rightful place within my chest. Fray kept his hand in mine, a smile fixed on his face.

"It's not over, you know," he said softly.

"I got that impression," I replied. "So we're okay to stay tonight, then? Is that what she said?"

Fray nodded. "I'm sorry you had to endure that," he told me. "Were you scared?"

I started to object but couldn't get the words out. Instead, I nodded slightly. I'd been a bit more scared than I wanted to admit. Now, I just felt exhaustion weighing me down.

"Didn't I tell you that you didn't have to be scared anymore?"

I let out a deep sigh as the room fell silent. It was bigger and more hollow than I imagined it could be without a group of angry Gwylis within it. I smelled the people who were here. Beneath all of that, I caught the subtle scent of the torches and even the wood and polish they'd used to scrub the floor clean. All the worry I had began to wash away, and I was left with a sense that even though this was not the world I was born into, it still felt familiar.

"The stars are out, and the dark is falling," I said reciting a song from my childhood. "And the wolves howl. They are not lost, so I am not lost."

And suddenly I felt a hand grasp my arm, nails digging into my skin. Sonia stood tall, her face mere inches from my own. If she weren't a Gwylis, I'd claw her eyes out here and now. But I'm sure I'd hold no trophies over an experienced wolf as she. Not when my place in the Den was undecided.

"Cross my path, and I'll be sure to challenge you," she muttered through a snarl. Her breath smelled of tobacco, and her delicate jaw was set. "Daughter of a traitor."

Fray forced her hand away, taking up position between us. He was just as tall as she but held more muscle than two of her combined. He threw back his shoulders and arched his neck. His blue stare bore into hers. It was not seconds later that she backed down, taking slow steps back, one after another.

The traitor in question was not my father any longer, but Aquarius. I had unknowingly aligned myself with a man who'd single-handedly cursed an entire people.

"You won't be able to protect her forever, Isosho."

I stared at her. The lack of sarcastic comments forming on my tongue rattled me. I must be more tired than I thought.

"Believe me, she doesn't need protecting," Fray said with an amused grin.

Sonia clicked her tongue. "We'll see."

With that, she left with the others until the hall contained nobody but the Fray and me. Fray reached for me. I hesitated at his touch. "Even now, I'm still the daughter of a traitor," I said. The words felt broken, filling my mouth and drowning me. I swallowed and recovered, speaking again before Fray could respond. "At least I know I can break free of it. Ms. Moody Wolf won't stand in my way."

Fray just stared at me, sadness in his pale blue eyes. The torches dimmed around us, and at the beckoning of Olio in the entrance, we started to leave.

"You're right, Izzy," Fray said. His words were a breath against my skin. "And I'll be by your side the entire way."

I shivered and remembered what I'd done all of this for. How, what seemed so long ago, I begged the gods for a life worth living. For something worthwhile and more than the stifling walls of that castle.

And I sure got it.

CHAPTER FOUR

Olio led us to where we'd be staying. At Kester's request, he took us to a rundown stand-alone home a little way from the main square.

The shadow of the imposing wall that surrounded the Den loomed over the house as we entered. What I saw first was

a bed fit into the corner underneath two windows that looked out from the front of the building. There was a fireplace with a worn wood table and two rickety chairs, a sink with a mirror beside it and another tiny window above, and a washroom essentially made up the space. There were shelves laden with dust and curtains soiled with dirt.

The entire house seemed to have been empty for quite some time—years and years, I guessed, based on the thickness of the dust. I counted my steps, running my fingers along the walls. Something felt off about the place. Maybe it was the way the dust motes gathered around me, as if glad there was finally a presence to latch onto. Or maybe it was the way I knew someone had once lived here, that there was a past etched into every wall and floor. Memories. Spirits. I searched myself for another meaning to the feeling, but I came up empty. Fray must have noticed my expression because his brows raised in question. I shook my head dismissively. Now was not the time to speak of ghosts.

I counted ten steps until I was at the far wall. The paint peeled and fell like ash at my touch.

"I'll get started on this in the morning," Fray said, running his finger along the dusty table.

I nodded, and we headed back outside.

The front yard must have once been beautiful with stone edging surrounding what must have been a garden but was now long forgotten. The front door hung on one hinge that Fray began to fix after Olio left. The air of something long forgotten flitted from the corners of the ceiling and the dirty floor beneath me. Someone cold and lonely had once lived here and left it just the same.

Exhaustion kept me from eating the last bits of food left in my pack. I stripped off most of my clothes and fell into bed in nothing but my underthings. I smelled, and needed someone to comb through the knots in my hair, but the allure of a real bed overtook me. Fray followed suit, albeit a little slower at undressing. Once his head hit the pillow, he fell into a deep sleep.

Sleep was elusive for me, as it had been for many nights before this one. Fray laid out beside me, his arm draped across my chest, his chin nestled into the place between my neck and shoulder. My breath slowed, matching his own. It was almost enough to lull me back to sleep, but I knew better.

I moved to sit up. Instinctively, Fray's hand moved to hold me, to keep me there with him. He tugged me nearer, closing the empty space between us. I moved onto my side, guiding his hand to my hip, and kissed the tip of his nose as he lay with his eyes shut. He smiled as he roused from sleep.

"I can feel that it's not yet dawn," he said to me. "Rest a while longer. Stay."

I closed my eyes only to find things I did not wish to see. Echoes of screaming and iron on iron. A battle far, far away, but I felt as if it were just outside the window. What could I do to make the visions go away? How could I distract myself?

I lay my head onto the pillow, our noses touching. The scent of sweet root. His lips on mine, tasting of the wild I'd always seen in his eyes. His hands roamed across my body, lingering just at the edge of my undershirt and brushing the skin beneath with gentle fingertips. I let out a breath, a soft moan that opened his eyes.

"Izzy." His voice a whisper in the wind.

I kissed him harder, allowing my hand to drag across his hips to his back. He responded by clutching me closer until there was no space between us.

Stop, I told myself.

I wanted him now in a way that I should not want somebody. When I wanted nothing more than to forget my past, I was mistakenly forgetting about my future. He could not be used as a distraction. He deserved better than I could give him. At least for now.

He pulled back, as if sensing my hesitance, and lowered his eyes.

For a split second, something dark passed over him. A shadow from the window, perhaps? A fleeting darkness across his light eyes? Sudden unease filled my stomach. Abiyaya said that there was darkness in my heart. Could it be contagious?

"What's wrong?" Fray asked, gripping my waist. "What can I do to help you?"

I couldn't help but smile. I searched his eyes and saw the man I'd fallen in love with. The one who'd saved my life over and over again. Who fought for me. Who loved me despite my many faults. The one who loved me despite everything.

Happiness and finding that peace and staying in it as long as I possibly could. Pyrus's words rang true and I remembered them now.

"I'm all right," I said. "But you need to explain why you used to eat flowers. That's really weird."

Fray grinned and fell back against the pillow. "There's a lot you don't know about me, Izzy."

I knew he meant it in jest, but his words made my heart stutter. He was right. There was a lot I didn't know about the boy in my bed. Was he pretty? Oh, sure. Strong and loyal? Check and check. But he had a past that he'd only lightly touched upon. I wanted to know everything.

"Tell me why Sonia called you Igosho," I asked him.

Fray's eyes flickered away. "Because I could never stay in one place for too long." Amusement slipped across his eyes. "It's the word for wanderer in the old language."

"And now?"

Fray sat up, gripping my body with two strong arms, and pulled me against him so quickly it took the breath from my lungs. Then he lifted me up and set me down. He eased his body between my thighs and brushed his lips against my neck.

"I know how I can help you sleep," Fray said, with a hungry grin.

I laughed aloud. "Get off of me, you brute!"

He smiled but did not obey. He looked at me as if I were extraordinary. But the way his fingers drifted from my skin gave me pause. The way his lips touched lightly—like I was glass too fragile to touch with even the slightest pressure.

I hadn't meant to keep Aquarius from him. It didn't feel like something we needed to discuss since I'd abandoned my kingdom and killed my own father. Such a small detail had been lost in the chaos. It had crossed my mind, but talking about it made me think of how I'd felt knowing Fray was going to die and the panic that almost seized me. I didn't think it mattered anyhow.

Apparently, I'd been wrong.

"Fray," I forced out. He sat back on his heels, watching me, his expression unreadable. "What I did, I did for you."

I knew it was the wrong thing to say the second the words left my lips.

Fray hesitated. We hadn't broached the subject in the weeks since we'd left Stormwall. I hadn't been quite sure who was to blame. Seemed we both were.

Fray retreated further and sat at the end of the bed with his legs crisscrossed and his eyes pointed skyward. After a few agonizing moments of silence, he finally spoke. "Don't remind me of what I put you through. Of what . . . I made you do."

"You didn't make me do anything." I made my own choices. He knew this by now. I slid myself up and sat facing him. "I don't regret it for one moment. What happened would have happened without you. With you, I'm alive. With you, I can—"

Fray leaned forward and placed a quieting kiss on my lips. "Let's not speak of future plans yet. One day at a time."

One day at a time. One sinking feeling of guilt at a time. Guilt for leaving my kingdom, for leaving my former guard Crim and my healer friend Pyrus. Guilt for abandoning what anyone else would probably fight for.

I would have to find a way to push aside these feelings and focus: find out what my brother Henry had been doing out here in the Old Kingdom. Find out how he became a Gywlis, and why and when. An anxious knot formed in my belly. Fray was right. One day at a time.

Fray laid down and pulled me against him again. He rested his forehead against mine. I breathed in his familiar scent and that of the space around us. From somewhere outside, I heard someone singing. Was it the same woman as before? The song had changed. But the voice was still hauntingly beautiful, drawing out emotion I didn't know laid dormant in me.

Tears welled behind my eyelids, but they were not of sadness. Despite my reservations, despite my fears, in this little dusty house, I had never felt more at home.

"Don't go—" The words slipped from my tongue, a surprise to us both.

Fray closed his eyes and shook his head, his lips to my ear. "I'm not going anywhere," he whispered.

Just before the sun rose, we lay, molded together, fitted perfectly like a lock to a key, and after, Fray drifted, his eyes closed, his body relaxed. I searched his face in that moment of peace: the line of his jaw, the curve of his nose and chin. How could I ever begin to tell him how much I feared losing him as I'd lost everyone else I had loved? How could I do it without completely breaking and him thinking of me as weak?

I am not weak. I will never be weak.

"I love you," I whispered, but he'd already drifted back to sleep. "Don't go." *Don't go.*

A KNOCK WOKE US JUST AFTER DAWN. OLIO FIT HIMSELF THROUGH the door and closed it behind him as if he were hiding us within. He had clothes on today: a light tunic and pants. His long hair was pulled back with a tie. He took us in, leaning against the doorframe, folding his arms across his chest. I'd thought he'd be disgusted by the two of us lying together—two innate enemies after all—but he seemed more amused than bothered.

"Nice hair, Castor," he said to Fray, who combed his fingers through his mussed-up hair.

I snarled at him and pulled the covers up to my neck. I was wearing nothing but my underthings.

"A little tidbit of information, Princess, but nudity truly isn't as big an issue as you think." Olio looked to Fray. His mischievous smile melted away in an instant. "Get up. Kester wants to see you."

Fray sat up, letting the covers slip, and stood. He was still clothed from the waist down, but he still drew my eyes to him. Olio whistled nonetheless, a half smirk on his face. Fray gestured something that made Olio burst at the seams. When he finished laughing, he turned to where I sat on the edge of the bed, pulling on my clothes.

"Not you, Rowan," Olio said to me. "You can come to breakfast with me, though." He cracked a smile at my apprehension, a wide mouth full of snow-white teeth marked by two overly long canines. "Don't worry. I won't let them eat you."

I pulled on my boots and stood. "If he's negotiating me staying, then I want to go with him."

Olio filled his cheeks with air and released it in a gust. Was he that bored of me? "He's not negotiating you staying." He turned toward the door, but before he shut it, he added, "He's negotiating his."

Oh. I looked to Fray for a reaction, but he kept his face blank. A pang of guilt hit me in the chest.

I bowed forward to fit my head between my knees and breathed deep. Before all of this, before leaving Stormwall, I hadn't considered Fray's status with his old pack. I'd been too worried about my place in it to even give it thought.

There was no denying what Fray was, but I couldn't let the word even form in my mind. If it bit at him the same way it had when Sonia said it to me, I'd be sure to never utter the word again for as long as I lived. Still, it forced through my subconscious.

Traitor.

Shaking that title would be far more daunting than my own. I only hoped for the opposite.

The mattress shifted under Fray's weight as he sat beside me. "You don't need to worry. It will all work out."

"I'm not," I replied, my head still buried.

"You're a terrible liar."

I lifted my head, and he kissed the tip of my nose and gifted me a wink that could have melted all the snow in these mountains. Gods, he was beautiful. What deal had I made in my sleep to deserve such a man?

"Don't do anything stupid."

I threw a hand to my forehead. "Me? Never!"

Outside, we parted ways. Fray walked off to wherever Kester lived, and Olio and I headed to the mess hall where, I assumed, the entire pack gathered for meals.

Seeing the Den in the day gave it whole new life. With its smooth stone walkways and houses built so close together, it reminded me somewhat of Stormwall. But unlike my former home, the construction of this city was not cut so precisely from a mold. There was a beauty in the variety of colors they used to differentiate the homes and businesses. Instead of stone pillars and statues of arrogant old men, frost-laden trees and expansive courtyards carpeted the area. There were even jagged walls of rock that I saw some younger pack members climbing. It was as if the city were built around the land instead of through it.

Over the wall, the snow-packed mountains jutted out like a hand holding the Den in its palm. As we walked, a cool breeze brought a familiar scent to my nose.

"Are we on water?" I asked Olio, who walked ahead.

"The Den was built on Lake Crestada," he replied, pointing east as if I could see over the giant wall. I looked, instead, to Olio. He shoved his hand into a pocket as he walked. "You came in from the west, which nobody really does, unless they're hiding or running from something. Or both."

I was doing neither. "So, your ancestors built the Den on a lake why?"

"Why does anyone build anything near water?"

It didn't take long to answer. I felt a sudden ache in my legs and realized we were walking uphill along a natural slope. "To protect it."

"Fray didn't tell me you were smart as well as cute as a button." The sarcasm in his voice wasn't lost on me. He poked the tip of my nose for good measure.

A group of four women rushed past us. One knocked into my shoulder, throwing me forward. She looked back, fierce eyes meeting my own. Sonia.

"She likes you," quipped Olio. He stopped and gave an exaggerated wave to the women before turning on his heels back to me. "She really likes you."

I glanced in the direction Sonia had gone. As much as I wanted to chase her down, shake her like a doll, and ask her what her problem was, I knew in order to be accepted I'd have to hold my temper. At least for now. I brushed myself off, tucked my hair behind my ears, and smiled. "We're best friends, didn't you know?"

"I hope you like meat."

Olio's voice was drowned out once we entered the building.

There was no order. Everyone ate and left as they pleased. It was a far cry from the methodical and stuffy meals I'd eaten back at Stormwall. This was the most loud and chaotic meal I'd ever seen.

All eyes were on me before I could even get my bearings. Some spoke under their breath with a not-so-subtle tilt of their heads toward me. Some snickered and shook their heads as if I disappointed them merely by being alive. They could stare all they wanted, but I wasn't going to give them the reaction they might have expected after last night. Not with Fray's life on the line.

I felt relieved that Olio quickly led me away to a table in the far corner and spooned some shredded meat from a large clay pot onto a plate.

The mess hall was arranged in more a circle than a square like most dining facilities and packed with more people than there were tables. Nobody seemed to mind, though. They gathered in groups in corners or around the long wooden benches, eating and talking. Some laughed. Some clinked and clanked spoons and cups. Some spoke under their breath with a not so subtle tilt of their heads toward where I stood with Olio.

"Maybe I should go," I told him. The teeter tottering of emotions was making me dizzy. Fight or flight mode was strong.

Olio leaned up against the wall, tipping a bowl of soup into his mouth. "Maybe you should," he replied, wiping his chin. "Maybe you should jump off a cliff like they want you to, too. My afternoon is open. I know a real good one. Rocky bottom. Sure to gouge internal organs."

I scoffed, wondering whether a punch to his arm would constitute a friendly gesture or not. He had wanted to kill me just last night, so I refrained.

I ate, but just enough to stop the hunger pangs. Though I had to admit, the shredded meat of whatever animal they'd killed was seasoned to perfection and rivaled even Stormwall's cooks. Olio slid some potatoes from his plate, and I shoveled them into my mouth without hesitation. After a week of eating charred or under-cooked meat (there was no in between), I savored this small taste of luxury. It gave me hope that I'd taste cake again. Hope that I tried to shove down in case it didn't happen.

Olio went back for seconds and took my sense of safety with him. I lingered against the wall, wanting to disappear into it. They sure didn't hide their displeasure of my presence. Their vile whispers echoed in my head.

I tried to steady the shaking of my hands and the heart that crashed against my ribs when a boy—skinny with shoulder length black hair, maybe twelve or thirteen years old—sidled up to me, one foot propped up on the wall.

"They can smell fear, you know," he said, leaning close. "I'm sure you can smell it on them, too."

"Why would they be scared?" I asked.

The boy grinned up at me. "Daughter of Aquarius, come on, now."

I cocked my ear to the boy. "They all know?"

"Word travels fast around here. You're quickly becoming legend."

Word has reached my ears. You are legend.

I disguised my sudden loss of breath and turned away. Those words were familiar, as I'd heard them in my dreams countless times. Dreams had immense meaning; Pyrus always told me so. Now words from them were being spoken in my waking life. The space around me began to shrink on itself. My chest felt tight. I looked down and noticed my hands were clenched into fists. I forced them open, but they felt tingly, as if my nerves were shooting sparks.

I couldn't lose it now. Not in front of the entire pack.

Someone called out to Ghetee and he waved a hand frantically in return. "That's Kap," he said. I followed his line of sight to a boy his age, skin the color of oak and dark eyes. Kap was the boy from the wall when we'd arrived. "We should go say hi."

Olio returned, shooting a glance to the boy beside me. "Ghetee, get out, would you? Don't you have some knitting to do?" He fit himself between us, shoving Ghetee aside. "Doesn't your mother need you?"

Ghetee leaned over to look at Olio and shot him a sour expression. "No, but she did mention something about you stopping by and cleaning out her—"

"Ghetee. Get. Out. "

The boy pushed off the wall and grinned, gifting me a slight bow before stepping away. "Oh, hey, are you going to take her to the Pits this afternoon?" he asked over his shoulder.

A few pack members heard this and cocked their ears in our direction. They stopped chewing, paused their spoons at their lips.

Olio reached over and smacked Ghetee on the back of the head. "After she jumps off a cliff to a very brutal demise, yes." He smacked the boy again for good measure. "You shouldn't get that in your head. You're just a pup."

Ghetee scrunched up his face. "I'm braver than you think."

Olio prepared his smacking hand, and Ghetee ducked under it.

"What are the Pits?" I asked as Ghetee scurried away, throwing the same insulting gesture up at the boy that Fray had given Olio just this morning.

Olio shook his head, shoving some meat into his mouth, and talked through chewing. "Nothing you want to see. Just a bunch of men vying for bragging rights by tearing each other apart. You know, typical men stuff."

Typical wolf *stuff*, I thought as a heavy-set man strode past, casting a menacing stare in my direction. Olio sighed, set his plate down on the nearest table, and made a move to grab my forearm, but thought better of it. "Let's go. This place is boring me."

I nodded in full agreeance, happy to be leaving. As we passed the tables, I summoned my courage, lifting my chin high and gifting some pack members with a glare of my own. Mainly to one pretty girl with an attitude named Sonia.

She met my eyes. An unfaltering flame burned behind them. I'd have to ask Fray about her. But in time.

CHAPTER FIVE

Olio led me around the city, describing how his ancestors built it along the lake because they liked to listen to the sound of the wind on the water. Since we were in the thralls of winter, most of the market stalls were closed. But I wondered if that was the real reason or if Gwylis simply didn't have a need for apples and greens any longer.

The full scope of the Den hit me as we wandered. I realized then why they'd built the walls so high. If this city were truly the last one standing in all the Old Kingdom, I would have done the same.

I walked through the city, running my fingers across buildings and walls. So much had been destroyed—entire cities, lives—but not this place. It was created with purpose, hands that chiseled stone and painted wood, leaving a mark on the world that would remain thousands of years after it was gone.

"I guess you could say this was a city, but there aren't many of us left these days," Olio explained. Despite that, the Den was still more than I expected. What *had* I expected? A compound of wolf caves filled with bones and droppings? My face reddened. They were human once. The tapestries in the meeting hall and the painted homes told a story of a people with more than magic in their blood. It would do me well to remember that.

He told me that the wall came after the city was built. After my own ancestors invaded and after Aquarius made the deal with the Uncanny for magic.

"You see, with the mountains and the water, you can't really take this place down," he told me as we walked. We wove through the higher levels, in and out of buildings that looked abandoned. Some were in a sad state of disrepair, mostly from the elements. A maze of alleys wound through and took us back to the lower level, to a place ripe with the smell of fire and iron. I felt people watching me from above, but when I looked, they disappeared behind the walls.

"I bet you're used to that," Olio observed. "Being the center of attention."

I couldn't lie. I liked it when people paid attention to me. More so when they listened to what I had to say, or at least pretended to. When I used to bring food to the Voiceless. When I stood on that dais with my parents in my pretty gowns with the city staring up at me. It was human nature, after all, to want to be admired—to be recognized for the good you do. Maybe even simply for the title you hold.

The scent of iron hung strong. As we turned a corner, I found a man standing over a forge in the open door of a blacksmith's shop. Even without the smells, I knew it by the rusted old sign creaking in the breeze. It depicted two swords crossing over one another.

"Jovi," Olio said by way of greeting.

The man waved as he spotted us. He was older than me, but not old enough to be my father. His face was red and slick with sweat. He was wearing only pants and boots, which left his bare chest glossy. I would have been worried for him, had he not been a Gwylis and prone to rapid healing if any burns occurred.

"Who do we have here?" Jovi asked, swiping his arm across his brow. He shook hands with Olio and waited expectedly for my introduction.

"This here is the wolf princess," Olio replied, shoving me forward. "Isabelle Rowan, meet Jovi, the blacksmith."

I held out my hand for him to shake, just as Olio had done, but instead of taking it, Jovi pulled me into a hug. It was nice and quick. Warm, albeit sweaty.

"It's nice to meet you, Isabelle," Jovi said as we pulled apart. This close, I could see the specks of yellow in his clear blue eyes. He wore his hair pulled back in a tail that ran down the length of his spine. He was handsome, as an untamed horse was handsome. Wild, yet gentle. "Have you come to tour my shop, or are you merely passing through?"

"Tour," I said, at the same time as Olio said, "Passing through."

Olio rolled his eyes.

Jovi snorted.

"Tour," I repeated, walking into Jovi's proffered arms again. He led me past his sweltering forge and into the building.

"Cute, smart, and rebellious," Olio quipped at my back. "I have my work cut out for me."

"You subjected me to the mess hall," I told him. At least it was quiet here. Plus, I wanted to see the weapons that Jovi made. If the Gwylis forged iron and steel the way they stitched and painted, I was sure to be impressed.

I turned and stuck out my tongue at Olio for good measure before skipping ahead with Jovi.

Inside was a museum of weaponry. Bows, swords, spears, knives, and other things I could not define adorned the walls. One object looked like a staff with an iron ball hanging from a thick chain. Another was a broadsword as long as I was tall. It stood on a freestanding display on the far side of the room.

A smile broke my lips. "I'd heard of such swords," I said. "You have to be very strong to wield one like this. Isn't that right?"

"Strong, yes," Jovi answered. "Also unafraid."

He took the broadsword and laid it flat against his palms. This was a two-handed sword, the pommel a fifth of the entire size of the weapon itself. I marveled over the craftsmanship, the way the double-edged steel glistened as if it were newly made. The state of its pommel, though, told a different story. There were deeply imbedded grooves, from other swords or axes perhaps. This sword had been used in battle, and brutal ones at that.

"Touch the blade," Jovi urged. "Don't be afraid."

I caught Olio in my peripheral, leaning in the doorway. But it wasn't his stare that sparked a thought; it was something Fray had once told me. *We fashioned weapons for hunting, formidable and ever-lasting.*

We imbued them with magic.

I laid my palm against the metal blade. It was warm to the touch. Was flame magic interwoven into it? The feel of it sparked in my mind like small firecrackers. Even without taking on the full weight of it, I knew why this blade was created. This weapon was not made for hunting. It was made for cutting down men.

"All right," I said, taking my hand back. Olio watched me carefully, having moved from leaning to standing with his arms folded across his chest. The air grew thick around me as shame built up, reddening my cheeks. The bows, the daggers: those were made for hunting, for feeding the Gwylis. Swords like that broadsword were made for killing. Nothing else.

I crossed the room, moving back to the displays on the walls. My eyes caught on a dagger that scarcely resembled the one Henry had given to me. Even more surprising was the collection of bows on the opposite wall. I took a closer look, letting the air thin out. One of the bows stood out to me. Like the daggers, this one was familiar.

"Rosewood grip," I noticed. "Mother-of-pearl, and—"

"Sabrecat sinew," Jovi finished, coming up beside me. I felt his eyes on me, but I kept staring at the bow. "How did you know?"

Biting my lip, I turned to Jovi. His brows were raised, his expression eager. "I have one just like it, given to me by a prince of the Peek Islands."

Jovi's expression softened. "The Peek Islands, yes," he said. "They are the closest descendants of the original people."

"Original people?"

"The first ones to live and breathe on this continent. The first recipients of the gods' power, so it is no surprise that they still hold true to tradition."

"Do they still have magic, as you once did?"

Olio shifted, and my stomach suddenly rolled. I hoped the words did not offend Jovi. He seemed like a nice man, one of the only ones so far who had not eyed me with suspicion.

"That I do not know," he replied. "They far removed themselves long, long ago. That history I am not well studied on."

Same here, I thought. All I knew of The Peek Islands was that they did not bend the knee to the self-appointed King of the New Kingdom, and my grandfathers had let them do so. It was only to marry me off had my father presented the idea of merging the kingdoms.

I wondered if by segregating themselves, the people of the islands lost their gods-given magic as well. I would have known otherwise, having known one Ashe Paratheon after all.

But did I truly know him at all? I thought.

Olio cleared his throat. "We must be on our way."

I nodded. Licking my lips, I pushed down my thoughts and offered my hand once again to Jovi. "Thank you for showing me your creations," I said. "They are a wonder."

This time, Jovi took my hand and squeezed it gently. "I'm sure I will see more of you, Isabelle Rowan." I thought.

Olio and I headed back out into the streets and began to walk without speaking. I was too lost in thought to form a coherent sentence anyhow. To think, I had traveled so far from my home, only to find it here in some way or another. In a song or a weapon. I was not as far removed as I once thought.

I looked ahead, ignoring the shame and the doubt that weighed me down. The past could be a jagged and dangerous thing if you let it take hold. I could not change what my family had done; I could only learn from their mistakes and hope that would be enough.

CHAPTER SIX

I decided that I loved the Den.

The city was more of a dream than reality. Soaked in the kind of magic you can only imagine in story books. It made me breathless. I couldn't tear my eyes from each vibrant home, each intricately carved statue or bright mural on long walls. Although it did lack the gods' small magic, there was no doubt the remnants of it would never wash away. The walls surrounding the city were so colossal I had to walk with my neck craned to take it all in. The watchtowers pointed skyward, stretching to the heavens. I could see figures moving across the planks of wood high at the edge of the wall.

Olio followed my marveled gaze. "Do you want to see the lake?"

I arched an eyebrow. "Are you being nice to me?"

Olio shifted his weight and rolled his eyes. "I'm appointed to you," he said with a dramatic bow.

"What, to make sure I don't run away or jump off a cliff?"

Olio kept a straight face. "Not really. I just do what I'm told."

"But why me?"

The answer was in the question. I knew Kester and many others didn't trust me. Was Olio one of those people?

But he brushed it off with feigned annoyance, rubbing the back of his neck as if I'd spent the morning hanging from it. "To drive me mad, no doubt."

"Are you not some sort of pack leader?"

"Hey, I'm a slave to nobody." He stared at me for a moment longer before huffing. "Whatever. You want up or not?"

I smirked. "Only if you don't push me over the edge."

We found a ladder near one of the closest watchtowers. Olio kicked off his boots and shot me a wiry smile before heading up first. The wood of the rungs creaked and swayed as he went. He had to be twice my size, but the ladder held up fine. Still, I waited until he was safely on the platform above before I started to ascend.

"Not afraid of heights, are you?" he called down.

I climbed, one hand, one foot at a time. The further I went, the more I decided that this was the highest I'd ever been. Even my balcony back at the castle was dwarfed by the height of the ladder. I swore the air smelled sweeter up here. I stuck out my tongue to wind-taste and I made the haughty mistake of looking down. My foot slipped, but I recovered quickly. I bristled at Olio's laughter.

"I'm not afraid of anything," I muttered and took Olio's offered hand at the top.

His face twisted in a grimace, and he shrugged his square shoulders. "Everyone is afraid of something. Here, come on."

We walked along a long stretch of wooden planks toward another ladder that lead to the actual watchtower, where a man stood with his arms propped on the edge of the stone. He greeted us briefly before yawning and allowing us room to stand.

Lake Crestada stretched out before me. Beyond it, the pointed mountains grasped at the clouds. Behind me, I could see the gate where we'd entered, the residential area and the smoke from the mess hall that I'd seen last night. The watchtowers spread evenly along the wall. At the end of the city stood a single structure, pointed like a tent, but solid with windows that opened out from the sill. They were the strangest, most beautiful buildings I'd ever seen. Now that I could see around, several smaller versions dotted the outer rim of the city.

From up there, everyone looked small as ants.

I closed my eyes and listened to the wind blowing through my hair.

There were whispers, if you listened hard enough. They told me that I had been wrong all along. It made my skin prickle to think of the stories I had heard. Ghouls and monsters and dark magic and nothing but ash and constant dusk. Thieves and liars and dealers of death, drinking blood and making bones into jewelry. The stories had been wrong. This was a city of magic—a place closer to my roots than any other. I tilted my head toward the sun and let it caress my skin. The gods may now stand at a distance, but they were here.

This wasn't the Old Kingdom I was taught to fear.

Even though I possessed the warmth of a wolf, I shivered in the crisp, clear morning. I looked out at the expanse of white, my breath steaming into the winter air. I laughed. The only thing dark and dreary about this place was Olio's sudden demeanor toward me. He stared, folding his arm against his chest, almost reading my mind. "What did Castor tell you about this place?"

I stared at the lake when I answered. "Not much," I said. "He'd been at a loss for words for a while. Quite literally."

"But you didn't ask him?"

"I don't press him."

Olio gave a disapproving sound. "You should have. You're too far from home, Littlewolf."

My body seized at Aquarius' name for me. First with the echo of Abiyaya's words and now this. There were too many things I did not understand, too many things that overwhelmed me to the point of anger. I let a snarl escape my lips without regret. "Don't call me that."

Olio laughed at my reproof. He threw up his hands and twirled around far too quick for being atop such an unstable structure. Barefoot and dancing. This man was insane. "Hey, listen, I brought you up here. I'm being as nice to you as humanly possible. " He snickered at that, but when I didn't laugh he sobered up. "I'd appreciate the same."

I lifted my eyebrows. "Nice? You wanted to kill me last night, remember that?"

Olio's laughter clouded the cold air around us. "I said as humanly possible, didn't I?"

I clicked my tongue and looked away. "So, why the watchtowers?" I asked. "What are you scared of?"

Olio stared deep into me, his face almost frozen. "What makes you think we're scared?" he asked, his lips barely moving with the words.

I gave him a look. "The watchtowers did. The way you built the wall to resemble mountain peaks did. Everything around here—"

My eyes snagged on something in the distance where, just above what I assumed was the meeting hall, there were two bell towers. I hadn't noticed them before. Iron, by the smell of them, the bells massive and ornate, reminding me of the ones at the temple in Stormwall. The vey same one I'd gone to bless when I'd gone hunting instead. I sent my cousin in my place. We'd gotten in trouble, sure, but the look on my mother's face had been so worth it.

"Lulu." The word was barely a whisper, but Olio caught it none-theless.

"What?" he asked.

I shook my head to dislodge the memories. "The bells . . . I was just looking at the bells."

"Ah, yes, you won't hear them ring any time soon. They're just for emergencies."

At that time, the heavy-set guard cleared his throat. "Looks like they're headed to the Pits."

I kept my eyes locked with Olio's for a moment longer before following the guard's line of sight to a trail of people leaving the front gate. They were too far to see exactly how many, but I estimated at least three dozen pack members. They hooted and hollered, jumped and skipped.

And then the drums came. They cracked like thunder and pulsed in rhythm with my heartbeat. I'd never heard something so terrible, yet so mesmerizing.

"What's that?"

"Change of guard," said the heavy-set Gwylis. He finally acknowl-edged me with a fleeting glance. "You should take her, Olio. See what she's made of."

"Blood and organs and maybe something dark and gross," replied Olio in a bored voice.

"Blood and organs aren't dark and gross?" I asked, looking at him.

Olio gave a toothy grin. "Not when they taste so good."

I rolled my eyes. "So what is this Pit?"

Olio pressed his arm to his forehead as if he were going to faint. "Well, it's a place we go to let out our frustrations. Us men are so burdened, you see. The weight of the world on our shoulders."

"I'm sure."

I imagined the Pits. If what Olio was implying was true, I bet it was a place to fight. We had those at Stormwall, but they were sequestered to the military barracks, and I'd never had the opportunity to see grown men duel. I imagined at Stormwall, it was like watching children fight, temper tantrums and all. But here, it was probably different. Men and women in their Gwylis forms, magic filling the spaces between their teeth and power. If their magic was anything like mine had been the day I saved Fray in the city square, that was something I'd like to see. Maybe even learn from.

I turned to the guard, who began descending his watchtower. I reached out and grasped his hand without thinking about what I was doing, but he seemed to hate me less than the rest of the Den. I took a shot in the dark. "Will you take me?"

Olio snorted. "I'm right here, you know. I can hear you."

The guard shook his head, lowering himself down further. I noticed a bald spot in the center of his head and wondered if, as a wolf, there was a patch fur missing between his ears.

"Olio would, but he's too scared," he said. "Got beat to a pulp last time."

"Branch cheated," stated Olio.

"Did he?" came the voice of the man now descending the main ladder. He disappeared before his laughter faded from the air.

I turned to Olio with nothing left to say, but he stood firmly and spoke before the silence could settle.

"Castor would kill me," he said. "You're not supposed to leave the Den. Besides, you'd have to ask him-"

"I may be with him, but that doesn't mean he owns me." I stepped down from the top platform and descended the first rungs of the ladder. "Besides, I don't think anything could make him like you any less."

CHAPTER SEVEN

"Have you killed anyone yet?"

We walked down a worn, snow-packed path west of the Den into thick forest with great, ancient trees taller than any I'd ever seen. We lingered behind the main party. Myself, still unsure if they'd want me there. Olio, unsure whether he wanted me there.

"I killed a man because he was trying to kill me," I replied.

"One? That's it?"

Light snow began to fall. I remembered snow angels and Lulu and the way she'd sneak snowballs into the castle before realizing how quickly they'd melted. Our fur coats, her laughter, her face. In and out of focus. I held out my hand to catch the flakes. Her face came with clarity.

Is it snowing where you are?

I started to walk again, boots crunching in the packed snow. I concentrated on that and said, "Just one."

"I know I'm not supposed to be asking this since they're probably digging it out of Castor as we speak, but what's your power like?"

I kept walking. "What do you mean?"

"We're all different. We all can do different things. Mostly having to do with the elements."

I thought of the day I leapt onto that stage to save Fray from the arrows intended to kill him. The way a protective bowl of magic had stopped them and saved both of our lives. It was not fire, ice, earth, or air. It was something else altogether.

"You're right," I said. "It's none of your business."

"Sorry," said Olio. His tone was meant to incite, but I wasn't stupid enough to fall for the bait. He could press all he wanted, but the only people I needed to answer to were the ones in charge. And maybe the gods for all the wrong I'd done.

Olio added under his breath, "Maybe it makes you nicer."

I smiled. "Keep guessing."

It wasn't hard to keep focused on the present, especially when I looked straight ahead and ignored everything coming out of Olio's mouth. I matched the footsteps in the snow until they became wider and multiplied. Wolf prints.

"Sure you want to do this?" Olio asked, wariness glazing his eyes.

I kept facing forward, even when I felt his presence inches away. "It won't be so bad," I said. "Maybe I can even learn something."

"Yeah, like what it feels like to have your face shoved into the snow."

"Did this Branch person do that to you?"

He shot me a look that forced me to hide my smile.

A chorus of howls broke the silence. Olio jogged ahead of me, speaking his chant quietly, as he undressed until he was completely naked. He leaped into the air and changed almost immediately. The massive black wolf with gray on his chest. I stopped, taking him in, and started walking again when I remembered who I was.

And then I entered a large meadow of snarling oversized wolves.

The snow was less packed here, trampled and soiled. The Gwylis arranged themselves in a circle, listening to one tremendous grizzled gray wolf. I backed up, disguising myself between the trunks of two massive trees. Olio gave a gruff, throaty snarl toward a massive wolf that stood a few feet from where we were, fur bristling. *That must be Branch,* I thought. *Also, it smells terrible here.*

"Stay here," said Olio, looking back at me. "Make yourself scarce."

"You're going to fight—" I took another long look at the massive wolf, "—that? Didn't that guard say that you got beat to a pulp last time?"

Olio eyed me and sat back on his haunches. "Must I school you on why you shouldn't question me? Especially since I'm not supposed to have you out here to begin with?"

I raised my eyebrows, and sighed.

"You're right. They've already smelled your stink from miles away."

I clucked my tongue. "I'll stay here if it makes you happy."

Olio rose to his feet. "Good. Stay. Quiet. Let the adults have their fun."

I watched Olio pad out in the circle. From where I was, I couldn't hear what was being said, but the way his stance changed, I was willing to bet the big wolf agreed to the challenge. The other wolves gathered, and two were chosen to battle first. The rest, including Olio and Branch, shrunk back outside the circle. But I wanted to creep closer.

IT BEGAN AS A DANCE. THE TWO WOLVES CIRCLING, PAWS MOVING in unison. One a dappled white and gray, and the other sandy brown. Then they were a blur, impossibly fast, snarling and catching each other in their teeth. The sandy brown wolf even spit some fur out. Growls of enthusiasm came from their pack. "Barbaric," I muttered.

"It's not so bad. Plus, we heal pretty quickly."

Somewhere between arriving and Olio leaving, I'd lost my senses and

hadn't heard or smelled the boy coming: Ghetee.

He dragged a log over to me before sitting down and patting the space next to him with a smile. I remembered his kindness from earlier in the mess hall and sat down.

"I thought your mother didn't want you here," I said. I shouldn't be here either, but what he didn't know wouldn't hurt him.

"She doesn't know. Besides, she's not really my mother, you know," Ghetee said. He looked at me for a reaction and continued. "They just appointed her to me when I came here."

"What does that mean?"

"It means she's the one who changed me."

I opened my mouth and then closed it. I imagined the reasons for Ghetee being here. Had his parents died? Was he . . . kidnapped? I shook my head inwardly. I couldn't see anyone here at the Den doing something that awful. Not even Kester. Ghetee had come at his own accord. Of course, I understood that. But the boy didn't offer up any more to his story, so I dropped the subject entirely.

Ghetee's eyes swept over the fight going on ahead of us.

He reminded me of a thief, the mischievous way his eyes gleamed, but also of someone's younger brother. He exuded a certain innocence, something that needed protecting. I laughed when he started hollering at the fight. Definitely more thief than innocent younger brother, but I decided that I liked him anyway.

He looked back at me when the fight ended. "So what's your magic like?"

"I'm not so sure yet," I replied with a shrug. "What's yours?"

He moved his hand from mine and held it out, palm up. Tiny sparks crackled and leapt from his very skin. "Just a little bit of lightning."

I smiled endearingly. "Just a little is a lot."

Ghetee smiled bashfully. "So what color wolf are you?"

"Black. Like my heart, apparently."

A flutter of feathers in a tree just above me caught my attention. Chunks of snow fell from the branch. I expected a small sparrow or even a hawk, but to my surprise, it was a black crow. At the sight of it, my mind immediately went back home to Stormwall. Pyrus loved his crows, Pax especially. But this wasn't Pax. It was a regular, run-of-the-mill crow probably waiting for someone's ear to come off during the fight. I imagined it would be a tasty meal for the bird.

"Sonia is black too."

I turned to Ghetee, unsure of how long I'd been somewhere else. "What?"

"Sonia, she's black when she's a wolf, I mean."

"Oh." I didn't care to share any similarities with that woman. "How old is she, anyhow?"

"Twenty-six."

I raised my eyebrows. "She looks much younger."

Ghetee made a face. "You don't have to be jealous, you know."

I scoffed. "Who said I was jealous?"

"Your eyes did."

I shot him a sharp look. Me, jealous? I'd never been jealous of anything in my life. Sonia may be beautiful and tall, and she may have that fierce female thing going on, but I had my own good qualities. Like, I'd always won cake eating contests with Lulu, and I used to pride myself on sleeping the days away. I bet she couldn't even shoot a bow. I bet she didn't even have a sense of humor. She sure didn't look it.

Ghetee rolled his eyes and sighed. "You don't have to worry about her. Sonia and Fray could never be together. It's impossible and kind of gross." He made a retching sound.

"Gross?"

"You don't know?" Ghetee cursed. "Geez. Sonia is his sister. Like, real sister. Thus the grossness."

Sister? Now I was more confused than ever. He'd never mentioned a sister. Though, he'd never mentioned who his mother was either, so why was I surprised?

"So why is she so mean to me and to Fray?"

"Family issues."

"Oh?"

Ghetee locked eyes with me and bit his inner cheek. "A story best told by your boyfriend, I expect."

I sighed. "Yeah, you're right."

Olio and Branch began to fight, and I sat forward, preparing myself for something incredible, but it ended before it truly began. Branch swung a paw into Olio's head and sent him flying into the mass of wolves outside of the circle. I promised myself not to mention the loss to him unless he annoyed me.

"So what do you know about Rixon?" I asked Ghetee.

There was a long stretch of quiet. I could almost smell Ghetee's hesitation. I should have taken it back. I knew I was treading a thin line with all my questions. I wasn't sure if I even deserved the answers I'd already gotten. I shouldn't risk losing Ghetee, but the question hung in the air, and I continued to let it.

Finally, Ghetee smiled good naturedly. "Just that she only speaks to the elders."

I looked away. "She spoke to a soothsayer I went to back at Stormwall."

Ghetee's eyes lit up so bright I swore his lightning magic was at play. "She did?"

I nodded. "She said that I was the one, and the soothsayer disagreed. They seemed to have a tense relationship."

"I disagree, too."

I narrowed my eyes at Ghetee. "You do?"

He sat back on his hands and stretched out his gangly legs. "Because premonitions are stupid."

I supposed that summed it up quite well.

"I like you, Ghetee."

He grinned. "I like you too. More than I'm probably supposed to." He looked off toward the fighting, though something caught his ear and he stood up hesitantly. "More than they will probably allow."

The fighting had ceased. In the meantime, the great gray wolf called out, "Who is next?"

I felt Ghetee's eyes on me. "I saw you in a dream once," he said, skipping backward, away from me. "Standing atop a mountain against a pale summer sky." I cocked my head and he frowned. "But you were alone, and you looked sad, as if there were nobody left in the world but you."

Before I could question him, a deep voice cut the air. It reminded me of storm clouds smashing against each other. "He needs practice," the voice bellowed.

At the thunderous voice, I slinked back against the trees, abiding by Olio's orders. I was sure they'd all picked up on my scent by now, but nobody made a mention. Even Olio involved himself as if I weren't even there.

"He's too young, Branch," came another voice.

"Thirteen is far too old if you ask me," said Branch. He was so close now that I could smell the wild on his fur. I began to wonder how his size matched up to Aquarius when he put a massive paw onto Ghetee's back and pushed him forward into the Pit. "Change."

Ghetee looked around hesitantly. Gone was the carefree boy I'd just spoken to. His hands wrung together, and his lips pulled in tightly. He was all elbows and knees and chattering teeth. I couldn't help but chastise Ghetee internally. A full-grown man like Olio had lost. What hope was there for a boy like him?

"You put your name in, did you not?" Branch snarled.

I started to rise from the log. Nobody caught sight of me. If they did, they didn't care. Unaware that I even began to move toward the other wolves, I suddenly stopped when Ghetee locked eyes with me. He shook his head. Was he telling me not to put a stop to this? Nobody else was. They should be protecting a child, not throwing him to the wolves. Quite literally. Regardless of my feelings, I stepped back just as he began his chant.

Ghetee transformed into a skinny cream-and-gray wolf. His tail tucked slightly, his back legs wobbly like a newborn deer. He was so young that he'd not yet grown a thick ruff. His ears were still a bit rounded from pup-hood. He had a wide-eyed innocence that reminded me of the young stray dogs I'd seen around Stormwall. He should be chasing sticks. Not this.

I eyed the other wolves. They looked at Ghetee like he was a meal. This would not be a fair fight no matter who it was he went up against.

And then Branch stepped up.

Compared to Ghetee, he was a beast in his own right. Too stream-lined, too bushy, too strong, and the way he demanded praise as he moved around the circle, sweeping his head up and down, showing teeth when he deemed it necessary, told me that he was a pack leader. A dangerous one at that.

Even though I knew nobody would be killed, it was still hard to watch. Ghetee backed away, leaping from Branch's paw swipes. He was nudged back toward his opponent when he strayed too far from the circle. The bigger wolf played with him as one would its prey before killing it. Branch the cat and Ghetee the cornered mouse.

But cornered animals could be the most dangerous, I thought. *Come on, Ghetee. Let him have it.*

Branch finally lunged forward, catching Ghetee's ruff between his teeth. The young wolf dangled there between Branch's jaws, almost life-less. Branch shook him like a doll. Blood sprinkled the snow; my nostrils flared at the scent. Ghetee finally broke a yelp that morphed into begging Branch to stop the fight. The other wolves encouraged it to continue, barking and pawing the dirt excitedly. It was the saddest sight I'd ever seen.

The sound of the chaos—it was unbearable.

And I couldn't see Ghetee anymore. Branch's massive form bore down on him as he whimpered and cried out. Branch snarled like something unworldly. The other wolves crowded around, growled and swept their heads up and down. Was that their form of cheering?

I couldn't believe what I was seeing.

Ghetee was only thirteen years-old!

I stood up. The pack was overwhelming. There were more of them than I thought, forcing their way closer to Pit to watch the fight. Some were bigger than others, and their colors varied from solid whites, grays, and blacks to sandy browns. All with blood-stained teeth, bared and chomping at the bit.

All with magic.

Ghetee whined again. Branch released him and threw him toward the other wolves just as he'd done Olio. They kicked Ghetee, even nipped at him, goaded him to get up and continue the fight. Blood ran down his ruff on both sides and onto his two front legs. A few more minutes passed before he decided to use his lightning magic.

It came in sparks from the ends of his fur and zapped Branch backward just enough for Ghetee to prepare his stance. But his disadvantage came in the form of the more experienced wolf, who formed shards of ice from his paws, sharp as daggers and just as deadly.

Out of nowhere came the human-sized Olio at my side. "It can get pretty dirty," he said, keeping his voice level. When I failed to respond, he nudged my shoulder like an attention-seeking child. "Lessons to be learned and all that."

"Why are they doing this?" I asked him. "This could easily have been over by now."

He threw a hand to his heart and pretended to faint. "Oh, you got a soft spot for the kid? That's so cute."

I looked back toward the fight. My heart beat rapidly against my chest. But I couldn't look away. Ghetee didn't stand a chance.

My fingernails dug into my palms, drawing warm blood that trickled into the snow. I smelled it before I felt the pain.

"Don't even think about it," said Olio, closer now that I could feel his breath on my skin. "I've got both eyes on you."

My eyes flickered from Olio to the fight and then back to Olio, who kept true to his word and locked his dark gaze onto me. He closed the small distance between us, his arm grasping mine, his body still warm, almost searing hot against my own.

I pulled away from his grip with a sudden strength that rippled through me. I shrugged off my cloak.

Olio grimaced, putting up both hands dramatically, pretending to look stung. "Fine, Princess. At least I can say I tried."

Branch closed in on Ghetee. The younger wolf had everything stacked against him. Ghetee used what he could—magic, instincts—but that alone wasn't enough to beat the older wolf. Snarls and whimpers erupted constantly, and before I knew it, I was talking under my breath, unable to control my limbs as I walked forward toward the fight.

"I am the wolf," I snarled through my teeth. "I am the beast."

Those four words echoed within me. I felt my muscles spasm and my skin prickle. Sudden heat engulfed me as fur sprouted over the fine hairs of my arms. There was no time to remove my clothes before my body started to lengthen and harden. My teeth elongated, growing sharper, thicker.

The second time felt worse than the first.

A flash of pain suddenly arched my back as everything that was human about my body vanished. Everything stretched, from my ears to my nose, and I dropped to my knees, shifting my spine to accommodate the new weight of my body. The rest of my clothes shredded as I completed the change.

When it was done, I bent low, my neck dipped, my paws digging into the ground beneath me. Every sense became crisp and clear. From the potent scent of blood to the voices of the Gwylis and the odor of their musty fur, which reminded me of old rain. I caught the flap of a bird in flight and heard heartbeats as loud as drums.

I felt so alive.

"Look here," came a deep growl. "We have another challenger."

Branch wheeled forward to face me. He was twice my size, more bear than wolf. It was like going up against something from my nightmares.

"Ghetee," I said, pressing myself against him. "Go."

When he didn't move, I took my head and pushed him. He felt as if he were feather-light and disappeared into the crowd of wolves, leaving a trail of red behind him.

I pivoted back to Branch, kicking up dirty snow with my back paws. "Some big wolf you are. Preying on little kids."

The older wolf laughed, his eyes black with wrath. He paced around me without breaking his stare as if he were deciding the quickest way to take me down. Or deciding whether to bother at all.

A snarl ripped from between my lips.

I lunged first, sinking my teeth into Branch's shoulder, tearing, tasting the blood beneath his skin. He threw me off seconds later, and we danced before he lunged, his maw wide and threatening, though he missed me by inches. A few dissatisfied howls erupted from the pack.

"Go away, little girl," Branch said, pawing the ground like a bull. "This is no place for you."

He made a move, and I leapt to the side to avoid it, but he caught my flank and bore down. A yelp escaped my throat. It took everything within me to push away the pain and throw him off once more. The older wolf was thrown several feet and landed hard on his side. This time when we faced each other, his eyes weren't so vengeful. *Back down,* I thought. *Back down, and this will all be over.*

Branch snapped his jaws, the only sound now besides our heavy breaths in the frosty air. He circled me, shaking his head, quick and jerky like a wet dog. I stole a glance to Olio, his look disapproving. Maybe even a little worried.

Pain came in waves, but I bore it down. I knew I'd done damage to Branch. He pretended it was fine, though I saw the slight tremble when he put weight on his shoulder. It was easily missed for someone who wasn't paying close attention. I was.

Adrenaline pumped into my body. I knew the moment to strike would be when he was distracted, if only for a second, but he kept his attention locked on me. There was no chance of making a move he wouldn't anticipate. That was when I knew I was in too deep.

Branch opened his jaws and laughed as if reading my thoughts. His teeth glistened, his breath like smoke from a campfire.

The second jolt of adrenalin threw me forward. My teeth found bone, and I locked my jaws around Branch's front leg, falling, landing hard onto my side. He came on top of me, his leg still in my mouth, the sheer weight of him taking the air from my lungs. I sighed through my teeth, still bearing down just enough to finally hear the tell-tale crack of bone breaking.

I let go, using all four paws to push Branch off me. I rolled and struggled to my feet, the blood dripping from my mouth adding to the soiled ground beneath my paw pads. *I can win this. Just a little longer . . ..*

Branch rose, limped toward me, and roared in such fury that it stopped me in my tracks. I could see the burning desire to kill me raging in his eyes, going against all judgments. All rules and laws.

Olio saw it too. He changed into a wolf and took up the space between Branch and me.

"Stop now," he said, facing Branch. "Let's make it a draw and move on." He then turned to me and said, "Get back to the Den. That's an order."

I relaxed and raised my head level with Olio's. He was right. Whatever it was I had to prove was proven. And the damage I may or may not have caused was irreversible. The maddening look in Branch's eyes cemented that fact.

"Fine." I remembered the pain in my flank and huffed.

"Let's go," said Olio. He muttered a slew of curses. "I have to figure out how to explain this to Castor."

Olio moved to reveal Branch, who hadn't moved an inch. His eyes, unblinking, met mine. Fury and pain were plastered across his face. He pulled back his lips and cocked his head to the side as if considering me. "No draw."

Branch curled back his lips, all teeth and rage. He shifted his weight onto his back legs and lunged. His claws barely missed my eyes before he toppled me over. His weight was crushing the air from my lungs so hard I swore my ribs would crack apart. I used all my strength to throw him off. He came again and again, and soon I was too weakened to even get to my feet. After one final push, he allowed me a reprieve, grinning at my sagging body. Happy to find that I was finally beginning to fear him.

As I slunk away from the pacing wolf, something shadowy streaked across my vision, moving and disappearing with an eerie grace. Were they ghosts? Had my brother finally found me? I waited for his figure to materialize, for his voice to speak to me, but nothing came. Nothing but the jeers of the Gwylis and the biggest, nastiest wolf I'd ever seen grumbling for me to concede.

Memories of Henry and of Lulu washed over me. The anger of what had happened to them flooded into me, filling up every empty space. I would not let anything happen to the innocent ones again. I would tear those who hurt them limb from limb.

The only thing I could hear was the sound of my own heartbeat and blood pumping into it, swooshing like a raging river. In that second, I felt the heat taking over, filling every space within my body.

I couldn't breathe. I couldn't make it stop.

In that same moment, Branch lunged with a violent roar. Everything happened so fast. Branch's four paws left the ground, and I slinked down, pressed against the earth. Fire sprang from my skin and blurred my vision. I anticipated Branch's body knocking into mine, but it didn't come. Instead, he dropped, yelping like a newborn pup.

I am the wolf. I am the beast.

I looked down at my paws. Flames licked them like smoke around a burning branch. I could feel the heat, but no pain.

What have I done?

Branch's roar of agony didn't stop even when he transformed into a human. He staggered to his feet, finally falling and burying himself in what little snow he could find in the Pit, extinguishing the flames and leaving his bare skin blistered, his body twitching from the pain.

I'm sorry. I'm sorry. It won't stop.

That only intensified the fire. I felt it rising and consuming me. Thoughts of seeing Ghetee being beaten, even thoughts of Lulu lying dead in my arms, seeped into my brain, and I was one with the fire. It surged through me, raging, catching onto the nearby trees, smoldering them. *No, I'm not consumed. I am the fire.*

And then it was sucked away, and I collapsed back into my human form. Arms pulled me to my feet, holding me up. The fact that I was naked never crossed my mind. I smelled Branch's burning flesh. He lay on the ground, curled like a caterpillar. My head fell onto Olio's shoulder, too weak to even say a word. I moved my legs and walked with him the best I could, the shadows and heat fleeting across my vision.

"Don't show them weakness now," Olio said softly into my ear.

I stared up at him, my vision in and out of focus. I was vaguely aware of how he covered me with his own cloak to spare me the indecency he thought I'd feel. He didn't know that I felt nothing other than terrified.

"Are you hurting?"

I shook my head, an automatic response. I wasn't sure where I'd been injured or if it was bad enough to actually feel pain.

"I can walk," I announced, my voice broken. But I fell into Olio the moment we were out of earshot of the Pit. A wave of dizziness swept over me, making me feel hollow inside. "I lied. I can't walk. I can't, Olio."

In a split-second, Olio effortlessly gathered me up in his arms. I hung there, my legs dangling above the ground as he walked through the forest. Part of me felt I should be ashamed to be carried that way, but there was no room to be upset. My head fell into his chest, and I breathed in the same wild smell I always smelled on Fray, and it brought me back. The depth of my anger seemed like a giant hole now, and suddenly I was aware of damn near everything that hurt. A veil of hopelessness fell over me.

CHAPTER EIGHT

I should have known something was wrong the second I conjured the fire. But it took Olio dragging Ghetee and myself back to the small home I shared with Fray to really ponder the weight of what had occurred.

I'd broken the rules, and it only took me less than a day to do so. They'd been simple rules: Do not fight. You will not venture outside of the Den. This was not like Stormwall where my disobediences were swiftly punished and then forgotten. This could cost me my place.

Nobody spoke of what happened. Olio went in and out of anger, muttering, cursing, kicking things he shouldn't be kicking since it wasn't his home, but I had no words to chastise him. He said nothing about my use of magic. Even Ghetee kept his mouth shut, which didn't seem in his nature whatsoever. Once Olio left, we both relaxed.

I found a basin of water and some cloth from a cabinet and sat Ghetee down on the only chair in the room to clean his wounds. The large one on his neck was still bleeding freely, so I cleaned it the best I could and wrapped it with some of the spare cloth. I wondered then whose home this had been before Fray and I came to live in it. The layers of dust told me it'd been a long time since anyone even stepped foot inside of it.

After I finished with Ghetee, I looked at my own wounds. One deep gash along my buttocks and another on my shoulder and side, just above my ribcage. Superficial wounds, none as bad as Ghetee's, but I cleaned and bandaged them anyway, wondering how long they'd take to fully heal.

Ghetee watched me through all of this. I felt questions burning on his lips, waiting to spill. I sat on my bed beside him after I'd finished and counted the seconds before he spoke.

"Are we going to talk about this?" he asked at last.

"I'm not sure what to say."

"How about, let's start with why you defended me."

I bit my inner cheek and lifted my shoulders. "I don't know," I told him. "I just didn't like seeing you get beaten like that."

Ghetee furrowed his forehead, a look of stubbornness I used to give myself. "I could have handled it."

"No, you couldn't have."

He jumped to his feet, grimacing from the pain. "Look, I didn't need your help, okay? Now we're both in trouble, you know. Rini is going to *kill* me."

"You don't think Fray will let this go with a kiss, do you?" I ventured.

"Yeah. Isn't it great how we'll both be killed today by loved ones? A family affair."

I laughed despite how badly I'd messed up. Something about the adrenalin wearing off set my nerves firing.

Ghetee sat down again, resting his chin in his hands. He shook his head, some internal monologue happening that I couldn't decipher. Finally, after a few harsh minutes of silence, he asked, "What was that magic?"

I didn't have an answer for him at first, but then it came to me.

"I think Aquarius gave it to me. He said I'd need to learn how to control it, but . . ." I sighed. "I think I screwed things up, Ghetee."

Ghetee stuck out his lower lip. "You shouldn't have let Aquarius change you."

I gave a tiny smile. "You're right. I should have just come here and had you do it."

Ghetee stared at me for a moment before his mouth formed a hesitant smile. "I still like you, Isabelle, even though you butt into other people's business."

"Thanks. I like you too. Call me Izzy, all right?"

Ghetee nodded just as the door clicked and opened. Olio stood like a hunkering shadow and motioned for Ghetee to exit the home. I gave his shoulder a reassuring squeeze before leaving. Olio stepped aside to let him through. That's when I saw Fray leaning against the threshold. There was no expression on his face to allow me to glean his mood. His light blue eyes watched me as I stood.

He said nothing, only shifted to let Olio and Ghetee pass through the doorway.

"I'm sure you two have a lot to discuss," said Olio. He winked at me before leaving.

Fray shut the door behind him. His face was still unreadable, his mouth turned down in his usual scowl. His eyes looked toward the ceiling as if finding the words written there. He stepped toward me to survey my wounds. I stiffened but allowed him to look. When he was sure I would survive, he drew me into his arms and held me there. My taut muscles relaxed at his touch.

"We were going to wait for Rixon to return to discuss us staying here," he said. "Now, we're going to her."

I swallowed hard. Suddenly my throat felt like it was coated with sand. "It's because of what I did, isn't it?"

Fray held me at arm's length and spoke through a grimace. "It didn't help things."

I had to admit, going to Rixon would be better than waiting around here. Who knew how many other messes I'd cause. But knowing this abrupt decision was influenced by something I'd done made me feel like a child being disciplined. My knack for mishandling situations preceded even myself.

"What did you tell them?" My words caught as if there were something stuck in my throat.

"I told them everything that happened at Stormwall."

I pulled away. "Everything?"

"Everything." He blinked a few times, sorting his thoughts. His eyes were more wary than outraged. "Izzy, what happened today?"

I wanted to make excuses. Tell him that I was defending Ghetee and that I wasn't trying to prove anything. But he'd know I was lying. I was lying to myself.

He took a thumb and ran it along the cut on my cheekbone.

"I told you not to do anything stupid."

"I live for stupid actions." I swallowed the memory of what I'd done to Branch. "Besides, why are we outside the city?" Olio made the Pit sound as though it was something secret. Maybe Rixon didn't like the fighting. But that didn't feel like the real reason. These Gwylis were not Voiceless. They had the freedom to change. But here, it was like they had to hide what they were.

Fray rolled his eyes, but his relaxed expression slowly receded. "Things are weird," he said. "Especially with them knowing that Aquarius is still alive. It may not have actually influenced anything, but I don't know for certain." He looked at me long and hard. "When I left to join Aquarius and his cause, I didn't know what I was leaving behind. I'd forgotten why I'd left in the first place. I thought our curse was a gift. It was only when I grew older that I began to realize why Rixon and the Gwylis here had split from their king. Being here reminds me of my shame every day."

My shoulders slumped. I hated seeing him in pain. "We both have pasts that won't let us go."

He knew I was right. But instead of reacting with words, he placed a calloused hand to the back of my neck and drew me nearer.

He pulled me into a kiss, and for a moment, I felt balanced, like things were going to be all right. Because with Fray, they couldn't be anything but.

I kissed him back, long and hard. My hands locked him against me, and I remembered the first time I felt his body against my own and how frightened it made me feel. It was strange to think of how things felt then, because he now felt safe. It gave me hope that he was right. Things may be scary now, but they would be all right in the end. I had hope.

Then his fingers brushed along the place where the arrow had shot me. It seemed like so long ago, as if it were nothing but a dream. A shiver ran down my spine at his touch, and I leaned away.

I signed to Fray because words would take too much out of me. *I'm not weak, but now I feel like I am.*

A groove formed between his eyebrows, and he signed back. *We'll be weak together.* He added, *I wish it were me that killed your father so you wouldn't have had to bear that burden.* The words that hurt him to speak aloud.

I swallowed the lump forming in my throat. "Don't apologize," I said almost sternly. I stared, uncomprehending, into his deep blue eyes. "He almost killed me. But Lulu . . ."

"Lulu wasn't your fault. The sooner you accept that, the better things will be." He looked off to the window in the front room where people passed by. "Don't let it haunt you, Izzy. You can't do any good if it does."

It'd taken less than a day for the world to tell me that life wouldn't just go back to normal. I was deluding myself. How could I think I belonged? How could I think my demons wouldn't find me here?

I was no longer able to contain it. I let the tears fall silently at first, until a sob tore from my throat like some long-caged animal being set free at last.

Fray watched me, almost apologetically, fearing he'd been the one to cause it.

"Let me," I said after he tried to hold me again. After a moment, I steadied my breathing. "I feel like I don't have a place where I belong. I feel imprisoned somehow. In some strange way."

"You're not. You never will be again, Izzy."

"You can't promise that."

Fray gritted his teeth and looked up from downcast eyes. "Maybe not, but I can sure as hell kill anyone who tries."

"Promise?"

"With whatever you did back at the fighting pit, you're not even going to need me."

I looked away. A feeling washed over me. Shame? Regret? No, not the latter. Not at all. "I don't know what I did."

Fray exhaled heavily and combed back his hair from his forehead. He paced the home as well as he could pace such a small space. Suddenly, I felt bad for the way he loved me. I was a doomed, black-hearted thing. Death and violence followed me wherever I went. How could he still love me after all of this?

"I don't suppose it matters," I said. "They're never going to trust me."

"They will."

"You sound so sure of everything, Fray. How?"

"Because what else is there to do but hope?"

"And if I'm shoved out?"

"Then I follow you."

"Even after almost killing Branch?"

Fray nodded. "Even then."

An uncomfortable ball formed in my stomach. I wished I'd never gone to the Pit. I wished this never had happened. "I don't know what I did," I repeated.

Fray dropped down in front of me, holding my hands in his. "We're going to find out. That's why we have to go see Rixon."

The idea of seeing that fire-woman from Abiyaya's home made my throat tighten. Standing in front of the queen of the Gwylis with the magic of the king in my veins was enough to make my body shudder. "Am I cursed?"

Fray grinned. "We're all cursed, Izzy."

For a long moment, we sat there with just the sounds of the people outside passing by and our own breathing to cut the silence. I was far too tired and confused to even think about the consequences of what had happened with Branch.

"If I were something else," I said, "would you tell me?"

He inhaled, held the air, then let it out. This was not giving me confidence.

"Fray," I said. "Would you tell me the truth about myself if I couldn't see it? If nobody else was brave enough?"

"I would," he said finally.

"Thank you."

I then thought about a lyric from a song I'd heard as a child. *A single tear, a single word could be enough to change the world, but in the time, you've closed your eyes, the changing world has passed you by.*

"Well," Fray said. "We'll hear the truth of truths soon enough."

CHAPTER NINE

"Have you seen her hands? Smooth, like a baby's ass."

The voice carried to my ears as I entered the mess hall with Fray and Olio on either side of me. The dinner drum had sounded no more than five minutes ago, but every seat was already taken. And all eyes were on me once again.

"I heard they're going to see Rixon," another voice whispered as we passed. "She must be real important."

I snorted. I probably ranked last on the list of importance in their pack. Probably next to yesterday's dinner and a hairball.

Another whisper, this time louder than the first: "Well, I heard she attacked Branch without cause. Can you believe the audacity?"

A growl rumbled in my throat. Gossip. How I hated it.

"They know you can hear them," whispered Fray as we neared the food line. "Ignoring them is best."

I balled my fists at my sides. "I could set them on fire."

Fray frowned. "Ignoring them is best."

I sighed, exasperated. I'd hoped to garner some sort of reaction from Fray but remained stoic. I hoped it was just the impending meeting with Rixon that had his muscles so tense. Perhaps when we returned and finally cemented our place at the Den, he would finally let go. I hoped.

We got plates of warm bread, butter, and more meat and looked to find seats. Olio used his girth to bully a few younger girls from their seats, and we sat down. Conversation grew louder, more mixed, and I relaxed, looking down at my plate, picking apart my bread. If I could only find my place in the Den, I could walk into a room and not have everyone look at me as if I was some sort of demon.

I looked across the room to find Ghetee sitting beside a young blonde woman. Rini, I assumed. He gave me a tight-lipped smile before Rini followed his line of sight. She gave his head a jostle. My circle of allies thinned.

"Why do we eat here like this?" I asked, looking around. "Like—"

Olio interrupted me. "Humans?"

I nodded.

"I suppose it's Rixon's doing. Making us appear to be normal."

"Is Kester going to speak to me, or are we just leaving tomorrow morning and that's it?" I asked Olio.

"Uh, I'm pretty sure they told Fray and I everything you need to know right now."

"Which is?"

"Pack your stuff and leave at dawn."

I opened my mouth, closed it, and opened it again. "Great, it's so nice to be in the inner circle, you guys. Way to make a girl feel at home."

Nobody reacted to this. I glowered into my bread.

"Oh, and we kind of have a little fellowship accompanying us," said Fray.

I narrowed my eyes at him. "You failed to mention this."

He went to speak, but Olio interrupted.

"Maybe because it's two of the people who probably dislike you and Fray the most."

Only two names came to mind. Sonia. Branch. Even better. Out of hundreds of pack members . . ..

Olio directed his eyes at Fray. "Work it out with her, Castor. She doesn't really hate you, you know. She feels like you abandoned her."

Fray's face remained impassive. "I did."

Olio laughed with his mouth full. "Honesty is a good trait, but stubbornness is not."

"And what of Branch? Is he going to kill me in my sleep?" I looked around the room. I'd yet to see the massive wolf in human form. My body shivered at the thought.

"No, you hurt his ego more than anything."

"Which is harder to repair." I sighed. "Kester did this on purpose, making those two come with us."

"Of course she did," said Olio. "They're all about testing loyalties. Yours and theirs." He gestured to my plate. "Eat. You need your strength."

I played around with the meat on my plate. It seemed silly to sit as a human, eating like one, when there was real game running around in the mountains ready to be hunted. I wondered if it was some sort of rule not to become a wolf behind the walls of the Den.

Branch picked that moment to walk by our table. In this light, and standing upright and not writhing in pain, he was even more threatening than I'd imagined. He wore a look of indignation under his salt and pepper beard with eyes so dark they could be night. I was pretty sure he was old enough to be my father, though he held none of the softness age usually required. He was built from agate stone, seven feet at least, with a walk that parted crowds.

"Cocky," I muttered when he'd passed far enough out of earshot.

Olio and Fray picked up their forks at the same time, shoveling food into their mouths the way men do, and said in unison, "No more Pits for you."

After dinner, Fray and I watched from atop a watchtower as the sun dipped low behind the mountains. The lake stretched out before us, still and serene. Beauty without a sound.

"Why does Rixon disappear like she does?" I asked, leaning over the wall, taking in the evening air.

"Did Olio tell you that?" asked Fray. I nodded. "Honestly, I don't know. I asked. Nobody seems to like straight answers around here."

"She wasn't like that before?"

He shook his head and looked out as the last of the daylight disappeared behind the distant peaks. The torches lit around us almost immediately. The night guard ascended the ladder to our right, nodded to the both of us, and took his place a few feet from where Fray and I stood. That closed the conversation for good.

Once on the ground, we headed home. From somewhere in the distance, the rhythmic beat of drums and chanting filled the night. I was suddenly reminded of the woman I'd heard singing when we'd first arrived. But this music sounded more enthusiastic and less like a mourning call.

"How about a night cap?" Fray asked, reading my thoughts once again. He smiled, a flash of white in the darkness.

We headed through the city, closer to the bass-filled drums. My heart thumped against my chest in exhilaration. A shrill voice sang into the air, followed by a chorus of lower voices behind him. *How strange and beautiful*, I thought. I'd never heard anything like it.

We made our way to the center of the city square. There gathered the entire pack, sitting and dancing in unison around the fire, like they'd done this same dance since they were born. Off to the side were the drum players, alongside others playing strange instruments I'd never seen before. The sound combined to form a melodious, almost haunting chant.

Artists, musicians, scholars. They had books older than the ones Farrell in Stormwall had shown me. I'd seen them in my room, their pages yellowed and brittle. Leather bindings torn and dusty. Was this song just as ancient? Did it trace back to the days before we were split by mountains in an even line down the continent? When my ancestors hadn't blundered the whole unity thing and started wars that never seemed to end. Or did it go further back, to when power did not divide us and evil did not exist. If that were even true. I didn't think it was.

We lingered behind the crowds, observing. I was drawn in, my eyes on the dancers, their bodies covered by almost nothing, content in their nakedness. Lost in the music.

"Your people are beautiful," I said to Fray. Tears formed behind my eyes for reasons I couldn't truly understand. "I never knew."

He smiled gently. "I knew."

"Why did you leave them?"

Fray bowed his head, almost ashamed. "More wolf than human," he muttered.

I shook my head and said gently, "That's not true."

From among the dancers came Sonia, alongside a handful of women. They dressed in tattered clothes, their hair braided down their backs, feet bare. They paused in front of the fire as the music changed, and then their feet moved along with the drums in such perfect rhythm it seemed almost impossible.

"Even she's beautiful," I commented, unaware I'd even spoke it aloud. I looked to Fray, who locked his sight on his sister, some distant memory creeping across his mind. I knew deep down he loved her. He just needed to work out how to tell her. "What are they celebrating, anyway?"

Fray blinked long and hard. "The death of your father, Izzy."

Oh.

"They're—" Fray paused, cocked an ear to his left. His body tensed. His chest stilled. After a beat, I heard it too. Someone screaming the word "intruder" from high atop a watchtower. "What's going on?"

The music stopped mid-beat as hundreds of wolf-tuned ears turned toward the main gate of the Den. Then all at once, they scattered, all yelling the same thing: "Intruder!"

Then, "Human!"

Human? A singular human? "Who—" I stopped, knowing the answer as soon as I began to ask the question.

How could I have forgotten?

Gods, damn him.

I raced past Fray, losing myself in the crowds. I pushed past them, nearing the closest ladder I could find. I climbed despite the many hands trying to pull me down. First onto the lower platform and then up to the highest that overlooked the path Fray and I had entered when we first arrived. Amidst the light of the moon and the torches, I looked down to a black figure below. I blinked and blinked, but I couldn't get a good look.

"Move it, girl!"

I was shoved as two men came, bows in their hands with arrows nocked and aimed. I looked across to the watchtower on the other side of the gate directly in front of me. More men. More arrows.

Come further into the light.

As if hearing me, the figure moved, sluggish, like a wounded animal. But this was no animal. It was a human male.

A sudden buzzing in my head. I looked to the men beside me, their eyes fixed on the man below. They were going to kill him.

"State your purpose!" one of them called.

"Name!" one of the men from the other watchtower called out.

A name to die by, I thought. They don't plan on letting him live. Not by the fire in their eyes.

I drew in a breath, held it, and leaned over the wall to call down, "Ashe Paratheon, Prince of the Peek Islands, why did you follow me?"

CHAPTER TEN

It felt strange saying his name; it brought back every horrible memory I'd ever had. It was a good thing I was so far away. I'd have probably attempted to kill him right then and there.

There was a moment of silence before a weak voice answered, "Izzy, help me."

I loosed a breath but kept my heartbeat steady.

"You know this man?" one of the bow-and-arrow men asked me.

"Yes, he betrayed me back at Stormwall. Fray bit his arm off." I cocked my head. "More or less."

I watched Ashe's form fall to his knees. Even from up there, I could tell how exhausted and beaten he looked. How he survived this long was a mystery.

"No arm?" the same man asked, a laugh escaping. "What does he think he's going to accomplish here?"

"Maybe he has news of the Greatwolf Pack," I said, not sure why I'd just justified keeping Ashe alive.

"Who is it, Rim?" called up a voice. I looked down to spot Kester.

"Someone named Ashe from the Peeks," Rim called down. "The princess says he may have news of the Greatwolf Pack."

"Can he be trusted?" Kester called up, the question directed to me.

No.

"He's missing an arm," I replied. "It was his sword arm. He's not dangerous." Not really.

Kester ordered the gate opened. I hurried down the ladders, mixed into the crowds again, and made my way to the front to watch Ashe being dragged in by two large pack members. He was limp. Like a doll.

"Stand," said Kester when Ashe was close enough to her.

Ashe planted both feet onto the ground and stood the best he could. His face was covered in dried mud, painted on like war paint, and he wasn't wearing armor. I sniffed the air. Nothing but layers of cloaks and maybe a fur from a fox. He swayed. I imagined a breeze would blow him over.

All that princely pride, gone from his body. In the darkness, by the light of the torches, he looked more or less already dead. Killing him now would be a deliverance.

I stood in his line of sight just a few feet away so he could see me fully. I met his bright green eyes. Something like a sob and a groan escaped him, and he bent forward at the waist, like he was succumbing to the weight of the past few weeks. I saw the pinned sleeve of his missing arm and smelled the rot beneath it. I felt a pang of pity. I remembered the way he screamed when Fray had bitten him. The way he begged to come with us when we'd left Stormwall.

Oh, coward prince, how the world has broken you.

But even before Fray had wounded the prince, he had turned against me, bowing to a father who demanded his son's loyalty lest it make him weak in his eyes. I understood grappling with one's royal obligations and doing what was right. But he had chosen a different path, just long enough to change the course of my life. Had he sided with Fray and I that day on the cliff, what would have happened to us all? Would things have played out the differently? Would I still be human?

The sensible Izzy knew my choices were my own, and that, while the events would have been different, eventually I would have broken the chains my parents had bound to me. But my mind kept going back to the cliffside, to the one decision Ashe had made that changed everything. His arrogance led him here, as if he thought I would be the one to absolve him.

His scent filled my nostrils. The wilderness and whatever sickness clung to him. He reeked. He reeked so badly that I barely had room to breathe. The smell took up the air around me. Air in the one place that I wanted to make a home. Home that he was invading.

I'd never been good at controlling my emotions.

I stalked over to Ashe and punched him the face.

"That's for everything, you traitor," I snarled as Ashe staggered, surprisingly still on his feet. My hand screamed in pain, but not enough to cripple me. With one more punch, he fell to his knees. "Everything."

"Seeing you hit that pretty face may have been the greatest thing I've ever witnessed," Olio said, punching my arm playfully.

An hour later and we were still waiting outside of the meeting hall, along with the entire population of the Den. Ashe had been brought in front of Kester, probably to decide his fate, just as had happened with me, except this time, the decision might have been whether or not to string him from the highest watchtower and watch him die slowly. From the palatable anger in this crowd, I took it they did not take to having a human in their midst.

Fray stood beside me, his eyes intent on the doors of the meeting hall, waiting. "He didn't have any control over what happened," he said to me.

"He could have put a stop to it," I replied, frustrated and breathless. I wanted to punch Ashe again. I'd do it over and over . . .

For the first time in weeks, I began my counting. One, two, three. One deep breath in and out. Just like Henry taught me. Fray watched me carefully, letting me soothe myself before he intervened. Luckily, my shoulders relaxed, and the need to break things dissipated.

"Archibald was taking orders from the king himself. Ashe had no say over anything at that point, Izzy, and you know it."

I glared at the closed door in front of me. Fray needed to stop being so sensible. "He still could have chosen my side."

"You weren't going to marry him. Why would he?"

I bit my inner lip until it bled. There was more to say about my feelings for Ashe—maybe the way I didn't know him, maybe the way I wish things had been different. Ashe held a piece of my brother, and I'd let it slip away. "I don't care. He's a criminal."

"His only crime was loving you, Izzy."

Behind us, the chattering went quiet as people started to listen. Great. I'd given them even more to gossip about.

Suddenly, the door opened, and I found myself confronted by the deep wrinkled face of Kester. "Branch Cushway, Olio Moore, and Sonia Castor. Could you also grace us with your presence?"

I nibbled on my lower lip as I looked back, finally seeing Branch up close and personal. His girth, his build, the way his dark eyebrows permanently drew together over sea glass colored eyes—even the way he walked—all of it demanded attention. He tried to make me afraid of him. I wasn't.

"Walk like snails, that's all right," said Kester. "It's not like there's sleep to be had. Why do you people always demand my nights?"

She led us to a small room off the main hall where the pack had gathered the night before. In the room, Ashe sat in a chair at a desk illuminated by bright torches on the walls. He smelled awful. His cloak had been removed, and he held a cup of water in his left hand. His face, full of cuts and bruises, turned to look at me as the door closed behind us. I took in his every detail, from his sunken eyes and his filthy fingernails, to his cracked lips and near frost-bitten nose. He looked away soon after. I felt the shatter in my heart.

He wasn't the prince I knew. His transformation was almost crushing.

"What is it with you royals coming out here?" asked Kester, taking a seat behind the desk. My ears perked at this, but Olio's laughter broke my thoughts.

"At least she smelled all right," he said, pinching his nose. "This one smells like rot."

I bent down to Ashe, my hand hovering above the stitched-over sleeve. "Let me see it."

He looked at me as a cornered rat would look at a hungry cat. Lifeless eyes, reddened where the white should be. The green dulled like dirty old bottles.

"You think it's his arm?" asked Fray.

I nodded. "Ashe, let me see it."

Ashe looked at me a moment longer, his eyes faded and distant. I could tell he was wondering if I were real. Then he nodded. I unfastened the folded sleeve and pushed it up.

I peeled away the soiled bandage that wrapped the stump. I held my breath at the stink that assaulted me. The wound had not healed right. The initial stitching had come undone at some point, and dirt and grime had entered through. From what I'd gleaned from Pyrus and his teachings, without proper care, an injury such as this was apt to infect the body and eventually cause death.

Stoically, I re-pinned the sleeve, turned my head for a deep exhale, and turned back to Ashe. I placed a hand to his forehead to the burning skin there and knew he did not have long to live. He would not survive this without proper care.

After composing myself the best I could, I turned to Kester.

"I was friends with a healer," I told her. "He taught me many things. I saw many things. This has been left untreated for too long. He's going to go into shock if we don't help him."

Kester looked over my shoulder to Olio, Sonia, Branch, and Fray. An agonizing silence filled the cramped room. The smell—I couldn't stand it. I turned and pushed past the others to open the door. Once in the main hall, I bowed, my hands falling to my knees, and called out to Ashe. "Do you want to live?"

"I do," he said.

"What say does she have in these matters?" The voice was Branch's. It was the first time I'd heard him speak as a human.

"I am the eyes and the ears," snarled Kester. "You'd do well to shut up, boy."

"Were you followed?" Olio asked.

"I don't know," Ashe said.

I stuck my head into the room, glaring at Branch. "My mother still lives, and so does his father. Do you really think they'll stop at Stormwall when they know both of their children have gone past the Archway?"

"They don't know we have," Fray said.

Maybe he was right. Maybe they had no idea where we'd gone. They may even believe we were dead.

I watched Ashe get to his feet. He stood straight despite the pain, putting on his best face. I wasn't surprised to see him standing tall in a room full of Gwylis. He always had that poise about him.

"Make me one," he said. A shudder ran through him, and his legs buckled. He fell to his knees at Sonia and Olio's feet. They both recoiled at the prince's actions. Branch left the room and stood with one leg propped up against the wall to the right of the doorway as if the whole thing bored him to tears.

"Make you one what?" I asked.

"He wants to become a Gwylis," Fray said, crossing his arms over his chest. "You should have told me that before you begged me to chop off your arm."

"It won't bring it back," I said to Ashe. "It won't bring back your arm."

"I don't care." Ashe's head fell between his legs. He sat there, huddled like a caterpillar. "I don't want to be me anymore."

"I won't." The words clogged in my throat. Emotion burned in my eyes, begging to be set free. The sudden sadness I felt for Ashe pooled in my gut. I fixed my sight on the ceiling, anywhere but on the prince.

Kester cleared her throat. "It's not up to us. It's up to Rixon." Much to my shock, she added, "If it were up to me, he'd be dead in front of the city gates."

But it wasn't up to Kester. Ashe didn't know what he wanted. He could not make such a decision, not in the state he was in. He needed to go back where he came from. Wherever that was now.

"He may know something that we don't," Olio said. "He was there in Stormwall, isn't that right? He spoke to his father?" I turned into the room just in time to watch him nudge his boot against Ashe's ribs. "What's his plan, boy?"

Ashe lifted his head but kept silent.

Fray exited the room at that moment and locked eyes with me. "If we keep him alive just for information, what does that make us?"

I looked away, afraid to remember everything involving Ashe that led me to this point. The last time I saw him, he was begging to run with me. The last thing I felt for him was hate. He betrayed me. He *betrayed* me.

I shook my head, but the memories remained. I remembered his gift, the beautiful bow, and the way he'd tried to kiss me by the springs. His light green eyes and annoying smirk. All of it gone. It may as well have existed in another life.

"I guess that makes us bad guys," I said. I glanced back into the room, where Sonia was moving away from Ashe.

"I say we put him down and scatter his ashes over the Pit," Sonia said, "so we can trample him for the rest of his afterlife."

"How about this?" Kester called from the room. "We treat him tonight, feed him, let him sleep, and tomorrow you take him with you to Rixon. Let her deal with him."

Push him off to someone else, I thought. *Great.*

"Great," snapped Sonia, echoing my thoughts. "First, we have to go to wherever we're going just for her—which, by the way, you never really asked if I wanted to go. But now we have to drag an invalid with us too?" She threw her braid off her shoulder and hissed. "Seriously, Kester, I think it's time to retire."

Kester picked up a book and threw it at Sonia's head. She dodged it by an inch.

"I never said he could return," Kester said, waving us away. "Leave it to Rixon. Be done with it. Go."

Branch glanced at me, sidelong and dark, a visceral snarl on his face.

Sonia brushed past hurriedly, making the most noise she could.

Olio just laughed, shaking his head as if the whole thing were a comedy—a play put on just for his amusement. "This is the most fun I've had in a while," he quipped.

Fray looked forlorn, uncertainty hanging in the air around him. He watched Kester take Ashe away with Olio's help, and after they disappeared, he cast his blue eyes to me.

"I think it's all unraveling," he said, holding his hands to his lips, his fingers steepled. "Him being here—how does it feel?"

How did it make me feel? How did he think it made me feel? My punches to the prince's face weren't enough to convey my feelings toward him?

"What can I do?" I asked. "I don't have all the answers."

"I don't feel right about any of this," Fray replied. "And I know I don't get much say in it, but if you want to keep the prince alive, I will have to trust in you."

Did he *have* to trust me? What sort of power could I wield against Fray if he had to bow to whatever I wished?

"I feel a lot of things, Fray," I said. I chalked that up to the human side of me. The side that I hoped was the most dominant. "But at least I can save a life instead of taking one."

Fray glanced in the direction Ashe, Olio, and Kester had gone. When he looked back to me, his jaw clenched and cracked—his resolve clearly teetering. "Just make sure you keep him away from me."

CHAPTER ELEVEN

Fray was already up and dressed by the time I opened my eyes the next morning. He sat at a small table, polishing my dagger—a very human action that elicited a smile from me.

"I'd ask how you slept, but I was there," he said when he heard me stir.

I sat up with a groan. Though my wounds from my fight with Branch were healed entirely, something ached my bones. Uncertainty, maybe. Gods, I was tired.

"Do you think he made it through the night?" I asked.

"I think there's a strong possibility," said Fray. "Our healers are like yours." He cocked his head. "Maybe better."

I smiled, glancing toward the window. I could hear voices, murmurs close enough to hear the words clearly. "They're already waiting, aren't they?"

Fray pursed his lips. "Probably."

"At least they're not barging in here without knocking," I said. "Bunch of brutes."

A smile split Fray's mouth. After I'd dressed and washed up the best I could, we went and met Olio and Sonia outside the house. From there we walked to the back gate where the rest of our group waited. Branch, and Ashe, the latter some distance away, stood beside a sleek black mare. There were several packs attached to the saddle. Clothes, I assumed.

Ashe looked better, washed and a little bit more alive than last night. I wondered how good the pack's healers were because he didn't seem to be in much pain. There was a hint of shock in his eyes, as if he'd only just realized where he was. His hand trembled as he arranged his saddle.

If ever I needed reminding of who I was, it was now. It didn't make a difference if Ashe was here or not. If he became a threat again, getting rid of him would be easier than before.

I could have loved him. In an alternate time when things weren't so strange.

The girl I once was, the one that always looked out into the sky and saw something other than the color blue, who dreamed of spreading her wings through the wind—that girl was gone. Now I found that I'd kill anyone who threatened the life I was building for myself. I'd never hesitate again.

Rixon's location wasn't far, less than a half day's journey along the lake. As soon as the five of us were ready, Kester came down to the square, her deep hood over her head. She pulled me aside, pressing herself close to me.

"If that boy comes back dead, I will know it was you, and I will not tell a soul."

I threw a glance over my shoulder to where Ashe struggled to mount his horse, a sense of dread twisting my gut. "What do you mean? What did he tell you?"

Kester replied with a shake of her head. I was in no position to demand answers—especially from an elder—and she made no indication that she'd divulge the information either way, so all I could do was nod. I pulled away from her slowly. She held my gaze. Something washed over her eyes. Worry.

Fear.

We set out, Sonia, Branch, and Olio transforming as soon as we were clear of the gate. Fray stayed with me, still in human form, a few feet ahead of Ashe and his horse. The path was dangerously narrow and only visible by the trail the others made as they ran ahead. New snow had come overnight and was falling still.

I looked to Fray more than once, but he avoided my gaze. Was he angry at my vouching for Ashe? I couldn't let him get to me. I set my focus on Rixon and Rixon only. She'd answer anything I needed to know. She'd make it right.

The snow fell more thickly, and the path grew deep. I knew I'd have to shift into wolf to navigate the ridge. My trepidation of Branch held me back. The incident at the Pit had been blown over by Kester, but Branch seemed the type to hold a grudge, and if something ticked me off, what would happen then? Would I set him on fire? Maybe burn the entire forest down? I groaned, wanting to fall back into the snow and lie there until everyone became my friend and nobody hated me.

Instead, I stuck my tongue out to catch snowflakes and cast sidelong glances at Ashe.

I found it hard not to speak to him. I wanted to pull him down from that horse and shake the answers out of him. Why did his father invade my kingdom? When did he ally with my mother? Despite the urge, I couldn't bring myself to get even a word past my lips. That was a first. Usually, the things in my mind came out whether I wanted them to or not.

Picking up on his feelings wasn't very hard. I swore I could smell them even. A wrathy scent of burnt wood and rotting flesh. When he thought nobody was looking, I caught a sagging, lost kind of feeling from him, and I found myself wondering what had happened in the time Fray was captured and the time I left my home for good. What did he see in Stormwall? How did he escape?

Around midday, the three wolves traveling ahead stopped and waited for us to catch up. The world was quiet, save for the bird songs that seemed to follow us. The forest grew thicker and the trees taller. Though I'd been in the Old Kingdom for weeks, it finally began to feel as though I were in a foreign land.

I'd grown up in the sheltered walls of the palace, going no further than the town proper. But today, I thought of Henry and how he'd come and tell me stories of his travels. I was reminded of the first time I'd laid eyes on the emerald necklace he'd gifted me, making me swear never to ask where it had come from. I drew my own conclusions. I knew it must have come from a far-off land. I pretended that it once belonged to an ancient queen and held magic so powerful that it could protect me from my father.

It hadn't protected me, but hope was not a thing that died so easily for me.

A strong smell cut the air. Even Fray leaned his head back, back, back. Nose in the air. Smelling. He then pressed one finger to his lips, signaling to both Ashe and me.

Save for Ashe, Fray, and myself, my companions had all been out this way, hunting and the like, but this smell wasn't an animal. Our adapted senses picked up on something far worse than what I picked up off Ashe.

Branch trotted close to us and bowed his head low. *Quiet*, the action said.

Fray turned to me and signed, *Can you change without a sound?*

I shook my head, unsure if biting my tongue as a wolf burst from my human body would be possible. I'd only changed twice now. I wasn't much of an expert.

Stay back with the prince, Fray signed.

What's out there?

Humans. Maybe dozens of them. Do you smell the iron?

I sniffed the air and nodded. *Soldiers?*

Soldiers. They might be heading back through the Archway. Word must have reached their ears about the king by now. Will you stay?

I nodded again. *Be careful.*

I watched Fray change, and all four wolves disappeared into the snowy wilderness. I lingered a few feet ahead of Ashe, digging my boots into the snow, creating shapes. I could hear his horse's unsteady huffing. *Must be hard, trying to control a horse with one hand*, I thought. After a few minutes of harsh silence filled with nothing but birds and his horse's frustration, I couldn't hold back. "Steady your horse, or I'll take it from you," I snapped.

"What are you going to do, eat it?"

I beared my teeth at this, focusing on Ashe's dreary face. He seemed smaller than before. So much less of a person. I couldn't tell how much of that was because of his malnutrition and how much was because he was a filthy traitor.

"You don't get to speak to me. Not anymore."

The prince exhaled long and hard. "I've more than paid for my sins, Isabelle."

I flinched at my name. Isabelle, not Izzy. He'd revoked the gift of my nickname all on his own. My shoulders slumped with what I felt. Sadness. Pity. Regret. But I could not let it show.

I straightened my shoulders, my heart beating fast. "What happened out there?"

"I saw what you did in the town square. I was in the crowd, though you didn't see me. But I saw you. I saw what you . . . did."

What I did. I ran toward where Fray was bound, in full view of the entire city and armed soldiers with arrows pointed at me from the rooftops. I'd conjured a shield to protect him. To protect *us*. And then I became a wolf for the first time. But what did that have to do with Ashe?

"I made a choice that day," he continued. "Seeing the lengths you went to protect that Gwylis, I vowed that I'd never hurt anyone ever again. I would never put anyone through that again."

"That's a bold promise to make to yourself, especially since you begged one of us to change you into a Gwylis."

He frowned. "Could you make the promise . . . as a Gwylis?"

I shook my head. "Never."

Ashe's mouth twisted. "If it makes up for everything, I'm going to try."

So that was it? Ashe's attempt at redeeming himself was never to hurt another person ever again? I wondered how many nights he'd spent in the mountains trailing us, shivering in the winter nights, battling his own demons. I wondered how he managed without losing another limb.

I frowned. Did he really matter? Ashe's days were numbered. Rixon would send him away at first sight. A human had no use in the Den, and I doubt she'd ever sanction anyone changing him into a wolf. It wasn't possible.

Ashe cleared his throat, demanding my attention without meaning to. "You're different," he said. "I mean—your eyes, your face, the way you walk. You're different."

I scoffed. "You have yet to see different."

"Change me."

I looked up. "What?"

"One of those wolf healers told me that you all heal quicker than humans. I'm so weak and tired." Ashe made a move to dismount his horse. My arm shot out, holding his leg in place to stop him.

Maybe he did not remember his incoherent babbling last night. *I don't want to be me anymore,* he'd said as he burned with fever. Maybe he was too embarrassed to say it now. Depressed ex-princes weren't the best of companions, after all, and he knew my weakness for the injured. Was he playing on that now?

"That's not a good enough reason," I said, dismissively.

"You're scared for me. Is that it? Is it so bad being one of those . . . things?"

Scared for him? Maybe so. Becoming a Gwylis was one of the scariest—yet easiest—decisions of my life. I'd had a reason, and his were?

"You're not thinking clearly."

His eyes hardened. "Were you?"

Anger slid through my veins. "Are you insane?" I snapped. "It wasn't something I chose. I had to do it. I had no other choice."

Ashe lowered his eyebrows. I noticed now how his normally short, ashy hair was now coming in longer, pieces floating above the top of his ears. The patches of red from where I punched him looked like a minor rash at best. I wish I'd put more strength into them.

He turned away, his attention floating toward nothing in particular. "There're always choices," he replied softly. "To think at any point in time that we're stripped of that portion of free will is mind boggling. What sort of hold does he—"

My stomach clenched. Did he want me to punch him again? "Choose your words wisely, Prince. You're still alive because of me."

Ashe locked eyes with me. "Is that really true, or is there something else out there paving our way, unseen?"

I rolled my eyes. "Did you become some sort of spiritualist out there all alone in the woods? I think I liked the arrogant, smirking Ashe a tad better."

He had the nerve to give me an all-knowing look. "The gods work through us, you know."

For a wild moment, I considered Kester's words. I could take him into the woods now, kill him and throw his body into a gorge and say nothing more about it. "Something else works through me now," I said. "They are telling me that you're not worth the air you breathe."

"You wouldn't be here if you had just married me. We could have worked it out. We could have sat side by side and ruled like rulers should. I could have worked with you. I could have stopped my father somehow. It wouldn't have been so difficult. We could have won it together."

Anger pushed in, but I let my composure replace it. "I meant what I said by the cliffside that day." *I hate you* echoed in my head. "I meant every word of it."

I turned from him and made my way down the path where the rest of my group had gone. I could smell them, so I knew they weren't far. I spoke softly, shrugged off my cloak and clothes, and tried my best to stay quiet as I turned from human to wolf.

I found the four wolves pressed low to the ground and crept beside the brown one, my head brushing with his. They looked down the ridge, where multiple scents now carried on the wind. Fray glanced my way, but all in all he was not surprised to see me there.

I must work on my unpredictability.

The camp wasn't big by any means. Maybe a dozen or two soldiers walked about, setting up tents and feeding horses. Fray moved closer. I felt his heartbeat thudding against me. He looked where I looked. His eyes fixed on one soldier's boiled leather. The Bear of Mirosa was etched on the chest plate, clear as day.

"We should probably kill them all," Olio growled.

Branch and Sonia made sounds of approval.

That was it, then? Killing was so simple now. Would it be just like breathing?

"I think we should move on," Fray said and turned to go.

One of the soldiers began laughing over a joke we had not heard. I trained my ears to listen, and that was when I heard my name.

"The princess?" one of the men said. "That whore. Who knows how many servants she'd slept with before that Voiceless. She was just like her cousin, I bet."

Just like her cousin. The unbidden thought of Lulu barreled through me. The way her eyes shone and her voice danced. The way she was never shamed for who she was. A spasm of anger racked my insides. These men did not know her. They would *never* know her.

I swiped away a tear and swallowed hard.

Fray's head rose and dipped low, concerned. He couldn't understand the need for revenge that tore through my body.

But I could. I peeled my lips back, my grin full of teeth, a savage thing, and turned to run toward the soldiers until I felt the earth blurring under my feet and the snow kicking up like dust.

CHAPTER TWELVE

We descended the ridge. Fray, Olio, and I went west, Branch and Sonia east. Every sense hummed as we all closed in. The smell of the soldiers burned me from the inside out. But I delighted in it. I would revel in the taste of their flesh on my tongue. I would show them who I was. Let them see the beast.

Our growls mixed with the wind and packed snow beneath our paws, surrounding the camp with howling war cries.

The soldier who'd spoken ill of my cousin saw me first and swung his sword instantly. It cut the air nowhere near me and almost fell from his grasp. He was young, Henry's age when he'd first joined the army, and still a little uncoordinated. I wondered what his father had been like, that he would push him past training so soon as to make such a clumsy play.

I lunged with open jaws, catching him by the midsection and clamping down until his wiggling body went slack. A blackness passed over me, cloudy and full of wrath. These were not the spirits of the dead here to pay me a visit. These were wrought with fury, making killing almost easy.

Yes, it was just like breathing.

The battle was only just beginning. I was willing to bet that none of these men knew what we were truly capable of. Didn't they know these mountains were full of monsters?

Soldiers rushed at me with swords drawn. I taunted them closer, my movements nothing but a blur as I took them down one by one. One of them landed a slice to my forearm and another to my hindquarters. It only made their deaths quicker. I almost wanted to tell them to run to save themselves the trouble, but the smell of death was too inviting. Something about it sparked my very being.

Amidst the chaos, a lone soldier confronted me. He stopped mere feet from me, sword catching the sunlight just right so that it shone like a gemstone. He saw where my eyes landed—right on the symbol I'd grown to hate, fixated over his chest—and let a smile split his face.

"Pike will have you obliterated," the soldier hissed. "He will level you."

Pike? Who was Pike? No time for questions. I rushed the man, who made a valiant attempt at defeating me, I give him that. A seasoned warrior, yet nothing compared to the fury I felt climbing to a crescendo inside of me. I rushed him, teeth bared, and tore his midsection in two.

A bark and a whine. I threw my head to the left to Sonia's scent. I couldn't see her at first, unsure of why she wasn't standing, until I saw the five men closing in on her.

The scent of blood. A hungry, warming sensation filled my belly, launching me forward. I reached deep inside, pulling out the magic I knew was there, finally gripping hold of it.

I saw the men. I saw Sonia. I saw the blood in the snow.

Bury them, I thought. *Kill them all.*

There was magic welling up inside of me. But it did not feel like the same power I'd used on Branch, or even on Fray back at Stormwall. This magic attached itself to every bone and muscle in my body, no longer feeling like the bits of muddled pieces it had during the Pit fight. It buzzed under my skin, surging until it finally poured out. I directed it toward the ridge, unsure of what would truly happen.

If it hadn't been for the trees that uprooted nearby and the sudden rumbling of snow and rock from the ridge above, I would had thought it a figment of my imagination.

I felt a rush of heat that moved from my feet to the core of the earth beneath me. My anger was an avalanche, and I would show them just what I could do with it.

The ground shook, knocking the men off balance. In that instant, Sonia snapped to her feet, taking down two while I took care of the remaining three. I steadied her wavering body and asked if she could run. She nodded just as the avalanche of snow skidded down the ridge.

Sonia howled as we retreated. Olio and Branch appeared from nowhere, and lastly came Fray, his fur red with blood. We cleared the camp, hopping from ledge to ledge. Once at the top, we watched the camp become drowned in white. Those who remained were buried, suffocating beneath several feet of impacted snow.

Fray pulled back his lips. This was the most emotion he'd shown in days, I thought. "I told you to stay with the prince," he said fiercely. "I told you to stay put."

I cocked my head. "I'm sorry, but you were right there snapping your teeth along with me."

"She saved me," said Sonia, directing her soft voice to Fray for the very first time. I wasn't expecting that. I half expected her to deny she was in trouble at all. "I could have been killed back there."

For a moment Fray and Sonia regarded each other with something less unsavory. Which was a start.

"It doesn't matter what happened," came the booming voice of Branch. Part of his ear was torn in a slit, like he'd taken a razor to paper. I wondered if it would stay that way. "We need to go if we want to get there by dusk. We shouldn't have stopped."

"Please," Sonia drawled. "You were the first one to suggest killing them."

The fur on Branch's back bristled into a long ridge along his spine.

"What were they doing this close to the Den?" Olio asked, padding between Sonia and Branch.

"One of the soldiers mentioned someone named Pike," I told them. "Does that ring a bell with anyone?"

Each and every one shook their heads.

Branch's body shuddered, ending with his back legs and tail. He craned his neck. I swore I heard bones crack. "It doesn't matter anymore, does it? Let us return to your prince, Rowan."

Fray and I walked side-by-side, but we didn't speak much. By that time, we were all in our human forms, either hoping to heal or merely just because it felt better than bloodied fur. Ashe said nothing. If he'd known what we'd done, he didn't show it. But I felt his eyes on me, an awareness that pricked my skin.

We continued for an hour or two before Olio hung back with me as Fray walked ahead.

"Are you all right?" he asked.

"I'm fine," I replied a little too quickly. I avoided his gaze, which was certainly lined with concern and maybe even some pity. He didn't speak again but kept in stride with me. I wondered if that was why Fray hadn't asked how I was. He was so used to seeing me as a girl, maybe he even still expected me to act as one. I wasn't even sure if I should, and that made me feel worse. Worse so was the presence of Ashe.

The sky grew cloudy with the threat of rain. I hoped it would rain. It could wash away the smells of death that permeated all around us. I thought the relief would come when we finally got to Rixon. Until then, I felt incredibly incomplete.

Nobody asked about the avalanche I'd caused. Nobody seemed to want to mention it.

How many men had I killed? My staggered breath elicited a glance from Fray.

What are you thinking? he signed.

I'm thinking that I'm more wolf than human, I signed back.

He turned away before I could read his face. *Are we so quick to kill?* I thought. *Is it in my blood?*

"It's just here along the beach," said Branch. He looked better. All salt and pepper hair, dark skin, and trademark scowl. No slit in his ear.

I nodded. Fray took my hand but grasped only two fingers and shook them like a failed handshake. "Just relax, all right?" he said. "She's nothing to be scared of."

I cast him a sideways glance. "Are you telling that to yourself?"

Fray smirked and looked over his shoulder. I did the same to see

Ashe only a few feet away, sitting like a statue upon his horse. He stared at us, a mix of confusion and disgust on his face.

"Something to say, Prince?" Fray growled.

"How does it work as a wolf?" Ashe asked. I was amazed at his gall and the fact that his forehead gleamed with sweat while he said it. His fever must have returned, but it sure didn't stop the arrogance from pushing through.

He shifted in his saddle and cupped his hand like one would a shadow puppet. "You know, like do you two just crouch and—"

Fray lunged first, followed by me on his heels. I tugged him back by his waist. It wasn't a strong hold, but it was enough to let the anger dissipate.

Branch, Sonia, and Olio approached, watching with amusement.

"That's a bet I'd make on Castor," said Olio with a grin.

"I wouldn't be too proud of that bet," replied Sonia, shifting her weight and crossing her lithe arms across her chest. "Even Ghetee in his human form could take down the one-armed prince."

"Don't come near me," Fray spat, ignoring the others. This sudden fury felt more like a weakness for him than something formidable. "Don't speak to me. Don't even breathe the same air as me." He shook me off with little effort and met my eyes. "Let me kill him now. Nobody will say a word."

Branch sighed. "We can't. Not yet."

Sonia clicked her tongue. "And why not? He is nothing but a plague, and he smells of decay. I can't stand it."

"She's got a point," Olio said, wagging a finger at Sonia.

'We're not killing him," I said. "He has information."

"What's your information, Prince?" Fray bounded toward Ashe, taking his leg and pulling him from his horse. He landed with a soft thud into the snow in a pathetic heap. He struggled to lift himself upright. For a brief moment, I felt pity for the fallen prince. Briefly.

"I say we let him run," grinned Sonia, advancing on the fallen prince, "and wait for the sun to set and make it a good ol' hunting party." She licked her lips. "We haven't had one of those in a long time."

"How about you act like civilized people?" I snapped, realizing the hypocrisy of my words straight away. I stood beside Fray's half-crouched figure and set a hand upon his shoulder. Ashe skittered away between his horse's legs, which wasn't the smartest idea, but up against four Gwylis, I supposed he'd taken his chances. "Forget about him, all right? Let's just see what Rixon says."

Fray shot up and faced me. "Don't tell me you really do want him here," he said, looking into my eyes. After a moment, he furrowed his forehead. "You're torn. Why? You killed those soldiers down there easy enough."

I watched the blood drain from Ashe's face. "Soldiers? Here?"

Branch shrugged it off, scratching his ear as if remembering his wound. "Running back home, most likely."

Ashe crawled into a sitting position behind his horse. "Not going. Coming."

"What are you talking about?" I asked.

Ashe lifted his chin in a weak attempt at arrogance. "Kester told me not to speak of anything."

I scoffed. "Kester does not rule you."

Ashe watched me quietly, his legs half-buried in the snow, his remaining arm buried within his cloak. I felt a pang of guilt even though my hands still wanted to strangle him to death. Why was I feeling sorry for someone who had forced my hand in marriage—who agreed to my tyrannical father's terms? *I'm going to help you, Izzy,* he'd once said, *Will you trust me?* Gods, why did I still believe him?

I reached out for Fray and pulled him close. "Fray," I said, leaning my forehead against his. He held both of my hands firmly. "Do you remember when Archibald had the axe to my throat, and you let yourself be captured?"

He nodded slowly.

"You knew you wouldn't die that day. You knew either I'd come for you or you'd use whatever magic you could remember to free yourself. Is that true?"

"I trusted the first," replied Fray. "Though this wasn't nearly what I expected. But I was willing to die to see you unharmed."

"You wouldn't fight for your own life?"

He pursed his lips and met my eyes. "Only for yours."

"I need you to do that for me again." I looked toward Ashe and exhaled. "Not the dying for me part. The trusting part."

For a moment, it appeared that he would answer, but then we lapsed into a silence. Our procession through the forest continued with little fanfare. I gazed at my companions, watching their movements, but they made no moves to ask me what I had done. How would I begin to answer them? We stopped briefly to eat and relieve ourselves, and I found myself thinking not of my magic, but of the soldiers. I knew my senses weren't as matured as the others, but I kept alert. We'd been lucky once. There was no telling if we would be again.

Less than an hour later, we came to a place on the north side of the lake where a mountain peak cut the sky like a knife. I wondered how far Henry had gone. He'd told me so many stories that I found it hard to recall each detail. I gazed out at the vast landscape, letting my imagination fill in the gaps. Hope dwelled in the pit of my stomach. If I were any other person, I'd think my comfort in the wilds stemmed from being a Gwylis. But I'd felt the pull from an early age. The trees, the water, the mountains, the open sky: they all called to me. If Henry were here, he'd tell me I was crazy, but knowing what I knew now, I knew a deep part of him would also feel that pull. I knew he never wanted to return to Stormwall. Gwylis or not.

As I stood at the lake's shore, gazing over the water, Fray sidled up to me, nudging my shoulder. If we were wolves, he'd probably be trying to tell me to focus. I looked at him, but he stared straight ahead, over the water and toward the sky somewhere behind the mountains. I no longer felt the air of frustration wafting off him. Now, he felt almost composed. I smelled the tangy scent of blood and heard boots crunching on packed snow as Olio approached. He bent down and tested the ice blanketing the lake and found it too thick to gather water from.

"Behind you, just there, you'll find a wonderfully suspicious cave," he said, jabbing a thumb over his shoulder. He gathered up a snowball and bit into it like it were a fresh loaf of bread.

I followed his thumb, past where Sonia and Branch stood, to the wide and gaping mouth of a cave. Rixon, the Queen of the Gwylis, lived in . . . in that?

"Welcome to our queen's winter home," Olio said, sitting back on his haunches with a grunt. Ashe stood, holding the reins of his horse some ten feet away. "How about you go on ahead, and we'll go hunting and make camp."

I turned to Fray. "Since it's your mother, I think you should go first." It only seemed right.

Fray opened his mouth, then closed it. Never had I seen him at such a loss for words. Even when he couldn't speak.

Olio intervened before I could work it all out, throwing an arm around Fray's shoulders and shaking him like an old friend. "I think it best you go first, wolf-princess."

My face reddened. I knew Fray had a tumultuous relationship with his mother, but how deep did it go? Did he fear her? Or was he ashamed of siding with Aquarius and coming back with his tail tucked, so to speak?

Did he even want to speak to Rixon at all?

I forced the thoughts from my head. I knew I had to focus on one thing at a time if I wanted to achieve anything. But the thought of seeing Rixon emerge from Abiyaya's hearth still made my skin crawl. There was no doubt that I was nervous about meeting the queen again. Maybe even a little scared.

Chin up. Back straight. Like a royal, but with wolf in my blood.

Fray, noting my sudden change of attitude, pulled me into his arms, talking into my ear, "Be brave, no matter what. Do you understand me?"

I stared into his eyes, somehow lighter and more blue than ever, and I poured over the past few months. The memories of everything I'd given up for him. And for myself. But most of those things, I'd never wanted to begin with. Being queen. Being married. Being . . . who I'd been before....

"I'll be right here waiting," Fray added before pulling away.

"Come on," Olio said, his words dragging. "I think I speak for all of us when I say the puppy love thing is getting real tiresome."

I smiled despite the stomach-twisting dread. I glowered, eyes wide, at the mountain, took a deep breath, and counted.

One.

I walked until I met the mouth of the cave.

Two.

I made a promise not to look back.

Three.

I broke my promise and stole a glance at Fray before disappearing into the darkness.

CHAPTER THIRTEEN

Silence and blackness.

That was what I walked into when I entered the cave. I let my fingers brush the stone walls, taking each step carefully. The floor was uneven, riddled with loose rocks and cracks, enough to break an ankle or an arm if you fell the right way. I breathed in the sweet air, glad to have a break from Ashe's fetid scent.

My senses came alive minutes later, and my sight adjusted. Now it was clear as day. I was not only in a cave but a series of caves, like a labyrinth of sorts. As I winded my way through the tunnels, sometimes through water from both under my feet and above, I beat back the fear creeping into my heart. I could at least appear to be in control, even when I wasn't.

Be brave.

The tunnel I followed opened up to a large room with two new tunnels on the other side. Both looked identical. Nothing beckoned me to follow either one. I pointed to them both, singing a song Lulu and I would perform when torn between two things. Wherever your finger landed when the song ended was what your decision or forced choice would be. But just as I began, a thin, cool wind swept from the tunnel to my right and drew me into its confines.

Water dripped from the cavern ceiling more frequently here, creating a miniature river at my feet. My heartbeat quickened so much that I had to stop, crouch down, and hug my knees. "Steady, Izzy," I told myself, my voice a dozen doppelgangers against the stone. Something colder than the breeze passed through me so that I shivered against it. "Gods, its cold."

"Always complaining about something."

"Lulu?" The name came on an exhale before I knew I'd even spoken. *No, it can't be.* She'd yet to come to me, but I expected her only in my dreams that were more nightmares. As much as I tried, the last image of my cousin would not be her smiling face, but her body soaked with blood. My heart seized. *Please let it be the Lulu I knew.*

My cousin appeared just as she had been weeks ago when she still lived. Raven-black hair, dark eyes, sweet, rosy lips. My twin through and through. She didn't look anything like a ghost. My Lulu. But she was dead. I saw her die.

She'd emptied out.

She didn't speak like a ghost either. In fact, I could almost smell that sweet scent of lavender she'd favored.

"I'm sorry for everything," I said, trying out my voice. It broke in places, but she heard me all right.

"It can't be helped now, Izzy."

"Were you waiting for me here?"

"Waiting, yes, in a dream, in a place between what is real and what is gone."

I shivered again. "This is like the dream you told me about—the dream I've been having, isn't it?"

I recalled the day like it was yesterday. I knew exactly where the sun was in the sky and the smell and sounds of my cousin as she immersed herself in planning my future. The way she'd grown solemn as she described her dream. How I took no notice of how much she believed it was real. As real as she felt at that moment.

Lulu flashed a pleasant smile. "Dreams are the best place to communicate with the living or those far out of reach. It's when you're most vulnerable and open to new ideas."

"You've been hanging out with Henry, haven't you?"

Lulu smiled again.

"But I'm not dreaming, am I?"

She shook her head.

I knew ghosts better than anyone, I expected, but it had been a while since one had come to me. Lately, all I'd been seeing was darkness. Leave it to me to long for the spirits of the dead to break up the mundane.

I smiled at my cousin. I could see the sparkle in her eyes, even the fine black hairs on her head. "Can I—can I touch you?"

At Lulu's nod, I reached out my hand, taking her cheek into my palm. Her soft skin had even the touch of blush it always did, except now it was cold as ice. I closed my eyes, and a feeling of dizziness swept over me. I squeezed my eyes shut tighter, forcing out warm tears. "I'm sorry," I said again and again and again.

"There's no more time for this, Izzy. Let's go."

I followed Lulu through the tunnel, watching the sway of her hips, the way strands of hair fell over her shoulders. She was too real. As if death had never claimed her at all.

"Stop," she commanded abruptly, "Do you hear it?"

I listened but could hear nothing.

Lulu pointed ahead to where a small blue light shone like a candle. "There."

I licked my lips, holding my cloak tight against my chest. "Is that where Rixon is?"

Lulu nodded. She turned and began walking the opposite way. "Remember, Izzy," she said, looking back, "not every queen needs a crown."

She disappeared too quickly. I turned and bounded the way she'd gone, my boots sloshing through the water. I called after her, begged her to come back. She couldn't leave me this way. Not after everything I'd put her through.

I begged for things to have been different.

I stopped and leaned against the nearest wall, heaving for breath. My body threatened to panic. The tears would not stop falling, and my hands shook like leaves in a gusty wind. I stared into the darkness, sorting through the shock and relief flooding through me.

There's no more time for this, Izzy. Lulu was right. I could stand here dwelling, or I could move forward. The latter was always the hardest part. The latter was why so many people failed.

If anything, coming here was not all for naught, even if Rixon did turn me away from the Den. I'd seen Lulu. I knew she was all right. She gave me strength.

Come on, Izzy, I thought. *Buck up. You're a wolf now. Act like it.*

I kept my hands still clasping my cloak and moved toward the light. The closer I came, the stronger it glowed. Without Lulu's presence, this tunnel felt dangerous. I kept myself grounded by the water soaking into my boots and the feel of the cold stone against my fingertips. But something waited for me up ahead. It kept itself hidden but whispered in hushed tones.

Like a secret.

"Come closer, let me look at you." The voice was soothing and echoed off the walls all around me like it was coming from inside the rock itself. "I know you. Yes, word has reached my ears. You are legend."

Oh, gods. It's my dream. "I am?"

"Oh yes, I know you." The voice traveled all around me. It pulled me closer and closer. I no longer heard my steps. I only heard the voice. "The princess who became a wolf. Now tell me, what possessed you to do such a thing?"

A woman came into view, long and lithe, wearing a robe of deep red. This time, I could see her resemblance to Fray. Same brown hair. Blue eyes, almost as clear as glass. She looked past me, narrowing her gaze. "Come closer. Let me look upon your face."

I turned, expecting to see Fray, but there was nothing but the cave and the dripping water. Who had been standing with me?

"I said come closer."

I counted the steps to Rixon and, once close enough, allowed her elegant hands to brush my cheekbones. "Any woman able to capture my son's heart is a friend to me and to my pack," she said. "Tell me, how did you cure him of his Voicelessness?"

I should have been intimidated, but I'd had my share of high royalty, and I knew to be fickle with whom I trust. She may have been beautiful, and she may have been Fray's mother, but I would not let my secrets go so easily. "I'll answer your questions if you answer mine," I said. When she nodded, I continued.

"I had a friend in Stormwall who concocted a cure for the Voiceless." I waited, expecting a reaction, but she merely watched me. *My turn.* "Why are you here?"

"I come here to seek peace," Rixon answered. "And to speak to the dead and those too far to touch."

"They told me to come to you."

"They were right. Come."

Her hands lowered as she walked toward the tunnel, where blue light shone in ripples. Closer and closer, the waves turned into rainbows, dancing along the walls of the cavern. When we stood in the center, I saw a naturally raised basin of water. No. A pool.

"We've met before," I said. "In Abiyaya's home. Except you climbed out of a fireplace and didn't have any clothes on."

Rixon smiled. "A useful mode of transportation, fire is." She looked up from the water and smiled slightly. "My turn. What are your powers like?"

"You haven't been watching me?"

"Not at all times, Isabelle."

"Fire," I said, then thought of the avalanche. "Earth."

"More will come soon, daughter of Aquarius. You have much to learn."

I sifted through my time with Aquarius and wished I'd had more. I cursed to myself. He didn't tell me who he was. He didn't tell me. It was partly my doing. I was the one who rushed into leaving Wargrave's. Would Aquarius have told me his story if I had stayed a bit longer? He would have taught me what I was. I would have learned to control it instead of acting without due consideration of my own magic.

Rixon smiled again, a less fearful figure than our first meeting. She took a finger and dipped it into the water, stirring the colors. I saw more than blues and greens. Now reds and yellows. And black.

"Graze the water with the tips of your fingers, Isabelle," she said. "Graze the water and let me show you what you really want to know."

I swallowed hard, fighting the urge to run. Something about the pool of water filled my stomach with dread. Almost like being in complete darkness surrounded by monsters, wondering when the first one would strike.

But a creepy woman was asking me to touch some creepy water, and I wasn't quite sure what any of this had to do with me staying at the Den. "Is this some sort of initiation thing? Does everyone have to touch the weirdest pool of water they'd ever seen?"

Rixon shook her head, almost in awe of my question. "Only if they want to see the truth," she said, her voice velvet. "But I understand your feelings." She leaned over the basin and flashed a tiny smile. "I was once afraid."

As kind as her words and face were, I was afraid of Rixon. Horribly afraid—but somehow, I managed to straighten and move my hand to the water where the tips of my first two fingers hovered along the top. "I am brave."

A faint smiled grew across Rixon's face. "Yes, you are."

I am brave.

I dipped my hands into the water.

It started slowly, a slight shift in the cavern as if I were tilting sideways. Yet I kept my feet planted, and the water never spilled from the basin. Rixon stood on the other side, now upside down with me, her hair still in place as if I were the only one moving. I gasped and drew my hand from the water, but it was too late. I closed my eyes, fearful of what was to come.

Why are you here? The voice came like a rush of air, but it wasn't Rixon's. It sounded as though hundreds of voices had overlapped on top of one another. Each unique, speaking the same words at the same pace, forming one singular question: *why are you here?*

Sunlight suddenly streamed through my closed eyes. I opened them to find myself standing on the front steps of Stormwall castle. A whole battalion of soldiers stood at attention, clad in new armor, swords at their hips, helmet visors down. They all looked the same when they stood like that, masked by their conformity. But I could see him. I could pick him out from a lineup of doppelgangers any day.

Why are you here?

I went to walk only to freeze mid step. A little girl ran out ahead, squealing, her arms outstretched, her black hair in a single braid down her back. She collided with the tall soldier in front, wrapping her little arms around his legs. A sword of pure Mirosian steel hung at his hip. Something on the pommel caught the sunlight and nearly blinded me. Blinking away spots of red, I watched them. He didn't move from his stance. A soldier through and through.

"Don't go," the little girl sobbed. "Don't go—"

Henry. Don't go.

I sank to my knees. When the first tear dropped from the little girl's cheek and landed onto Henry's boot, I was suddenly lifted from the scene. I squeezed my eyes closed, awaiting the fall.

It didn't come.

I opened my eyes to find myself in front of my mother's chambers. The same little girl stood with her ear to the door. Sobs came from within. The girl kept silent, a stoic look of suppressed sadness etched on her tiny face. A sudden darkness floated between us, blotting out her face. The same shadow took me again.

I found myself in a different place entirely. A very large tent, and inside of it, a large table with maps covering its every inch. A chest in the corner, a sword, a shield, a cot, a banner depicting the bear of Mirosa, and my father with his head lowered, both palms pressed against the map in front of him.

I felt the blood drain from my face and felt my heartbeat throbbing in my ears. Soon it receded. This residual fear was short-lived. I no longer had to bow to him. I now had power, and he could not take it from me.

"Didn't think I'd see you again," I said, taking a furtive step further into the tent.

"Come in," he said, his gaze still locked on the map in front of him.

"If you'd paid attention, you'd see that I'm—"

I got a good look at his face. He hadn't received his scar yet, and his beard was much shorter, less gray. He looked past me, and I turned to see my brother stepping into the tent. There was blood on his uniform. I could see it speckled on his face where his frown lines had deepened. His large Mirosian steel sword hung on his hip.

My father offered him a seat, but he didn't take it. Why was I here?

As if reading my thoughts, Henry's eyes sharpened. "You called for me?" he asked. His words were toneless, like a soldier's. Not like a son's at all.

"The battle of Highyard was too close for my liking," our father said, straightening from his maps. He paced the tent. "How many did we lose? A hundred? Two?"

"Three-hundred and ninety-six."

I gasped, cupping a hand to my mouth.

"How many for you, son?"

"I lost count, sir."

My father smiled that cruel, cold thing, and I shuddered at its appearance. If Henry was proud of his kills, he didn't show it. How could he be so emotionless?

"I've called you here tonight to divulge something that can end this charade once and for all," my father said, stopping not inches from my brother. He slipped something from the pocket of his pants and held it up.

"What is it?" Henry asked. His body was frozen still, but he moved his eyes to look at the thing my father held.

I moved closer, my eyes widening at the vial on my father's hands.

"This is liquid loyalty. You want to stop fighting, don't you? You want to go home to that gal of yours?"

Henry finally reacted, his mouth twitching at the corners, and my father smiled.

"I know about her, Henry. I approve. You didn't think I would, did you?"

"I wasn't planning on asking for your approval."

"Thus is your right as a male." He nodded and looked away. "Thus is your right."

Finally, Henry shifted. "What does it do?"

My father held the vial level with his eyes and turned his back to Henry. "This will take away their voices. No voices, no magic. No magic, no power."

Henry considered this, swallowing hard, his throat bobbing. He looked off, blinking as if thwarting away tears. My brother was not as cold-hearted as he appeared while in uniform, and in that small moment, I saw the Henry I knew. The Henry who still had a heart.

When my father turned, he smoothed out his features yet again.

"It will make them human and the fight a fair one, do you agree?" my father said. Fair fight, my haunches. He divided them and turned them into hapless slaves!

Don't agree to this, Henry, I thought. *You can't agree to this.*

In the dim light of the tent, I could still make out Henry's expression. I expected it be questioning, but it was far from that. His eyes flickered my way, and I stepped back in horror.

"I agree," said Henry, and I bent forward, wanting to vomit. "When?"

"Soon. We will need to infiltrate close enough to get it to their water supply and then no more war."

"Infiltrate how?"

But I didn't hear the answer. I was dragged from the tent with such force that I closed my eyes again. My body filled with shivers, and my mind rushed with memories. By the time I heard the soft dripping of the caverns, I'd fallen onto my butt, my arms wrapped around my knees like a child. He didn't know. He couldn't have known.

"He knew," Rixon said.

I opened my eyes to find her crouched at my side. She shouldn't be here looking as if she wanted to comfort me. My family made her who she was. The Rowans.

But she didn't look angry. She looked concerned. She took both her hands and fit them under my arms, lifting me to my feet, and there she held me in her arms. "Don't fret," she said softly. "It wasn't your doing."

I may not have tipped the vial into the water, but my own flesh and blood did. By proxy, I was as guilty as them. No matter how many times I'd heard it, I knew I'd forever be to blame.

"That's why they hate me, then," I said, my voice cracking. "My family, they poisoned them and poisoned Fray, and they will forever hate me."

"Is that why you're here? Because of my son?"

I nodded into her shoulder. "I love him. I did it for him."

Rixon pulled away gently, took a finger, and brushed away the solitary tear from under my eye. "No," she said. "It wasn't about Fray. It never was."

CHAPTER FOURTEEN

Princess Isabelle Victoria Rowan, heir to Stormwall and the New Kingdom. Sister to Henry Yuel, daughter to Queen Chelsea and King Hugo Rowan. Relinquished of all titles forthwith. Isabelle Victoria Rowan. Stand up.

My new, shorter name put a smile to my face as I walked through the caverns. It quickly faded as I thought of Henry. Would the pack accept me now, or would they only tolerate me still? How long would I have to work for them to see me as a different entity than my father and brother?

Henry, why did you do that? Were you changed as punishment? Did you get caught?

I shook my head. It didn't matter. Not anymore. I had a lot of work ahead of me.

You need a teacher for your magic. Branch will be that teacher. You come back here whenever you feel that you can't control it. I will help you.

Branch. The man who I'd almost killed was going to show me the ways of the Gwylis magic. Great.

Rixon had dipped her finger in a paint mixture and swept it across my forehead. I touched it long after it'd dried, unsure of the color.

I could stay, and that was what mattered most.

I walked out of the cave and back outside where the sun had already begun to set. I could see my group on the shore of the lake. Sonia was nowhere in sight, but Branch stood still as a statue not far off, and Olio was hopping on the balls of his feet with a long stick in his hands, seemingly attempting to knock a mass of snow from a higher point. When it finally fell, he dodged it artfully and managed a cartwheel before hollering success. When he saw me watching, he padded my way, but Fray beat him to it.

"Are you all right?" he asked, eyeing the mark on my skin.

I nodded, pulling my hair over one shoulder. "More than all right."

"Was she well?"

"She misses you. You should see her sometime."

Fray's upper lip twitched in a brief scowl. "Maybe so, but not yet." First, he had to repair things with his sister before tackling something so large, but I had the feeling that Rixon would be a little more forgiving than Sonia. "The prince?"

I cocked my head, opening my mouth to question Fray when Olio answered for me.

"Princeling of the Stumps has been beckoned by the queen," he said, with a flourish. "Hopefully she doesn't allow him to stay. I'm not changing him." He sighed dramatically. "Imagine having a three-legged wolf in my entourage."

I imagined it too and managed to snort.

All jokes aside, how would life at the Den be if Ashe was permitted to stay? I could not imagine Fray taking kindly to the news. Maybe that was why he stood off with his arms folded across his chest, locking them in so they didn't accidently flail out and choke the prince.

Ashe struggled to his feet as soon as he saw me coming toward him. "Do you have a lantern?" I asked him, surprised at how steady my voice sounded. He nodded. "Good. Get it and watch out for ghosts."

Ashe fetched his lantern and walked away toward the cave without a word. If he was scared, he didn't show it.

I turned toward the lake and closed my eyes. I walked over to Branch, keeping the breath in my lungs until I spoke.

"She wants you to train me," I said.

I turned just in time to see Olio falling from a tree. Sonia, who had just returned, gave him a reproachful look as she passed without offering a hand, stopping just where Fray stood. I couldn't garner an expression from any of them. It felt as though we were all holding our breaths at the same time.

Branch crossed his arms across his chest. I fought against the immense weight in my belly as I waited for him to speak.

"If it's the will of the queen," he said at last, "I will."

I nodded. "I'm sorry," I said. "I didn't ask for this."

"Lesson one. Stop apologizing all the time."

I watched Sonia fist her hands and hop to her feet. She shot one poisonous look to me and stomped away. It wasn't long until her lithe form became a black wolf that disappeared into the ridge above us.

"Lesson two," Olio said, brushing himself off. "Don't piss off the she-wolf."

Guess she was hoping I'd be turned away. She guessed wrong.

"She's always going to hate Fray, isn't she?" I asked. "I mean, she doesn't have to hate me too. I saved her life, after all." The last bit was a grumble, but Olio heard it all.

"You'll find that it's hard to make Sonia do anything she doesn't want to do." He slapped my shoulder.

I frowned as Olio grinned ear-to-ear like a madman. All this drama must have had him rubbing his hands together in anticipation of what was to come next.

"Thanks, Olio," Fray said, giving him a vulgar gesture.

"I think you should talk to her," I told him. "At least try."

Fray shrugged casually. I took my hand and traced it along his chest and around his waist when he pulled me in. For a moment, we forgot about Olio and Branch and stood, breathing each other in. He relaxed, little by little.

It wasn't until that moment that I realized how much I missed having a family. It didn't have to be by blood, as I felt closer with Crim and Pyrus than anyone, barring Lulu of course. But to think I could have something like that again, albeit a little strange and temperamental, stirred something inside of me. I wanted to belong. I *needed* to belong. To do that, both Fray and I had to deal with our pasts, bit by bit.

That was what mattered to me: the people I love and those whom I could grow to love.

I nibbled on my lower lip and watched Fray work his jaw. I smiled. Something inside of me had lifted the moment I stepped out of the creepy cave. For the first time in weeks, I felt like the old Izzy. "Remember that time I saved your life—twice?"

He grinned wolfishly. *Someone's mood has also improved.*

I pushed off him, but he caught my arm and tugged me back.

"When we're alone, I'm getting you back for this," he said in a dangerous whisper.

"You'll thank me," I said as he turned to leave.

He held up a hand in a farewell gesture and said, "Later."

At Olio and Branch's stare, I felt heat rush to my cheeks. 'What?"

"Can I call it puppy love just one more time?" Olio asked. His lower lip jutted out like a forlorn child. "Can I, please?"

I shook my head, dismissing him, and sat down. The moon rose in the blue-black sky, an argent silver orb reflecting off the frozen ice of the lake. With my new senses, I could hear the water beneath the ice and even smell the smells of animals probably buried dozens of feet underground. I'd been to lakes before, but never like this.

"Well, you're part of the pack now." Olio sat beside me, his smile cutting the dark.

I took in his words, repeating them in my head. Part of the pack. I was part of the pack. Should I call it *my* pack or *the* pack or just *pack*? I thought I'd ask Olio, but he'd make up some inane nickname for it, like Wolf Warriors or Frost Fangs. He'd probably give me a new nickname as well, one worse than Little wolf or wolf-princess.

I shook the thoughts away. "I guess so," I said. "As long as I don't kill anyone, I guess I'll be fine."

"True." Olio laughed and then looked to Branch. "He's not so bad, you know. Most pack leaders are sullen like him. But they're not so bad."

I groaned inwardly. Not only had I wounded him in a fight I shouldn't have been anywhere close to, but now I had to train alongside him, every day perhaps. I hoped my patience for temperamental old men still stuck. Otherwise, I wasn't sure how Branch and I would fare.

I sighed long and hard. Just when I thought things would be okay, I began to worry again. "Are you trying to convince me of something here?"

"No." Olio shook his head and looked off. "You don't need convincing of much."

"So you're saying I have a chance here?"

"I think you need a place to belong and that you're still not really sure where that place is." He looked at me, his gaze bordering on thoughtful. It was a strange look for him.

I touched the emerald tucked under my shirt. "I think I just need to forget who I was before."

Olio tipped his head back and forth and stretched his lips to the side. "That may be so. I think you just need to remember who you are now."

Ashe had returned during the night when everyone had fallen asleep. Except me, of course. I heard him approach the place where Fray and I lay upon our cloaks just under a large cluster of trees. He stopped only a few feet from me, whispering my name. I made sure Fray was still asleep when I left his side.

In the moonlight, the lakeshore was a vast and ghostly thing. The tips of the mountains glowed an eerie blue where they met the sky in the distance, and just above that, the sky was an inky canopy with only a few scattered stars. The scene was almost magical. The sky, the landscape, the water: it could almost swallow me whole, but it also made me feel comforted. The waning moon was a yellow half-orb between two peaks, and I stared at it for a long time as I moved further away from Fray.

Shadowy slivers of clouds floated toward the moon, and I finally turned to Ashe.

"You should sleep in the cave," I said as I approached him. "It's too cold—"

"I'm leaving," he interrupted. "Away from everyone. Isabelle, I promise you won't see me ever again." He took a daring step toward me. "If that's your wish."

I breathed in his scent, and it hit me. It wasn't the wound, and it certainly wasn't Fray's sweet-root musk, but it was sweet and almost pleasant. My eyes snagged on Ashe's face, where the lack of weariness that drew dark circles beneath his eyes had vanished. He no longer seemed hollow. Not whole, of course, but not hollow. "She took away the rot."

He nodded.

"Well, that's good for you, Prince."

Ashe blinked a dozen times as if trying to find the right words. "I'm not a prince anymore."

Rixon had relinquished his name as well. Good for him.

"Well, we have something in common then, don't we?" I clicked my tongue and looked away. "At least there's that."

"Listen, I'm sorry about that day. I was caught up, confused. I didn't know what I was doing."

I nodded, knowing the truth all along. "I know."

"I never meant for any of this to happen."

"It wasn't your fault."

"If I had only known what my father was doing—"

"It wasn't your fault, Ashe."

In that moment, something passed between the two of us. Understanding. Compassion. Pity. Saying his name made it all spill out, and suddenly he was reborn. Not a prince. Just Ashe. A stranger I'd met once again. His smirk, a ghost and a memory.

"You know, I don't think my father will hunt us like I thought he would," he said. "I think we'll be all right."

"What feeling is that based from?"

He shrugged, pulling his cloak tight. "Faith, maybe." He smiled to himself and turned away. "I'll find a new home. Hunker down until winter is over and cross the mountains. Somewhere that doesn't stink so much like wet dog."

I smiled, remembering what Abiyaya had said that day in the market square. *I see love and many, many children. All boys.* Picturing Ashe as a father almost made me want to take back those punches to his face. Almost.

"I want to make a home here," I said. "With Fray."

"I get it, Isabelle."

"Good."

Ashe stepped forward, but then backed away as if an invisible wall stood between us. Maybe one did. Maybe it was more than a wall.

"You know, I'd sit by the sea and watch the ships come and go and wonder when it would be my time," he said. His lips thinned into a hard line. "To fight. To prove myself. And I'd wait and wait, and that time finally came. And each minute felt like a year stretching slowly, like pulling back a bowstring, and you just sit back waiting for it to snap back at you because that's what I found life really is."

I caught his glance, and I debated asking him to stop. I didn't need to hear about his life on the Peek Islands. That life was gone for him, just as my life in Stormwall was. He'd do best to remember that. But I let him continue anyway.

"Life is a collection of moments and memories, and eventually they're going to snap back and hurt you, and we're forever pulling at them because we don't know how to let go. And I don't know how to really make you forgive me."

I wanted to tell him that I didn't think I ever could forgive him, period, and that we may never be friends again no matter how hard I tried.

I wanted to tell him that I still had his bow. That I remembered his kindness and that he made his choices based on the events that happened, choices that protected himself. I could not fault him for that. I made the same decisions. He hadn't been so quick to break from his poisonous father, but he still broke away nonetheless. And I, the only familiar thing left in his world, had all but wanted him gone.

But instead, I looked to my boots and listened to my heart thumping in my ears.

"I don't know what you want me to say," I said finally.

Ashe's blew a laugh from his nostrils. "There's nothing for you to say."

"So, we're done here." I thrust out my hand for him to shake. "Good-bye, Ashe."

He looked at my offered hand but didn't take it. Was he remembering the first time he'd held my hand? I had been on my way to escape the castle, and he'd kissed it ever-so-gently. I remembered it. I liked him, and there was a spark of something that could have grown. He'd seen the loss of my brother in my eyes, and he had it too. But I left him, and I left everything.

"I speak to him sometimes," he said, not meeting my gaze. "Henry. I think he'd be proud of who you are, Isabelle. He wouldn't think you were—"

"Henry was a Gwylis when he died." I diverted my eyes from Ashe's reaction and shook my hand in the air, begging him to take it and be done with this.

This was my choice, and the shame of it tugged at me. I knew he would not forget this moment. The moment he was truly alone.

"Goodbye, Isabelle," he said at last. "Perhaps life will treat us better in the days to come."

I nodded and watched the lines of his mouth crease in a small smile. The day he'd come to Stormwall, I'd not yet found myself, and if I hadn't been attacked that night—if I hadn't met Fray, and if Ashe had asked for my hand in marriage—I would have said yes a million times over. It made me sad to think of it because I wanted to forgive him, but more than that, I wanted to move on, and the best way was for him to disappear and for me to forget.

I watched him walk toward the cave to bed down for the night. It wasn't like watching him before, walking with that straight, rehearsed strut of princely upbringing. This was the walk of a human with a space in his soul so large it may consume him whole.

CHAPTER FIFTEEN

Three days later, I lay awake with the remnants of a dream edging over my subconscious.

Sunlight streamed through the window over my bed. The day before, I'd dusted and wiped down every surface and even washed the curtains, which lay drying outside where I'd forgotten them. I was exhausted, and my body ached, but it felt good to finally call somewhere home.

Nobody truly reacted to Ashe having disappeared the morning after we'd last spoken to each other. We could smell him, but his trail went east, away from the lake and away from the Den. By now he could be near the distant mountain range I saw from the towers every day. He got all the way through the Archway and to the Den on his own. I was sure he would be just fine.

I sat up slowly so as to not disturb Fray. He lay on his back, his growing hair swept into his eyes. I brushed aside a strand caught against his lip and smiled. This was our home. Home.

There came a gentle rap at the door, and it eased open all the way and bounced back gently. Branch caught it with his boot and lingered in the doorway, leaning against the frame. I drew my blanket to my chest. *Is there a such thing as privacy in this place?*

Branch shook his head and turned to allow me a sliver of privacy. He turned back just in time for me to finish pulling on my boots. I didn't expect anything different from him. His look was pure indifference—or maybe even annoyance that I wasn't ready and waiting at his beck and call. I wasn't used to people besides my parents telling me what to do.

He led me through the front gates of the Den and past the watchtower guards, who made no attempt to hide their curiosity. We headed west toward the Pit, but a little further up a high ridge that overlooked the Den. My legs felt boneless by the time we got to the top. Once there, I reveled in the crisp morning breeze and the sight of a bird of prey soaring overhead and dipping down into the mass of trees that guarded the Den's walls below. The blue mountains glinted against the rising sun, which shot an orange dagger through Lake Cresteda. The world looked unconquerable, that vast snowscape. Untouched by humans. Or so it seemed.

I took a moment to take in the view before turning to Branch, awaiting his instructions.

I took a deep breath. One day at a time.

He stood, three times my size, hair dusted with morning snowfall, his brows pulled tight. He was stone—a thing to be feared with eyes glazed with violence. A leader through and through.

I gave a weak smile, remembering our first encounter. "What do we do?"

"First, you're going to wipe that damn smile off your face." He kept still as he said it, as if the words just came out of thin air. "I don't care who you were before or who your daddy is."

Daddy. I could have laughed, but I didn't, Daddy.

He continued. "We're not here to fight. I'm not going to hurt you unless you give me reason to. I'm here to harness your power and gauge it."

"Gauge it?"

Branch stepped toward me, his upper lip twitching. The heat coming off his body could melt a mountain. "You do understand what Aquarius was, don't you?"

I nodded. "The first Gwylis."

"The first, yes, but we're overlooking the details. He was the man who traveled into the pits of darkness to strike a deal with the Uncanny. Tell me what you think of that."

A trick question, I was sure, but I said the first thing that came to mind. "He lacked cowardice, that's for sure."

Branch hissed a laugh. "Now tell me what the difference is between stupidity and bravery."

"I didn't do my homework. You tell me."

Branch's eyes widened at my response. I was willing to bet not many people spoke to him that way before. Part of me regretted it, but the memory of Ghetee lying bloodied on the ground made the regret go away.

"Aquarius made a decision for thousands of his people," Branch said. "He did not refer to them when he went to make his deal. He did not ask permission, though a leader rarely does. He decided for us. Do you understand?"

"Rulers will do that for the good of their people."

"But how can you know what is good for your people?"

"That is why rulers are appointed. We trust them to make the right choices."

"And when they don't?"

I lowered my head as thoughts of my father attempted to jog through. I shook them away like a wet dog. "War."

"Correct. The Uncanny gifted Aquarius with powers I cannot begin to fathom."

I lifted my head as a staggering realization set in. "They gave you power, but what did they take in return?"

What had Aquarius promised the Uncanny? No deals were made without the other getting something in return. The thought never occurred to me, but now it bit like a rapid animal.

When Branch refused to answer, I offered another question. "What sort of power?"

"The power to topple castles, I expect. That's why we're here." He yawned. "Let's see what you got. Change."

I obeyed, and Branch changed simultaneously. "Show me that fire," he said. "Without directing it to me."

I dug in to whatever I knew was lying dormant inside of me. I tried, I really did, but no matter how deep I reached, I couldn't grasp it. It was like dipping a hand in the ocean with my magic fathoms below.

"You're really going to make me stand here all morning?" Branch growled, digging up snow with his paws. "Do it."

I stepped back, realizing I'd tucked my tail between my legs. Had I ever done that? Gods...

Branch's ears flattened. "Come on, Princess. I heard you killed your own birth father. I also heard you were going to let him go before he tried to kill you." His voice was thunder, shaking my very bones. "You're a pathetic little thing."

I shuddered as a rush of heat surged through me. I spread all four legs apart to steady myself. "How did you know about that?"

"I'm a pack leader. I know everything about everyone."

And then he lunged.

I cemented my feet to the frozen ground, bracing for his attack, but for all his quickness and ferocity, he stopped mere inches away, his eyes aligned with mine, his breath like clouds in my vision. It was an intimidation tactic.

He pulled back his lips. "I also know you got your cousin killed."

A fierce urge. One half of it wanted to sink my teeth into Branch's neck and rip him apart piece by piece. The other half wanted to see him suffer slowly, bleeding out from a well-timed hole in the belly. I let the magic bubble to the surface and melt the snowy ground at our feet. *He wants me to sing. I'll show him my talent.*

But that wasn't me. Those thoughts were not mine. I couldn't think such things, even when goaded. My vision pulsed with blackness. I sucked in smoke and ash and blinked away the darkness, reeling it in as quickly as it came. Shadows danced and spun on the edges of my vision. Teasing. When I tried to look, they vanished like smoke in the wind.

Were they ghosts rather than shadows? No. Ghosts did not run from me. They did not taunt me that way. They spoke to me. Maybe they were residual magic. Illusions.

"Good," Branch said, stepping away. "Anger brings it out. I can work with that." He swung his head away. "Tell me, what do you see when you feel your magic surfacing?"

I swallowed, counting to ten in my head as my temper faded. "I see .

. ." I stopped, unsure what Branch's reaction might be if I told him the truth. Would he think I was mad? Would he refuse to train me? I swallowed again. I couldn't fear him. I was a Gwylis, and no matter what our relationship would turn into, Branch was part of the pack. And he was now family. "I see shadows."

Branch snapped his head back. "Shadows?"

"Yeah, like they're the ones bringing me the magic." I stopped and looked at Branch. "Is that not normal? Please tell me it's normal."

"No, it's pretty normal." There was a pause in his words that made unease crawl up my spine. He turned and shifted back into his human form. He picked up his clothes and dressed as I averted my eyes. "Tell me about this thing you cast over Castor back at Stormwall."

I flinched at every word. He said it so plainly, as if we were sitting around sipping tea in front of a fire. He saw my hesitation and reiterated, "I know everything."

"Do you know about my brother? Henry Yuel Rowan was his name."

Branch's eyes kept a steady gaze. He was still as stone. "I do not know that name."

I wished there was a magic that could tell me if someone was lying. Now that would be handy. "I would tell you what it was if I knew."

Branch's nostrils flared. "Tell me what you do know."

I shifted back into a girl, picked up my cloak, and looked over the cliff's edge. *Tell me what you do know.* That was such a loaded question. "I know that when I saw Fray, I couldn't control anything that was happening to me," I said. "I thought of nothing but saving him."

"So you conjured this shield of sorts?"

"I did what I had to do to keep him alive."

"And Aquarius told you nothing of his powers?"

I shook my head.

Branch cursed. "Shameful. A stain on this world."

"If you were kept locked in a tiny room in your Gwylis form, you'd be closed off too."

Branch clicked his tongue. He looked noticeably more docile than minutes ago. I bet that was his way of getting information from people. I smiled. The crease between his eyes stayed.

"These questions are just wasting time," I said.

"They will help me understand," Branch replied.

I sighed heavily, remembering what Aquarius had told me. *I won't have time to teach everything to you, but when you get away, make sure you find someone who will.* I supposed Branch was my "someone who will," so I told him everything I knew, which was everything he knew, but down to the details: how I felt, what others seemed to feel, and, most importantly, what I thought about all of that.

"He said nobody needed him and that many will want my magic for themselves." I watched Branch's expression go from emotionless to almost insulted.

"You're nothing great." He snorted and turned away to squint against the sun.

"That's something we finally agree on." I laughed as Branch turned back to me. I could have sworn I saw amusement in his cold, dead eyes. "Hey, for an old bastard, you're actually not that bad. I do see why people hate you—but again, not that bad."

"I don't need friends."

"*I* don't need a friend. I need a teacher."

Branch's nostrils flared again, and he gave me one good shove to my shoulder in a show of dominance. I smiled instead of shoving back. He then turned to leave without a word.

"That's it?" I asked, jogging after him. "Is class over?"

Branch held up a hand by way of goodbye. "Same time tomorrow," he said. "Bring your dagger."

My dagger? The question hung in the air, unable to leave my lips. Branch did brag about knowing everything, so he must have known the importance of it. *He'll use it against me, I'm sure,* I thought. This was going be tougher than I imagined.

I stayed on that cliff for a while longer, scanning the horizon. I'd been told of a great ruler who had decided that he had made a mistake and exiled himself, leaving his people broken and lost. One half became voiceless, and the other, hiding behind their walls, pretended life beyond the Archway was no concern of the others. Maybe it wasn't. Maybe the half who abandoned fighting should have left the war to those who wanted it to begin with. It seemed only fair.

I guessed what I didn't understand was how desperate Aquarius had been when he went to the Uncanny. How a king could damn his people that way was beyond my comprehension. He damned them all and left them cursed for eternity.

I could see how some of the pack would see people like me and Ghetee as dumb. We'd chosen what they had no choice over.

Still, all I needed was time. Time to learn my magic. Time for the pack to accept me. Time for Fray to mend his family and, for myself, time to learn about the time my brother spent out here. Most of all, I needed to let go of the fear that something more than a one-armed prince followed us through the Archway. Sometimes I wondered if I would ever stop looking over my shoulder. When all of that was completed, there would be a home in it for us.

CHAPTER SIXTEEN

I dragged myself home the next evening, half-dead under the burnt glow of the setting sun, mentally and physically drained from my lessons with Branch, wanting nothing more than my soft bed and Fray there to say this was all worth it.

What I got was Fray sitting at the table looking exactly how I felt, a half-eaten plate of food before him. Another full plate was set at my seat. His eyes were weary, rimmed in shadows.

"Did you just get back, too?" I asked, pulling off my boots and tossing them by the lit fireplace to dry out.

He nodded. "I cooked."

I threw off my cloak and plopped down in my chair. I inhaled the food. Buttered biscuits and rabbit with gravy. It smelled exquisite. I vowed to learn how to cook. It was the least I could do to pull my weight around here.

"See, I can do more than wash dishes," he said. His tone was not meant to hurt, but it still gave me pause. I'd never thought of him as a lesser person for being a servant, Voiceless, or lower caste whatsoever. Why did I feel my cheeks go hot?

There was silence as I ate, a little too fast and without a moment to spare. There were candles lit, casting a calming glow in the room.

Outside, the moon peeked through darkened clouds against the blue-black sky. When I finished, I glanced to Fray, whose portion hadn't changed since I walked in.

I set down my fork and folded my hands on the table. I hadn't told him about what Branch and I did every day, and he hadn't asked. I supposed he already knew and understood, and it wouldn't make a lick of difference to waste time talking about it. What he didn't know was that I didn't care what he talked about. As long as he was talking.

So, I told him how about the soreness in muscles I never knew existed, and he told me how boring his guard shifts were, but he became animated when discussing the metal works and how they pounded steel into weapons and cookware alike. For a time, it felt . . . good talking about nothing life-threatening.

"Ghetee's mother Rini wants to teach me to sew," I told him, picking up my fork. I shaped the congealed gravy on my plate into what I thought looked like the outline of a wolf. I smiled. "I think it's her way of telling me to get new clothes."

After a long pause, I put down my fork, positioned myself on my knees, and leaned across the table on my elbows, clattering the dishes. "What do you think of this? This life?"

"I think you should get down from the table." He smiled through his words.

"Oh, you're boring." He laughed and absentmindedly brushed his hair back off his face. As soon as the action was done, he peered at me, moving his hand to block it, but I'd already seen it—the purple mark of a terrible bruise just along his cheekbone.

I will kill them.

I jumped from the table, breaking a plate in the process, and moved to his side, my hands on my hips. "Who did that to you?"

Fray stood up, pretending to clear the table. "It was nothing. Just an alpha male fight."

I frowned. "Were you at the Pit?"

"No."

I groaned. "That makes it worse."

"It's not that bad, Izzy." He picked up the pieces of my broken plate and threw them into a bin. He then collected the dishes and piled them into the sink. I watched him. The way he pushed in the chairs. The way he smoothed out the tablecloth. It threw me into a rage.

"Fray, you're not a servant any longer," I snapped. My eyes wandered to the stain on his face. I balled my fists until my knuckles whitened.

He clenched his jaw. "I know, Izzy. I know."

I couldn't find words for the anger bubbling up inside of me. "Then stop and look at me."

He stopped and glanced my way, his hands at his side.

"Who?" I managed to ask at last. I couldn't stop staring at the bruise and pondering how to mimic it on the person who'd given it to him. Maybe not mimic it exactly. I could add on a few extra splotches.

"It's fine," Fray insisted. "I'm fine."

"If by fine you mean beat up, then yes, you're fine."

"It doesn't matter, Izzy."

"It *does* matter."

Fray stepped back, and I stepped forward, closing the distance. The bruise looked worse the nearer I got. I touched my fingers to it. He winced.

I remembered the moment Fray let Archibald and the Peek soldiers capture him on the cliffs, and I remembered the defeated, almost lost look in his eyes. I saw the same look now. What did I do back then?

I'd solved the problem.

I made for the fireplace and began to pull on my boots. If Fray wouldn't tell me, I'd go around the city and ask. It may take me all night, but so be it. *I won't let this happen.*

"Izzy," Fray said.

"Then tell me, Fray," I said, straightening. My boots were still wet on the inside, but I paid no mind.

"It's going to take time for them to accept me," he said. His eyes squeezed closed, and he pinched the bridge of his nose. "Some of us don't have a clean slate to build from."

I looked away because if I looked at him any longer my heart would shatter. It physically pained me to see him hurt. I searched the entire world of a million answers to give him, but nothing came. It wasn't long before the tears finally formed behind my eyes. I squinted against them and toward the light of the closest candle on the window sill to my left beside the front door.

"You want to belong here, don't you?" I asked.

If he hadn't seen the tears, he heard the sob that shuddered my voice. Knowing what Fray went through, joining Aquarius in war, being raised as a soldier from birth, and seeing him now, in this house, docile and cooking dinner: it was more than I could bear. He did not seem comfortable doing it. It was not him. It was not fair.

"You do because you're just like me," I continued, despite the wrenching in my heart. "You spent your life as a prisoner, led by someone you discovered was not what you thought he was."

"I was not a prisoner. I made my choice."

Since the moment I'd first met Fray, I'd been afraid. I had been afraid long before that, of course. Afraid of my potential marriage. Afraid of what my father would do to me if I did not obey him and produce an heir. Afraid that my mother did not care for me and now afraid that she did. Before that, I'd been worried that the Den would not accept us and that my unchecked magic would fatally hurt someone. But most of all, I was afraid that Fray regretted ever meeting me. I wasn't before. What changed?

Here I was, trading fears for fears. It was an endless cycle that I could not break.

But I dealt with it in the only ways I knew how. Most of the time I ran, hoping that when I returned, all the problems that weighed me down would disappear. When they didn't, I used wit and occupied my mind so I could pretend they weren't there or that they did not bother me. What could I do now? I could not help Fray. He wouldn't let me. Not anymore. I had to trust that he'd be all right without me. Besides, what help could I be? I was still finding my footing.

My eyes wandered back to him. "Do you regret leaving the Den?"

Do you regret meeting me?

Fray opened his eyes. He drew close enough to sweep my hair from my shoulder, glancing to where the poisoned arrow had hit me. "The only thing I regret is not saving you sooner."

I felt warm everywhere. Fray wrapped his arms around my waist and pulled me closer. I wrapped my arms around him. I breathed him in, the scent of sweet root and wilderness. With my face buried into his neck, he whispered into my ear, "We're different now."

He relaxed his grip on me, and it felt like he was slipping away entirely.

When I'd met Fray, he was Voiceless and contracted to the palace. When I first caught him taking food to the Voiceless camp, I thought, *There is so much more to this boy than I know.* He hadn't wanted my gratitude for him saving my life, like it was normal for him to save the lives of foolish princesses. But he cared for me. He saw more than the gaudy gowns and the extravagant braids. He saw past the glamour and the hair and saw me.

What did he see in me now? A girl who did not know who she was. Again. A girl doing her damn hardest to find a place without letting the past drag her down with hurt and sorrow. I'd lost my cousin. I'd lost my brother. I'd killed, I'd left my home. I needed time.

He was right. I was not the same person I was before.

I worried that Fray would not be able to outrun his past. I saw it long ago in the way he did not smile and the way he fought. I worried now because he still no longer smiled, and the bruise on his skin told me that he was no longer fighting back. And I did not know how to help him.

Yes. We are different now.

CHAPTER SEVENTEEN

The air knocked from my chest. In a rush of pain, I fell onto my side, where Branch took me by the neck and shook me until I caved in and yelped. He released me and sauntered back. I clawed my way upright and shook myself, tail to muzzle. The snow was tinged with brown and red from dirt and blood. The sun was hidden by clouds, darkening an already dingy type of day.

Weeks had passed. My fighting as a wolf greatly improved in that time. I'd even managed to change without as much as a whimper. Much to my surprise, I'd grown accustomed to nakedness and even forgot some of my clothes before leaving my house. I was sure if Fray had been home during those times, he'd advise me to stay with him.

Fray. I missed him. We seemed to only see each other in passing or when we were too exhausted to speak before falling into bed. I tried to tell myself that it was all worth it. That soon we'd find our place in the pack and maybe even find our places with each other.

Not long after I discovered Fray's bruised cheek, I'd sought out Olio, one of the few pack members I'd considered a friend. When I told him what happened, he pretended not to care, telling me that wolves fight and not to worry, but I could see the twitch in his jaw and the way he clacked his teeth together.

"I know this isn't my fight," I told Olio when I'd cornered him in the mess hall. "And I know Fray is a big boy and all, but could you do something for him? You're a pack leader, right? Maybe put in a good word? Get him some real shifts instead guard duty all the time? Something useful."

Olio had chortled at this. "You think guarding our home isn't useful?"

"I didn't mean—"

He slapped a hand to my shoulder, the once-wounded one, and my legs nearly buckled. "I'm joking with you, Princess. Castor is tolerated here, I'll give you that, but if your lover's turmoil is affecting you, I will not stand for it." He said the next words a bit louder. "It is tearing you up inside, isn't it?"

I winged my eyebrows at Olio, slow at the uptake. "I don't think—" Then I got it. I looked around and saw eyes on me. Ears trained to listen in. "Absolutely. I cannot sleep. I cannot eat. How am I supposed to control my magic? I'm afraid I might explode!"

Olio bent down to my ear. "A little too much there, but effective nonetheless. I'll talk to Kester."

I could hug him, if he hadn't tried to kill me that first night we met. I shrugged and went for it anyway. Besides, who hadn't tried to kill me?

"Do that again, and I'll string you from the towers." Although his face was stern, I could hear the hint of jest in his words.

"You need a woman," I said.

He frowned.

"Man? No matter, we'll get you situated."

"Go away. Crawl back to your pathetic servant boy."

"You mean pathetic serving boy who isn't doing guard duty any longer?"

Olio stared at me for a moment, then laughed. He had a nice smile, I noted, genuine and open. "Princesses always getting what they want."

I'd been so deep in thought now that Branch spared me a bored look.

"Bite me. Act as though you want to tear me shreds," he snarled, taking in my every move with dark eyes. I looked at to Branch's massive height. I'd already slashed him once with my claws. A flesh wound. He never even flinched.

I knew I should focus on Branch, but I was so tired. He'd come to wake me before the sun rose. By the position of the sun, it was now early afternoon, and I'd yet to eat. I staggered back a step, light-headed and gasping for breath. Branch took that moment to put all he had into threats and demeaning comments about my family and how weak he thought I was. He knew his words would cut. They always did.

The thing was, it wasn't so much his bullying but the thought of that bruise on Fray's cheek and how I'd burn down the world to protect him. My magic poured through me when I thought of him in danger. It flared, red-hot and fierce.

My fire took over, and when it did, I was a single entity. The world around me faded in and out of view. I watched it all through a veil of smoke and ash. I tasted it. I felt it turning my skin to grit.

I made a move, my jaws clamping around Branch's forearm, and bit down as hard as I could. His head flung back. I could see the whites of his eyes. He was hurting, and not just because of my bite.

He shoved me off into the dirtied snow, and I let him. I panted away the magic, feeling it extinguish almost immediately. Like a candle in a breeze. The world became clear again.

Branch licked his wound just as the clouds moved and the sun peeked through. "Your teeth were hot as the depth of all hells."

My heartbeat slowed. Unlike my fire, the warmth of the sun set me at peace. I shifted back into human form and stood, naked, bracing one hand against a tree, gulping down air as if it were water. "What does that mean?"

"That fire is a part of you and probably the most dominant aspect of your magic."

"Was fire Aquarius's dominant power?"

Branch squinted against the sun. "The Uncanny made a deal with him. He was closer than the fire to any of us."

Well, I'd have guessed that was that. I knew more about my magic than I had weeks before and my fighting rivaled the old pack leader, so why were we doing this? If I'd known any better,Branch was out here all day just to spite me.

I was afraid to ask before, but now the words flowed freely. "When are we going to be done with this?" Without all this time away, I could work on things with Fray, or else the rest of the pack. I hadn't seen Ghetee or Rini—or anyone for that matter—in days.

"I'm doing what Rixon instructed."

I whirled toward him. "I know, but why? I could just promise not to change form again if she's really that concerned about my stupid magic. I could probably do without it anyhow."

I was too much wolf and not enough human. I needed a rest.

Branch tilted his head. He looked offended. "You're a Gwylis now. The quicker you accept it, the quicker we can get through this."

I already *had* accepted it. More than he'd ever know. I was already beginning to forget who I was before. What I even looked like without my hair in tangles and my skin unblemished. Branch kept me in a constant state of anger. I was too scared to even see how dark the circles under my eyes were or how the creases between my brows had deepened. I hadn't been eating much, so my limbs felt sinewy. I may have been as strong as a Gwylis, but I was liable to disappear if I did not tend to the human side of me.

I needed a human touch. Fingertips, not claws. Lips, not teeth. I thought of Fray and nibbled my lower lip. Okay, maybe *some* teeth.

"Change again," Branch ordered. "This time—"

I was beginning to forget my life before. It was what I wanted, wasn't it?

I did remember Lulu, though. The way she'd sneak into my room at night and the way she'd smile. When Henry was alive, the three of us were a force to be reckoned with. The future of Mirosa. Three crazy children with dreams bigger than the world.

Now two were dead, and to the people of Mirosa, I might as well be.

Branch roared closer to my ear. "Change now."

I got to my feet, facing the large wolf, steeling myself. "Don't bark orders to me. I don't answer to you, old man."

"You do while you're here. You are part of a pack. Know your place."

I winced at the intensity of his voice. Each word was a growl that shook me to my bones. But true to my nature, I let my mouth run before my mind could warn against it.

"This is not why I'm here—to take magic lessons from you. I'm eighteen years old. I don't need school anymore."

Branch prowled the area, making circles in the snow. "You are eighteen, that's clear." He shook his head as if shaking out debris from his ears. "Castor will hear about your disloyalty."

I bristled. Loyalty to the Den was why I dragged myself out of bed and away from Fray's warm body. It was why I felt the distance between us stretch and stretch. Loyalty was why I gritted my teeth against Branch's insults each and every day. I pledged loyalty to the Gwylis the moment Aquarius bore his teeth down on me.

I was not disloyal.

Branch looked me dead in the eyes. "You're nothing but a spoiled little girl with daddy issues who has no sense of responsibility. Loyalty is beneath you." His expression softened, but his words stung. "Just like your brother."

My heart pounded in my ears. I knew a trap when I saw one, and Branch's words were merely to entice me. I knew I should have ignored him, but each taunting grin, each flash of his teeth, sent my blood boiling.

I bit my lower lip until I tasted blood. A familiar shadow passed before my eyes, and for a moment, the world covered itself in gray. I could see Branch's form, but it became muddled around the edges. I blinked, but it did not change. Despite everything I told myself, despite pushing away Branch's words, the darkness took me into its depths, slamming down on me like a tidal wave.

But I was not changed. Still in my human form, my heart began to drum against my ribs, and my throat tightened against the onslaught of the magic I felt filling me up. This was not possible. Was it?

Abruptly, I was nothing. Limitless, weightless, a cloud, a leaf riding the wind in a sea of black. Branch's outline became nothing until he disappeared entirely. I no longer felt the snow beneath my feet. I no longer smelled Branch or the forest or the breeze.

Was I dead?

But I was breathing. I could hear it—the only sound in the void. A deep, heavy breathing that was...

...not my own.

Someone was there with me.

I felt it against my skin, not like the wind, but more like the heat of a fire, and it stank of charred flesh. Overhead, the sky grew darker, almost black, but beneath my feet, it glowed a searing crimson. I knew this was not right. The shadows that had been haunting me had taken me somewhere against my will. Where was Branch?

"Help me," I whispered. If this was the Underworld, they had to take me back to Branch. I wasn't ready. Not yet.

A voice sang, almost melodious and comforting if not for the words it spoke: "We've been waiting for you in the fire. You brought us closer. We are you."

For all that was happening, I knew it to be true. I saw the darkness long before I began to acknowledge its presence.

The Uncanny made a deal with him, Branch had said. *He was closer to the fire than any of us.*

My belly tightened. I clenched my fists against it as my knees hit the ground beneath me. Heat ignited my skin, flickers of flame dancing up from my thighs to my arms, setting me aflame. But I did not feel pain. I was engulfed within it. The fire was part of me. Maybe the whole of me.

Disoriented and sick, I managed one thought. I was close to the fire, by proxy, and these shadows, they were the Uncanny.

And then the visions came.

First, the scene blurred, like an unfocused dream. Slowly, I rose to my feet, bracing myself for what was to come. When it cleared, I came face to face with Stormwall Palace. And it was on fire.

Warning bells rang out and horns blew, loud and urgent. But the flames poured from every window all the way to the tops of the towers. People screamed, the bloodthirsty and the pleading alike. Mingled, overlapping. I covered my ears to block out the sound, but it was in my head already, and I could not unhear it.

A cold sweat broke out over my skin as the vision faded. I shook away the bells and keening from my skull, but it was no use. I would hear them for my entire life.

Another vision came. This time it was a single figure. It walked from the blackness, coming closer and closer until it took the shape of a man. My father looked at me, his face twisted with rage and disgust. His belly was torn open, spilling blood and guts onto his feet so continuously that I wondered how a body could hold so much.

But I knew how. My father was dead and had been sentenced to life in the fire of the Underworld, reliving his death over and over. And I had done it to him.

I screamed. I closed my eyes against the terrible sight.

Open your eyes to it, the Uncanny spoke. *Open your eyes and see. We welcome you, Princess of the Gwylis. We welcome you to the fire.*

Behind my eyes, I saw the demons. Oozing black with eyes of red. I saw myself in them. A girl with black hair with eyes of pure hatred. *No. You cannot have me.*

It is too late. We already do.

As soon as the words formed on my lips, a flash of light streamed across my vision, forcing my eyes to open and filling this black world I'd somehow transported to with brightness. It blinded me as if I were looking straight into the sun—burning, searing my eyes.

I opened my eyes to see the snowy winter mountains and Branch, now in human form, standing only a few feet away with a cloak in his hands. I felt the breeze, chilly against my skin, and inhaled the scent of everything familiar. My belly rolled over on itself, and my head grew light. I lowered myself to my knees and bent my head. Soon, I felt the heaviness of my cloak draped over my naked form. I shivered within it. "What happened to me? I croaked. *Please tell me there's an explanation.*

Branch waited a moment before answering. "I don't know."

Bile rose into my throat, but I managed to rock back onto my heels and fix Branch with a leveled gaze. "What did I do?"

Branch made no move toward me. "You opened the sky and plucked out the sun."

I sighed, long and hard. I could still hear the warning bells. I could still see my father's insides puddling around his feet. "In simple terms, Branch. Please. No riddles."

Branch's eyes softened into something resembling pity. "You opened the sky and plucked out the sun."

Fray wasn't home when I arrived, which gave me time to collapse into the screams I'd held back the whole walk from the cliff to the Den.

What have I done?

I bent over the table, knocking my fist against the wood as I thought about my next move. There was something about Aquarius that I did not understand. I knew for a fact that he was the first Gwylis, which made him the most powerful. From what I'd gathered, the Uncanny gave him magic beyond anything I could imagine. The same magic flowed through my veins. Much of it still lay in waiting, allowing me time to harness it. That is, if I wanted to harness it.

The fire. The earthquake. What had I done this morning? I could not have taken away the sun as Branch had told me I had. Old men talked in metaphors. Pyrus did it all the time.

That was not a dream. What I'd set foot in, the Uncanny had brought me there for a reason. They wanted to show me what I'd become... what they had given Aquarius. But why me? Fray had never spoken of such things. Was I special because I'd been bitten by Aquarius? If I had known, would I still have gone through with it?

"The Uncanny must have haunted him too," I said aloud. "No wonder why he secluded himself." I cursed. This thing I was, it was demon-born. Cursed. Brought to earth from the depths and thrown into mortal men who did not know any better than to deal with monsters.

But I was not a monster. No, I had created that shield to rescue Fray back in Stormwall. That magic was used for good. It was not all meant to destroy.

I pressed my palms against my temples. The weight of the emerald necklace between my breasts suddenly felt heavier than stone. I pulled it out and grasped it tightly in my fist.

Henry had done it. He'd become a Gwylis. Had he struggled with his magic as I did? Did he have visions like that? Did he feel alone? Gods, I hoped he hadn't died knowing nobody loved him. I had. Did he remember me?

I felt the quiver in my hands, a tingling beneath my skin. I counted to three. I counted many times, but the panic would not subside the way it always had. My throat squeezed until my breaths were nothing but tiny gasps. I clawed at my neck. *Fray*, I begged, *help me.*

But he wasn't there. He never seemed to be there. I needed to do what I'd always done and deal with this on my own. No matter how hard it was.

I knew what I needed like I knew the stars. I needed to run.

I staggered about the house and packed my things. Henry's dagger on my hip and Ashe's bow slung onto my back. I then swept myself into my cloak and almost broke the door from the hinges as I slammed it closed behind me.

I didn't know where I was going, but I didn't care. I needed to get away. If only for a little while.

I left through the main gate, steeling myself against the stares of the guards on the watchtowers. The tears hadn't even dried by the time I'd gotten to the path Fray and I had taken on the way in. I veered from it, scaling the snowy slopes, tempted to shift to make the climbing easier.

But Aquarius had cursed me more than I'd expected him to.

I lost track of how far I walked, lost in the thoughts that wouldn't shut up. I couldn't let myself use magic. Not anymore. Not when I had no clue what it was. Not when it terrified the people around me. What if I saw the same eyes I'd seen in Branch in Fray? What would become of me if I terrified the very person I loved the most?

With sure footing, I entered the depth of the forest. By then, I could breathe again, and my thoughts were not so addled with worry. I let the trees surround me. I let the calls of the hawks and the scurries of the rodents in the underbrush take over the sounds I had heard in the void. I allowed the sunlight to seep into my skin and my boots to sink within the snow. I felt myself become who I was before—the one who followed her older brother outside of the palace to teach her how to hunt and remember that she was more than a title and a crown.

I fed the Voiceless. I was a hunter. I learned to sign. I was kind.

I was human once and I could be again. If only for a little while.

I spotted a deer not long after, amongst the trees at the top of the slope. I crouched, drawing Ashe's bow and notching an arrow. The morning was quiet save for the sound of animals in the brambles and ice falling from the trees. I breathed, calming my heart, and smiled as I let the arrow fly.

And frowned as it hit a nearby tree, sending the deer fleeing.

"You're not very good at that."

I swung, another arrow already notched, and pointed the weapon toward the voice. Straight at Ghetee.

"What are you doing here?" I lowering my bow. *I could have killed the kid. Ugh.*

He arched an eyebrow, eyeing the bow suspiciously. "Following you, of course."

I scoffed and placed the arrow back into its quiver. "I'm afraid I won't be much entertainment."

He frowned. "What are you doing out here anyway?" The question was really *Why are you hunting like a human?*

"Just out for a little stroll," I lied. I even tossed my bow to the ground as if he hadn't already seen me using it. *Foolish.*

He guffawed loud enough for me to crack a smile of my own. He then went serious and said, "Right, and I'm here to find the Uncanny and break our curse."

That struck me more than I thought it would. I frowned. "You're a weird one."

Ghetee didn't skip a beat. "I'm not the one trekking through the mountains in the snow like a human."

"So are you."

He smiled. "Got me there." His smile faded as he looked at me. "You weren't leaving, were you?"

"You think I'd leave without saying goodbye?"

"No, I guess not." Ghetee frowned, as if not believing his own words.

He didn't say anything else, so I picked up the bow and started trudging through the snow again. "You can go home, Ghetee. I'll be fine."

"I know you will."

I stopped and turned to him, and I was struck at the realization of how young he was. Smooth bronzed skin, unscarred, his wide eyes still holding an innocence that I'd last seen in my cousin as she lay dying. A look that held hope that things would be all right. How could I tell him otherwise?

"I'll be official day after tomorrow, you know," he said. "We're having a big old party."

"Official?"

Ghetee smiled bashfully. "Part of the pack. I guess they thought it was time. I'd done my part, you know?"

I nodded, not unsure of why the invite had passed me. It made sense. I wasn't "officially" part of the pack. I was probably less than that in the eyes of some of the members. Especially the one with the intense stare by the name of Sonia.

Ghetee's voice snapped me back. "Are you coming?"

"Of course. I wouldn't miss a party for the world."

A party may be the type of thing I could use to my advantage. The comradery that comes with a group of people gathering for a singular reason always had a way of furthering relationships. If anything, I could meet the rest of the Den and possibly gain a few friends out of it.

But what if it doesn't go the way I planned? What if everyone shunned me, and I ended up having one of my panic attacks? Would I run, just as I'd done today? A sense of panic pressed on my chest, making it hard to breathe.

Castor will hear about your disloyalty. Branch's words clouded my head. I shook them away inwardly, just as I planned to shake away Ghetee. If he'd let me. But instead of reading my sullen expression, he ignored it and motioned to the bow slung over my shoulder and grinned.

"Can I see that?"

"You've never seen a bow before?"

Ghetee scoffed. "Did you make it?"

I shook my head and handed over the weapon for him to inspect. He looked at it the same way I probably had when Ashe had first shown it to me that day by the water. "No. I can shoot them well enough, but I don't have the type of skill to carve such a thing." Not like your people, I thought, recalling Jovi the blacksmith and his array of weaponry. "I can hardly draw a straight line."

"I doubt that."

I blinked. "You do?"

Without looking up from Ashe's gift, he replied, "Will you teach me someday?"

I let out a thin laugh as I tilted my head to the sky. "Yes, Ghetee. Nothing would make me happier."

He smiled as he always did and handed over the bow.

"Want to go somewhere with me?"

I frowned. "Are you supposed to be out here alone?"

"Don't worry. It's not the Pits. It's somewhere less bloody. We'd have to change, though."

Change... into a wolf? I blew out a gust of air and blinked through the hesitation. I'd come out here to take a break from wolfy things. But I couldn't tell Ghetee that. Not with his bright eyes and constant grin. Not when he didn't see me as anything but Izzy.

I looked back to where the deer had gone and then back to my young friend. "Would your mother approve of this place?"

Ghetee grinned nice and wide. "Yeah. She would."

My next smile was genuine. "Fine," I drawled. I removed my pack and cloak and stripped behind a tree. Once I smelled Ghetee in his Gwylis form, I relaxed enough to do the same.

I should have been afraid, being a wolf again. But I felt nothing but rapt hunger like a child discovering how large the world really was. I was running side by side with Ghetee, the forest quiet as death. Without the threat of violence or eerie shadows trailing me, being in this skin almost felt freeing. Our paws dug up the soft snow like a whisper. I wanted to run forever. Deeper and deeper into the mountains, away from the Den, and I wanted more Gwylis with me. I wanted them to fly with me. Would it be so bad to do this forever? Was this not what wolves were supposed to do?

I opened my jaws and gobbled up the wind.

I was no longer straddling the line between human and beast. If I had to choose now, I would choose beast.

It was afternoon by the time we got to the top of the highest peak I'd ever seen. Taller even the one Branch and I practiced upon. The Den below seemed so tiny. I saw snaking rivers far in the distance and landscapes that stretched past the horizon. I even swore I saw green. Quite the contrast from the wintery white I swore would never end. Up here I could almost touch the clouds. My fur rustled in the wind. If I thought running through the forest tracking deer was freeing, I knew nothing at all.

Ghetee spoke to me as we walked, telling stories about the other members. Some made me laugh while some gave me a deeper sense of who they were as a people.

"I don't see you with Castor that often," Ghetee said and gave me a quick, cautious look. As though it were something I didn't want to discuss.

"How do you know that?" I asked him, staring straight ahead.

"I've seen more of Castor than you."

"Well, Branch has been grinding me down every day," I said. "You can imagine how that would affect one's home life."

I meant the words in jest, but they made my belly recoil.

Ghetee leapt over a fallen tree and sauntered ahead. "You know, you both should make time for each other."

I paused in my step momentarily. "Are you giving me relationship advice, Ghetee?"

Ghetee gave me a wolfy grin. "I just think you two are good for each other. We don't see much of that here."

"Much of what?"

Ghetee stopped lengthwise and cocked his head ever-so-slightly. "Devotion."

A warmth filled my chest. "I love him, but there's so much I don't know about him."

"Ask him."

I shook my head. "It's not that simple. There are some things—"

Ghetee threw his head back. If he were human, I expected he'd have roll his eyes. "It is simple. Communication is the foundation of a healthy relationship."

"You're thirteen."

Ghetee grinned again. "We're here."

Waiting for us were a half a dozen young wolves, all of whom were oblivious to our presence and conversed as if we weren't there at all. I smiled. It was nice to not be stared at for once.

I looked to one who suddenly looked back at me, his eyes a warm golden brown, the afternoon sun reflecting off his chestnut fur. I waited for the snarl, the quip, even an attack, but it never came. Instead, he nudged the nearest wolf, and that wolf nudged the other until all of them were looking my way.

I cleared my throat, which came out more like a growl and resolved itself in a, "Hello." I didn't realize, until Ghetee pointed it out, that my tail was low and almost tucked, a passive stance for a wolf.

The chestnut wolf bowed his head. "We're all friends here," he told me.

Together, we walked to the edge of the peak to a place that jutted out from the rest, creating a sort of bridge to nowhere. Below were meadows and valleys, forest and canyons, all blanketed in white. My new home never looked more stunning and terrifying all at the same time.

Ghetee touched my nose gently with his own. "You're not human anymore, Izzy," he said. "But you don't have to confine yourself to one or the other. If you want to free yourself, start now."

"Yes, free yourself," said another wolf before she threw her head back and howled. The others followed, forming a chorus that cut off in a crescendo that would have shattered me had I not been in my Gwylis form.

From somewhere far off, a lone wolf answered back.

My eyes shot to Ghetee. "Gwylis, or—"

Ghetee interrupted me. "Normal wolves?" His chest rumbled in a laugh. "There's no difference. We are them, though Rixon and the elders seem to think we aren't."

"Rixon went against everything Aquarius wanted," another wolf chimed in. "He wanted wolves. She wanted humans. You can't really be both."

Ghetee's throat rumbled. "That's not true."

You can't really be both. I was reminded of something Fray had once said: more wolf than human. Yet I had changed into a wolf more times than he had since regaining his voice. He'd broken from Aquarius's pack but had spent so long in silence within a human's skin.

Another howl broke the silence and seemed to lift the tension. The young wolves nipped at each other's heels and tumbled into each other like playful pups. I couldn't help but feel lighter than I did before Ghetee found me stumbling through the forest in a mad panic. Gwylis like Ghetee need protection. Seeing him in the Pit that day should have alerted me to that fact. If I could teach him what I'd learned from Branch and also show him how to shoot a bow, maybe the shadows would not find me. Set my focus on what mattered. Here and now.

I had to continue my lessons with Branch, and I had to accept how things were now. If I couldn't, then I'd find a way. I always did.

I struggled with the boundaries of being an animal and being human without knowing that the differences between the two were not so distant. We craved family, and we hungered for things beyond our grasp. It made me think that no matter what we were—be it bird, fish, or beast —we would always struggle within our skin because the world demands it of us. And I existed here: tame and wild, an integration of two hearts, each wanting to belong to one world. Nothing else would do.

I bit down on the wind and let loose a howl from my throat, so free that it could rival the best of dreams, and I let the sound of my own anguished voice break through the hurt in my heart. For all the things lost and gone and the things yet to come.

I carried that feeling as I hiked back to the Den, to my home, where I found Fray. He stood in the center of the room as if he'd just arrived to find me gone. He turned and ran a hand down his mouth to his chin. There were shadows beneath his blue eyes filled with a weariness that caused a slip in my heartbeat.

I slid the bow and quiver from my shoulder, and it hit the floor with a resounding thud. He stepped toward me just in time to catch me in his arms. I sank into him, counting our heartbeats, feeling the pulsing warmth of his body against mine.

"They said you left," he whispered into my ear. There was a hint of fear in his words and they sank into the pit of my stomach.

"No," I said. "I wouldn't leave without saying goodbye."

He pushed me away gently, his eyes an ocean touched with panic. "Is there a goodbye in there somewhere, Izzy?"

I clicked my tongue. "Goodbye? We've barely had our hellos."

I turned away and stopped right in front of the cloudy mirror above the sink. I gazed at my reflection, at my dark eyes and my black hair, and for a moment I saw the Isabelle I'd always known. For a single heartbeat, I was that princess of Stormwall.

"Maybe this won't make sense to you," Fray said. The weariness in his eyes spread to his voice. "But maybe it will. I dreamt last night that I woke to find you gone, and I didn't know why. You--" He stopped, setting his jaw, and looked away. *Don't look away.*

"You didn't tell me why you left," he continued. "If you only told me, I would try to understand. I would try—"

I grabbed his face with both hands and forced him to meet my gaze. "No," I told him, desperate and pleading. "No, Fray. I'm not leaving. I run. That's what I do sometimes, but I always come back. I do." *You were the one I feared leaving. Trust me. Believe me. Please.*

I closed my eyes and felt his arms wrap tightly around my waist. I placed both hands on his and squeezed them back with the same intensity.

His arms never broke contact, but I drew back as he pulled me closer. I stared into his eyes. He was more than a strong and kind man. He was a force that took hold of me. Blue eyes and tawny brown hair. I placed my hand over his chest. His heart.

Fray leaned in, kissing me softly. For a moment, my heart panicked, and I almost pulled away until I remembered where I was. There was no reason to be afraid anymore. I trailed my fingers up his back and around his neck, drawing him closer. There was never a reason to be afraid while I was with him.

My fingers trailed the hem of his shirt and slipped beneath, following the silky skin of his stomach to the strong slope of his spine. He felt so strong. I dug my fingers in insistently, and his chest heaved. "Izzy," he whispered onto my lips. A warning that he was going to lose control.

"Sorry, sorry." I slid my hands from beneath his shirt and rested them against his chest timidly. But I wanted to be brave and reckless. I touched the waistband of his pants and his abdominal muscles contracted as he took a breath.

"Why do you have to look the way you do?" I asked.

Fray hissed a laugh that tickled my cheeks. "Are you complaining about my looks?"

I shook my head.

He smiled. "Good."

But despite his words, he pulled away from me, lengthening the invisible boundary between us.

"I feel you tremble whenever I touch you," Fray said, so low I almost didn't catch it. "I know the things your father did—"

It only took a second for my mind to refocus from my inner thoughts to what Fray was saying. The words hurt, but they brought me back to reality. My father had been a monster who used violence when simple words could have sufficed, but it was my grief that kept me from being with Fray in... that way. It didn't seem proper. It felt like it would be more of a distraction than anything, and this made me sad.

I let out a heavy sigh and lifted my eyes from the floor. For a moment, we stood there, two teenagers who wanted to be free, but probably never would be. I didn't mean to hurt him; I never truly did. Maybe everything that weighed on us, this roiling hurricane that was always above our heads, maybe it was all we knew, and we'd have to live with the darkness that came along with it.

"It's not that," I said. "Branch makes me use my magic every day, and it's draining. The things he says to me...."

I trailed off, but I got the feeling Fray was going to interrupt anyhow.

Fray's body tensed taunt as a bowstring. "Is he hurting you?"

Define hurting. "No. It's something I need." *I'm trying to find my strength.*

Fray looked unconvinced, but we both knew there was nothing we could do about it. Taking on a pack leader meant taking on Rixon, Fray's own mother, and from what I gathered, that wasn't something high on his list of things he was excited to do.

It was with that thought that I recited the words I wanted to ask Fray. *What was your childhood like? How well did you know Aquarius? Do you miss being in battle?*

Who is the man I fell in love with? The man I want to build a life with....

But I was not so brave. "Did you know that there's going to be a party for Ghetee?"

Fray's shoulders sagged, all tension dissolved. His words were muffled against my skin as he trailed the length of my neck. "I do, and we'll go, but not before this."

I laughed. "I do miss the days when I'd sooner punch you than let you near me."

His mouth was an inch away from mine, but I dared not kiss it. That impulsive heat that penetrated through our clothes was enough to weaken my knees. Who knew if I'd be able to stop.

"I do love everything about you, Isabelle Rowan."

"Subject changer."

"Wolf lover."

I started to laugh, but his mouth on mine left no room for anything else to be said. I felt him as I felt the very air in my lungs. I felt his strength and smelled his scent. Fray. Fray. Fray.

I gripped against the tremendous hold he had over me. "I love you," he said as his tongue broke through my lips, over and over until the room was quiet with nothing but our heaving breaths.

He placed one hand behind my back to support me and kissed me gently. "I know this life is hard for you, but I hope I can make it easier."

Hard was an understatement. But instead of expanding on it, I went for what I leaned heavily upon in the past. My undeniable sense of humor.

"There's a joke in there somewhere, you know," I said with a laugh.

He smiled with his eyes closed, and a grin tugged at the corners of his mouth. "You're the world to me, Izzy," he said. "I want this place to be all right for you. I need to know that I am doing everything within my power to make it so."

I nodded. "You are." He relaxed his grip on me, and I smiled to assure him further. "You are."

I could still feel the warming in my core even when he stepped away. As I did, I stole a glance at the mirror above the sink. Less than an hour ago, I'd seen a princess in that reflection. Now the wolf inside of me emerged in such clarity. Smell, sounds, the taste of Fray on my lips.

I closed my eyes, and I saw a girl.

I opened my eyes and saw a beast.

CHAPTER EIGHTEEN

The next day, I sat in front of the fireplace, my fingers hovering over the flames, making them dance as sparks tickled my skin. It didn't hurt in the least, and my skin didn't burn. I wondered when I'd be able to start a fire without the use of matches, but Branch was reluctant to even give me a timeline.

The windows rattled against the wind, loose in their frames. I swore this old house was going to blow away, what with how strong the apparent shift in weather had been. That, or at least rip the roof off. It brought a laugh bubbling up in my throat at the thought.

The door slammed open and Fray came in, pushed by a gust of snowy wind. He shook himself free of snowflakes, as if he were in his wolf form, and gifted me a dimpled smile full of teeth. "A blizzard is rolling in," he said.

I scooted over to let him sit as the heat of the fire melted the snow from his clothes. This was a rare day off from getting mauled by an old pack leader, but instead of lying around doing nothing, Fray suggested he finally teach me to hunt. As a wolf. Great.

"Is practice canceled?" I asked with a sense of hope.

He barked a laugh. "We're wolves, not skinny little children."

With a sigh, I pushed to my feet and tied my hair back. "Let's get going then."

~

We moved through the drifts, fast in our wolf forms, and pulled ourselves toward the forest. When we reached the place where the trees grew the thickest, we hunkered down low and listened to the sounds all around us. Fray's paws were light as he moved. He barely touched the ground.

"It's not fair," I said. "It's like you're practically walking on air."

Fray's lips pulled back and his body shook to loosen the snow from his thick coat. "Branch hasn't been teaching you the right things."

I may have been a fair hunter with a bow back in my human days, but when it came to prowling for food with tooth and claw, I was in the same class as a newborn pup. When we'd left Stormwall, Fray had done most of the hunting. Once, I ate the raw flesh, though when I changed back into a human, the taste almost nauseated me. Fray joked that I'd get used to it. I wasn't quite sure if I would and hadn't eaten uncooked meat since.

I scanned the trees through the wall of snow. My ears pricked and my nostrils filled with scent. A small rodent. Weasel or rabbit.

Normal wolves hunted in packs. They used this to surround and take down their enemies. What they lacked in size, they made up for with smarts. Despite their limitations, they seemed to have made a reputation for themselves.

Fray called it 'the frenzy'. It was when a group of four or more wolves were on a hunt and got the taste of blood, which put them in a blind rage upon their kills, leading them to tear and eat without a thought. He said it was as if they were transformed into demons, even attacking other pack members if they drew too close to their teeth. Gwylis were bigger, stronger, faster—but that risk was always there.

"If you feel that you're losing yourself, tell me," Fray said, sniffing the air. "We'll keep it small for today, just in case."

I nodded and followed Fray forward, my muzzle to his tail, keeping low. The snowflakes tickled my nose and frosted my fur. Still, I was warm and happy to have a day alone with Fray.

Fray growled low, swinging his large head to mine. "Go."

"I can't—"

"You've watched me many times. Go."

I nodded and pushed through the snow ahead of Fray where, between two trees, gathered a small warren of snow rabbits.

I moved silently, pushing smoke through my bared teeth. I kept low, training my ears to every sound, even that of my own beating heart.

A bird's fluttering wings, snow falling from tree branches, and the sound of air from my nostrils. The creaking sound of my paws compacting the snow.

I willed myself invisible.

I paused and waited, the scent growing stronger. I felt the hunger. I felt the thirst.

I moved forward and stopped again, my tail stiffening in a solid straight line.

Then I attacked.

I fit the rabbit between my jaws and bit down with a fierceness that was both bloodthirsty and unabashed. So strong and so proud I was of my kill that I dropped the carcass from my mouth and howled. Fray joined me, and side-by-side we stood, two massive beasts in the blood-stained snow. Black and brown, darkness and light, becoming one. For the first time, I felt the deep-pitted strength of the creature that I was: a hurricane of intelligence and loyalty, created to kill—but I had found a better use amidst the war. We were not good or bad. We were not innocent or guilty. We just were. In that forest, paws in the snow, noses to the sky, we were.

Fray yawned and laid his head atop my ruff and nuzzled me there. "Shall we head home?"

I licked my lips and tilted my head to his. I hadn't felt this relaxed in a long time. It was intoxicating.

"Alphas eat first," I said, pretending to move aside, but I stepped in front of him at the last second. The blizzard began to roll in, faster and stronger. I licked his cheek. "I said alphas."

At the sound of a branch breaking, our breath stopped, leaving the air empty around us. For a long time, there was silence. Not a bird's wing or a heap of snow falling to the earth. Nothing but the stench of a human in the forest.

"The prince, you think?" Fray asked, his voice low.

Or perhaps my mother finally came looking for me, I thought with a sudden pang of fear. She had the Greatwolf Pack on her side. Her and Dal both. "There are many possibilities," I said.

A rumble shook Fray's chest, and his tail raised. I hadn't thought of Ashe in weeks. I'd done pretty well for myself with keeping the past where it belonged. Fray's eyes darted right and left until they settled just ahead of us. He remained unmoving. "Izzy, move."

I flattened both ears against my skull. "What?"

Fray turned and ran. I skirted and followed, leaving my kill behind. We made a path through fresh snow and into a tight cluster of trees that led us farther away from the scent. And from the Den.

"If there's more of my father's soldiers," I said, "we should do what we did before and kill them now before—"

Fray's entire body tensed. I watched the fur along his spine stand tall. He sniffed the air and didn't speak for a moment as we waited. There was silence in the forest, save for the snowfall. Silence, but something was moving closer.

Only something trained for stalking prey could move that way. Light on their feet. And it wasn't the prince.

When I had first become a Gwylis, back at Stormwall, my senses were not as keen as they were now. Though I had not distinguished the Greatwolf Pack from the thousands of smells around me that day, it was Fray's reaction that solidified what I'd assumed. Men we could take on easily enough. Even the Voiceless of our enemy pack. But there were still some that had defected from the Den who sided with Dal Paratheon and my mother. There was hatred in Fray's eyes. Fear in the tremble of his muscles.

His eyes flicked to me. "We must lead them as far away from the Den as we can."

I cursed inwardly. "What are they doing out here, Fray?"

The question went over his head. "They already smell us. Let's go, Izzy."

But before we could take another step, I caught a whiff of something at our tails.

To our right. To our left.

We were surrounded.

My heart dropped as the soldiers came into view.

They appeared through the blizzard like sunlight through the mist. Their swords gleamed and glittered, their uniforms leather-boiled, black and tough. All bore the Bear of Mirosa upon them.

But it wasn't those soldiers that elicited the thunder from Fray's chest. It was the Gwylis that stood with them.

The world had gone quiet, the air stagnant. Although the Gwylis dressed as everyday soldiers, I could smell them. They stunk of wolf, and also of human—but it was the sight, not the smell, that turned my stomach.

The Gwylis should not be used this way. They all deserved freedom. Not more bondage. Did they not see what their king was doing to them?

My cheeks flared with heat. What I wouldn't give to feel Dal Paratheon's flesh on my tongue.

We looked to each other, facing off in a silent battle, one or the other not knowing which move to make. The Gwylis sneered, kicked up the snow with the heels of their boots. I willed them to see that we were their kin, that they did not need to attack us. But they were too far gone. The Uncanny had created monsters. Men kept them that way.

Every second bristled my fur. They raised their swords.

My ears pricked to the distinct sound of an arrow being notched.

I turned my head as more men materialized.

"Commander, those are the biggest damn wolves I've ever seen," one of the human soldiers said. He sounded young—too young to know any better.

A tall soldier at the front moved forward, unafraid, medals adorning his chest. "Gwylis." He said the word as if it were poison on his tongue. He gripped his sword, unaffected by the sight of us. "There are rumors that the Peek prince is with you. Tell me where he is, and you will live."

Such bravery, I thought, *to stand in front of Fray and I and demand answers as if we were prisoners.*

The Voiceless men with them began to sign, but I did not care to pay them attention. If they were signing, they could not change into wolves. They had no magic. We had an advantage.

Fray dipped his head and lifted his jaws, roaring spit and smoke toward the soldiers. I knew what he was thinking. He'd die before becoming a prisoner again. He'd die before seeing harm done to me.

I showed them my teeth, but they held still. They were as ready to fight as I was. "What do you want with him?"

The commander merely cocked his head. I saw him clearly. Dark hair with dark eyes, with mouth lines that branded him older than he probably was. His eyes lied. They were the type that appeared calm and composed but housed ill intent that smelled like charred meat.

I knew the name now. How could I have been so stupid? Pike Ivo had spent his military career beyond the Archway alongside my father. To say he was perhaps a good man never crossed my mind. To sustain a friendship with a monster made you one just the same.

"I want no fight," he said plainly. "Nobody has to die."

Someone will, the voice in my head replied.

"We don't know where he is," Fray said. The tips of his fur began to ice over as his power begged for release. I'd yet to see it in full force, and this moment seemed as good as any. "He is a wanderer now. Track him yourself."

Commander Ivo regarded Fray but for only a split second before turning his attention to me. He studied me and settled on my teeth that still tasted of flesh. His eyes filled with an emotion I couldn't identify.

He'd only seen the princess version of me a handful of times. He surely knew what had occurred. He carried out Dal Paratheon's bidding, after all. But did he know who I was even in my wolf form?

As far as any one human knew, the Gwylis were rendered voiceless long ago.

But they knew better now, and the defectors surely knew where the Den was located. It was that thought that chilled my heart. My blood.

We have to kill them.

"Have you seen him, then?" the commander asked. He leaned back, taking in the entire situation as if it bored him to tears. This casual stance only infuriated me further.

"What do you want with him?" I snapped. I felt Fray's eyes on me, but I dared not meet them for fear of losing my false bravado.

Commander Ivo slipped a smile onto his face, his mouth lines deepening. "His father wants him home safe and sound." He raised his nose to the air as if breathing in our scent. "You didn't eat him, did you?"

I shook the snow from my head and growled. "He'd be a measly meal." I looked to the men standing behind the commander, the blood draining from their faces. "You look like you have a bit more meat on your bones, though."

Pike Ivo barked a laugh, unperturbed by my threat.

I knew my temper well, and the swelling of hate for this man was clouding my mind. Thank the gods Fray was there to guide me through before I ended up killing myself.

"Tell him where the prince is," Fray said as softly as he could, his eyes boring into mine, though I still refused to look at him.

"What will you do to him?"

Fray turned back to me, his jaw slack. His look was clear. *What does it matter what they do with him?*

He was right. Sacrifice one life for the many. Could I do that? Could I honestly hand over Ashe to our enemies? If it kept my pack safe, I would. The decision was clear.

My pack. *My* home.

"West. In the mountains," I said and heaved a great sigh. "Hunkering down like a rat until spring."

Commander Ivo nodded and turned to go, but he hesitated. He scratched an invisible itch on his chin and narrowed his eyes at me. "You're her, aren't you?"

It felt like the world slowed to a creep, stretching the seconds between the moment Pike Ivo discovered my identity to the moment I answered him. "I am no one."

The commander made a bizarre noise that sounded like a cross between a laugh and a choking cough. "So they say."

Terror settled into my bones. I felt Fray lean into me as if I had started to tip. But it was not enough.

"Iz—" Fray caught himself, but his words never formed enough for anyone to hear. They sounded more like the hiss of a snake. It didn't matter. Pike Ivo was grinning, almost ear-to-ear, like he'd discovered the meaning to life itself.

"Princess Isabelle Rowan of Stormwall," the commander said, drawing out each syllable.

My ear twitched, and my skin grew hot, searing from within. My name traveled amongst the men and Voiceless alike. They all took note of the girl in their midst. The girl who they probably thought was dead and gone.

The commander turned, flicked a gesture to his men, and at once they lowered their weapons. He exuded power, having traded one loyalty for another. I wondered how Dal Paratheon trusted such a man to carry out orders.

"Are we going to let them live?" asked a soldier. His voice shivered and stuttered in the cold.

I braced myself against what would come next.

The commander withdrew his sword and said very quietly to the soldier, "Speak again, and I'll gut your entire family. Move out!"

The surge of magic continued to fill me even as the soldiers began their retreat. I dared not let my eyes off any of them. Even as their backs turned to me.

Fray's clear blue eyes finally found mine, and the coil of magic began to slowly unravel. A strange sound erupted from my throat, and I realized it was only my breathing. My chest heaved for more air, and I managed a soft whimper. They knew me. They knew my name. But they were leaving. We were safe.

"I thought you weren't going to give him up?" Fray's voice was a menacing growl. He moved in front of me, forcing me to meet his gaze. His fur stood on end, his eyes glazed with icy fury. "You were protecting the prince."

"I wasn't," I snapped, and pulled back my lips. At the sight of bare teeth, he stepped backward. Hurt flared across his face briefly before he thrashed his head side to side, cursing aloud.

Shame tugged at me. Why had I taken it out on Fray? *Ugh.*

"Let's go," he seethed. "Away from the Den. We'll come back at dark."

He refused to look at me when he spoke. I'd bared my teeth at him. The fact that he still spoke to me was more than I deserved.

Neither Fray nor I could have ever expected what happened next.

A howl tore through me, breaking me away from my thoughts and echoing through the air.

Both of our heads snapped in the direction Commander Ivo had gone. The scent of our own hit me straight away. My legs were moving before I had time to consider whether running toward a battle was the best idea.

We came to a place where the trees were cleared. There, we saw the archers who had been behind us initially and heard the hungry barks of several Gwylis. Four, my senses told me. I caught sight of Commander Ivo holding out his hand to stop the men behind him from aiding. He merely stood there, watching and listening to the screams of his men dying before his very eyes.

They stood and waited as their comrades died.

Fray barreled into me and pushed me backward into the protection of several large trees, away from the scene. My magic thrummed as I breathed in a familiar scent. Sonia.

Through a curtain of falling snow came four snarling wolves, snapping their bloody jaws as they approached us. The stark black body of Sonia led the charge. Her teeth dripped red into the white snow. The others crept behind her, ready to tear into the men before us.

I could smell the blood, and my body shook with a sudden lust. Suddenly, the men smelled so appetizing that my saliva dripped from my open jaw. The pack pressed against Fray and I, standing in a neat line, a picture of pure terror that made even Commander Ivo shiver with sudden fear.

It was time for the frenzy.

Sonia attacked first and took down the young soldier in the front while the others scattered, each taking their own victim. The men formed a wall, protecting their commander as he fled. Swords flashed as bright as the teeth of my pack.

Fray stiffened and did not make a move to join the pack. "This will only end badly," he said. "This is a mistake."

The bloodlust and rage inside of me wanted to disagree with him.

But my loyalty told me he was right. Attacking them could mean danger for the Den, especially if some of them escaped. Even if they didn't, word would reach Dar Paratheon, and he would send more and more men, and before we knew it the Old Kingdom would be overrun. Again. It would be as if nothing had changed since my father died.

We were risking everything.

One by one, the screams of the dying filled the silent forest. The battle began to disperse, and the Gwylis gave chase. Fray stayed where he stood, though his legs shook with anticipation. I stayed beside him, watching the scene unfold with mute horror.

"Sonia, stop!" Fray suddenly called out, his tail swinging furiously. He dipped his large head and let loose a howl to call them together, but nothing was stopping them now. Fray was not a pack leader. He had no authority here. Sonia disappeared in pursuit of the commander, and a sudden emotion stirred in my stomach.

Jealousy. I wanted him.

I tried to convey my apologies to Fray with a glance, though I wasn't sure he recognized the look, and ran ahead through the snow, following the scent of Pike and Sonia, who'd trailed him.

Pulling together all the strength I had, I pushed through as snow fell around me, until I finally came upon trickle of red upon the snow. Wolf or human? I bent down and sniffed.

Wolf.

I howled long and hard and ran through the world of white until I came upon a form just below a large drift of snow.

"Sonia." I practically leapt upon her black body, where it lay lifeless. I nudged her head with my muzzle. She opened her eyes and lifted her head to reveal a missing ear. Another wound bled into the snow near her back paws.

There was too much blood.

"He's...." She stopped, her head flopping to the side. Her eyes drifted closed. "He's... still here."

With all the blood, I hadn't picked up his scent, but there he stood atop the snow, materializing like a ghost. I snapped to my feet. Heat gathered in my throat. I felt so hot that I could spit fire.

The commander brandished a small knife, but the courage wavering in his eyes was so clear, I found myself reveling in it. Just for a moment.

I readied my lunge.

The commander gestured with four fingers. *Come and get me.*

A smell hit me, quick as a blink.

An arrow suddenly bit the air.

I crouched, fearing it was meant for me. I turned, looking for the source, but a grunt took my attention back to the commander. The arrow was in his flesh, sticking out from where his heart would be. He stood for a moment and then fell down the snowdrift, down to wherever the ridge sunk. Gone.

I didn't know what shocked me more: the fact that Ashe Paratheon appeared from nowhere, or that Sonia was still alive and whimpering.

I tore myself away from the advancing prince to Sonia. I nudged her awake, tightening my own grip on my composure. I laid my head on her neck. "Don't you die on me," I whispered. "Fray needs you more than you think."

"Isabelle?"

Ashe. He wore heavy furs and such a beard that I hardly recognized him at all. As he approached, I felt Sonia change beneath me, shrinking into her human form, naked and frail.

"Give her here," he said. If he were frightened by my wolf form, he didn't show it. That is when I noticed the remainder of his arm was unclothed and around the stump he'd fashioned a cuff with an attachment dangling down with a hook at the end. Was that how he managed to fire the bow? He tossed his bow to the ground, and bent down, positioning Sonia's arm around his shoulder. In one swift motion, he gripped her waist and brought her up with one arm. "I'm not far."

Just then, Fray and the other wolves caught up to us. As soon as Fray saw me safe, he whirled to the others, releasing a roar that shook even my bones. Compared to the other wolves, he appeared monstrous, more ferocious than I'd ever seen him.

"Go back to the Den and warn the others," he told them. "I swear to the gods, if I see you back out here, I will tear you apart."

"You're nothing, Castor," said one dirt-brown wolf, curling his lip.

I watched in despair as Fray's tail lowered and his back arched. Submissive. Weak.

"Fray," I said. My eyes drifted over the members of the pack. The dirt-brown wolf held his eyes on Fray until Fray finally looked away.

His pain was mine, and it crushed me.

I want this place to be all right for you. I need to know that I am doing everything within my power to make it so. Fray's words were an echo in my mind. He was trying to help me. But what about himself?

As he stood there the way he did, defeated, I finally knew the deeper truth of it. Fray would never belong here.

In that moment, I realized how wrong I had been.

"Argue all you want, but she needs help," Ashe said. "And my arm is getting tired."

"Go," came the feeble voice of Sonia from Ashe's arms. The other wolves looked at us another second, then went without another word.

"Fray—"

He blew out a long breath into the chilled air and turned to follow Ashe.

CHAPTER NINETEEN

Ashe's dwelling turned out to be more than the cave I expected. He kicked open the door of a small home that may have been used as a hunting lodge long ago and brought Sonia inside, where he set her upon a neatly made bed.

The doorway was too small to enter in wolf-form, so Fray and I changed. Seeing as we'd left our clothes somewhere in the forest, Fray moved to block me as we stood just inside the home. Ashe glanced our way and closed his eyes briefly.

"I've seen more of you naked than any woman in my lifetime," he said to Fray and retrieved two oversized cloaks from the corner. They were made of fur—bear, maybe—but it was better than nothing. Fray growled at Ashe's proffered hand but took the cloaks anyway.

The house smelled like death and was clad with furs and antlers upon the walls. A large fire blazed from the hearth, casting a warmth in the home that reminded me a lot of where I lived back at the Den. Except this house was composed of one larger open room that served as a single living space. I watched as Ashe took a bottle and poured a bit of its contents into a cup that he forced down Sonia's throat. I strode around the dwelling, willing myself to come to terms with what had just happened.

"She'll heal, right?" Ashe asked, true worry etched on his face. When Fray and I failed to answer, he turned away and let the piled furs drop from his shoulders. The prince was thinner than when we'd first met; I could see the hollowness in his cheeks and the leanness of his arm. Something about that panged my heart just as it had when Ashe had come to the doors of the Den, freezing and begging for death.

Fray paced the home, taking in the horrible decor. He passed a torn-up armchair, a wobbly table with a single chair tucked against it. "She will," he replied plainly. He wore the angriest of expressions. He was furious with me for joining the battle—that much I was sure about. But was he thinking of how the other wolves had treated him? I couldn't be sure. He was too closed off.

Ashe nodded and scratched his face. His beard was full and wiry and matched the length of his hair. He wasn't fooling me. The softness in his eyes betrayed the wild look he seemed to have worked so hard at achieving. A man stripped of his royal status should have looked a little more lost after being alone in the mountains for months. Ashe didn't look lost. He looked more found than any one of us.

Tearing my stare from Fray, I said to Ashe, "Did you shoot your bow with that cuff on your arm?"

"I fashioned it with scraps I found around this cabin," Ashe replied, without expression. He awaited my response.

"A skill," I said.

Fray grumbled, but I ignored him.

"I've learned a lot," he replied. "Much you don't know."

"That's enough," growled Fray. He strode across the room and leveled his gaze with Ashe's. But the ex-prince was not deterred. He stood tall before the Gwylis, his expression unflinching. "I noted Fray clenching and unclenching his fists. They were like ice and fire. "Who was that man," Fray asked, "and why did he want to find you, prince?"

Ashe lifted his chin, his look placating. "I don't know. Someone my father sent, I assume."

Fray snatched Ashe by the neck, making the prince gasp in surprise, and squeezed softly, as one would when kneading bread. "You're not the only one who can lift a human with one arm."

Ashe drew in a long breath and held it. Despite the unfortunate predicament he'd found himself in, his eyes never left Fray's. There was no fear in them. I could have applauded the prince if he weren't about to be strangled by my angry wolf-boyfriend.

"Fray, is this necessary?"

Ashe stared coldly at Fray, almost daring him to squeeze harder.

Fray's fingers sunk into Ashe's neck in response. My fingers itched to the do the same to Fray if he didn't let up. Ashe craned his neck, like he was trying to work out a kink rather than the hands of a Gwylis.

That only made Fray tighten his grip further.

It was only then that Ashe began to panic. He grasped Fray's wrist in a feeble attempt at pulling it from his neck. His face was turning a sickly shade of blue. "Call off the dog," he choked out, using precious air.

My heart stuttered. My loyalty was to my pack and to Fray. How could I intervene and simultaneously avoid a fight with Fray? I bit my inner lip. A fight was inevitable after today. I had nothing to lose.

Fray's anger was misdirected. This wasn't about Ashe. But I did not have time to talk him off the ledge just yet. First things first.

"That was Pike Ivo, commander of Stormwall and friend of my father's," I told Ashe. "He's switched allegiances, that much is clear." I steeled my gaze. "He was looking for you."

Fray released his grip and practically threw Ashe to the floor. The prince recovered quickly, even brushing himself off casually before straightening. "I expect my father wants his heir home."

"Sonia shouldn't have come here," I groused. We should have gone back to the Den with the others.

Fray cast a strained look at me. "I'll deal with Sonia."

I glanced at Sonia's unconscious form and then to Fray. I thought of what the wolf had said to him—*You're nothing, Castor*—but instead of feeling sad, I now felt protective. Which was another way of saying I was about to do something really stupid really soon.

My temper flared, making my face hot. "You better deal with the other wolves too, before I do."

Fray bristled. "You have your own issues. That's not your concern."

My own issues?

My body shuddered with anger. Anger for feeling pity for Fray when all along maybe I shouldn't have. He'd been the one closing me out for so long. He'd been the one ignoring... everything.

"It is," I countered. "We're all family now, Fray. We should try to act like it!"

Fray scoffed. "Family. Right. These Gwylis are not my family."

Well, if he'd stop moping around and letting people beat up on him, he'd probably find a place in the pack. I'd been up before the sun daily to spend my days with Branch. At least I was trying. I was doing my best. Frustration built up inside of me, pooling in my gut and flooding out from my tongue. "That's because you're not trying hard enough!"

I'd done the stupid thing.

The hurt that flashed upon his face was fleeting. Emotion rose inside of me. Guilt. Shame. *Take it back, Izzy,* my mind begged. But I pushed it down and replaced it with a feeling I better understood. Anger.

He was to blame, after all. If he wanted to fume, he should fume, but not strangle princes while his sister lay almost dying. And he certainly should not attempt to butt heads with one of the only people on his side.

Fray stormed off, throwing open the cabin door and disappearing into the blizzard. Ashe stood up and closed the door behind him ever-so-gently, like an old man or someone at peace with the world. I stared at the space where Fray had been in disbelief that he'd gone, just like that. Should I have been more offended that he didn't care to leave me alone with the prince, or that he never cared to look at me before he went?

"He seemed more pleasant when he couldn't speak," Ashe said. He rubbed the muscles of his neck and grimaced.

"What do you smoke out here, Ashe?" I asked, a hint of amusement ebbing into my voice, just for him.

Ashe furrowed his brow and looked to his feet as he crossed the room back to Sonia. He sat on the edge of the bed and wiped away blood from her skin, so tenderly I'd think he were a healer in a past life. I watched him set the cloth he'd been using into the basin by the bedside. He glance toward me. The soft look in his eyes almost took away the sinking feeling in my gut after watching Fray leave me behind. Almost.

"I didn't think it was possible," he said, "but I think you got more beautiful." I wanted to frown, but a slip of smile tugged at my lips. "Your wolf seems a little too threatened by me, seeing as I only have one arm and all."

"Nothing to lose then, Prince?" I quipped. He smiled but said nothing. "Fray and I both seem to flip opinions when it comes to you."

"I don't know what to say about that."

"There is nothing to say."

"You're in danger, too," he said. "Your whole—" He gritted his teeth. "Your pack."

"Pike said he wanted you and you only," I said.

"Do you truly think my father would stop there? After today?"

"Pike is dead."

"He's not."

"He looked dead."

"I hit his shoulder. He's not dead. My aim isn't perfect."

I breathed in deep, taking in Ashe's scent. He smelled of musk and mint, no longer the humanly smell I associated with him. It reminded me of the forest and the Den. It calmed my nerves, that was for sure. I wanted to hug him, thank him for what he'd done, but my instincts warned me against it. He was not my friend. He was not my enemy. He just was.

As if sensing my change in mood, he stood up and neared me. "You're still the same to me," he said, so low I almost thought I misheard. "I know you don't hate me. I know you once felt something for me and that . . ." He blew a laugh through his nostrils as he gestured toward the door. "That is the life you chose? You don't deserve that."

I made no move to rebuke him. Fray had acted like a boy throwing a temper tantrum. "How do you know what I deserve?"

I bore my teeth as he took another step closer. He was now so close that I could see the specks of brown in his green eyes.

"Because I know you."

"You said we didn't have to worry out here," I said, taking in his face. It was a miracle he'd survived this long in the wilderness. The prince was full of surprises. I wondered if he'd tell me he'd built a new castle for himself, just over the ridge. "My father's army is pulling out of the Old Kingdom. Isn't that right?"

Ashe's lips moved, but no words came out. He did take a step closer to me, though, and that was unacceptable.

My arm shot out and pressed against his chest. "Don't think you can use Fray's behavior to come into my good favor, Prince." Did he think I was so fickle? "They will find you and bring you back to Stormwall, and you will stand beside your father, a puppet with one arm, dangling crookedly for the rest of your life."

He locked his green eyes onto mine. "I would die first."

I lowered my hand. "Then do it, and leave us out of it."

I couldn't miss the way Ashe closed up. It was a physical thing, the way his mouth snapped shut. The way he diverted his gaze. I felt him go deep into himself, touching my words with every piece of who he was as a person. Just as the night we'd said goodbye at Rixon's cavern, he was broken, and I had done it to him.

I was no better than Fray. This was all falling apart.

Ashe turned and spoke with his hand cupped to his lips like he was trying to trap his words within. "It was your wolves that attacked first. They would have let you go."

"Do you really believe that? After all of these years?" My father hated the Gwylis and made us all do the same. For all I knew, all of Mirosa wanted us dead.

Well, not all of us. There was still the Greatwolf Pack who had helped Ashe's father. Mostly Voiceless, but still a threat. What did Mirosa think of the Gwylis now?

Ashe pursed his lips, something—pain maybe—pinching his eyes closed. "When she wakes, you all can go."

"Gladly."

Ashe placed his remaining hand on his chest. "I'm sorry."

I gritted my teeth. "You keep coming back into my life, Ashe Paratheon."

"Just Ashe, Izzy."

"Still Isabelle."

He nodded. "Well, don't get too attached. I'm leaving soon, as far away as I can get."

How far? I wondered. Deeper into the Old Kingdom? Before I had time to respond, Sonia began to stir. *She's bound to lose it when she wakes*, I thought. "It's good for her to see me first," I said, stepping past Ashe. "She's a bit temperamental."

Ashe didn't care to argue. He crossed the open room to the other side as if he couldn't get far enough away. "Of course."

Sonia slowly sat up, holding her head and groaning as if hungover. She immediately lifted the blanket to survey her wound, which had already begun to close up. She then moved her hand to her right ear and sighed, unconcerned that she was stark naked.

Ashe gave a sigh of exasperation and busied himself. He knocked over pots and pans and whatever else he could. A line formed between Sonia's brow as she watched him.

"That's a human boy," she said, matter-of-fact. She groaned long and hard, but still did not attempt to cover herself. Ashe glanced and then looked away again. What a gentleman.

"Stupid human," Sonia muttered. "I will save you from him, even though I don't like you one bit."

"That stupid human saved your life, Sonia." I looked back at Ashe, who stood so frozen in terror that I had to laugh. "You don't need to ruin a perfectly clean floor."

The blood drained from her face. "I didn't ask him to."

Sonia swung her legs over the bed and stood up. Her body was sharp curves and angles, but she wasn't fooling anyone. I knew she was far stronger than she let on. Ashe came back with water and handed the cup to her, his eyes on his boots. Sonia scoffed and shook herself, as if she were still in her Gwylis form.

"You won't get out the door as a wolf," I told Sonia.

Sonia sneered. "I'll make a new door, then."

Sonia snatched up her blanket and covered herself before getting to her feet. She nearly fell back over. "They're all better off dead," she said. She glanced at Ashe, who still held the cup of water, though his eyes had turned toward the floor. She didn't take the glass from him. "Most humans are."

"At least we're not all impulsive," Ashe said under his breath.

A low growl came from Sonia's throat.

I broke into a half-smile.

Sonia went for the door, bored of the entire thing. I watched as the blanket around her shoulders dropped, and I listened to her chant. She went in a human and out a wolf. "I'd keep moving, prince," she said, glancing back at Ashe. "It's harder to catch moving prey than a cornered one."

"Cornered prey is the most deadly," Ashe responded, still avoiding meeting our eyes. He tilted his head to the ceiling.

"Not prey with only one arm."

His jaw ticked. "Not wolves with only one ear."

The blizzard was just ending, it seemed. The snow dusted up behind Sonia's paws as she darted away. I watched from the open doorway, lost in the thought that what happened today was only the beginning. If Sonia reported this to the Den, would they begin a hunt for Ashe? If Pike Ivo was alive, would he and Dal send more soldiers? More Gwylis? I shook my head. I left to avoid war, not to bring it with me.

"Kester will hear of this," came a low voice. "She'll be the first one Sonia will go to, no doubt."

I glanced over to find Fray. He leaned against Ashe's house, chin to chest with his eyes closed. There were snowflakes in his hair.

"Would you ever tell them where the Den was?" I asked, turning back to Ashe. I knew he could never promise such a thing. Torture could bring out any secrets a man had. "Pain of death?"

I felt Fray behind me as I reentered the house. Although I prided myself with handling things on my own, my love for Fray transcended all my stubbornness, and I almost forgot the small rift between us. He was a powerful presence when I needed it. *Although his attitude sure stinks.*

Finally, the prince leveled his gaze. "Isabelle..." Ashe said. He was still holding that cup of water. He finally set it down.

"He would," Fray said, but before he could add to it, I cut in with, "That's enough out of you. You and I are not okay."

I expected Fray to simmer at that, but he merely nodded.

Ashe straightened his spine, his eyes flitting from me to Fray and then back to me. "I would never put you in danger, Isabelle." He glanced back at Fray, his expression mournful. "Nor anyone you love."

I remembered how horrified Ashe had been when he'd first seen me with Fray that day on the cliffs. An image filled my mind at how even then, when I'd made my choice, he still tried to save me. He was always doing that, putting himself in harm's way for me. I admired that about him, and I still did. I hoped he got as far away as he could. I hoped, for his sake, that he was not dragged back to Stormwall.

I wondered if he truly would die before standing beside his father.

Fray said nothing and turned into a wolf once back outside, but I lingered behind.

"Thank you," I said softly over my shoulder. Ashe nodded that he'd heard.

With that, I walked into the blizzard and became a wolf too.

CHAPTER TWENTY

That day's sun hadn't yet set when I walked into the meeting hall. My stomach curled in on itself with anxiety, my mind filled with questions and fears. Fray stood beside me. He barely looked at me. I felt his fears too.

The hall was packed so tightly we had to squeeze our way to the front. A few of the pack nodded to me and let me pass nary an insult or complaint. Olio spotted us and yanked us through. The din of the room was so loud that I almost didn't hear him when he said, "You can't go one day without stirring up excitement, can you?"

Kester strode in, her cloak floating behind her like a bedsheet in the wind. She looked as though she had already been deliberating what Sonia and the others had reported. She was calm. Too calm.

The hall quieted, but still beat with a fierce pulse. They demanded to know what happened. They wanted answers.

"Let your fears be quelled. They want nothing from us but the human prince, and once they have him, they will not return to the mountains. They are no danger to the Den."

That trickle of fear in the back of my mind was not quelled by Kester's words. How was she so sure we were not in danger? Pike knew who I was, and if Ashe was correct, that man was still alive and dragging feet back through the Archway. We should have gone down the ridge and hunted him. We should have ended this.

I looked to Fray, who kept his face stoic. If I spoke up now, they'd think I was inciting terror. Thinking back, I wasn't even sure I was convinced Dal Paratheon would pursue the Gwylis. Nothing was certain. What I did know was that the thought of it rolled over me like a wild sea.

Kester opened her arms and walked the circle of room as if embracing each of us. She stopped when she came to Fray and me. "I am glad you are safe," she said and moved on. I turned to Fray.

"I don't trust her," I whispered.

For a moment, we just stared at each other, and I remembered how anguished Fray had looked when the brown wolf had disparaged him. Guilt wrapped around me so tightly that I suddenly felt as though I couldn't breathe. Fray wanted nothing more than to belong, and here I was blackening an elder leader's name. Would he think less of me now? Had I gone too far?

Fray glanced at me with his usual silent intensity.

I raised my eyebrows. "What are you thinking?"

His eyes narrowed, shadowing his gaze. "I think you should increase your training with Branch."

That night, I told Fray I wanted to go for a walk, but instead I headed to the meeting hall and slipped inside undetected. I knew where Kester's office was, but when I reached it, I found the door open and the room within dark as night. I continued down the hall, where I saw a light against the far wall. I turned the corner and came upon several rooms, one of which held the light in question.

There were voices inside, though I could only see one shadow. I pressed my ear to the door and listened.

"... and it's putting doubt into my heart," Kester's voice said. "She is strong-willed, and so is he. They could convince the entire pack of anything if they wanted to."

I heard nothing after this. Not the shuffling of feet, not even a breath until Kester spoke again.

"What more can I do?"

Another voice, this one louder, more commanding. "You will do as I command and nothing more," a woman's voice said. I knew this voice. It was cold and hard as steel, and at the same time warm as a scarlet fire. "You will tell them they are safe, and they will think they are."

"Are they?" Kester asked.

"That I cannot be sure of."

I heard Kester exhale loudly. "You can see all, Rixon, but not this?"

Fear slashed through me. Rixon was here. How long had she been back? For all I knew, she normally did not call the Den her home. What did her presence here and now mean?

The unmistakable sound of a roar of fire shot out like a furious exhalation. "Not all things are crystal clear, Kester."

I gasped and slapped my hand to my mouth, remembering my first encounter with Rixon. She'd come out of Abiyaya's hearth, walking as fire. Was she doing the same here?

I moved away, remembering that Kester still had the senses of a Gwylis even though she appeared as something much more fragile. I should not have come here. I pushed on down the hall in a crouch as fast at my feet could carry me. My thoughts swallowed me up as I went. What reason would they have to lie to the pack? Why not be prepared if a direct attack did come? I was so lost in thought that I didn't sense another person behind me.

I turned to face the woman: Kester. She stood at the other end of the hall, narrowed her eyes, and walked toward me.

"Strange place for a stroll," she said.

"If I said I was here to spy on you, would you believe me?" I asked, coming up from my crouch.

Kester grinned. She must had been beautiful in her day. I wondered how far from 'her day' she really was.

"No," she said.

"Then I was here for a stroll."

We regarded each other as adversaries.

I folded my arms across my chest. "I heard you speaking to someone."

"On your stroll?"

I nodded, maintaining direct eye contact with her.

"I am in contact with the queen from time to time."

"What does she say of what happened today?"

Kester's mouth twitched. "I cannot divulge that to you."

"Why not? Don't I have a right to know?"

"You have a right to know what we tell you."

At that moment, I knew I was beat. Kester was one to die standing, her beliefs shackled to her ankles. I was the last person she'd ever confide in.

I swallowed the anger I felt pulsing in my muscles. Silence was my friend.

Kester wore a small smile. "It was nice to see you, Isabelle. Shall I see you out?"

"I think I can find my way," I said.

Kester turned away before I did. I left the meeting hall, feeling more perplexed than when I'd first come. I hoped Rixon wasn't lying when she said she couldn't see the future of the pack. But was that better than knowing?

I stood outside in the streets and looked up to the half-moon. The truth always had a way of uncovering itself. Maybe I just had to wait.

When I finally fell asleep, I found myself back in Abiyaya's home. I moved through it, pushing aside the scattered items from the floor and hanging from the ceiling. Nothing had changed. The home was still filled top to bottom with knickknacks and useless junk. As useless as the piles of jewelry on the old woman's neck, ears, and wrists. I found her by the little table where she'd taken a drop of my blood, her back turned to me.

She spoke lowly. "Arrogant. Untrusting. Beautiful and cruel."

I recalled what she'd said about me at our last meeting; it did not sting any less the second time.

"I am not cruel," I said firmly.

She turned, her eyes like deep wells of black and teeth red as rubies. Like blood. "The princess with stars in her eyes and darkness in her heart. You will bring nothing but death!"

I woke up screaming.

Something coiled in my stomach as a sob broke through what little resistance I had. It was a few minutes before I'd even realized Fray was standing with his back to the far wall watching me as if the horror would spill out and claim him too.

"Izzy . . ." he said, pushing off the wall. Whatever argument we'd had before, it all trickled away as he crawled across the bed and gathered me into his arms.

"It's broken," I said through sobs. "I'm broken, Fray."

He shook his head. "No, you're not. You're the most put-together woman I've ever known."

He held me tighter, and I sunk into him like a frightened girl afraid of the shadows beneath her bed. A girl who didn't know that she'd soon become the monster.

Another sob broke through, and with every tightening of his strong arms, I felt all my strength seeping out. I couldn't hold onto my bravado any longer. It was crushing me, and it was crushing Fray. So I cried. I cried for Lulu and for Henry and maybe even my mother. I cried for the friends I'd lost who still lived. I cried for the uncertain future that even Rixon couldn't see.

It was only then that I realized how heavy the burden had been. All these days that I'd thrown myself into training with Branch and all the times I should have spoken to Fray—they piled up and up, and here I was, toppling over. It was a funny thing, having a voice and refusing to use it.

"We're going to deal with this together," Fray said. "I'll keep you safe. As safe as I can."

I took a deep breath and nodded, believing him. But could I say the same? Could I protect him from the darkness that blocked the sun and spoke to demons? I felt the presence of my magic in my human form, like a pulsing light behind a veil. Waiting. Was this what drove Aquarius to madness? This feeling that he was never alone, even when he was?

I pursed my lips. "There's ghosts here," I said. "In this very room. All around us. Branch said I am in my father's shadow. I'm afraid I'll never be free of it."

Fray exhaled and guided me to lie down. My anxiety melted away bit by bit at the press of his body against mine. I counted our heartbeats and felt his eyelashes on my skin until he closed his eyes. I held him. He held me, and for a moment I forgot everything outside of that little house. The soldiers, Ashe, our fight, everything.

I drifted into a dreamless sleep.

CHAPTER TWENTY-ONE

Kester dipped her fingers into the paint on the pedestal beside her. With two fingers, she drew three red streaks across Ghetee's forehead and cheeks.

"With the power given to me, I hereby name you Ghetee Ranser, official pack member."

Ghetee stood tall atop the stage they'd erected in the city square. There, we'd gathered by the light of the moon to watch Kester drape a woven robe across the young boy's shoulders. He wore it well, adopting a skip to his step as he descended the steps, where the pack waited, cheering and embracing him as he passed.

Tables had been set up and a grand feast prepared. Torches blazed, music sounded, drums beat softly, and guitars strummed lazily. There was an air of relaxation that even I caught on to.

"Just wait until after supper," said Olio, who sat beside me. "That's when the real party starts."

Olio wasn't lying. After eating, several of the pack began building a fire and stoked it until the flame reached far over our heads. Soon enough, most everyone was either singing or dancing, and when the drinks began to flow, the music grew faster and louder. Memories of the grand parties at Stormwall forced their way into my mind. As with dinners, they were organized and stuffy, with stiff rules that dancing-hands were never allowed below the waist (gods forbid anyone have a sense of individuality). Here, the people were as loose as their decency. I smiled at a couple molded into each other, locked by their lips, and snorted as I imagined my mother seeing such a thing on the ballroom floor.

She'd completely lose it.

A hand landed on my shoulder, and the scent of sweet root filled my nose.

"You'll have this soon," Fray told me. A faint smile tugged at his lips. Small, barely there. "I'll make it so the party last two days long."

Sweet lies from sweet lips, I thought. I would never accept induction into the pack before Fray. He had more a reason to be here than I did.

Unbidden, my thoughts drifted to Ashe. I knew—at least for tonight—that we had to pretend we believed everything Kester had told us. Maybe she wasn't lying. Maybe she honestly thought the Den was safe.

But only three of us that had been in Stormwall had also passed the Archway. Only three of us knew the truth of it.

There was a cruelty in Dal Paratheon that may supersede that of my father, given the time. I'd give him credit where credit was due. He waged a siege on Stormwall and took the throne of Mirosa. But for all his planning, he could not capture me. Nor could he keep his own son by his side.

If he truly wanted Ashe, as Pike had said, I knew Mirosa's new king would stop at nothing.

"I know how the law works," I told Fray. Ghetee had told me earlier that day: each and every pack member had to cast their vote, and it must be unanimous. One vote against acceptance would lead to another vote months later, and so on and so on. "I can think of a few who'd vote against me. One for sure."

Fray followed my gaze to Sonia, who writhed among the dancers like a tendril of smoke.

"Give it more time," I said.

"That's your answer to everything."

"Better than telling you to suck it up and move on." He returned my glare with a smile. "See. I was right."

I hung back while Fray did his part and integrated himself among the party guests. There was no way to tell which wolves had been there on the day the commander attacked us, but I liked to assume they were the ones chatting him up. One had short brown hair, so he could have been the wolf who belittled him that day, trying to make amends. I worried at how he was getting along, but it did not seem as bad as imagined. Or maybe he was pretending to enjoy the company of others, for my sake. There had been no talk of relieving him of his guard duties, but Olio promised it would take time to work Kester up to allowing Fray to integrate properly with the pack. Guilt tugged at me when I thought of it. Would he want me butting in? He'd be furious, that I was sure of. Men did not like when women fought their battles. But perhaps not: Fray was not like other men.

There had been an apology in his eyes ever since our clash in Ashe's cabin, but he had yet to utter the words. I wished he would. So I could do the same.

I grasped the emerald laying against my skin. I'd done my brother wrong by forgetting him and the reason I'd come out here to begin with. So much had happened between the moment I'd asked for Fray's help in getting through the Archway and tonight, as I sat amongst a Gwylis celebration. But I knew deep inside of me, burning like embers, there was something bigger. To get to the truth about my brother, I had to trust in my new family. I had to mend myself. I had to learn to love those who deserved to be loved. I had to learn to live again.

No, I had not forgotten. I was merely veered away from my path.

Still, the path was a lonely one. I'd kept so much locked up inside that confiding in anyone seemed a dauntless endeavor. As I watched Fray, I knew why. He'd regained his voice and returned home. He also needed to learn to live again, and I could not stand in his way.

As alone as I felt, there was one other toiling in obscurity.

Kester, with her hood drawn, stood by the stage where she'd announced Ghetee's membership. At first it looked as though she were looking at nothing in particular, but as my eyes adjusted, I saw she was looking at me.

My father had always taught me that to be respected, you had to be feared. He used power and cruelty to enact what he wanted. My brother had taught me differently. He taught me that respect went both ways—to gain loyalty, you must also give it.

I often wondered what part of my family's blood would take the strongest hold over me.

Kester didn't know it, but I'd spent my entire life recognizing evil. Sometimes it was clear as day, and sometimes it hid in the darkest corners of the room. My judgment about her was skewed. I didn't like not trusting myself, but I found myself in that place then. Kester was a storm cloud in the shadows, and she made my skin crawl.

"I didn't tell Kester."

I started at the sound of Branch's voice. He stood beside me, chewing vigorously on some sort of meat. He wore a loose tunic and even looser pants tucked into high leather boots. *It's weird*, I thought, *to see him fully clothed*. I laughed inwardly. *He's old enough to be your father, Izzy. Gross.*

I pushed out my chair and stood. "What?"

"I didn't tell her about what you did."

Oh. After the incident this morning, I'd nearly forgotten what had happened on the cliff. What he said I'd done frightened me enough. Knowing he'd hidden it from Kester gave me a renewed sense of anxiety. It had to have been bad to keep it from his own pack. I really was a monster.

Branch grunted when I failed to respond. I kept my eyes locked on the dancers, having reminded myself of the first and last time I'd danced with Fray at the Voiceless camp so many moons ago. I was a different person then. Maybe not unburdened, but different.

I blinked away tears. Thank gods it was dark.

"I saw you leave after," Branch continued, undeterred. "Like a rabbit trying to outrun a fox."

My mouth twitched. "Of course you saw me. You know and see—"

"Everything."

I nodded and managed a faint smile. Henry had taught me to hunt, and I could never let that part of me go. No matter what sort of beast I was. Imagining his face did nothing for the tears. I let one fall and pretended to scratch my face to rid of it.

"I don't see him anymore," I said before I thought better of it. Branch was aware of my brother, but what he knew started and ended with his life and ultimate death somewhere out here in the Old Kingdom. He'd spoken to me in my dreams and at his empty gravesite back at Stormwall. Why not here? If I was so close to where he lost his life, why was it that he didn't speak to me the way he used to?

This may be the last time you will ever see me, he'd said. But I hadn't believed him. I didn't want to.

Branch cleared his throat and licked his fingers. "We will continue your training," he said simply as if I hadn't said anything about Henry at all. "I don't care about your past. If you want to run, do it on your own time. But come back."

I nodded and watched the older man stroll away, perhaps in search of more of that meat he was feasting on. Somehow, even with such few words, I felt Branch understood me more than he showed. Maybe he even cared a little.

Not about Henry, but maybe about me.

In the minutes I stood there, I soaked in every person's presence. From those whose names I did not yet know, to Fray (who was cracking a smile at some unheard joke), to Olio (who danced hand in hand with another man). The way they moved and laughed, I knew their connection was so deeply rooted that no storm could ever break it. Fray's eyes met mine from across the crowd, and I felt the same.

"How about a dance, my lady?"

I felt my cheeks redden as Ghetee approached. He bowed dramatically—unnecessarily, but how could I refuse?

"Only if you're better than that wolf over there." I jabbed a thumb at Fray and his two left feet.

Ghetee grinned. "No promises."

He took my proffered hand and led me away into the thrall of dancers. There, the drums banged faster and louder, and the singing rose and fell with the flames. The young boy laughed and moved as if he had no bones, and it took a moment to remember that Ghetee was once like me. Now he was truly where he belonged.

It wasn't long before I picked up the rhythm and got my feet moving enough to almost mimic Ghetee. My cheeks flushed. I felt oddly out of place. It was then that Sonia appeared and took up the space between Ghetee and me.

"The pyre is for pack members only," she said, her face mere inches from my own. I felt the toe of her boots against mine. Her hair was down, but it covered both ears.

"From where I'm from, a pyre is for burning corpses," I said. My mouth twitched into a smirk that would make the prince of the Peaks proud. "How about you start?"

I felt a pang of pride at my words, but it was short lived.

"Why don't you go help your human friends? You know, the ones that almost got us killed."

Ghetee moved to play mediator, but Sonia tugged him away. I seethed. "You did that to yourself, Sonia. We had it under control."

"Did you?" She shifted her weight and crossed her arms across her chest. "You were going to turn in the prince, then?" At my silence, Sonia cocked her head, a thin smile lifting her cheeks. "You're just like your brother, you know? Selfish and stupid."

I flinch. "How do you . . ." I hated how shaken my voice sounded. I drew in a staggered breath and started again. "You're lying."

I imagined myself as a wolf. Lips curled back, baring my fangs. Snarling, leaping, and thrashing. I even began to mutter the chant before I felt the attention of a few hundred Gwylis eyes on me. They were watching, slipping out from whatever reverie they'd been in, waiting for the inevitable explosion. They knew me by now, and they knew the reputation I'd been building since the day I visited the Pit. They were expecting a show. *They just may get it.*

"I wouldn't lie," Sonia said, her voice softening. Over the music, I almost missed it. Over the thoughts raging in my head, I almost didn't realize how close I'd stepped toward her. "Your brother, on the other hand—"

My body jerked forward again. "Stop talking about him. You don't know him at all."

I didn't want to believe it. I couldn't believe it. Sonia knew Henry. Henry was here.

Sonia pushed back, snapping her teeth. "Your brother was stupid and selfish."

"Henry." His name comes out at the exhale. My brother had been here. How? Did he live at the Den? A breeze ran through me like a slithering serpent, and I dipped my chin to my chest. The words came from cruel lips. How could I trust them? "Don't tell lies about the dead," I said. I choked out the last word.

Sonia's face, usually as agitated as a storm-tossed ship, collapsed into something resembling . . . sadness. Her shoulders slumped forward, and her breathing slowed. I recognized the look. I saw it in myself every day. A frail thing. A carved mask of loss.

I lifted my chin. "Tell me what you know about him, Sonia."

But the small sense of shared loss was short-lived. In the moment it took me to see past Sonia's bravado, it transformed once again, as if she knew I sensed weakness. As if I'd use it against her.

"Shove your laws, Kester," Sonia said, though Kester was nowhere in range to hear her. "I knew him. Most of us did, and most of us want to forget, so we don't talk about it. Then you show up and ruin everything." Something fierce tore at the woman, and she screamed, "We don't need your help. We never did!"

Each instrument stopped playing at different times, causing a sudden upset to the music. It stopped alongside my heart. This was all happening too fast. Like being caught in an ocean's undertow.

I was suddenly aware of my own vulnerability. If Sonia was lying, she at least knew the right things to say to disarm me. But would she do something so incredibly cruel? Did she hate me that much?

I shook my head at her. "I didn't come here to help you." I felt a sudden pang, and I grasped at my chest. I had to start counting, but I couldn't remember the numbers. "Did Henry—" I stopped, taking each word slow and calculated. It felt as though the air was being sucked from my lungs. "Did Henry live here?"

"In the very house you live in, Rowan," Sonia said, my surname grating against her tongue. She smiled viciously. "You're sleeping in a dead man's bed."

She was a liar. I hated every word that came out Sonia's mouth. I hated them so badly I willed the universe to reverse time and stop her from saying them.

Because it wasn't true. It couldn't be.

Sonia widened her eyes, the look predatory. I imagined ripping her throat out. I *wanted* to rip her throat out.

The world began tilting at a strange angle. My blood turned hot, searing against my skin. Voices droned in and out, but all I heard clearly was the blood flowing in my ears. I found a small piece of me that wasn't beyond my control and willed it to slow my racing heart. But things weren't going so well by the time I located Olio in my blurring vision.

"You didn't tell me," I demanded of him as my head began to spin. "Why?"

Olio looked as though he wanted to comfort me. His hands outstretched for just a moment before one went to his hip and the other scratched a non-existent itch on his chin. "It wasn't my job, Isabelle."

"Wasn't your—" My words caught in my throat as I lunged toward Sonia, but Olio intercepted at breakneck speed, hugging me from behind as I kicked and shrieked. "You didn't tell me!"

"A little help here, Castor?" Olio shouted.

Fray bounded forward and with two strong arms grabbed both of my forearms and held them tight against my sides. There was sadness somewhere in those blue eyes, but I looked past it. Did he keep it from me too?

"I didn't tell you because it didn't matter," Olio said into my ear. "It was the past, Izzy."

My entire body trembled, and I couldn't make it stop. All around me, people stared. I diverted my eyes to the ground, waiting for composure that didn't seem to want to come.

"It matters," I said. Maybe it was the heat coming from Fray's body, or else the tension. I felt like I was going to ignite. "It matters a lot."

"Olio," Fray said roughly. I could feel the racing of his heart. He was just as worked up as me. His muscles pulled taunt, his teeth grinding against one another. "You shouldn't have kept that from her. I should kill you for this."

"Yeah," Olio said, giving Fray a nervous look. "I know."

I blinked and swallowed, but my throat was dry. Fray loosed his grip as the rage slowly eased from my body, but Olio lingered behind me, ready to intervene at any moment.

"Leave her alone," Fray told him. He placed a hand at the small of my back in typical male dominance. But I didn't need him to help me through this. This was all on me.

When Fray let me go, I shook myself like a wet dog and stepped away. At first it was like my legs had turned to rubber, but then I quickened my pace. I ran away from the party. I ran away from Fray.

I just ran.

CHAPTER TWENTY-TWO

I burst through the door of my house and began a tornado of destruction.

First, I went to the sink and swept every dish from the counter. They were dishes he'd eaten from. Washed. Dried.

Then I whirled toward the stacks of books on the shelves and watched as they tumbled and bent at my feet. They sent up clouds of dust that erupted from the pages and hung like shadows. I choked and clawed at my chest.

There was no bout of counting to three that would calm me now.

I ripped up the covers off the bed I shared with Fray and stuffed them into the fireplace, which I promptly lit. Tears blurred my vision as I struck the match and watched them burn. The grip of anger weakened my body. I crumpled, and with my cheek pressed to the floor, I closed my eyes.

Henry had lived here. Somehow, I had to have known.

I'd felt the presence of something long faded from the world within those walls. I thought they were memories of its former occupants, defectors, killed in battle perhaps. Faded like a speck in the sky.

I spread out my fingers along the floor, making shapes from the dust. *It looks like ash*, I thought. Now that I let Sonia's words settle, I knew it to be true. I could feel him here. In every crack, every corner. I wanted it to be true. I clung to it like mist in a dark, troubled sea.

It was true that he had become a Gwylis of his own accord, having betrayed my father. Knowing Henry, he'd tried to gain penance for what he'd done. He didn't concoct the potion, and he didn't give the order, but he'd created the Voiceless indirectly. It was not in my brother to sleep soundly.

But he'd lived here. He touched these walls and walked this floor and stoked the fire that now burned the blankets he'd slept on, and even though I sat amongst broken glass and ruffled books, I felt him, and I couldn't help but blink past the tears and smile.

Because he was here.

"I don't know what to say, but seeing you cry tears me apart."

I blinked the blurriness from my eyes, letting Fray's outline coalesce into a solid figure.

I stood up slowly, bent as if I'd been broken. He came toward me, blue eyes blazing. The broken dishes crunched beneath his boots, and the loose pages of the books I'd tossed wafted in the breeze his movement left behind. He took the extra weight in his hands and hoisted me upright. He pulled me into him with a fierce urgency.

"He was here, Fray," I spoke into his chest. He felt warm as sun. "He was here."

I inhaled, my breaths steady with the rhythm of his heartbeat.

"I won't let this tear you apart," he said firmly. His chest vibrated as he inhaled. "I won't let it."

"It won't," I said, my voice muffled against his shirt. I lifted my head. Those eyes that I'd learned to lose myself in, the soft curve of his nose, the way his lips still moved wordlessly as if he'd forgotten that he now had a voice. "It can only help."

"Help?" Fray asked, leaning back, confused.

"There was something Henry was trying to do here."

I felt Fray's eyes on me as I paced around the ruined home. "I think you should sit down," he suggested. I shot him a look. "You've just learned something life-altering, Izzy."

I ignored him. I didn't want to cry anymore. Nor did I want to destroy our home more than I already had. Acceptance was the only logical next step. "Tell me what you think for once, Fray."

His brow crumpled like a cliff to his thoughts. "I think he was lost in his grief about creating the Gwylis and decided to lose himself completely." He paused briefly. "By becoming one."

"No—I know him. He wouldn't abandon me if he knew he could change something." Henry was calculated, smart in ways I could never dream to be. What was he doing in the Den?

"I don't think he planned on dying."

I inhaled deep. "But he couldn't return as a Gwylis. Ever. There was something else, Fray. I just know it."

Fray took a long, hard breath and stared at the ceiling. I counted the seconds. One. Two. Three—

"Where do we start?" he asked.

The answer to that was simple and came to me as if it was waiting for my attention all along. My older brother had brought shame upon himself and indirectly me by obeying my father and poisoning the Gwylis. Henry would never have rested until his penance was made.

My brother was born to hate them. But he was also born with the freedom to choose. He would not have abandoned me the way he had if he knew he could reverse what he'd done.

Olio stepped through the open door. He looked around the small space, taking in the mess I'd made, and sighed. "You're one for theatrics, Rowan," he said. He bit his inner cheek. "What you're looking for is under the floorboards."

THE THREE OF US SAT AT THE TABLE. FRAY AND I IN THE CHAIRS and Olio on a stool from the washroom. In front of us sat a leather-bound book without a title brought up from a space between the ground and the boards at our feet.

"Why don't you open it?" Olio asked. He'd been nursing his mug of ale for what seemed like hours. He tapped his fingers impatiently and bounced his knee.

I stared at the book and hovered my hand over it as if it were on fire.

"Ten years it's been," I said. "And I'd spoken to his very ghost, but somehow this is harder. Somehow this is more important."

"Open it," Fray said.

I raged against my toiled heart and pulled the book toward me. I opened it to the first page, which was blank. and then to the next. I recognized Henry's writing right away. He started off describing where he was, which sounded a lot like the mountains around the Den. He described waters and plants, and the way the sun shone differently, and he swore he could hear a thousand voices different from his own in his mind.

From the very beginning, he knew where he belonged.

As I read, my heart swelled, and soon the pages were wetted with my own falling tears. Henry had seen creatures and colors and felt the warmth of the Old Kingdom's light, and he loved it. We were alike. We both yearned for something much more brilliant and incredible. It made me smile, yet it was so oddly agonizing.

I'd wiped away most of the tears, but one hung there as if reluctant to fall. Fray leaned over, trying to catch my eyes, but I'd directed them to the ceiling. "I can't," I said within a sigh, but he cradled my face in his hands and left them there until the tear finally released, and he swept it away with his thumb.

For a moment, I pretended not to feel it. I even convinced myself that it never existed, but Fray pushed his chair to mine and placed his head into the hollow of my shoulder where the arrow had pierced me. I laid my head onto his.

My mind took me back to Pyrus's workroom in the catacombs of Stormwall. He'd told me of Henry and his urge to be rid of his dreams. My brother had fought between what he wanted and what life expected of him, and I was a bystander to his struggle. That, all along, was what tore at my heart. Why couldn't he have told me? Why couldn't he have let me help him?

"He wasn't coming back," I said between sobs. "He never was."

"I know," Fray said. "I'm sorry, Izzy."

"He loved you," Olio said.

I wiped my cheeks and looked to Olio. Sadness somehow touched those dark eyes.

"He talked about you all the time," he said gruffly and cleared his throat. He gestured to the book with a sweep of his hand. "I'm sure you're mentioned on every page in that diary. I knew you before we even met."

"Yet you still wanted me dead."

"You can't blame me. You Rowans have done a lot of damage."

"Not as much as you've done to yourselves."

Olio slapped the table and stood up. "You and me wouldn't be here in this room had your family not wanted to slaughter us," he said with sudden tenacity. "None of us would be here. Have you ever thought of that?"

"I try not to think of a lot of things that could have been," I said. "Mainly because it takes up space in my mind meant for more useful things."

Olio locked eyes with me for a moment before glancing to Fray. "You really know how to pick them."

Fray grinned. "I'm glad you think so."

I turned another page, and another, and by the time I'd burned through an entire taper, I'd read over half of the diary. Olio was asleep at the table, his head cradled on his arms, and Fray had moved to the bed, which was void of blankets, and began to snore.

"Olio." I waited a beat to see if he heard me. He didn't. Soon enough, though, he snorted in his sleep and startled himself awake.

I held up a page of the book on which Henry had drawn three stones —or gems. "What are these?"

Olio looked through narrow slitted eyes and groaned. "I don't know."

"You're lying."

"Your brother had ambitions that few of us believed."

I pushed the page closer to Olio's face. "What did he think these were?" I asked, rewording the question.

He straightened and stretched. "He had a knack for sticking his nose where it didn't belong. Sort of like you."

I set the book down and folded my hand atop it. Slowly. Breathing.

Olio rolled his eyes, clearly bored of my theatrics. "He believed in an ancient tale of three stones meant for evocation. He thought that this would break the deal with the Uncanny and make us human again."

I wasn't sure if Olio was afraid of anything except maybe dying in a horribly boring way, but the way he spoke about Henry gave me pause. What about this made his voice quiver?

"Evocation?" I asked.

Movement from behind me. Fray spoke. "Summoning gods and demons."

Oh.

Olio nodded and pursed his lips. "These gods would battle the Uncanny, and when they won, the curse of the Gwylis would be broken."

"A war," I whispered almost silently.

Olio nodded and pointed to the drawings one by one. "Emerald. Ruby. Celestite. Emerald for the green of the earth and the youth of all mankind. Ruby, the flame that cannot be doused and the stone of kings and queens. Celestite to call upon the heavens. Obtain all three and see their demands, and you have yourself a war."

"I don't believe it," I said. "It doesn't seem plausible that mere stones could do such a thing."

Olio leaned back in his chair. "You are in a land of ancient magic, Rowan. Anything is plausible."

I cleared my throat and remembered the emerald lying against the hollow of my neck.

Nothing was coincidence.

"Celestite," I said. "I've never heard of such a stone." I looked over my shoulder to Fray. "Have you?" He shook his head, as did Olio. "Who would know about this?"

Olio cocked his head and shot a glance to Fray. "You're not thinking of looking for it, are you?" he asked. "It is folly."

"My brother didn't think so," I said with no room for argument. "And he was the greatest man I'll ever know. He didn't want to fight. He wanted these wars to end."

Olio smirked despite his uneasiness. "So we put you on the throne and fret no more."

"I would die before setting foot back in that castle."

Olio wiggled his eyebrows. "Strong words."

Fray rounded the table and stood with his back to me, looking out the window. *Please, don't close up now, Fray. I need you.*

"So you want to be human again?" he finally asked, his voice thick with emotion.

"I want to help you," I said. I wanted to finish what my brother started, but somehow the words didn't come out that way. "I want to stop the Greatwolf Pack from siding with Dal and threatening my friends here—and there. Kester is lying to everyone. We are not safe."

They were not lies. I knew Henry well enough to know that whatever he put his mind to was as important as anything in the world. Maybe more so. If he were trying to break the Uncanny's curse, he must have had a reason. I looked to Fray for understanding, but his face remained neutral.

"And if I say that I don't approve, what would you do?" he asked.

I raised my chin and sniffed. "I will do it anyway, but with a piece missing because you are not beside me."

Fray turned, leaned against the sink, and closed his eyes. "I won't stop you."

But will you stand with me?

I could not ask so much of him. Our relationship was new, like a bud in spring, delicate and fragile. How much more could I demand of this man? He loved me, and he would tell me so, and he would do it for me with no thought of himself.

Olio cleared his throat unnecessarily loud. "What are your thoughts?" he asked Fray.

Fray opened his eyes, first looking to Olio, then to me. "My thoughts are this. When I was Voiceless, I wanted nothing more than to regain my magic, but it was for revenge. It was for the malice I felt in my heart, which is what drew me to the Greatwolf Pack to begin with. Since you cured me, I no longer feel that malice and hate, and I no longer want to kill, but I will to protect you, Izzy. There are times when I miss the simplicity of being human because I felt as if I were mortal. The feeling that tomorrow is never promised is what draws the world together. It was moving, and here it is stagnant. I fear that this will only hurt you further, and that is the last thing I want for you."

I failed to speak to that. I could only stare down at my own hands as they trembled. I sighed quietly and looked out the small window above the kitchen sink. There was a vine of ivy creeping along the pane, wanting to join in the conversation.

"This is bigger than you and I," I said. "But if we succeed, maybe we can finally have peace."

"Peace." Olio said the word through a chuckle. "Only death will bring me peace. Same for you, Littlewolf." He leaned back in his chair. It creaked under his weight. "And dead is what you'll be if you take on this task. I've never heard of celestite, but I'm assuming it's somewhere far off and dangerous, as most things are that you need the most. This is a classic fairy tale. You're fast becoming a moral."

I said slowly, "Everything I have done in my life I have done to please my parents. Henry knew how evil my father was, and he was not wrong. He could not be wrong about this. I won't waste years of my life thinking otherwise."

"Are you saying you're going to risk your life for a page in the journal of a dead man?" Olio countered.

"I'm saying that I trust a dead man more than I trust even myself."

Olio shook his head. "Castor, I do feel for you, brother."

"Izzy is all our problem now," Fray said with a smirk. "Where she goes, I go."

Olio clicked his tongue and rapped his fingers along the table, uncharacteristically at a loss for words.

Fray was quiet for some time before speaking again. "If you wish to break the curse, you must understand one thing, Izzy. There are those who do not wish it to be broken. They would much rather stay as wolves."

CHAPTER TWENTY-THREE

The crow could not have arrived at a worse time.

Meals grew increasingly less awkward as the days passed—not because my presence was becoming less of an annoyance, but because I was constantly covered in cuts and bruises. Branch used my unfocused mind against me, knocking me down at every turn. He was aware of what happened at Ghetee's party (who wasn't, after all?). Three days later, and I could not get Henry's journal out of my head. I ate, drank, and slept with it. I had a piece of him. I wasn't letting it go.

There was a certain joy behind some the Gwylis' smiles that suggested they liked seeing me beat to a pulp, rather than because they were happy to see me.

I walked back to our house side-by-side with Fray. He placed a hand along the small of my back and drew me closer. It was a rare morning off from everything. I was glad to let my body heal from training—or wolf-training, as Fray called it. I wasn't really sure he understood the extent of my magic, and I didn't divulge it. We were doing well without anything sitting between us for the time being.

Each day that went by, I saw them less and less as Gwylis and more as humans, but more forgiving.

"What shall we do today?" Fray asked. His hand dropped lower, and

I slapped it away playfully. Several people greeted him by name, and although he pretended not to notice the significance, I did. He hadn't come home with any new bruises or scrapes, so I assumed Olio's good word had finally been put in. Things were going to be all right.

"Fray Castor," I scolded. I looked back to two women a couple paces behind us. I stopped to let them pass, aware of their sidelong glances. "Behave."

He swung me forward so that we faced each other. "I have a crazy idea."

I frowned and brushed the hair back from his eyes. It was growing wilder and longer than ever. I smiled. "Does it involve a haircut?"

He furrowed his brow and squinted one eye against the sun. "Will it make a wedding day better if I did?"

I sucked in a breath. I'd read Henry's journal every night. For clues. For anything to show me where to start. As the days wore on, I pushed it from my mind, though the idea of breaking the curse lingered there like a nagging insect buzzing. Quiet, but present. This proposal was like a beautiful flower torn up by a mighty wind.

Fray and I were like mountains and rivers where we met and parted. We could love each other one day and the next act as though we could not be further apart. How could he ask such a thing?

I took an involuntary step back. "You're lying to yourself," I said softly. "We both are."

"I thought maybe this was what you wanted," Fray said incredulously. He raked a hand through his hair and tugged at the ends. "A new life—"

I snorted. "Fray, we hardly know each other."

The second the words left my lips was the second I beheld the truth of them. They hung heavy in the air between us. Though it had been months since we left Stormwall—far longer than most dalliances in the New Kingdom—such a thing never crossed my mind. Not with Dal Paratheon slinking around the Old Kingdom. Not with Kester and her secrets. Not with Henry . . . No, it was not possible. Not yet anyway.

Coming up and out of my thoughts, I registered Fray's reaction. But he let nothing show. He remained impassive. His look, remote as a hidden star. A chill of icy fear ran my blood cold. Would he walk away from me now the way he had in Ashe's house?

Would he not return this time?

But I couldn't say anything else. Not a word to make him stay or even a word to make him leave. Instead, I signed, *I love you.*

He did not sign back.

I braced myself against the heavy blow of emotion, but I didn't have much time to let it crush me.

A voice called out to me by name. Olio jogged up to us, breathless, and placed a hand on my shoulder. "A crow," he said, softly beckoning me away. "A crow for you."

Fray and I exchanged a look as the words sunk in. The black birds were used by royals to pass messages on to lords and ladies of the land. There was a small chance that this was random or sent by someone other than a high-born. Yet nobody knew where I was. Save for Pyrus—and Pike Ivo, had he made it back to Stormwall in one piece.

We ran toward the house where the crow waited, perched on the overhang of the front door. It turned its tiny black head to me as I approached and hopped down onto the window sill.

Fray grasped my arm. "Is that one of yours?"

Yours. Meaning from Stormwall.

I advanced toward the bird, my heart thumping wildly against my chest. Crows were very much alike in their black feathers and beady little eyes, but this one I knew by heart. For some strange reason, I could pick this one out from a lineup of hundreds of birds.

He cawed at me, loud and annoying.

I exhaled a gust of relief. "Pax?" I whispered to the bird. "Pax, what are you doing here?"

"Come, let us go inside," urged Olio.

Once inside the house, I untied the note bound to Pax's leg and handed it to Fray. I looked at him, feeling the desperation that had to have been clearly stamped upon my face. Pax brought news from Stormwall. Stormwall was no longer my home. That piece of paper could only hold grim news, and I could not bear it.

"Read it," Olio said, leaning against the kitchen sink. His knee bounced with nervousness despite his casual stance.

Fray sunk down into a chair and placed the neatly folded note onto the table. "It is no longer your concern," he said to the note. He then looked up to me. "Whatever it says, it is no longer your concern."

"Read it," Olio repeated.

"Leave," Fray ordered.

"You do realize I'm probably your only friend."

"He can stay," I said, biting my lip. I nodded. "Read it."

Fray expressed his disapproval with two narrowed blue eyes and unfolded the paper. Pax cawed from his place atop the bed post and flew to perch on my shoulder.

"'Dal Paratheon has destroyed our home,'" Fray read. "'In the days after your exit, he managed to infiltrate the army, which he now has made his own, and I am afraid to bear the news that your mother has accepted his proposal of marriage. Though they are not without heirs, I wouldn't put it past them to create another. Your mother hasn't requested her potion in quite some time.'

"'But I digress. This may be the one and only letter I send, for they have discovered the Voiceless cure, and I count down the seconds until I am interviewed. Your maid informed me that she destroyed the contract your cousin was carrying. I do not believe anything will be traced back to the Barge.'

"'Everyone is well, including Crimson. I do not know what else to say besides to run further and further until this place is nothing but a bad dream, but I write this in the case that our new king decides to pursue you or his son, which I would not put past him. He doesn't seem the forgiving type, and there are still soldiers beyond the Archway. I hope you're safe and well, and most of all, I hope you are happy. Pyrus.'"

There was a long, strained silence where the only sound was that of Fray crumpling up the paper within his fist. A grimace pulled at his mouth. If we had a fire going, I'm sure he'd throw the letter into the flames. I didn't blame him one bit. We were moving on, but the world kept bringing Stormwall back to us.

Pyrus was alive. So was Crim and Pedoma. The names that once weighed me down seemed to float now. Without their deaths on my conscience, I breathed in deep and fell back in my chair. Tears pricked the corners of my eyes. It wasn't until that moment that I realized how badly I wished to hear from them and to know they were safe.

Olio moved away and crossed the room to the sink yet again. He pinched the bridge of his nose and shook his head. "If you're wondering what I'm thinking, you'll be disappointed," he said. "I care nothing for the New Kingdom's plight, nor for yours or that of your dead brother. If you wish to go be a hero, do it someplace else and leave before anyone gets attached."

I blinked. "Like you?" I asked. When Olio turned back to me, I raised my eyebrows. "Are you getting attached to me, Olio?"

But something passed between us that it was more than friendship or even the magic inside of our bodies. It was a bond that I had begun to feel with many of the pack who I'd encountered. It was as if we were all connected with invisible tethers. A root that grew in strength and love. This was what it meant to have a family. "Olio—"

He raised his eyebrows and cocked his head. "Sooner rather than later."

"I care nothing either, Izzy," Fray said.

The block of ice and cold that had numbed my thoughts suddenly gave way like snow melting at the first sign of spring sun.

I'd killed my own father. I'd torn him to shreds. I'd tasted his blood. I still tasted it to this day, a memory burned inside like a hot wind, and even though I should no longer think of my home as mine, I still bore the name of my ancestors. Their blood still ran through my veins. My title ran across my mind like claws. Princess.

I care about my old home, but I don't want to.

"What are you thinking?" Fray asked, noting my hesitance to speak a word.

"I'm thinking that it's not my problem any longer," I said despite the nagging itch inside my brain. "Dal can run the world into the ground, and I will stay here with you."

Fray let out a groan of relief, and Olio made for the door, satisfied in his own right. He turned toward us before leaving and said, "Speak not a word of this to anyone."

I nodded to Olio's back as he closed the door behind him.

"I'm sorry," Fray said. He drew me into his arms, and his smell transported me to a better memory than the ones that filled my head upon seeing Pax.

"Don't be sorry," I said, nestling myself into the space between his neck and shoulder. "Don't ever be sorry."

Sorry was for people who regretted what they'd done. Fray made it quite clear what he thought of the New Kingdom and his intentions of never returning. So why did his words hang heavy and break apart the already ruined heart inside of me? Had I become so good at lying that I'd started to believe the lies I'd told myself?

But I could not risk the Den, and I could not risk Fray. I couldn't plummet now that I'd flown so high.

During the night, I found Pax. With one finger, I stroked his little head. I left the Den and traveled to the cliff where I practiced with Branch and said, "Do not come back here." With that, he took flight. The note, tied to his leg, bore only seven words. *I am well. Do not write back.*

The thing with my magic was that it heightened with my emotions. Pyrus's note had caused a rift that split apart in me the very moment I encountered Pike Ivo in the forest. The memory of the arrogant man made my skin itch. There on the cliff, I removed my clothes, uttered my chant, soft and slow, and changed. In my wolf form, I pointed my nose to the cold white moon and howled, loud as vicious thunder. I howled for the life I had lost, for the memories I'd resigned myself to never forgetting.

As much as I tried, it would never be. The person I was now was far more complicated than the one I'd left behind in Wargrave's dirty little shop in the Barge. I howled again, less mournful. Fray may say that was stagnant, but I was not. I was a life in motion.

Sweet as love and strong as steel.

But I could not ignore the turmoil rising through me like dawn over the lake. It would take more than a few thoughts of positivity to unravel this road before me.

CHAPTER TWENTY-FOUR

"We made good progress today," Fray said.

I stood on the watchtower, staring off into the night sky. It had rained that day, leaving that fresh smell that seemed to wash away everything bad that ever existed. Three days ago, Pyrus' letter awakened something within me. So for three days I thought on it, and for three days I concluded that it was better to pretend that it had not affected me rather than let it take up space in my mind. I had more important things to focus my attention. One was standing next to me.

"I'm getting better with the dagger, as well."

Fray leaned over the wall and smiled thinly. "I'm glad."

"My magic, too. I can change without screaming murder now."

Fray breathed a laugh and looked at me. "That's good, Izzy."

"What's good is the way I can harness my magic. It's like I have control now." That wasn't entirely true. Though I could control the fire portion of my power, I knew there were other aspects that needed reining in. Although I had not been overcome by the shadows again, there was still the threat of it. The darkness lingered in the corners of my vision. Ever present. I lowered my gaze. "Not completely, though. I feel like Branch doesn't know what to do with me sometimes."

I felt Fray's eyes on me, so I pretended the lake was more interesting than it was.

"There's something else on your mind," Fray coaxed. "What is it?"

I worried about the Den. I worried that Ashe may have been right and that war would come to us. I feared that people I loved would die, and I feared I would meet the same end.

I feared for Pyrus and for Crim. I'd left them behind. I was guilt-riddled.

Fray sighed. "Izzy."

"There's a lot of my mind, Fray. I can't sleep again and I'm just . . . tired." Excuses.

"Go sleep. I can take the watch on my own."

I watched Fray for a moment. Three days ago he had asked me to be his wife. More or less. But Pyrus' letter had interrupted the entire moment and he hadn't brought it back up since. I wished he had. It would had been a nice distraction.

"That's all right," I said. "Sleeping alone feels way worse than being tired and awake." More excuses.

Fray frowned. "Sleep here, then."

"It's all right, Fray," I insisted. "Tell me a story."

"What kind of story?"

I looked off and bit my inner cheek. "How about the one where you decided to leave the Den?"

Fray's eyes flashed to mine, dark under the light of the torches. "You don't want to hear that one."

"I do."

He looked off as if the memory were playing out before his eyes. "I was taught that fighting was the only way to survive," he said. "I was ten years old and could already kill a man. I'd already had many kills. Like most things, sooner or later it takes hold of you, and if that's the only life you know, that's the only life you know."

I opened my mouth, but I wasn't sure what to say. To begin with, I hadn't expected him to answer me. I expected the stone wall that had become Fray Castor. All I could do was stare at him and hope he would continue.

He did.

"The pack was disintegrating, and Aquarius wanted nothing more than to cross the Archway himself and stain your father's fields red. Our camp was stationed further out than where we are now. That was when the water was poisoned and we lost our voices. Soon after, Aquarius disappeared, and I decided to do the same."

"All by yourself?"

"No, there were others, and we helped keep each other alive for many years. We grew into the routine, and soon, we all gotten jobs and went our own ways."

"Did you know Crim?" My former guard was a hard man to miss, big as he was. Thinking about him now and knowing he was safe made my heart hurt. I was such a sentimental fool.

Fray nodded. "He was a kind man. Always."

We fell into a silence, and when I was sure Fray wasn't going to continue, I reached out and threaded my fingers between his. "I'm thinking about leaving the Den and heading deeper into the Old Kingdom."

He nodded knowingly. "Why am I not surprised?" He sighed. "After winter is over, then?"

I didn't know what I expected him to say, but it wasn't that. The relief that came with his words alleviated the weight on my shoulders, and with it went the strain on my heart that I'd grown accustomed to. Hope was a strange thing, and sometimes it didn't make much sense. But right here, right now, I felt as though I could take on the world.

"If you don't get up, I'm going to make you."

Branch stood over me as I sat on the cliff's edge the next day, blocking out the sun like a storm cloud. I fell back onto my haunches and felt my form shrink and shrink until I was nothing but wind-swept skin and brittle hair. I grabbed my cloak and draped it over my shoulders. It wasn't until I closed my eyes that I realized the extent of my tiredness.

My heart was no longer in these long days. I had to remind myself more than once that I did not have to put on a brave face. I did not have to practically remove ribs to squeeze into silly overdone gowns any longer. An undefined sadness seemed to overcome me like mist on a mountain peak. A weakness bled through me. As I sat there, I tried to place where my spark had gone. Where my heart truly was. But it was hard to comprehend much more than that with Branch breathing down my neck.

"You're done when I say you're done!" the enormous man growled. "Get up."

I stood up, brushing the snow from my butt and legs. "I think I'm done," I said, my voice calm and level, which did nothing to quell my teacher's volume.

"You don't have a say in this pack, Littlewolf," he growled.

I faced him, almost chest to chest—or more like his chest to my head. A challenge nonetheless. "Tell me about my brother."

Branch's ears flicked. He knew Henry. He'd been lying to me all this time, along with the entire population of the Den. Still, nobody seemed to want to talk about him—save for Olio, and that was only after much pressing. Olio hadn't been close to him; nobody truly seemed to be. Henry had been an outsider, just like Fray and me.

I could tell that Branch was considering changing the subject, lying or merely staying quiet, but instead he gave a great sigh and locked up all his attitude, if only for a moment. He turned away, shifting behind a large snowdrift, and came back wearing nothing but a pair of torn trousers and boots. He stood to face me.

"Your brother tried to reason with his . . . your father, but there is no reasoning with one who has his mind made up," Branch said and stopped mid-thought. All of his gruffness returned in an instant. "What is it you wish to accomplish by knowing? He is dead. There is nothing left to know."

"The dead can speak. There is much to know."

"So you wish to speak to your brother?" He waved a hand in the air, dismissing me. "Go."

"He hasn't come to me since I left Stormwall, remember?"

"Spirits stay where either they fell or they lived, and sometimes both."

I looked at my feet. "He lived here for a short time."

Branch cocked his large head. "His spirit is stronger where he fell. Probably."

I looked up. "Do you know where he fell?"

Branch didn't need to say anything. The answer was there. A heavy boulder of grief sunk into my stomach. Tears threatened to fall, but I bit my tongue to keep them at bay. I watched the wind rustle the tree branches behind Branch. They moved and swayed like my thoughts. I remembered the day I'd heard my mother sobbing, when I'd been too young to understand death. I remembered how it shaped me into a stronger person. A stronger woman.

I took a breath. "Will you take me there?"

"The dead should stay dead. You should not play with the afterlife."

I whirled toward him, my cheeks going hot. I stood with the big, broad man, an ant against a mountain. "I'm not playing, Branch. I'll burn down this entire forest if you don't at least point me in the right direction."

For a minute, my heart leapt with the possibility of Branch hitting me, and I braced myself, fists curling and jaw set. Instead of a blow, he gifted me a smile, teeth gleaming white against his dark skin, and suddenly the air around us lifted.

"I could do for a trip," he said. "How about it, then?" He looked off into the distance.

"This is a trick, right?" I said. "You're going to lead me into some wasteland and leave me there for days to teach me some sort of lesson, aren't you?"

Branch glanced my way. "A wasteland, yes. Leave you there? No. There are worse things than ghosts in the Old Kingdom, Littlewolf. It'd be right to show you."

I watched Branch walk away, his arms stretched out over this head. "That's not funny," I called out after him.

Branch shot me a bemused glance. "I wasn't joking." Before he disappeared down the cliffside, he called back to me, "Be ready before sunset. Make your feet like a baby bird's."

I let out a holler and yanked my boots on. As I made my way back to the Den, I held my breath, waiting for Branch to jump out at any moment to tell me how gullible I was and that we'd work through the rest of that day and night until nothing got past me. But the more I thought about it, the more that seemed more up Olio's alley. Branch wasn't the type to joke around.

I ate my dinner at the mess hall as I waited for Fray to get off guard duty. The conversations around me drowned out the thoughts in my head. I was weary and uncertain, but most of all I was frightened. What would I find out there? I'd done what Henry had asked. I'd killed our father. But it did not stop a thing. Dal Paratheon was making a mess of Mirosa. Of my home. Tears pricked my eyes, but I swept my sleeve over them. I could not cry now. Not when there were decisions to be made.

I arrived home before Fray.

I stood in front of the mirror and rubbed my fingers over the scar above my breast. The willing memory surfaced in front of my unwilling eyes, but I let it stay there for a moment to test out my courage. As soon as my heartbeat slowed, I squared my shoulders. *I am fearless.*

I'd come so far. There was no need to be scared. If I did this now, I could move on and not wonder what really became of my brother's body. I'd spent so many years talking to an empty grave. It was time.

I dropped my hand and stared at my reflection. I'd done my hair in a long braid, but I found myself undoing it and letting my hair down so it flowed over both shoulders. Time to go.

"Izzy?"

I turned to see Fray standing in the open doorway. He looked beautiful in the candlelight. For a moment, I forgot all about the widening distance between us and remembered the kitchen boy I'd first come to love. That scowling little brat who challenged me at every turn. He still did.

If he stared at me any longer, I'd never leave.

He balanced on one foot and traded off to the other as he removed his boots. He let out a weary sigh and hung up his cloak, kicking the door closed behind him. He slumped into a chair at the kitchen table and lowered his chin to his chest. "Where are you going?"

"Branch is taking me to see my brother."

I didn't know what I expected Fray to say, but it wasn't what came next.

"I'm coming with you."

That moment, the smell of him—which was a mix of sweet-root, untamed forest, and a nineteen-year-old boy—filled my head. I bit on my lower lip, almost hard enough to draw blood. He noticed, and a smile tugged up one corner of his mouth. *Bad wolf,* I thought. *Not here. Not now.*

"No, you stay," I said.

"I will not."

I sat down beside him. "I have to do this alone."

Fray hung his head, depriving me of seeing his eyes.

"I hope you find what you're looking for."

His voice was flat and emotionless. Why had he not put up a fight?

Was a fight what I wanted?

"I hope for closure more than anything," I said. I only hoped closure didn't mean forgetting.

"I doubt you will ever forget Henry." Fray lifted his head and tucked his hair behind his ears. I longed to reach out and touch a strand—to remember the first time I'd done so when I'd been a human.

But I was no longer human. I could not show weakness. Not even now.

"I know what you're thinking," I said.

Fray narrowed his eyes. "What am I thinking?"

"That I'm going to get into trouble somehow."

Fray laughed through his nose. "I think that no matter where you're going or what you're doing. Trouble always seems to find you."

"I guess you'll find me no matter where I am, then."

He shook his head, and the corners of his mouth dipped. "Don't do that. Don't make me laugh when I feel like you're slipping away from me."

"Fray—"

He met my eyes, which was the worst thing he could do at that moment. I could see everything in there: the hurt, the longing, but most of all I could see his loneliness. My love was not enough to keep it at bay.

"I don't know what you want, Izzy," he said. His voice broke the way it did when he'd first regained it. "But I know it's not me. Not entirely." I opened my mouth to respond, but no words came. "You didn't need me to pass the Archway with you. All you needed was a map and a good push. You wanted me with you. But now . . . now I feel like I'm following you and not the other way around."

I swallowed hard. "Is that so bad?"

"No, you're strong. You always have been. But I don't want to be behind you." He blinked and looked at me from downcast eyes. *Not behind,* I knew he meant to say. *Beside.*

I caught movement from the corner of my eye and saw a blot of darkness creeping across the floorboards. It slinked under the table and climbed the wobbly wooden legs to stretch out to where Fray sat. It blanketed him in shadow before vanishing entirely.

"Izzy?"

My mouth had been hanging open, so I promptly closed it. He had not seen the shadows. He did not see the Uncanny or their taunts. They'd come to touch upon Fray, not by coincidence. No, they came to remind me who I was and what they could take from me.

Gods. I pulled in a breath and shoved my fists into my closed eyes. There were things that could be fixed and things that could not be replaced. I was being careless with Fray's heart, keeping him at a distance this way. Maybe it was my fault that we felt so far apart. Had I been doing it all along?

Lulu would have shed light on this. She knew her way around romance better than anyone I knew. She'd tell me I was being selfish. She'd say that if I ever doubted myself, to remember what brought me here to begin with, and that even though I felt that I was not enough, he stayed. Fray stayed. I smiled inwardly. She'd also chastise me for not bedding the Voiceless servant yet. *No time like the present, Izzy!*

"Will you come back?" Fray looked at me with wide, hopeful eyes that nearly inspired tears.

I forgot all about the shadows and held onto Lulu's voice in my head. I ducked my chin to hide the water surely filling my eyes. "No matter what."

∼

It was still dark when Branch and I left the Den. We said very little to each other. It was my first time venturing through the mountains deep into the Old Kingdom of Mirosa.

What I expected what just what I saw.

The territory beyond the mountains was deserted and colorless. The plains, as I assumed they were, crunched beneath our feet. The grass was dead and blanketed the landscape in muted browns. Scarce trees silhouetted the grey sky. Nothing else stretched along the horizon. It made the world eerie and vast.

The lack of sun there left us in a perpetual dusk. As much as I didn't want to admit it, my father was right. It was a wasteland. It was nothing.

After the plains, we walked upon ground cracked with the roots of the trees we'd seen in the distance. Up close, I could see that they were bare of leaves, grabbing the air with pointed limbs sharp as daggers. There were no sounds. No leaves to rustle. No birds to sing. Not even the whistle of a breeze.

But even with the absence of wind, the air felt full with the memory that something once thrived here.

As we moved deeper, signs of civilization appeared. Broken fences and remnants of long-abandoned homes. Every now and then, we'd come upon whole towns filled with weeds and vines rising up and tangling through empty windows like snakes.

The longer we spent walking, the more I thought about Fray. *It wasn't always like this*, he'd said. There were once great cities here, led by great lords, invaded by kings who razed and tore them up until they resembled nothing more than ruins.

"Welcome to the land of the City of the Dead," Branch said.

"Battles were fought here?" I asked.

Branch nodded his great head. "Fought and lost."

"It must have been a great place if my family wanted it so badly."

Branch locked his dark eyes with mine and raised his head high. "It was."

We fell silent for the rest of the day as I took in everything I saw, trying to imagine it as something rather than nothing.

I saw green and blue and yellow. The colors of fresh grass, clear skies, and glaring sunlight. I saw livestock and men on horses and children at play. I saw lives playing out in front of me—lives that were stolen. These images danced in my head as we crested a large hill that seemed eerily familiar and looked out at the scene before us.

The field was once a thing of beauty but had since been remade. The long green grass I'd seen in my dream was nowhere to be seen, replaced instead by reddened soil. There was no grass to be seen. I stood atop the hill where I once stood with Henry. I could still hear horses and the clash of steel. I could still see the carnage like it were happening right before my eyes.

I felt my courage melt away. This was where my brother had lost his life.

As we descended the hill and drew closer, I saw small markers about the height of my calf, scattered everywhere.

Here it is, finally, I thought. The place I'd seen in my dream.

I stepped like I were walking on glass. Branch walked behind me, his eyes intent on every reaction I made.

"Did you fight here?" I asked him.

"I did," he replied.

I took a shuddering breath. "What is it called? This place."

"The Lonely Fields."

I bent down and took the dirt into my hands, letting it sift through my fingers. So many people died here. They did not have to. All of this could have been avoided if only one of Mirosa's kings had said *enough*. If only they had grown tired of the fighting and the lust for power.

I stood up and followed Branch's gaze to a man standing by a cluster of trees—the very same I'd seen in my dream. The figure faded away, dust in the wind. *Henry*.

"We are in a place of deep, broken magic," Branch said, his hands tightening into fists. "Do not trust everything you see."

"But we are magic."

"This magic is not controlled or claimed. It is wild and unharnessed. Too much of the dead and not enough of the living."

"I wonder if my father knew he'd destroy the very place he wanted to rule."

I neared the place where the figure had appeared. Every step echoed the ones I'd taken when Henry had brought me here. I felt myself drawn toward the clearing and to an unnatural rise in the dirt. I felt something worse than sadness. Worse than the initial loss that the seven-year-old me had endured. Years and years of hoping my brother was alive—wishing he'd come into my room one night and whisk me away to wherever his dreams took him. Even when I knew the truth of it, I still held on to that single delicate thread. I felt that thread breaking.

This was a devastation that made everything so real.

The world fell away around me. One moment, I was standing beside Branch, and the next, I was there in the moment my father confronted his son. I was in my dream.

I saw it all just as I had when I'd first come to that place. My heart clenched, and a single gasping breath shook my body. My brother bound by two Mirosian soldiers, my father, in his armor, the cold look in his eyes. My brother transforming into a Gwylis as my father's sword cut his heart in two.

I screamed until my throat burned, but there was no sound, and the scene shattered before me—but not before my father turned and crossed through me like I were nothing but smoke. With each step, he faded further and further from sight.

Then I was standing in the clearing again.

I was back in the present with my face in the dirt. I'd fallen to my knees. How long had I been there, clawing at the ground? Inching my way toward the mound of dirt that marked where my brother had fallen?

"Did you find what you came for?"

Branch approached, hand outstretched. I didn't take it. The wild look in his eyes told me he was shaken by this place. Maybe more so by my outburst. Or did he think I'd seen the shadows again?

A rough wind broke some of the brittle branches of the trees surrounding us.

"At least they buried you, my brother," I said and lay with my cheek to the ground. "At least they did that one courtesy."

"Izzy."

I squeezed my eyes closed and felt myself smile. Just before Henry had gone into his initial military training, he'd come to me with a story. The story was about a princess named Isadola whose step-mother became jealous of the love she received from the king, so she cursed

Isadola to become a serpent to live out her days beneath the ocean of their kingdom. For years, Isadola watched her castle as it warred with the neighboring kingdom and eventually fell to ruin. She could not help —being confined to the water, after all—and the guilt nearly stole her life, until one day, not long after the destruction of her kingdom, she came upon a ship.

On it was her father and step-mother.

Her father marveled at the sight but did not do what men do and try to capture her. Instead, he leaned over the rails of the ship and watched her swim, and Isadola showed him her iridescent scales and how she could leap from the water with her entire serpentine body. Seeing this, his wife filled with rage. She had turned Isadola into a monster so she would cease to be beautiful in her father's eyes, but she still was. In a fit, the step-mother pushed the king overboard into the raging seas, but Isadola was there. She rescued her father just before he drowned. When she peered up at the ship and saw her step-mother looking down, she rose her great body from the depths and, with her father upon her back, gobbled up the queen and swallowed her whole.

The reason I remembered such a haunting story was not for the heartbreak and the destruction of the tale, but because Isadola's father had called her Izzy. And so, the first time Henry read the story, he decided I would be Izzy, and I decided I liked it. But only to those whom I trusted and those I knew would not change me into a fish.

That was why, when I heard my name, I started to cry. It started out as a whimper, then transformed into laughing sobs. Almost giddy in the way they shook my shoulders and stretched my lips into a smirk wider than anything Ashe Paratheon had stored up.

After so many long months, I'd found my brother here.

"Well, look at you, little sister," he said. "You're very far from home." Henry was clad in his dress uniform, pressed and polished without a wrinkle in sight. There was no blood dotting his face or his clothes. It set my memories humming. I watched his chest rise and fall. He breathed like a sea at rest. Like he was alive. I felt my hopes wrap around me, tightening like a vice around my heart. *Please, be real. Don't be a dream.*

I took a tentative step, aware of Branch watching me—perhaps even the both of us. If he saw Henry too, that meant I was not dreaming or merely imagining things. A thought leapt into my mind; along with it came a sense of panic. I'd been able to touch Lulu in Rixon's caverns. Could I do the same with Henry, or would he feel like a wisp of smoke?

I fought to keep my voice steady. To pretend I wasn't saddened at the possibility.

"Can I touch you?" I asked him.

He nodded. "My energy is very strong here, Iz."

I reached out and brushed my finger along the lapel of his jacket. The day I'd begged him not to leave had been the very last time I'd touched him. Had I known it would be the last, I wouldn't have let go. I would have tried harder.

I pressed my palm onto his chest and felt for his heart. He was so tall and so strong. He'd fought so hard and for so long. From what I'd learned, he brought battles home to Stormwall with him. They kept him awake. They raged within him and tore and ripped. I knew the feeling now, this hurricane.

I felt for his heart, but it was not there.

Something broke inside of me, a dam against a raging river. I pressed against him. He was so solid, but it was not really him. This magic was a lie.

"I told you not to go," I said softly, pressed against his chest. I could smell him! Tobacco and campfire. He murmured an apology against the top of my head. I wrapped my arms around him, tighter and tighter, willing this moment to never end.

"Izzy, there's still work to be done."

I pulled away and took his face in my hands. I had to get onto the tips of my toes to do it. "Tell me what to do, Henry," I said. "Tell me, and I will do it."

"Even if it takes you far from here? Would you do it?"

This gave me pause. "This is about your journal, isn't it? I found it under the floorboards in the Den." I watched him smile.

"You made it there. I should be surprised, but your tenacity is legendary."

"Why did you want to break the Gwylis curse, Henry? Is that why you joined them?"

He shook his head and stepped apart from me. He scratched his chin the way he always did when his thoughts were conflicted. "I didn't poison them," he said. He met my eyes to gauge my reaction before continuing. I merely nodded, as if I'd known all along. "When our father found out, he threatened to reassign me somewhere in the New Kingdom, as far from Stormwall as he could. But I couldn't because . . ."

"You grew to love them," I finished.

"I did, and if you look and if you ask the right questions, they will tell their history, Izzy. There is so much we did not know and so much my father did. He feared magic and sought to destroy it, only he created a darker form of it in the Gwylis. This magic we have now, it is not the magic that used to fill this land. They traded light for dark. We are wrought with demons."

Light for dark. But all this, I already knew. "I feel like this is a segue for something—"

I saw the shadows then, puddled at my feet, begging for attention. Henry saw them too. He stepped back, his arm flung behind him like he was going for a sword that was not strung to his back. But when his arm flew forward again, there *was* a sword. The steel was brighter and hit the light so that it seemed to glow. He let out a strangled cry as I jumped back. I heard the scrape of steel on ground as he dragged the weapon across the dirt.

The shadows made no sound as they fled.

I stepped back, struggling to maintain composure. I couldn't meet Henry's eyes, afraid he'd look at me the same way that Branch did that day on the cliffs.

I'm a monster because Aquarius was a monster, and he passed it on to me.

"Izzy."

I flinched at the feeling of Henry's hand on my shoulder.

He was beginning to leave, his skin becoming translucent, the warmth of his touch cooling. *Look at him,* I thought. *Look before he's gone again.*

"Those eidolons will not leave you be," Henry said, his tone soft. He still held the sword. It was unmarred, like it was just forged and polished. "They are mere shades of the Uncanny, but they are their servants. I don't have much time."

Panic reared its head. I clutched the emerald at my chest, summoning courage from it. "You gave this to me because you knew it was up to me, didn't you?" I didn't give him enough time to answer. "Even then you knew you would die, didn't you?"

Henry looked away, forlorn. "I knew I wouldn't have time to find the stones. I left one in the place I knew it would be safest, and the other . . ." He held out the sword to me, proffered in his palms. "The other comes to you now."

I handled the sword, heavy and intimidating though it was, holding it point down, like a crutch. At least at that angle I could get a better view of the ruby set inside the pummel. The deep red of the stone reminded me of the Lonely Fields. Like a drop of blood.

"Aquarius and Rixon are hiding something," Henry said. "You know what the Uncanny gave them, but in exchange for what? They took their souls, Izzy."

Olio was right. The gods were not with us. They'd abandoned this land long ago. When the demons came to claim its people. They traded their ancient magic for that of the underworld. They could make flowers bloom and forge blades imbued with strength. Blessed by the heavens. But no more. No. They'd lost their souls.

Soulless.

"But not entirely," Henry added. "As humans, we still own the rights to our souls. The Uncanny may have a hand on them, but they cannot take over unless we give them up willingly."

"Why would anyone do that?"

The answer was in the question. The answer was power.

"Like anything made of darkness, it grows. The more Gwylis, the stronger the Uncanny. And things of darkness do not need permission."

My knees buckled, but Henry caught me. "I didn't want to think they . . . *we* were giving up our lives." But now . . . now I began to feel it, like I'd finally pinpointed the empty space where my grip on my resolve had weakened.

"We must break the curse," Henry warned, "or our people will fall into shadows. We must reverse what our ancestors pushed them to do. We must make them whole again. It is our duty."

I clicked my tongue. "You always ask so much of me."

Henry smiled despite the fear and worry that creased his eyes. "You came for me, Izzy, all the way out here.

Henry looked past me to Branch, who I'd long forgotten was standing there. "You have strength behind you," he told me. "It's nice to see you again, my friend."

Branch regarded Henry with a slight nod. Or was it a bow?

"We fought side-by-side, Branch and I," Henry said, regrading me again. "Trust him with your life."

Tears pricked my eyes, but I made no move to stop them.

"Henry, our home is gone. What you were trying to do—break the Gwylis curse—what good would it have done? It only renders them weak, yet again. It was the only thing they had keeping them alive."

"But they divided themselves. Don't you see? They became leaderless when Aquarius abandoned them."

I knew what Henry was saying. It was impossible to ignore no matter how hard I tried. "As long as there is a king of men on the throne in Stormwall, there will never be peace."

My brother pulled his eyebrows together. "Unfortunately, so, little sister. The more power a man has, the more he has to lose, and a man with something to lose is a ruthless one. The Gwylis against you will lose their power with the curse broken, but there is still a king to worry about. Wars on all fronts."

I shook my head furiously. "I can't go back there," I protested. "I can't lay siege on Stormwall and retake the throne. If that's what you're insinuating, it's impossible."

Henry looked taken aback. His face began to putter in and out of view, like the sun from behind a cloud. I didn't have much time left.

"I'm not saying you need to personally take up arms and lead the soldiers, sister," he said. "But when the time comes, will you join those who do?"

A wave of guilt crashed over me, bringing everything together. The letter from Pyrus, Pike Ivo's invasion, the way I tried to forget my past, only to see it every time I closed my eyes or looked in a mirror.

My feelings were as selfish as my answer: I didn't know.

I'd run away from my gods-given right to the throne. But what was the reason? I'd claimed it was to find out more about Henry. I'd claimed

I could not be part of a family that slaughtered and poisoned the inno-cent. But what if none of those reasons were true? What if I was just a coward?

I once thought I'd been born to be a queen, but I'd since become a wolf, and there was no room for both.

Henry cleared his throat to get my attention, but he did not repeat his question. He more than saw the answer in my eyes: I would never go back to Stormwall.

Henry's eyes landed on Branch, although his words were directed at me. "You seek the celestine. What I am about to tell you may cause you to rethink this quest."

I straightened. "Tell me."

"In the city of Hassara lies a mine and in it, the stone, if you dig deep enough."

I looked to Henry, narrowing my line of sight. "Hassara is—" I stopped and took a breath. "Hassara is in the New Kingdom, Henry."

He nodded knowingly. "Far west, yes."

I looked away, paced. Getting the celestine stone meant crossing back into my home. There was no way around it unless I secured a ship and sailed around the continent, but that presented a whole new set of dangers. Every scenario played out badly, and I began to think aban-doning the task altogether would be better for everyone.

But only because I feared for my very own life.

If I acquired the missing stone, though, I could break the curse, and the Uncanny would have no choice but to remove their grip from our souls. The gods would return to the Old Kingdom. It would be like it was long ago.

Henry touched my shoulder. "I must rest now, sister," he said. "Take my sword and keep it safe with you."

I was reminded of the moment I knew what the Gwylis were and how I came close to begging on my hands and knees for Fray to help me. I could never ask the same of him now. Not when he had so much riding on reestablishing his place in the pack. Not if . . . if it came down to me removing Dal Paratheon and my own mother from Stormwall.

Would I do it? *Could* I do it?

Alone?

"But how will I know what to do?" I asked.

"I will help you," came the voice of Branch.

His voice came as a relief. A bit of a light in a dark, dark night.

I looked to Henry for confirmation, but he was close to gone already, the shape of his body and the colors of his uniform swept away like a brushstroke. I dropped the sword and reached out for him, hoping for something to hold. Something to keep with me that was tangible. But there was nothing, and the air stilled. The world felt empty.

It was all too much to handle. Crossing back through the Archway and journeying south to Hassara, a place that may or may not have taken allegiance with Dal, and breaking the Gwylis curse, whether they agreed or not. Could I do such a thing and go behind the backs of those I considered my family? Aquarius had spoken for them all when he'd made the deal with the Uncanny. Would I be doing the same?

But I could do it. I *would* do it, because, despite everything, I knew deep down who I truly was. My brother shaped me in teaching me to hunt and to be kind. My father taught me that cruelty could be beaten. My mother—that I could still love those who turned against me. And Lulu—that love comes with sacrifice, whether you mean it to or not, and that no matter what, death was not the end.

CHAPTER TWENTY-FIVE

I started a fire.

Branch went out hunting and must have eaten as a wolf, because he brought back only a small rodent for me. I skinned and roasted it over the flames with a stick.

"Do you eat often as a wolf?" I asked Branch, who'd been busy turning in circles the way dogs do before they decide to plop down and rest. Except he was in human form.

Feeling my eyes on him, he looked up but said nothing.

The stars were out in full force that night. The sky was blue and black and the moon the shape of a hang nail. The air was calm and smelled of nothing. No pine. No water. It was as if this place took it all away. I wasn't even sure where Branch found animals to hunt. He was stitched quiet, basking in the heat of the fire.

Finally, he said, "More human than wolf."

He'd been quiet for so long that I'd forgotten what I'd even said to warrant that response. I looked down at my hands. More human than wolf. Fray was more human than wolf, or so said Olio. Ghetee and the younger wolves seemed comfortable being animals. I wondered if there was a happy medium.

As if reading my very thoughts, a call, long and mournful, came from far in the distance. My head raised. My skin prickled. All the while, Branch did not so much as twitch a muscle.

"Regular wolves?" I whispered to him.

To my shock, he shook his head.

"Gwylis."

It was decidedly hard to glean anything from that one word. Were they Gwylis from the Den? Had they followed us?

Before I could utter my slew of questions, Branch heaved an exasperated sigh and said, "Did you truly think the Den was the only standing city in the Old Kingdom?"

I didn't. Or did I? I wasn't sure what to think anymore. Maybe I'd been the same as when I lived in Stormwall, living in my little protective bubble, never seeing the world beyond. I wasn't so naïve as to think my father and grandfathers destroyed the entirety of the Old Kingdom, but from what I'd seen so far and from what I knew of Fray's ancestors I assumed as much.

"Nobody speaks of them," I said, marveling at the images that popped into my head. Were their cities just as unique as the Den? Who ruled over them? How many were there? I felt as though I'd discovered a long-lost family member. I felt warm at the prospect.

"Not everybody joined in the war," Branch said. "They did not bow to Aquarius and therefore escaped the havoc your family wrought."

But . . .

"But they could not escape the curse."

I bowed my head in dismay. "They hate him, don't they?"

The chorus of howls faded into the night and stopped altogether.

"It goes without saying."

"If I break the curse, what then?"

"They will live out there, and we will live at the Den. Nothing will change."

I didn't believe that for a second. "Things could never stay the same."

Branch made a sound low in his chest. "You're wayward, Isabelle Rowan. You always will be. Do you honestly think your actions will affect anyone in the future?"

I bit the inside of my cheek. He was baiting me. I knew it, but I took it anyway. "I think that we all make impressions on someone at some point. If someone sees you pick an apple from a tree, maybe they will do the same, and so will the ones behind them, and so on and so on." I smiled, recalling Pyrus' words. "We could move even the stars."

"So you think you're a leader."

"I think I am what I am."

Branch rubbed his eyes with the palms of his hands. "What do you wish to accomplish by breaking the Gwylis curse?"

His question felt like it was part of a lesson. The answer, he already knew.

"Would you rather that your souls be bound up by demons?"

The was a silence so thick, I found myself holding my breath.

"You need to realize two things, Littlewolf," Branch said. "One, breaking the curse will make us human. Two, the king on the throne in Stormwall may not be a Rowan, but that does not mean that he will not retaliate for what you seek to do. The Greatwolf Pack made a pact with the foreign king for power, and in exchange he seeks to capitalize on their magic. Take away the magic, and that pact is broken."

He leaned forward. The fire danced in his eyes. "And who do you think he will come after?"

"We cannot risk losing our souls to the Uncanny," I said. "This is another thing entirely."

"No. It is one and the same. Do not break the curse, Mirosa—old and new—is doomed. Demons will walk in mortal bodies and raze the world beneath our feet. Break the curse, and war will destroy everything you hold dear. Either way, we lose."

I took the roasted rat from the fire and set it down, my hunger gone. "What if we don't lose? We will all be equals again. We will have the gods on our side again. You will regain everything you—"

"There's much you need to learn, Littlewolf. There are no equals in this world. Only in Hell and Heaven. Only death makes us equal."

I tightened my jaw. "I don't believe that."

Branch leaned back on his palms and tilted his head back. "You're free to believe what you wish."

"Do you think I'm crazy?"

"Why do you care what I think?"

"I—" I stopped mid-sentence and sighed. I didn't care what others thought of me. I was who I was, despite my mother's attempts at grooming me and even suppressing the things that she found unsavory. Pleasing everyone was an impossible task.

I cared at that moment because I respected Branch.

"I think of you as my friend," I said finally.

"I'm old enough to be your father."

I snorted. "Grandfather, maybe."

Branch choked on a laugh. "Just don't call me that."

I smiled. "Deal. So what *can* I call you?"

"Branch."

"You can call me Izzy, if you'd like."

Branch merely nodded and went back to staring at the fire. I threw the rest of my rat into it, having lost my appetite entirely. My skin prickled, and my mind warred with itself. Part of me knew to trust my instincts, while the other part of me wanted to deny the thing that I'd always been destined to be. A leader. A ruler. A queen.

It dug at me, clouding my judgment. I'd come out here to find Henry, and I did. He'd tasked me what he had failed to do. But I'd asked for this. I took on the burden in every choice I made, from the moment I was shot by my arrow in the woods to the moments leading me to this place. To deny it now would make everything I had done inconsequential. I'd accept the quest and its aftermath. I would find a way.

"You don't have to help me," I said. "If I decided to do this."

"I will, whether you want me to or not." Branch's words were stern and cut the night air, but I could tell he was afraid. I could see it in his eyes the moment Henry had come to me. If he believed the curse could be broken, I knew he'd stand with me, just as he'd once promised Henry. He was a man of honor. "Do you want to hear a story?" Branch offered abruptly.

"Please." Anything to take away the thoughts raging in my head.

"There was once a man named Rydell who dreamed of being a bird. So much so that he climbed to the highest mountain peak and asked the gods to give him wings. He did this every day for thirty-seven years."

"Dedicated," I quipped.

Branch continued, "After a while, the gods decided to hear him, and one day they touched his shoulder and changed him into a bird. Rydell was so happy that he couldn't wait to try out his newfound body. He leapt from the mountainside and spread his wings—" Branch looked up from the fire, his eyes dancing with amusement, "—and fell to his death."

I clicked my tongue. "There better be a good moral to this story."

"The moral is that you can wish and wish to be something other than what you are, and you may even achieve it. But before you step off that cliff, make absolutely sure that you learn how to fly."

"So you're saying it's not the right time."

"I'm saying the gods will let you know when it is. Trust in that. Do you understand?"

The gods? "They left your people. We cannot rely on them any longer."

Branch pushed himself to his feet. "I think we should head back."

I stayed where I was. "When will I know?"

Branch was quiet for so long that I wondered if he'd fallen asleep standing up.

Finally, he said, "Spring is only weeks away. The snow will melt and make traveling easier and faster."

With that, he sat down again, and soon he was lying with his back toward the fire, sound asleep. I sunk down, using my pack as a pillow, and fingered the emerald on my collarbone.

Henry's sword lay flush beside me, a testament to my brother's bravery. *What would be mine?* I wondered.

I recalled the image of Fray lying broken and close to death on the day I found him while hunting with Ashe. I would have done anything, *given anything,* to see him live. I now felt that way about the Den and everyone in it. What I wouldn't give to see them flourish as they once had. To see cities built up without walls. Without fear.

I fell asleep with the most profound sense of duty. It blazed hot as a fire and bright as a thousand suns. I would not dare douse it, not this time. This fire would lead me. It would take me to a past that laid buried and would help me to unearth it, even if it may destroy me.

I would do it anyway. I would burn.

CHAPTER TWENTY-SIX

"You're brooding. What's wrong?"

I sat on the ground in front on my home, shaking out the snow from my boots. I'd planned on reading some more of Henry's diary, but the sun was out, and I couldn't waste the day. Ghetee found me after breakfast, his face coming into view only when he moved to block out the glaring sun.

I think the gods will tell you.

I replayed Branch's words in my head. They gave me solace and calmed the heaviness in my belly. Seeing Henry did the same. For once, I felt as though I had a purpose.

How I'd go about fulfilling that purpose was another story.

"I think I might be happy," I said, pulling on my left boot. Branch had given me the day off since we arrived back at the Den in the early morning, and I slept in well past sunrise. The thought of seeing Henry the day before calmed my soul. "Crazy concept, I know."

"Nah, it can happen to the best of us." Ghetee sat down beside me and handed me my remaining boot. "A bunch of us are going hunting. Do you want to come?"

"Am I allowed to?"

"You're a Gwylis like us. You can do anything you want."

I pulled on my right boot and gave a *humph* of approval. "I guess you're right."

"Where's Castor?"

"Noticeably absent."

"Well, come and meet the guys."

We walked through the city until we came to a large snow-crusted courtyard behind Rixon's looming structure. There, a dozen pack members were gathered. They all looked about my age, with Ghetee being the youngest and by far the smallest. I'd seen some of them around but never traded words with any of them. There weren't any girls in sight.

Ghetee led me to a tall, gangly boy of sixteen who went by the name Claw, which I suspected wasn't his real name. He looked kind enough, but he had an air of superiority that told me he was the leader.

"You're the only girl here," he said, doing some sort of weird stretch with one arm completely hugging one side.

Ghetee scoffed. "She's not a girl."

"Woman," said Claw, a bit sarcastically. "Sorry. Still, she's the only woman."

"Nothing gets by you," sighed Ghetee and leaned into me. "His father—like, his *real* father—is Branch. You'd never know it by looking at him. Looks like a breeze would blow him over."

I jabbed him with my elbow. "You're worse than a woman."

Ghetee smiled. "You work the kitchens, you'll find out differently," he said. "Do your best to avoid that job. Hey, Kap!"

A stocky, square-shouldered boy walked over to us. He looked about Ghetee's age with wiry hair and dark eyes. He spoke through one side of his mouth and walked as if he had a ball between his legs. I recognized him immediately. Kap.

"Hey, Castor's girl," he said, looking at me. "Welcome to the Den, formally."

I shifted my weight. "Thanks. My name is Isabelle."

Kap grinned. "You hunting?"

"Seems like a good way to pass the time."

Kap raised his eyebrows. "You need a job? Branch could hook you up. I'm surprised he hasn't already."

I looked away. "Yeah, me too."

"How old are you? You don't look very old."

I was a bit taken aback by his candor, but I answered anyway. "Thanks, I guess. I'm eighteen."

"Well, you seem fit already. Done a lot of outdoor activities?"

"You mean before I was changed?"

Kap swallowed. "Well, yeah."

"I used to hunt with a bow and arrow." Sometimes a dagger.

Kap nodded, impressed. "Did you do it in those clunky dresses you royals like to wear?"

I flinched, setting my jaw. Did he really think I hunted in a dress?

"Somebody say dresses?" asked Claw. He looked me up and down and frowned at my simple tunic and trousers. "Who's wearing a dress?"

"Kap, if he keeps on acting like an idiot," said Ghetee.

For that, Ghetee received a jab to his shoulder from Kap. They fell over, laughing like . . . well, like children. I couldn't help but smile.

"So you're joining us then?" asked Claw. I nodded. "All right, men and lady, let's go."

We headed out in a tight group through a back gate I'd never seen before. Unlike the main entrance, this one was small, just big enough for Claw, the tallest in the group, to walk through. The closest watchtower had to be about twenty feet away. A single guard, an older woman with a crooked nose and a severe frown, stood at ease. She stared in our direction. I was the last to leave.

"Feel the wind on your face," she said and broke into a smile as I passed. I imagined she was the most beautiful silver wolf. "Run free."

IT HAD ONLY TAKEN A FEW HOURS TO BRING IN ENOUGH FOOD TO feed our respective families. A few deer, one stag, and a mess-load of smaller animals—good for stews, Ghetee informed me. We sat in our wolf forms around our bounty, taking a moment to relish it.

"You did real good, Isabelle," said Claw. He was a pretty, long-legged dappled wolf with a crooked ear.

I cocked my head. "Don't say it," I said. "You were going to say, 'for a girl' weren't you?"

Claw barked and snorted. "I think we need to give her a formal welcome," he said, calling over the other wolves. "No drawing blood. She's with Castor, and he'll murder us."

"Why do you say that?" I asked.

"Well, you see, even though Castor left our pack, he still went to war, lost his voice, wooed a princess, and got his voice back. He's sort of a hero to the youngsters, but in a more hushed way."

I wanted to leap to my feet but kept my joy contained. Olio's rumors had finally circulated. The thought of Fray finally being accepted into the pack played havoc on my heartbeat and distracted me from

Claw and the other wolves, who suddenly closed in on me. There was no maliciousness to their intent, only mild amusement.

One by one, the wolves snapped and nipped at my forearms. I knocked them back with several swift kicks, but they kept at it incessantly. After each had taken their turn, I was left with several bite marks, none drawing blood, just as Claw had ordered.

"Is this some kind of initiation?" I asked. "Or the equivalent of a wolf-kiss?"

"No," said Kap, pulling back his lips. "You more than proved yourself here. You're one of us now. This was strictly ceremonial."

I shook myself from head to tail to rid myself of their saliva. "Oh, good."

"We better get the meat back before supper," said Claw, turning away.

I looked up. The sun was low, marking the onset of dusk. My stomach growled. The dead animals were smelling really good about now.

Just as we gathered our kills, a scent rode in on the wind and hit my nostrils, causing me to drop the deer in my jaws.

I knew the smell. Humans.

I stood as the other wolves passed me, unable to find my voice. They took no notice of the strange scent. Why would they? They did not know human scents. Either they thought it another animal, or they simply did not care.

Both were mistakes.

Shaking off the paralyzing fear, I bounded ahead and stopped lengthwise. Although I did not hold a leadership position, I hoped my size would carry its own weight. "Turn back and run as far from the Den—"

Only Ghetee fixed me with a stare; the others were too deep in conversation to hear me. They began to skirt around me.

"Izzy, what is it?" Ghetee asked, watching the others walk ahead.

"Humans."

With that, I sucked in as much air as was possible and let loose a howl.

The others jerked in my direction, but it was too late.

Soldiers came, breaking out from behind the bare trees. There were only a dozen or so men. They wore armor—some of the Peek Islands and some of Mirosa—but none bore their weapons. I noticed one held a trekking pole, while another clutched a folded sheaf of parchment at his side. I knew what that meant. I'd sneaked into too many war meetings in my younger days not to remember.

This was a scouting party.

They carried maps with notable locations on them, probably of abandoned villages or other vaguely specific areas: animal tracks, game trails if they could see them in the snow, bodies of water. They may even go as far as journaling strange sounds with dates and times.

Although these men did not pose as much of a threat as the ones led by Pike Ivo, we knew they could not live.

Claw and the rest of the younger wolves sidled up to me. We watched the men freeze in their tracks upon seeing us. I wondered if we could get by pretending we were normal wolves. They must have heard my howl. If we did not speak, maybe they would forget they saw us.

My insides churned. Pike may have said they were out here for Ashe, but I could not risk putting the Den in danger.

I arched my back to release a kink. There were only a dozen men. *This will be easy.*

Claw cast a sidelong look at me. We didn't need words between us. Just a wolfish instinct to protect the pack.

The command spread through the wolves.

The Gwylis bore their teeth, almost in unison, to meet the soldiers, battle ready within seconds. The man holding the map nearly tripped over his own feet as he backed away from the advancing wolves. The one holding the pole brandished it as a weapon. Only four of the men drew swords, the rest backed away into the cover of the trees.

We clashed in a collective sound of steel and teeth.

Roars and screams.

Five of the men died valiantly defending themselves, while the mapmaker fled into the trees. Claw gave chase, returning with a bloody red grin. The others barked and yipped as they trotted amongst their kills. *These boys*, I thought, *have spent time in the Pit.*

But the fight was not nearly over. The remaining soldiers who'd fled earlier now had a change of heart. They advanced through the trees. These men were skilled. They set their feet and looked on us, pretending that they did not feel the fear that was etched on their faces. One even whistled at me like he was calling a dog home for dinner.

"Get the princess!" one of the sword-wielding men commanded.

"Ghetee, go!" I growled and turned back just in time for the sky to darken. "Split up. Don't go home right away!" I saw the pack, Claw and Kap colliding with the surviving enemy. I snapped at a soldier trying to sever my head and felt the air hiss as an arrow sailed overhead. Right toward Ghetee. It missed, thudding into the tree just to his right. I let loose a howl, but the young wolf was frozen with fear.

I froze, reaching deep down to harness my magic, taking another injury on my back in the same moment, but the magic didn't come. Something inside me shook and splintered, leaving me with nothing.

I was overcome by fear so intense that I hardly fought off the soldiers nearest to me. I almost sank to the ground until Kap came smashing into my ribcage and jostled me back to life. I didn't understand what was happening, not until I saw more arrows flying by. My world shifted out of focus.

A wail from Kap, followed by an ear-piercing yelp of pain, and I finally heard Claw's howl, calling us to retreat.

Retreat? Why are we—

A stark white Gwylis stalked forward, barely glancing at the dying soldiers around it. It snapped its jaws, attempting to startle us. Its golden eyes—no, one golden and one blue—were wide, and its tail was held high. Even without its long, pointed ears, this wolf was bigger than any of us could handle.

Its eyes were fixed on me, intense and terrifying. A hunter's stare.

My first instinct was to not show fear. I was a Gwylis, just like it was. I was not prey, and I would not be made to feel like it. My second instinct was to retreat. This wolf was too big; it was bigger than Branch, even, and there was no telling how powerful. Magic radiated from the tips of its fur, and the clouds churned in the sky above, sending winds straight toward us, so forceful that several of the young wolves nearly lost their footing.

This was one of Dal Paratheon's traitor Gwylis. We did not stand a chance.

It took a short step toward me. "Aquarius," came a low rumble. It raised its large muzzle and sniffed the air. "Where is he?"

The fur on my neck stood on end. I matched the giant wolf's steps, even though my legs trembled beneath me. "He is dead," I lied. "I killed him."

The Gwylis widened its eyes, its jaw hanging open, letting saliva drip to the ground. It focused on me, trying to decide whether it believed me or not. Whether I was worth killing over it.

This Gwylis knew who I was. I would not give it the answer it wanted.

I could not risk the lives of my pack.

I made a run for it, sliding as if I were on solid ice. Fear slammed into me, making me clumsy as a newborn deer. The rest of us reunited with Ghetee and fled the scene. The air smelled of death and was heavy with the agonizing screams of the men we'd maimed.

As I ran, I could not get the white wolf's gaze out of my mind. It's mis-colored eyes, the way it watched me as if I were familiar, spellbound by the sight of me . . .

"Who was that?" asked Claw as we ran through the trees. Everything looked unfamiliar.

"What do we do?" asked Kap. He ran directly in front of me. There was blood on his haunches. I couldn't tell if it was his. I could smell his fear. Or was it my own?

I tried to think, but my fear overtook me like a fog. Every moment that passed without an answer felt loaded.

I sniffed the air. The humans weren't following. Neither was the Gwylis.

"Back to the Den," said Claw. "Through the mountains and around the long way." We followed him without question, all of us caught off-guard, injured and confused. Ghetee met my eyes, a look of disbelief and terror on his face that mirrored my own.

It hit me like a ton of bricks.

I stopped, frozen in my tracks. "We can't go back there," I said. "They'll track us, whether we go the long way or not."

"She's right," said Ghetee.

It was then that I noticed the extent of Kap's injury. His back paw was nearly cut off. Hanging by a string, I thought.

"Yeah, she's right, but what other choice do we have?" said Claw. His muzzle looked as though it'd been dipped in blood. "We'll die out here. Besides, they can't get through the passes, not with the snow and the steepness."

"Isabelle, what happened?" Ghetee sidled up beside me, his eyes wide.

"I don't know." I felt drained, as though my magic was gone all together.

If I couldn't defend the pack's young from humans, how was I supposed save their souls? They'd all been wrong about me. And even worse: I'd been wrong. I wasn't as powerful as they thought.

"We should go." Kap's wolf form dissolved slowly. Fur became skin. Limbs shortened until he was nothing more than a scrawny boy, sobs racking in his chest. "I'm not doing too good over here."

Claw changed back into a human and took Kap onto his back, holding him under his knees. He adjusted, bending forward under Kap's weight, and then we went, leaping through the snow, scattering our prints, dashing in and out of trees, onto fallen logs and rocks.

CHAPTER TWENTY-SEVEN

E*veryone is afraid of something.*
That never seemed truer.

I followed Claw and Ghetee as they lead me to their healer. Fray met us soon after, and we all gathered outside their small infirmary.

First Fray held me; then he looked me over inch by inch and pulled me into an empty infirmary room to examine my wound. He lifted my jacket, revealing a straight-lined gash alone my spine.

"Looks worse than it feels," I said. I peered expectedly at Fray, determining whether he bought the lie.

He didn't.

Instead, he looked pale. "I can't leave you alone, can I?"

I tried to laugh, but it hurt. He pulled off my jacket completely and found another injury just below my collar bone. This time, he went ghost white.

"I'll heal," I said, tugging my tunic down. "It's fine."

I got down from the bed and turned to my reflection. My hair was in knots, and my face was lined with blood and dirt. I looked like I'd be to war. I didn't look fine.

Knowing Kester, she'd take the news of the attack with a dismissive wave of her hand. There'd be no warning bells, no meetings. She'd tell us how safe we were, and most of the pack would believe her.

My voice was so small compared to hers. What could I do to convince everyone otherwise?

Kester would only say this because she hadn't seen the white Gwylis. If she had, would she recognize him as one of the Den's traitors? How many were there?

I forced a smile. "You don't have to look at me like that."

Fray straightened. He held himself like a stone statue, trapping his emotions tightly inside. "Like what?"

"Like you think I'm a piece of glass ready to shatter at any given moment." I sighed and looked at the wall. "You can stop acting like, when you're not around, that I'm going to get myself killed."

"You look at me the same, you know." I turned to find him frowning as he continued: "As if you don't believe this is all real, and that one day you're going to wake up back at Stormwall, and everything will be just as it was before." I scoffed and started to walk away, but Fray grabbed me, one strong hand on my elbow. "This is real, Izzy. I'm real."

I turned back to the mirror, seeing past my reflection, and for a moment I saw something I didn't like. The urge to reach through the glass and shake away the person looking back at me was strong. I wasn't powerful. I wasn't able to use my magic to save Kap's foot. I couldn't love Fray the way he deserved. I'd failed him. I'd failed myself.

"We need to hand him over," Fray said, his voice cutting through my thoughts. He held my gaze. The words make me ill.

Him. Ashe.

"I think he moved on, Fray," I said. I was ashamed at how small my voice sounded. It splintered around the edges, like ice thinning over a lake. "I don't think it matters, anyhow."

"Why doesn't it matter?"

I released a breath, remembering the soldier's voice. Every word raked across my memory. *Get the princess*, the soldier had said. Gods, they knew I was here.

I rubbed my temples, allowing the thought to sink in. My entire body ached, especially my chest, where it felt like my lungs were going to burst from lack of air. I tried to remember the last time I didn't smell of sweat and blood. I just needed time to think—and maybe a bath.

Fray wasn't going to let me go so easily, though. "Izzy," he said, staring at me. "Why doesn't it matter?"

I'd been so lost in thought that I'd forgot what the original question was. I thought of Kap and how weak and powerless I felt. I shook my head as the memory faded, but I still found it hard to speak. "Because he's an afterthought, Fray."

Fray opened his mouth, probably to ask me to elaborate, but the door to the room creaked open. Claw eased in. "We can see him now."

At that moment, the bells sounded, melodious ringing filling the air. *You won't hear them ring any time soon. They're just for emergencies,* Olio had once said. The startling sound caused a dread within me, and the dread widened until it was nothing more than a black void. Gathering along the edges of everything within sight. Did I do that? Did I bring war to these people?

"I DIDN'T LOSE IT, SO THERE'S THAT."

I looked over Kap's bandages and forced a smile. He'd stayed in his wolf form so he could heal faster. The Den's healer, a middle-aged man named Brix, was cleaning up, collecting his basin of red-tinged water, several vials, and his tools. Behind me were Fray, Kap, and Claw.

"Thank you," I said to the healer. He reminded me of Pyrus, and I felt an ache in my chest. The same hefty build, the thoughtfulness and precision of his words. He even wore glasses. He left us with a nod, closing the door behind him. "Does it hurt?" I asked Kap.

"Not much." Kap shrugged and repositioned himself on the bed so he was propped up on one elbow. "By the way, thanks for protecting Ghetee."

I leaned against the wall, saying nothing.

"We should get our story straight," said Claw suddenly. We all looked at him.

"Story?" I asked.

"I mean, everyone is going nuts."

"With good reason," Fray said. Being the largest of the group, his mere presence in the room thickened the air. "What did you think? This place would stay hidden forever?"

"You didn't really think it was hidden—"

Fray shot Claw his typical intense look. "You don't really think much, do you?"

For the first time, I saw why Fray left the Den. Deep down, he must have known that sooner or later the Gwylis of the Den would be faced with war. It was hard to avoid even now.

Fray pushed past Claw and Ghetee, clenching both fists. When we were alone outside the room, he drew me nearer, his breath in my ear. "I knew we weren't safe."

For a few seconds, I just stared at him. I could feel the heat surging from his body and the way his blue eyes danced. I knew he was deep in thought. He knew as well as anyone our numbers would—*could*—not hold against an invasion, would Dal Paratheon dare one.

We were not as safe as we thought we were. We were delusional.

I cleared my throat. "This is my fault."

Fray took a finger and held it to his lips. He signed instead of speaking. *Why doesn't it matter?*

When I failed to respond after a few beats, he reiterated, his hands moving faster this time. I held up my own hands and signed slowly.

Because they were looking for me.

Fray dropped his hands to his sides. A deep crease appeared between his eyebrows, so tight I thought it would never come undone. "So you couldn't use your magic *why?*"

I pressed my lips together and shook my head. "I don't know."

"I think I do. I think you're afraid."

I nodded, because it was the only thing that made sense, and I felt no shame for it. "Fear can suppress magic?"

"Fear can suppress a lot of things."

My nervous words transformed into something like terror inside of me. What was I if I couldn't control my emotions? I'd be as useless of a Gwylis as I was a human girl.

Fray pulled me into him, and we left the infirmary, walking through the Den arm-in-arm. The bells had faded, but the pack doubled their guard watch and formed security groups groups. As we walked by, I heard the pack leaders barking orders.

"What are they doing?" I asked.

"Deploying the pack to guard the Den. Stay close to me."

"Where are we going?"

"Keep staring forward."

"Fray?"

He looked ahead.

"Fray?"

He stopped, our faces nose to nose. "Pack your stuff," he said softly. "We're going to find the prince."

I wanted to scream at him. I wanted to shake him until he understood that everything I feared was coming to fruition. Finding Ashe would not fix this. The Den was in danger because of me. Because I was here. Hunting down a one-armed prince wasn't going to change that.

Ashe would never give me up. He would die before then.

"Castor!"

Olio jogged up and fell into step beside Fray and me. He was out of breath, his eyes wide with excitement. "Don't tell me you have something to do with this, Rowan," he said to me.

"It's always me," I mumbled. The feeling of guilt was overwhelming. Not only did I always find myself in the center of conflict, but now it truly was because of me.

"If you have something to say, say it now," Fray said. "I don't have time for this."

"A meeting has been called," Olio said and began to quicken his step. Part of me wished he'd stay so I wouldn't have to deal with Fray's attitude alone. But maybe it was for the best.

We stopped just at the center of the city, where we could watch the pack descend from all roads to head toward the meeting hall. Fray stood with his chin to his chest, saying nothing for so long I almost couldn't stand it.

"It is always you, isn't it?" he asked.

"Is that an accusation?" I said. I shook my head as all thoughts about the attack this morning pushed to the forefront of my mind. "It seems to be, anyway. Kap almost died out there, Fray. It would have been my fault."

Fray lifted his head but looked elsewhere. "Is that it then? You want to leave forever?"

"It's not that easy—"

"You'll find that it is."

"Real easy," I said. "You don't truly think I'm like that, right? That I'd abandon something I'd grown to love?" Whether he meant it to or not, I could see the amusement dance in his eyes. *Foolish Izzy, they seemed to say. You run away from problems as often as I blink.* Frustration built almost to the point of tears. "It's not as easy for me as it was for you. You did it, what, twice?"

His gaze slipped from mine. "Leaving my pack wasn't easy. Don't ever think it was."

"I do think it's real," I said, redirecting the conversation. "All of it!" My voice was louder now, bordering on screaming. My throat felt raw. "Which is why I can never rest. I will never be at peace."

Fray glared at me, furious. "We will never rest. We will never be at peace as a people. These are delusions."

My heart pounded. I felt light-headed. I'd dug myself so deep into a hole that there was no hope of coming out of it now. "I'm delusional now?" I snorted. "Great. One more thing to add to my long list of issues."

Fray let out a frustrated growl and turned away. I wanted to tell him that I needed him more than I showed. That I wouldn't have survived this long if it wasn't for him. Instead, I watched him walk away, feeling the empty space between us widen.

CHAPTER TWENTY-EIGHT

"Let's have quiet!"

Branch stood in the center of the meeting hall. He was naked from the waist up with his hands clenched at his sides, pacing the room like a rabid animal. Kester stood behind him, huddled in a cloak.

I stood in the back with Olio. Sonia wasn't far off and eyed us sporadically. Though it still held an accusatory spark, something had softened in her gaze. Ghetee stood just in front of me. He glanced over his shoulder sporadically to give me either a smile or a wink.

"By now most of you have heard of the incident this afternoon," Kester said. "It was confirmed that, yes, the attack did come from soldiers of Stormwall."

Murmurs from the crowd. Surprisingly not one accusing eye turned to me.

"We are awaiting word from our queen on what the next step will be," Kester said.

"The next step is burning their asses." Ghetee leaned back. "Right?"

I looked sideways to the younger boy as he reached up and patted down my hair. I hadn't bathed. He frowned at me, and I frowned back.

As I looked to Ghetee, then to Olio—and even Kap and Claw, who I'd just met—it hit me. In the little time I'd spent in the Den, they'd become my family despite keeping Henry's existence here a secret. My fear for their safety vastly overcame my anger toward the soldiers. *Harness it with all emotions*, Branch had once said. But how?

Kester continued. "While the reason is up for debate, one thing still stands. We will not participate in a war with humans."

All at once, my body filled with heat. "She's sentencing them to death. Rixon would never allow this."

Rixon, their invisible queen. She was more than useless.

"Rixon may agree," whispered Olio. "She did before and will again."

"They have the Greatwolf Pack on their side." My voice was higher than I expected, spoken over a lull in the crowd. "They're mostly Voiceless, but not all of them. I saw one. It had mismatched eyes." I looked to Kester and raised my voice. "Did one of your traitors fit this description? How many left the Den, Kester?"

There was a collective breath from the crowd. Kester drew her eyebrows together, her eyes scanning her people. Outside, thunder sounded, followed by the sound of rain upon the rooftop. The pitter-patter like a lullaby, slackening my tense body. If only I could sleep, and think of nothing for a few hours. If only.

"We don't know for sure whether the Greatwolf Pack—"

Fray stepped forward, having entered the hall without me knowing. "I told you they were there," he barked at Kester. "I told you the night Izzy and I arrived. I told you each and every thing that happened at Stormwall, and you did nothing to stop it." He plowed on, not bothering to wait for Kester to answer. "I told you there were wolves amongst them. You did nothing. We were attacked, and Sonia almost died. You did nothing."

I caught Sonia's face as she listened to Fray speak. Her look was fragile and composed as she took in every word her brother said. I imagined I saw love flit across her face. Maybe I just wanted it to be true.

"Stories," Kester countered. "Nothing proven." She kept her face blank, but I saw past it.

I knew the look well. It was the one my mother wore after Henry died. One that she kept fixed upon her countenance until it became who she was, swimming in denial day after day after day. There was something far worse than your son dying: pretending that he hadn't.

There were murmurs from the hall, but nobody spoke up to rebuke Kester's words. Not even the wolves who were with me this morning. The very ones who had seen the white Gwylis and the scouting party. Did they really follow Kester so blindly? I shook my head in disbelief.

"We all know what you've been through, Isabelle," Kester said. Her patience with me was wearing thin. "Nobody can deny the effects it has had on your person. Same with you, Fray Castor. But I am the voice of the people, and I speak for Rixon. For now, we will not pursue war."

"You are sentencing us all to death," I said, my fingernails boring into the skin of my palms.

But I couldn't tell them what I feared: That I was the reason for the scouting party. That my mother wanted me back—for whatever reason that may be. Could it be because of the Voiceless cure? Pyrus hadn't mentioned it in his letter, but that had been weeks ago. And that white wolf had asked about Aquarius. Did his survival pose a threat to Mirosa's new king? If so, what sort of threat?

Henry lived here at the Den long enough to form bonds with the pack. Whether he confided in them about the gemstones and his quest to find them remained unknown. Olio knew about them. What if others did too? Breaking the curse was a threat to Dal; without it, he did not have the power of the Gwylis on his side.

With the cure, the Voiceless in Stormwall and beyond would regain their power.

Dal would imprison them, no doubt. He would torture them and force their allegiance. The Gwylis would either die or side with their king. Either way, there would be losses.

And I stood in his way. I had the Voiceless cure. I also had two of the three gems. I laughed inwardly. The feeling burned in the center of my chest. Never had I felt so powerful.

"If the king takes the Den, he will either slaughter you or chain you up to make him more Gwylis," I said. The latter sent a shudder down my spine. I hadn't thought of that as a possibility until the words left my lips. Dal could create an even greater army, if he hadn't started already.

But I had the Voiceless cure. So could I.

Branch caught my eyes. He shook his head slightly. *Not here*, the action said. *Not yet.*

"I promised peace to my people," Kester said, her look softening. "If it is the prince they want, perhaps soon they will find him and leave us be."

At least she wasn't ignoring the fact that Dal Paratheon was a threat —that she did care for the wellbeing of the Den. There was that much, but it wasn't enough for me. The new king of the New Kingdom had already had plenty of time to rally up his army and march past the Archway, and it was increasingly clear that it wasn't for his son alone.

Dal Paratheon wanted me, and when men like him want something, they eventually got it.

I'd heard enough. I left the meeting hall before Kester was finished. The door slammed shut behind me, leaving me in the night surrounded by nothing but the rain and stars above.

In that moment, I wished I had Henry to speak to. But his grave was too far, and he'd been absent in my dreams since I'd encountered him. What had changed?

"I know this isn't what you wanted."

My throat tightened at Fray's voice. He passed through the doors, stepping aside for other pack members to pass. *Guess the meeting is adjourned.* "How can they live in such illusions?" I asked.

"It's not their fault," he said. "It's hard to come to terms with something that you believed was true."

I turned to Fray. His hair was rain-soaked against his forehead. The water trickling down his skin reminded me of a world I'd once longed to be a part of. A world that could be fought for.

I closed the space between us, letting the commotion around me fall away.

My fingers trailed his shoulders and down his back. He shivered at my touch—which should have offended me, but I could not blame him. Loving him was a wild, desperate idea and something I could maybe do right someday. We could fly on the wind, him and I, soar over what was impossible and meant only for dreams, feathers splayed against the sky. Forever. He took away all the doubts and the pain and the years of uncertainty, the dashed thoughts that the world may never see me in any sort of light at all.

It was only when you gave up that the light stopped shining.

I wouldn't give up on us. I would never let our wings fall.

Fray took my face in his hands and rested his forehead to mine. I met his eyes, flickering blue in the torch light behind us. His voice, deep and soothing, said, "I'll be right beside you." He held me in place with his stare, and for a moment I felt more alive than I ever had. That was, until Olio bounded out from the doors behind us.

"Whatever you're doing," he said breathlessly, bouncing on his heels. "I'm doing with you."

GETTING OUT OF THE DEN WAS EASIER THAN I THOUGHT IT WOULD be. The three of us trailed a group heading out the main gate and broke off from them the second we had the chance. Then we shifted into wolves.

Picking up Ashe's scent proved more difficult. I knew from what he told me that he was heading out of the mountains, but how far he'd gotten in a few days had yet to be seen.

Two hours passed before we picked up the scent of another Gwylis.

I didn't hear anything besides the rain, but out from the darkness to our left came Sonia, skulking from the trees like a shadow.

At the sight of her, our shoulders all sunk with relief.

"You could have just said something," Olio snarled.

"Where's the fun in that?" She nodded her large head toward Fray, and I gave Olio a headbutt to his chest. "You're off to find the prince, aren't you?"

Fray's face leveled with Sonia's, and for an instant it looked as though something passed between them. Understanding? I would have thought I imagined it, had I not seen the same look in the meeting hall.

"It's nothing against the pack, Sonia," Fray said. "We're just questioning him."

"Fray," she said, suddenly circling him like a vulture. Her tail flicked back and forth. "No need to convince me. I believe you. I think Kester has gone mad. Same as you."

Fray made a choking sound, like he'd swallowed a bone. I couldn't help but grin.

Olio laughed and dropped his head in a curtsey. "It's an honor to have you with us, my lady."

We set off again, following Ashe's scent deeper into the mountains. By dawn, we reached an abandoned camp, where our noses sifted through the embers of a long-dead campfire. I knew the prince's scent—same as they did, if not better. Ashe had been there.

"Where is he going, anyhow?" Sonia asked. "There's nothing out here."

I looked off into the distance, where the sun was beginning to rise. Given my internal compass, I'd say he was heading deeper into the Old Kingdom through one of the only paths there were, as he'd mentioned at our last meeting. As we walked, my suspicions proved correct. Ahead was one of the main roads my father and his soldiers would have taken, according to Fray. Snow-covered but littered with fresh prints.

"How many?" I asked.

"Hundreds," Olio said, sniffing the air. "Far from here."

"And Ashe?"

"He's not with them. He's much closer."

I hoped he was right. The thought of Ashe teaming up with his father again was more than I could bear. I hoped he'd abandoned that part of his life as I had, even if he wasn't the wolf he wanted to be. *He's smart*, I told myself. He wouldn't go back. Because as far as I could tell, he still cared for me. Dal was now king, I reckoned, and he had my father's armies and the Greatwolf Pack on his side. Ashe would have no place there. No future.

He'd been safer with me at the Den, but that couldn't have happened.

"Smells like death," Sonia said suddenly. Her lips pulled back into a sneer. I bet she wished to find the prince dead.

"Up ahead!" Olio cried.

We burst across the road following Olio's voice and through a cluster of trees. My mind twisted with images of Ashe being dragged off, bloodied, beaten. Maybe Sonia was right. Maybe the soldiers had gotten to him. He was a traitor, after all. Just like me.

But just ahead, I caught wind of his familiar scent. Musk and mint.

My nostrils flared. If I were human, I think I'd sob with relief. "He's alive," I said. "Over here!"

We broke through the trees and arrived at what I could only describe as a ghost town. Small houses jutted from snow piles so high, they reached the tops of the doors on some. Some were small and flat, others larger with pyramid roofs. Their outer layers pulled back like peeled skin revealing the brick underneath. I spotted a stable, a church, and what appeared to be a stone fountain in the center of the dead town. Broken shutters. Broken doors. A grain tower knocked from its feet. Broken fenceposts sticking out from the snow like fingers grasping for help.

I felt too large for this place. I was disturbing its slumber.

What I imagined was Ashe huddled in on himself, living off roots and carrion. But what I found instead was a small, abandoned village within the trees and Ashe opening the door of a quaint, snow-topped home, looking as though we had just interrupted supper.

We advanced side-by-side toward the front stoop, four massive wolves in a straight line.

"I sympathize. I'm alone, I promise." Ashe's voice was steady. He stood between the door and the darkness behind him. I spotted the flicker of a single lantern and the gleam of a sword resting against the inside wall. Beyond Ashe, I smelled meat. "I don't want to die," Ashe continued. "Take what you want, and let me go."

"You're in no place to demand we do anything," Fray said.

Ashe scratched the back of his head and slinked back into the home. Judging by the windows and the poorly made door, he had to know shutting us out wouldn't keep us at bay. Still, fight or flight tore at him—until he caught my eyes and recognition eased the tension in his shoulders.

I took a step forward. "What are you doing here?"

"Surviving."

I hesitated in a fleeting moment of self-doubt and fear. I'd learned in the months I'd spent at the Den that forgiveness would only move my life forward, and the first person I'd have to forgive was standing in front of me.

I'd prepared myself for that moment. Still, it was harder than I thought it would be.

I lowered my head in a slight bow. "Ashe."

Ashe blinked, keeping his voice steady. "It's nice to see you again, Isabelle."

"So let me get this straight. First, it was all right when Pike Ivo wanted only me, but now that you're in danger—as I said before by the way—you've come for, what? My help?"

I nodded, no shame in it whatsoever.

Judging by the look on his face, Ashe seemed content at that. Maybe even a little gleeful. "So what do you want to know?"

Once inside Ashe's cabin, Sonia, Olio, and Fray had changed to human. Olio fetched some spare clothes from a chest long forgotten in the abandoned home to spare Ashe our naked company.

"I wish to know what your father planned beyond taking over Stormwall," I said. "Does he really plan on attacking the Den? When?"

"Well, he has his own Gwylis with him," Ashe said, leaning against a beam by the rear of the house. It looked ready to topple over at any moment. "They know exactly where your pack is."

"But why?" Olio asked. "We aren't hurting anyone. We want nothing to do with them."

Ashe narrowed his eyes at me. "Maybe it's because you know something he doesn't. Or because you have something he wants."

The words, spoke aloud, were a confirmation of what I'd already suspected. Hearing it now, truly knowing it, felt like a weight on my chest.

With slow hands, I signed to Fray: *The cure. He wants the cure.*

"What's that?" Ashe asked, pushing away from the beam. "What did you just sign to him?"

Fray advanced. "None of your damn business," he growled. "You're only alive because we kept you alive."

Olio snickered.

I clicked my tongue. "Fray, please."

"Question anything again, and I'll rip the other one off." Fray's eyes lit, alive and dangerous.

Ashe lifted his hand in a surrender. "Forgive me for not raising the other."

Silence fell over the small room. The tension thick and excruciating. I watched Fray, his jaw moving, molars grinding against one another.

"Enough of this," Olio's voice boomed, and he threw a hand to his forehead. "I'm going to make an educated guess on something here. I'm going to guess good ol' daddy wants the cure that Fray used, thus why they're after Izzy." He tilted his head toward me. "Because . . ."

"I have it." The words slid from my lips before I had time to think them over. "But it doesn't make sense. They have Pyrus."

Olio gestured dramatically. "Pyrus was . . ." he said, fishing for completion.

Fray answered. "The best healer in all of Mirosa."

"It's not the only reason," I interjected. "That white wolf, it asked me where Aquarius was. What would Dal want with him?"

"What do you think?" Olio asked.

I released a slow, controlled breath. I'd done well to suppress the weaved illusions that the people I knew were safe. Crim, Pyrus, Pedoma —even Abiyaya and Wargrave. *The people you love are your weakness, Izzy, and sometimes it will cloud your judgement.*

Deep breaths. One, two, three.

"That's one thing I don't know for sure," I said, a new confidence to my voice. "I don't know Dal Paratheon. I don't feign to understand his reasoning."

Olio cleared his throat and leaned against a wall with one foot propped up. He pointed a finger at Ashe. "But he does."

"My father is not a violent man." Ashe spoke the words like he believed them.

I snorted. "Show them the scar, Ashe."

"He wouldn't kill innocent people, Izzy. He wouldn't."

"Show them the damn scar, Ashe."

The prince looked at me, begging, a horse on his way to slaughter. He then lifted his tunic, revealing the long-healed wound his father had dealt to him. "My father. Drew a sword and slashed my flesh when I was just twelve years old. He told me that pain was part of life and to know it well."

"Your father did that to you?" Olio asked. He pushed himself away from the wall and stared in disbelief. "To his own son? What monster do we deal with?"

Ashe told me once that I could trust him, and he'd broken that promise; yet now seeing him dressed in piled furs, dark circles under his eyes, his once smooth skin chapped and dry, I couldn't help but replace all doubts with pity. If my gut felt anything, it was the need to trust him at that moment.

"If he wants the cure, he'll stop at nothing to get it," Sonia said, speaking for the first time. Her eyes were wild and alive. She was already preparing for a fight.

"But how does he even know I have it?" I asked. "There's no way for him to know."

"Unless he got it out of Pyrus," Fray said, his fists still curled. "Men will say or do anything at the threat of death or dismemberment."

I shook my head. "He wouldn't. He'd rather die."

Olio rubbed his chin. "Do you know this?"

A deep dread filed my belly. If they got it out of Pyrus, they'd know about Wargrave and, ultimately, Aquarius. They wouldn't need the vial I had. They wouldn't have bothered.

I nodded. "I'm sure of it."

"It doesn't particularly matter anyhow," Olio dismissed.

We all looked at him. He paced in and out of the shadows, stopping at the open window and peering up to the moon.

If Dal Paratheon wanted a war, let me bring it, but not before we did everything in our power to stop it.

"Will it help if I do give myself up?"

I blanched at Ashe's words and the sincerity in them. I truly believed he would give himself up if that was what it came down to.

"Yes," Sonia said at the same time as I said, "No."

I thought of how all of this could have been avoided if he had given himself up the same day we met Commander Ivo. Kap wouldn't have been wounded. We wouldn't be out here discussing war at all.

But I knew in my heart none of that was true. If I accomplished what Henry set out to do, there would still be a false king on the throne in Stormwall. There would be a war. Now or later. Eventually.

I had to return to my past to make right for my future. Returning to Stormwall was the only way.

The thought came undaunted by my unwillingness to accept it. The Den was at stake. Our very souls hung loosely in the balance. Uncanny. Dal Paratheon. Pike Ivo. Even Kester and Rixon.

Enemies snapped at me from all sides, and it was too much to bear.

I walked from the house and into the frigid night. I leaned against the house, briefly closing my eyes. and then opened them to see the stars shining like beacons against the black sky.

My faithful friends, I prayed, clenching my fists together. *Guide me in the right direction.*

My fingers loosened at the sight of a falling star. I watched it fade, then stared down at my torn boots, the remnants of a life long gone.

And looked out into a world that was my future. Ahead, mountains and stars; behind me, death and darkness. A sob threatened to shake loose, shuddering my body, and I jolted forward, breathless, until two strong hands caught me.

I knew his face, and I knew it well. I'd done this all for him, hadn't I?

"You can't fall apart now," Fray said. He pulled me closer, and I slipped into him. "We need you. *I* need you."

I nodded into his shoulder.

He went on, "If you want, we can leave. Like Ashe. We can go far and find a place, just the two of us."

"That's running away." Something I used to do best.

He looked at me, running a hand over my cheekbone.

Sometimes I wondered how free it must feel to think of nothing but happiness. To have hope for the future when all seemed so bleak.

"Then this is the moment we make a decision," said Fray.

I didn't have to ask him to elaborate. I knew what he meant.

"Going back wasn't high on my list things to do," I said. "In fact, it was nonexistent on said list."

"I know." His blue eyes met mine. "Together we can make it. Olio, Branch, even Sonia will join us. That's a pretty formidable pack. But I need the Izzy you were back at Stormwall, the one who fought for what she wanted, no matter what. That is the only one that will get us through this."

"And if we die?"

"If the odds are against us, we will die together." Fray slipped his hands into mine. "Hand in hand."

Death. Such a final word. I'd seen it in many forms. My father torn, dying in fits of screams between my teeth. Lulu lying peacefully as her heart stopped beating. There was nothing to stop it. No magic spell. No cure.

"We don't have to talk about it tonight."

Fray flinched, and we parted, his hands dropping from mine. "You're right, we don't."

"About dying, I mean. I don't want to talk about it anymore."

I turned from him, my hands cupped to my mouth, catching my breath. I looked to the stars again, this time not asking for their aid but realizing that they lived to die just like the rest of us.

Not long after it was my turn to keep watch, Ashe came to me. I stood outside the house, one leg propped against the door so that, when he opened it, I nearly fell. He caught me just under an arm and hoisted me upright.

Falling wasn't the thing that caught me off guard. It was the way I didn't flinch when he touched me.

"Shouldn't you have sensed me coming or something?" he asked, closing the door behind us.

"Your scent is constant," I replied. But maybe I'd been too deep into thought. Too distracted by . . . everything. "Plus, I'm kind of a defective wolf."

Ashe smirked, and something jolted inside of me. I found myself watching him, committing him to memory in a way. Was part of me admitting to myself that we all may not live through this? Or was it something else entirely?

"What are you doing?" I asked, when he caught my gaze and held it.

"I should be asking you the same thing," he replied. He kept his tone light, though the tension furrowing his brow was deep. "Running straight into danger. It's classic Isabelle, but it doesn't mean I have to like it."

I frowned. "Good thing I didn't ask you."

He sighed long and hard. "Gods, Isabelle."

"Ashe, what?"

Ashe's face gave nothing away—an unfortunate trait to have for a royal- so when the blanket of arrogance that I'd come to know finally dropped, I saw fear in his green eyes. "You can't take on my father from the outside."

I begged to differ. I had Uncanny magic. I could do anything. "Don't worry about me, Ashe. We have it under control."

He moved so he was facing me. I looked hard to see if I could find the prince in there somewhere, but he was gone. Long gone. Just as the princess was in me. "I know you, Isabelle. You jump into things without thinking, and if you do think, it's for a split second."

I stepped away from him, in disbelief of his unsolicited candor. "You don't know me, Ashe. Not anymore. Probably not before either."

"It doesn't matter," he said. "I'm going to offer you something, and I want you to listen and consider it." He stepped forward to reclaim the few inches I'd stepped back. Hope glistened in his eyes.

He better not try to marry me again.

"Are you listening?" he asked after a moment.

Except, this wasn't a proposal. No, this was something much more intense and much more dangerous. The prince had never been the cunning type, not when I first met him, but he had grown since then. Surviving not only in the mountains alone, but with one arm. No family. No friends. Nothing.

But I was there, right in front of him. *I* was his family. *I* was his friend.

Pressure built behind my eyes as I finally nodded. "Yes, Ashe. I'm listening."

CHAPTER TWENTY-NINE

Someone shook me awake.

I opened my eyes to find Olio hovering over me. I mouthed a question, but he slapped a hand to my mouth and placed a finger to his lips. Silence. Something was here.

I sat up slowly to see Fray and Ashe on either side of the door, a sword in the former prince's hand, a chant hanging on the lips of my temperamental suitor.

Emotions ran with abandon on Ashe's face when he met my gaze. Fear. Apprehension. Maybe even doubt. I ran my fingers along the scar on my shoulder. *It will hurt now*, I told myself. *But it will be worth it.*

I looked away because I could not face him. I could not face the decision we'd both made. I wished to change into a wolf and run as far away as I could.

We couldn't all change. Not in that tiny house. We'd break enough furniture to wake the dead. Olio might even burst through the roof itself.

"What's going on?" I whispered, shoving my feet into my boots.

"Soldiers," Sonia said. She crouched, holding her chin in her palm thoughtfully. "There's a back door."

Nobody responded. I gritted my teeth and willed Fray to look at me.

They will kill us or capture us, I signed to him when he finally looked my way.

I'd die before sitting in another prison cell, he signed back.

He'd never told me what happened to him after he'd been captured at Stormwall, and I turned away, trying not to think about it.

I crouched and peered up through sheer curtains at the dark forms walking against the dusk. One after another. An army marching three lines deep. They stopped to search houses, but were as silent as the dead.

"They haven't seen our prints." Olio took a minute to slow his heartbeat. "I think we're good."

I agreed. Our prints were long trampled by the soldiers marching through, or else already buried by the dusting of snow overnight. Still, as they neared, the relief turned to dread that something would go wrong. There were too many of them for the five of us to fight. We were outnumbered, and I doubted we'd encounter the same negotiations we had before. They would slaughter us.

"Shit," Fray drew looks from Ashe and Olio. "Change of plans."

"Back door?" Sonia asked, arching an eyebrow.

Fray nodded. "Back door."

We all got down on our hands and knees and crawled. The rear door of the home opened up to a cluster of trees, maybe fifteen to twenty feet away. If we ran quickly enough, we'd be able to hide within them.

Ashe went first. His furs were too heavy for the movement, and he stumbled, crawling the rest of the way. Once he was safe, Olio and Sonia followed, lightning fast.

Fray hovered in the doorway and met my gaze. "Go."

"You first."

He planted a kiss onto my forehead. "Don't make me beg, Izzy."

I stuck my tongue out. "But I like it when you beg."

He looked at me for a second longer and said again, "Go."

I ran forward, wondering if we'd made the right choice in running. Deep down, I knew the five of us could never bring down an entire army, but it didn't stop my brain from trying to convince me that I could.

Once Fray safely broke through the trees, he took my hand, and we cut through the woods. One by one, we changed into our Gwylis forms.

Ashe struggled to keep up, but had the common sense not to call after us.The trees hid us from sight as we climbed a slope to get a better view of the army. I wished we hadn't.

There were thousands of them, a black stain snaking its way through the wintery white landscape.

In the direction of the Den.

"We have to fly," Sonia said.

But something stopped us all suddenly. A scent creeping into our nostrils. Fray lifted his head, his nose working hard as he looked toward the trees. We smelled it too. Steel. Leather. Human.

"Don't move."

A man stepped forward from the cover of the trees. He had a firm grasp on Ashe with one hand, while the other held a knife to his throat. It gleamed in the moonlight. Mirosian steel.

A deep growl thundered in my chest.

"Let him go, human," Olio sneered, inching forward. His ears laid flat against his head. I hadn't expected him to defend Ashe that way. "Let him go, or you die."

The soldier, his face hidden by his visor and neck scarf, seemed to hesitate. Voices rose behind him, and he began to back away, dragging Ashe with him. "We just want the prince," he said. Fear shook his words. "I'm just following orders."

"Leave him," Sonia roared. Though she spoke the words with such vehemence, there was no denying the uncertainty in her eyes. She wanted to repay Ashe for helping her, but not if it risked the pack.

"Don't worry," Ashe said, his voice splintered. His chest was heaving, but his jaw was set. "I can do this, Izzy. Trust me."

Time slowed to a crawl as I looked to Ashe in desperation. His eyes were pleading with me, the clear green of the seas of his home. His jaw tightened, steeling himself, accepting this defeat. I took one more step, but he shook his head. Last night, before we'd fallen asleep, we'd decided on this, and I could not go back on my word. Nor would he. I took a step backward, and he nodded with relief. The knife cut a thin line into his skin with the action. Blood dripped into the snow.

"We have to go," Olio urged.

"I'll be fine," Ashe said and repeated the same words he'd said to me so long ago: "I'm not one to give up easily."

I watched him, the last piece of my former life.

Now I knew why he'd suffered so much. I knew why he'd followed me. He knew there was a way out of the life we'd grown into. He left to avoid war, a selfish action. But now it meant something different.

Now it was for something so much more than himself.

He nodded to me, permission to leave him. To let him go. "I love you, Izzy," he said against the blade on his neck. His bright green eyes widened, as did my own. "I'll be fine."

"Please," I gasped, still backing away. Please what? We'd made this choice. No going back now. I dug my claws into the snow, fear curling its way in my belly. Ashe, who had only one hand to defend himself with, who begged me to change him so he wouldn't feel the agony of betrayal, so he would have family again—who agreed to our plan without so much as a hint of hesitation . . . I had to trust in him. There was no other way.

But it wasn't supposed to be this hard.

I begged for my magic to come, to betray this moment and get him back. I willed it so. We'd find another way. But nothing came, and I had no time to acknowledge my disappointment.

Arrows began to fly. One struck the center of Olio's shoulder blades before he launched himself from the cliff. Sonia and Fray followed seconds later. I lingered there, watching as the men took Ashe away, replaying his words from the night before in my head.

Will it help if I do give myself up?

I launched myself from the cliff just as I felt the first licks of flames on my feet. It had come too late.

CHAPTER THIRTY

Olio ran ahead growling, quickly running out of curses.

"They'll torture him," he said. "He's going to tell them everything."

"He can't tell them anything they probably don't already know," Fray said.

My body felt heavy, hardly able to move through the deep drifts of snow. A shiver of icy panic shot through me. I was cold, so cold. All I could see were Ashe's eyes, pleading with me to trust him. The knife at his throat.

Are you listening?

He'd barely questioned it last night as we both stood guard outside the house. Fray, Olio, and Sonia had dozed off, promising to wake in a few hours to take over. I'd seen how cold Ashe was and offered him my cloak, but he'd refused, pushing his chin beneath the collar of his coat. He was a broken man, but a stubborn one nonetheless. As they all were.

It was he who'd initiated it.

"I can kill him," he said, staring out into the night sky. He licked his lips and blinked away the urge to take it back. There was no taking back those words. "I can get him to trust me again and then . . . then I can kill him."

I let out a breath that curled in the chilled air. It wasn't something that hadn't crossed my mind, but I could never have asked such a thing. Not to someone who I'd pushed from my life. Not from someone who owed me nothing. "Ashe—"

The line of his jaw hardened. "Let me do this," he said. "It's safer for me behind the city walls than you. I know my father better than anyone. I can . . ."

He trailed off, but I knew what he was going to say. He was going to say that he could take back Stormwall from within. It was a grand notion. A dangerous notion.

I bit my lip, terrified of the way I agreed. "I need to know what his plans are," I said. "But after that, I do not care what happens to him."

I'd told him everything I knew about the Uncanny and the curse and what Henry had been doing. Said it all aloud as if telling a very scary bedtime story. He'd listened, committing everything to memory. At one point, the clouds shifted from their place over the moon, and I could see the outline of his profile. I'd forgotten how handsome he was underneath all that beard. The Peek Island men were once thought to be indomitable warriors, but I knew now that they were only men, and they felt fear just as I did. Despite everything, Ashe was a prince, and some of the pride remained in the way he held his gaze. Focused and undoubting.

"He might kill me," Ashe said. Something changed in his tone that made it seem like he'd thought of this already and had come to accept it.

"He won't," I said. "Don't you remember what that soothsayer said?"

Abiyaya had once told Ashe that he would have sons. Someday, he would be happy.

Ashe met my eyes and chortled, no longer so stoic. "You don't believe that, do you?"

I looked away. There was a lot I didn't believe that proved to be true.

I closed my eyes and listened to the sound of my own heart beating and that of Ashe's. If he were to suffer . . . if he were to die because of me . . . I'd lost Henry, and I'd lost Lulu. I could not bear it.

But I could not stop him. Ashe was going to do this. He did not need my permission. Only my support.

"When your band of wolves arrive, send a crow," Ashe said as we delved further into the plan. I knew for a fact that Fray would come with me, and so would Branch. Olio would probably tag along just for the fun of it. Either way, I would not be alone.

"Be safe," he said, as if it needed to be said. It probably did.

Inside I wilted, but outside I nodded. Although I tried to push the facts away, I knew it to be true: Ashe and I were the children of kings. We could no longer run from what we were born and bred to do—and that was to protect our people at all costs. For the heirs to come, we had to be brave.

It still wasn't supposed to hurt this much.

In the present, Olio skidded to a stop, swinging his body to face us.

"They don't know about Rixon," Olio said. He sniffed the air. "Looks like we're taking the long way. Your friend made a humble sacrifice for us."

I snarled and snapped the air near Olio's muzzle. He hopped back, surprised by my violent gesture.

I swallowed and then nodded. I had to get a hold on myself. The wheels were already in motion. I could not stop things now. I bowed my head to Olio. "I'm sorry."

"It's all right," he said, shaking himself. His tone was far softer than I deserved. "He's your friend."

I neared him, licking his wound and resting my head against his neck. *I'm sorry, Olio. I'm sorry.* I'd taken my anger out on the wrong person. I hated that part of myself. "You are also my friend."

A burst of crows from the trees overhead set us moving again. My anger propelled me forward, and before long we were crashing through the smaller east gate of the Den, still in Gwylis form.

Many approached us, wondering what had happened and where we had gone. I wondered how many had fought in the war with my father and how many actually knew how to fight. I thought of the young wolves —Ghetee, Claw, Kap, and the others—and how disorganized they'd been. There were more like them here. Those who would fight to the death, though not very well.

Get ready for war, I thought. *Get ready or run.*

We moved straight through the city, past the main square. We stopped briefly to change and snag some clothes from home before approaching the meeting hall. Kester waited there, her hood pulled over her head and her hands folded together at her chest. She looked too calm. The sight of her made my blood burn.

"You knew," I said. "You knew this was going to happen."

After what seemed like the longest moment, she nodded. Her body seemed to sag. Her secrets spilling out and making her lighter.

"Tell me it'll be all right." Fray approached her. Her body language resembled something about to shatter. "Tell me there's a plan, and it will be all right."

"She won't." My voice was louder than anticipated. "She'll let us all die."

"No." Fray turned, holding his head in his hands. "You won't do this again. Not again."

"Not again?" I stopped, and so did my heart. Ten years ago, an eight-year-old Fray had left his pack, immersed himself in a war far too old for someone far too young, and begged fealty to a king who abandoned him.

His king had betrayed him. And now his queen.

I stepped forward, anger boiling in my blood. "I can't let you do this. You have to lead them. There is nobody else!"

Kester regarded me without expression.

"There is an end to us all," she said softly. "If this is it, so be it."

Suddenly, Branch was at my side, shirtless, with two stripes of red paint under both eyes. Or was it blood?

"I will lead them if she won't." He cast a glare at Kester that would have subdued the strongest of foes. "If I go down, I go down standing."

With Fay, Olio, and Branch in tow, I made my way past the uneasy crowds that gathered in patches around the city and into my house.

Once the door shut, I located my necklace. Two jewels hung on a chain, side-by-side like siblings: the ruby from Henry's sword that I had placed into bezel setting hanging beside the emerald. I fell to my knees, gripping them tightly. *This is it*, I told myself. *You have to fight again, Izzy. Stand up.*

From beneath the bed, I pulled out a small bag containing the two vials. One that cured and one that killed. Side-by-side. I'd have to be the same. A healer and a destroyer.

Part of me wanted to run—to sneak out the back door and leave all of this behind. But the thought of leaving Fray and the family I'd made here tore me apart. I could never live with myself. How could anyone forgive me?

Stop being selfish, Izzy. You've been given the power to save your family. Stand. Up. Now.

I stood. I looked from the unmade bed to the fireplace to the rickety old table. Even though it was small and old and dusty, this was the first home I'd shared with Fray, and that counted for something.

If I never returned, at least my ghost would have a quaint little space to rest.

Commotion from outside turned my head. Someone was yelling for me. From the window I saw the top of a head attempting to push through Branch, Olio, and Fray. I snorted. Only one wolf would try to do such a thing.

Branch had him by his arms, lifting him from the ground like he weighed nothing. Ghetee kicked; one booted foot landed straight in the pack leader's groin—a blow that even the strongest men would bow to.

"Ghetee," I scolded, pushing past the boys. "What are you doing?"

Branch, still bent over in pain, finally released Ghetee. I saw Olio off to the side, cupping a hand to his mouth to suppress his laughter. The crinkle of his eyes and the tremor in his shoulders gave him away. I shot him a look, which only made it worse.

"I can't," he said through tear-filled laughter. "This kid is my hero."

I fixed my stare to Ghetee. Like Branch, he had painted his face. Black swirls looped across his cheeks, around his eyes, and met on the bridge of his nose. His bare chest was decorated with red orbs that I assumed were supposed to be moons. They reminded me too much of blood, and I had to look away.

I'm braver than you think. I recalled Ghetee's words on the day we'd first met before his attempt at fighting in the Pit. I admired his determination then. I still did. But this wasn't the Pit. It was not play. This was more real than a bunch of wolves battling for bragging rights. Now we were battling for our lives.

"You're not coming," I told him. I had to grit my teeth to speak. I was going to crush the boy's hopes. "Get it out of your head, Ghetee."

"I know I choked up yesterday, but I'm ready," he urged. He

gripped at his pants, flexing what little muscle he had. He reminded me too much of the story of Rydell and his prayers to the gods to make him a bird. He fought so hard, but leapt before he was truly ready. "I'm a pack member. I have to defend my home."

"You will, someday," Fray said, taking the burden from me. "But not now. Find Rini and get to safety."

Ghetee frowned. "It's not fair," he grumbled.

Branch finally straightened. "Go," he barked to Ghetee. "Get out of here before I snap your head off."

I thought that'd be the end of it. Orders from a pack leader were set in stone. But Ghetee barely gave Branch a glance. Instead, he looked to me before finally walking off. By then, Olio had finally composed himself enough to give a semblance of his battle-readiness.

"Let's go, pups," he said. When I came up to walk beside him, he leaned into me. "I'm going to crack up every time I think about it. I'll be killing one of those humans, and then *bam*, Branch gets kicked in the groin."

He looked straight ahead as I glanced his way. "Right in the groin," he mouthed.

At the watchtowers by the main entrance of the Den, several men were racing up and down the ladders, unsure of where to go.

Branch called up to the men stationed above and ordered them down.

"Is that the Rowan girl with you?" a voice called out.

"Are you leading an army?" asked the other.

Branch called up, "Yes to both. Would you like to join?"

Two heads peered down. "With you leading, I'd walk into the depth of the hells," one of them said.

They both descended and, along with Olio, accepted Branch's orders to call together more men and women. He climbed the watchtower, Fray and I following behind.

"They'll funnel through from here," said Branch, pointing out into the wilderness from the highest platform. A voice called his name, and he looked down. "Archers up here. As many as the towers can hold. Bring fire."

I placed a hand on Branch's arm, and he turned his dark eyes toward me. "I'll take care of the fire." I hoped.

He smiled, a snarling, toothy thing, and left the tower, leaving Fray and I alone. A strong gust of wind moved through, fluttering Fray's long hair into his eyes. He stared at me through the strands. Did he know what I was thinking? I'd always thought he could read my mind. I hoped to the gods now that it wasn't true.

"What are you planning?" he asked. How right I was.

"I'll hold off the soldiers as long as possible, and once Branch gives the okay, I'm going to kill the commander." Take out the leaders. Rule number one of war.

Fray scoffed. "You can't go alone."

"I'm going."

Fray nodded. "Just not alone."

I smiled. "Just not alone."

We waited there, looking out, waiting, hoping for a reprieve. It never came. Along with the sight of the first line of soldiers breaking across the ridge, the smell of something foul yet familiar wafted toward us.

Soon enough, we saw them. Calls from the watchtower directly across from us confirmed our fears.

They started out as dots that slowly resolved into wolves, trotting along the ridge in single file. The path to the Den—though still narrow and dangerous for humans in large numbers—could be navigated in small groups. With the Greatwolf Pack defending them, Voiceless or not, they had an advantage.

Men could not navigate the ridge easily. But wolves could.

But we had the high ground.

"There were not that many defects from the Den," I said to Fray. "Where did they come from?"

I begged my mind not to think of the worst possibility: that Gwylis were changing humans. I shook the thought free. That would be ruthless. That would be inhumane. That was against all the rules.

But what rules had I played by this whole time? Were rules even present anymore?

Not a minute later, urgent voices from all around us filled the spaces between the bells' ringing. The ladder beside me shuddered as Olio climbed to greet us. Once he found his footing, he froze in place, the grin falling from his face.

"That," he said. "was not what I was expecting."

~

THE STREETS BEGAN TO FILL WITH THOSE POISED TO FIGHT AND those running for the safest place to hide. Branch and Olio darted through the city, recruiting as many they could as quickly as possible. Near the meeting hall, I nearly collided with them.

"We need to evacuate the city." Branch's pained look glanced over us. "There are less of those who want to fight and more who don't. We cannot risk their lives."

This is how a kingdom dies. "No." I turned away and pushed open the doors of the meeting hall, where I found half of the pack waiting and Kester in the center. Holed up like rabbits in a warren. "Kester!"

The volume of the room hushed to a dead silence that prickled my skin. Kester neared me, her face expressionless and cold. As cold as the words that fell from my lips.

"You are a traitor." We were face to face now, breathing in each other's air. "The enemy is at your gate, and you're having meetings. The time for talking is over. Take me to Rixon."

At first, she cocked her head as if she hadn't understood the question. As if I didn't know.

"I know you can speak to her," I said, this time calmer. A little sweetness never hurt the cause. "Take me to her."

"If I don't?"

"Then I will kill you and parade your head through the city streets."

A collective gasp rose from the people, but nobody made a move. Not with Branch, Olio, and Fray behind me. They wouldn't dare.

Kester blinked. "This way." She led us past the room where we'd reached a decision on Ashe the night he arrived. My eyes lingered there even as we passed, looking back as if I'd never before seen the chair where he'd sat or the floor where he'd begged for his life. The memory was a ghost.

I turned my focus ahead.

Moving forward would be the only way I'd survive.

The hallway took us to a room with nothing but a fireplace in it. My fingers pulled at each other, my throat lumpy, my legs feeling as though they were about to fall off. I felt Fray behind me. His temper smelled strong.

"Light the fire," I demanded.

Kester obeyed.

Fray grabbed for my hand, whirling me toward him. "What are you doing?"

"I want to have a word with Rixon," I said.

"Let me be the one to do it." There was a quiver in Fray's voice. Did I imagine it?

I loosed a breath. Fray had not wanted to see his mother but had prepared himself for the confrontation nonetheless. As much as I would never come between a son and his mother, this was not the time for reunions.

"No, Fray," I said. "I would never ask that of you."

Fray's throat bobbed as he swallowed. "You don't want to do this. Let me."

"You don't, either. Please, Fray, let me take this burden from you. It's the least I could do after—"

"Izzy." He pulled me into the curve of his body. His hips settled against mine, and my mouth went dry. This was the closest we'd been in a while, and I wasn't sure what to expect.

"Trust me, will you?" I said.

He leaned down, and for a moment I thought he was going to kiss me, but he pulled back and nodded. This small rejection stung, whether he meant it to or not.

Focus, Izzy.

I turned toward the lit fireplace. I started to ask what to do when my gaze snagged on the flames.

When the realization of what I was seeing sunk in, the words died in my mouth.

A hand made of flame reached out toward me, its fingers grasping the air. I screamed, stumbling backward in a panic. I moved so quickly that I lost my footing and fell onto the floor, only to find it cold and wet.

I was no longer in the room with Kester, Olio, Branch, and Fray. I was somewhere dark and damp. I felt a presence. Watching. Waiting. I could smell my own fear, thicker than quicksand.

I blinked and became encased in darkness. The smell and the sound of that place were familiar. I was in Rixon's labyrinth of caves.

I pushed myself to my feet, my eyes adjusting to the pitch black.

"You're not really here, Izzy."

I looked around, Lulu's sweet voice reverberating against the stone.

"Just a part of you is here," she said. "Like scraping the burnt edges off a loaf of bread."

I strained to listen. "So you're saying I'm crust from a freshly baked loaf of rye?"

Lulu appeared now and smiled widely. "I'm saying you're in two places at once."

"Was it you that brought me here?"

"Rixon isn't here." She pointed down the tunnel, where the blue light flickered. "But they are."

"They?" I looked around, wondering whether I'd end up by the sandy shore of the lake if I turned back.

No. I couldn't leave. Not now.

I needed to save them. I mouthed the words and headed down the tunnel, deeper into the caverns.

Which family are you saving, Izzy? Lulu's voice was in my head, taking up every space in it. *Don't go there.*

I have to. There was a rush of cold air. Lulu stood in front of me. "Why are you helping me, Lu?" I asked. "Why aren't you at peace?"

At the mouth of Rixon's cave, she turned. "I was murdered, Izzy." She shook her head. "We don't rest."

I let out a pained breath.

"I'm scared for you," she said. "And for Fray."

"Why are you scared for us?"

"Because, when the time comes for you to die, I want you with me, even if I am in-between. Not . . ." Her head whipped to the right at something I couldn't hear. "Not there."

"What's there? Where would I go, Lu?"

She looked back to me and frowned. "Somewhere not so beautiful."

My skin grew warm with the thought of spending an eternity in the depths of hell. Worse so under the stare of Lulu's desperate, pleading eyes. I wished there was a way to tell her to leave and let me do what I had to do. Just as she'd done for me.

I approached the well of water, mindful of the colors dancing along the walls. "I'm glad you're here, Lu." But when I turned to smile at her, I found her look grave.

"Behind you."

My head had barely turned when a hand grasped my forearm and pulled me down into the water.

CHAPTER THIRTY-ONE

The darkness of Rixon's cave instantly turned into the empty, one-window room with the fireplace, but instead of Kester, Fray, Branch, and Olio being there, I was all alone. I went for the door immediately but found my hand went straight through, as if I were nothing but fog.

The door opened, and I gasped at the sight of Rixon. Through the filtered sunlight from the open window, she looked as though her edges were lined in gold. That was what she was. Edges. Tall and slight in a white robe, made of bird bones, I expected. The way she crossed, it was as though her feet never even touched the floor.

She didn't seem to notice me.

She moved a delicate hand to the hair that drifted across her shoulder and turned as the door opened again. Kester walked in, not quite as lightly as her queen, nearly slamming the door behind her.

"You've been gone too long," Kester said, practically seething.

Rixon cocked her head on its hinges. "I took a trip to Stormwall."

"What did you find there?"

"The girl. And Aquarius."

Kester stopped midway through her stride. "He's alive, then."

Rixon nodded. "Very much so."

Kester smirked and shook her head disbelievingly. "And the girl led you right to him."

"It's surprising what a little lust can do to a young heart. My son did quite well."

I tore my eyes away, shaking my head. *No time for anger now, Isabelle.*

"Astonishing," Kester said. "The soothsayer—"

"Warned her." Rixon faced Kester with pursed lips. "Against my wishes. It probably scared the pants off her. Time will tell what happens next."

Kester tilted her head. "But you know what happens next."

Rixon furrowed her brow and placed a finger there to quell an imaginary hurt. "In order for peace, they must all die, and you must make it so."

They all must die. Did she mean the entire population of the Den? That didn't make any sense!

Kester looked as though the wind had been knocked from her lungs. "We don't fight the humans?"

"Have we ever, Kester? We won't start now."

"Even if it means . . ."

"Even if it means your death."

Kester lowered her head, but it was brought back up by Rixon's touch.

"Do not fear death," Rixon said. "You will not be alone. The entire pack will be by your side. The ones that do not die in battle will die by my hand, and I will burn the city to the ground as if it never was."

I took a step back as my muscles tensed. My pulse drummed in my ears as the world grew muffled around me. I stepped back as far as the wall, but instead of coming against it, I fell through.

The cave materialized around me. I stood on one side of the pool, gasping for air, gripping the edges of the rock surrounding the water. With my last gulping breath, I threw back my head and screamed.

Rixon had known the humans would come for us, and she still let it happen—told Kester to deny any danger, make it seem safe, so when the danger came we'd be snuffed out like candles at midnight. Everything that had happened was because of her. Everything. Down to the smallest of details.

But why?

With an explosive exhale, I squeezed my eyes closed and dropped to my knees. I let my forehead touch the damp rock beneath me, grounding myself. The world was still muffled. The silence felt infinite and then—

Water dripped from the ceiling of the cave. Drip, drip, in perfect rhythm with my heartbeat. I smelled the water, the rock, the soil. I felt the chill against my skin.

"Come out, come out," I whispered. A shadow crossed before my eyes.

I pushed to my feet in a surge. My body tensed like a drawn bow. My nerves rattled against my skin. Rixon was here. I knew she was.

I heard her, soft like a breeze against a curtain, and she stood before me as I'd seen her minutes before in my dream-like vision.

The Queen of the Gwylis.

CHAPTER THIRTY-TWO

Rixon rounded the pool of water, running her fingers along its edge, looking down and away from me the entire time.

Even though I couldn't see her eyes, I could still read the betrayal, the cunningness, dripping off her.

I hated that I once trusted her. I hated that I still feared her.

She stopped and raised her eyes to me. Calm and tired as if she'd just woken from a nap. "Are you going to stop me?"

I closed my hands into fists. There was no stopping the spasms that ran through them. "You want us all to die. Why?"

"Because we weren't meant to be on this earth. Not like this." She looked at me as a mother would right before she might stroke my hair and tell me it was going to be all right. "This is our fate for what Aquarius has done to us. We are cursed, Isabelle. You and me both."

Suddenly, I didn't fear her. I didn't feel much of anything when she spoke in that soft, breezy voice meant to lull me. I saw past the mask.

"There is a way," I said. "My brother—"

Rixon hissed a laugh. "Even if it were true, there wouldn't be time, Isabelle." She took a finger and dipped it into the pool. Colors blended and reflected off the cave walls. "Your best chance is to leave if you want to live. Make amends with your mother. She thinks about you often."

"Don't talk about my mother." I scowled. "She doesn't exist to me."

Rixon eyed me from the other side of the pool and sighed. "I don't believe that's entirely true."

"When you told the soothsayer 'I could,' what did you mean by that?"

"I told her you could be the one to change the world."

"Abiyaya didn't think so."

Rixon lowered her eyes. "Nothing is certain in life. Not even a soothsayer's word. Nothing."

"So, you're saying we should give up?"

"You don't have a chance," Rixon reasoned. "Don't you see? We are outnumbered. We will all die by fire and become dust, then nothing. No legacy. Nobody will throw our ashes to the wind. They will trample them. We are doomed to become no more than shadow. We will never win. We never could."

I refused to believe that. I was not doomed. I once thought I was; then I woke up, and I realized that the place I stood was not the place I would end up. My heart grew calm. My soul was on fire. I felt the world expand, and my vision cleared, and all that I thought about life shifted. The scar on my shoulder was a symbol of strength. I was tired, but I was full of hope.

I am not doomed.

"I'm sorry it ended this way," Rixon crooned. "I wished more for you, dear girl."

She studied my reaction. I swallowed and pushed the air from my lungs. I wondered how she'd ever have led someone, never mind hundreds. A ruler was strong, hopeful, and protective of her people. Rixon wasn't any of those things. She may as well have been a passerby who knew nothing, wanted nothing, merely watched as the world burned. I knew then that I wouldn't die that day. Not without a fight.

Rixon didn't move when I walked toward her, my dagger drawn in my shaky hand. She positioned her body to welcome me as I rounded the pool. I let out a gasp. "You saw this," I realized.

"My entire life," she said, her pale eyes focused on my dagger.

I shook my head, warring with myself. What was I thinking? This was Fray's own mother, and I was intent on killing her. He would never forgive me, no matter how he felt about her. This would tear us apart forever. I would lose him.

But deep inside, I knew there was no other way.

Closer I went. Every step left my heart heavier and heavier. "I can't let you do this."

Rixon nodded. Too calm. "I know," she said.

"You're Fray's mother," I said. I hated how small my voice sounded. How it was almost begging. "Don't you want to see him?" I offered her my hand. "Come with me and you can."

Rixon shook her head, and I clearly heard the words she didn't speak: *The ones that do not directly die in battle will die by my hand, and I will burn the city to the ground as if it never was.*

My mind was swimming. I tried to see past Rixon and into the cruel thing she really was. I walked forward, dagger gripped and pointed, feeling it become harder and harder to breathe. I finally understood what Branch told me when he said sometimes it was hard to make decisions when the future was so uncertain.

It had all been to prepare me for this day.

At that moment, I would claim my certainty. From that day forward, I would never bow to anyone ever again. I was in no one's shadow, and I was no one's slave.

Before another thought could cross my mind, a sudden jolt wracked Rixon's body, and she twisted, eyes rolling back, mouth opening in a scream. I stepped back, my boots skidding on the wet ground. Blackness pooled in her eyes, filling the whites until there was nothing left. Tendrils of shadow rushed from her open mouth like a cyclone, and I cried out, brandishing my dagger as if such a mortal weapon could fight them off. It was an asinine thing to do. A useless thing.

I could not defeat the Uncanny. I was just one person.

My magic lashed out so suddenly that I nearly stumbled. Heat pricked the tips of my fingers, surrounding the handle of the dagger. It swirled, red and yellow with a blue center. How could this be? My magic was Uncanny-born. It would do nothing against these shadows. If anything, it would embrace them.

It would overwhelm me.

I called upon my own humanly strength, but it struggled to respond against the magic pooling from my skin. The shadows continued to stream from Rixon's body. I cried out and felt my body turn itself over to me. The decision was born in my human heart and was propelled of my own volition. With a fury born of desperation, I launched myself toward the queen and thrust my dagger toward her heart with all the strength I had left.

Like the fearful girl I was, I closed my eyes and turned my thoughts inward. I expected this to shatter me. I expected a wave of devastation. I thought of Fray, who loved me despite my shortcomings, who loved me without knowing what I would do to tear his world apart. He would hate me, and I would accept it. I felt my body burning like living coals as I sunk the dagger into his mother's flesh.

Her body sagged as I drove the dagger as deep as it fit. A cry of agony, full-throated like the sea, echoed off the cavern walls. The pain in my throat told me it was not Rixon crying out, but me.

Her eyes were her own, bright as a blazing star. I sank down with her, cradling her body against my own. She laid across my lap, unmoving. Blood drenched her white robe.

Rixon looked smaller and frailer now. This close, I could see the resemblance to Fray in the straight slope of her nose and the fullness of her lips. It was her eyes that unsettled the beat of my heart.

"I'm sorry," I said softly.

Her gaze was pointed at me, but her eyes were far away. Her face grew pale as wax.

I forced her eyelids closed and pulled my dagger free. Her blood flowed, streaming into the cracks of the cave floor, filling them with red.

Before the weight of what I'd done could settle on me in full, the pool began to bubble like boiling water. I rose to my feet, dagger still dripping with blood, and watched the pool glow.

"I know what you are," I said, sheathing my dagger. "And I do not fear you."

Isaaaaaaabelle.

I swallowed hard, my fingers drifting above the water as the voices called my name. "I wish to speak to you," I said.

You wish to speak to the Darkness and the Death?

Chills ran up my arms. "You speak of darkness and death as if they're the worst things to happen to a person."

I went numb.

I knew what my problem was. I was afraid of letting my power consume me. Afraid I might fall into the darkness and never come back. But what was fear good for?

I knew what I had to do.

For the first time in my life, I finally understood what I was and what I was capable of doing. I knew that anything was possible. The pack may hate me for what I'd done—Fray may hate me—but for the good of Mirosa, I made the right choice, even though I might be the only one who understood it.

I would give my life to save my family.

I'd do everything in my power to keep them safe, even deal with the Uncanny.

I dipped a finger into the water. "I've come to speak about my people," I said. I swallowed hard, knowing once the words were out, I could never take them back. I closed my eyes and plunged my hands into the water. "I've come to make a deal."

CHAPTER THIRTY-THREE

I*zzy.*

I opened my eyes to a void. A gray, barren wasteland stretched out before me, obscured of color. Above matched below and made it difficult to distinguish the earth from the sky. There was no source of light to be seen. No sun. No clouds. No wind. I was in the Nothing.

Something darted across my peripheral. The thing moved like a shadow, black and shapeless, and its eyes glowed red. It called my name in a harsh, grating whisper:

a disembodied voice from the depths of my nightmares.

"Are you the god of the seven hells?" I asked.

The thing laughed, long and hard, the sound like scraping nails along sandpaper. Its body ebbed and flowed.

"You came looking for a god?" it asked. "Did it ever cross your mind that you might come across a devil instead?"

I inhaled. Its voice was neither male nor female. "I did."

"But you came to us anyway?"

Exhaled. "I'm not afraid."

"Oh, yes you are. If you weren't, you wouldn't be here." The demon dipped right and left like a metronome. It stopped, making a sound of breathing in deep, then gave a groan of pleasure. "You reek of fear."

I scowled, and the demon laughed.

"You fear us, and you will find us everywhere. I'm already inside of you."

"You inhabit men and feed off of them," I said. "And they let you because their hate makes them strong." I steadied my heart and began to move, circling the shadow demon.

"Deals come with a price."

"I know how you work, demon. You can take my heart, and you can turn it black. But I will fight you every step of the way."

"We will take it anyway."

"If that is the only way. I will let you."

"What do you wish of us, girl?"

"I wish for power beyond the mortal world. I know you can give it to me. I saw some of it in myself. You gave it to—"

"The King, Aquarius. Yes, we remember him. Locked himself away, didn't he? He doesn't know that we can find him."

I stopped circling. "If only just for an hour. Just to save my people."

The demon laughed, a grossly wicked thing. "Which people?"

Time stood still as the question laid boulder-heavy in my belly. Lulu's ghost had asked the same, and I still didn't have an answer.

No, stop, it's trying to confuse me. "The ones you created," I said. "They are my family now."

The demon hissed. "It's your lucky day. But only because you brought someone with you."

I looked around. "Who?"

The demon interrupted, putting space between us now. "I will take you."

"Take . . ." I lurched forward, clutching my chest, the place that felt the most pain. "You want to drag me into your hells."

"You will invite us into you, and when we've weakened you, you will hand over your body to us. You have power in this world, Isabelle Rowan, and it will look very nice in my hells. We will welcome you on a path of fire, and you can rule with us. A queen."

On a path of fire . . .. "How long until I'm weak enough for you to take me?"

"Weeks. Months. Maybe years."

So I still had time. These demons were not yet strong enough, and I could hold them off long enough to find the celestite and break their hold on the Gwylis. But what if that failed to break this deal? What if I still . . .

The demon dipped its head in a nod, swimming legless inches above the dirt. Sacrifice one to save hundreds. Sometimes one action—even one death—could spur a movement, sway the cosmos, and move the stars.

No. Pyrus was wrong. No matter what I did, someone would always die. But then, sacrifice was the greatest of acts. What movement of stars would occur after such a thing? When I closed my eyes, I saw stars exploding, leaving the sky starless for evermore.

"Your heart belongs to someone," the demon hissed. "You won't be the same after this."

"You speak so candidly, demon. Almost like you're trying to talk me out of it."

The demon's hiss sounded like dropping meat into a hot pan of oil.

"I only wish for you to understand the terms," it said.

"I killed . . ." If I couldn't say it now, how would I ever confess it to Fray? "I killed the queen, and her son—the one who holds my heart—will hate me forever."

I saw it play out in my head. The very first time I'd seen Fray in the stairwell while trying to sneak back into the palace, the way he tripped me up, quite literally. The gentleness despite his strength and the way he let me stand on my own without acting on a constant need to protect me. He treated me like the person I had not known I was, even then. Strong. Determined. Fierce and loyal. I was everything because of him. But life was an ocean, and I'd left him on the surface while I dove deeper and deeper.

I was so afraid of him leaving me that I'd done it first. I hadn't realized it until now.

I've lost him. I have nothing to lose.

In my head, I imagined the screams of my pack as they were slaughtered one by one. I saw Olio, Sonia, Branch: all lying dead, the Den gutted by fire and blood.

Maybe Abiyaya was right.

I was a queen of death.

But I couldn't let them die.

My eyes fluttered until I was back to staring at the demon. I would have sold my soul to this demon wholly, my heart as well. Would I no longer love? Would I cease to care for anybody, just like Aquarius?

I saw Fray again, this time in his demon mask at the Black and White Ball, and I considered how he'd risked his life to come back to me.

"I will—" My raw throat forgot how to shape the words forming in my mind.

"You wiiiiiill?"

The images flickered unbidden through my memory. Henry. Lulu. Crim. Pyrus. Pedoma. The wolves of the Den. Ghetee. Olio. Branch. Two lives, both of which I did not belong in. Pieces of me scattered across two sides of the mountains.

I ground my teeth and stood up straight, making myself appear bigger, more threatening. For a moment I thought it worked, because the demon flittered backward as if a wind had kicked up. "I will agree to your deal."

My legs should have given out beneath me, and my belly should have turned itself inside out, but I felt nothing. I lifted my chin to the demon.

The demon sighed, nearing me with five dark fingers reaching toward me. He spoke on a breath. "Your presence will be welcome. There are far too many men here."

I inched away. "Bring me back to Fray," I said. "Bring me back to the Den."

The demon flittered closer. "Not before relinquishing my part of the deal."

This time, I let the demon touch me, and for a moment everything was still. I dared to look, meeting the demon's eyes—that glowing red that resembled flames and death. I sunk into them, drowned until I began to choke. My body filled up with something hot, worse than magic, searing and painful. I fell to my knees as the demons slinked away.

It spoke as it watched me cry out in agony:

"Princess of wolves and men, bringer of life and death. On a path of fire, you will walk. And out of the flames, a beast will rule. But this is only a mortal land. You are bound to the Uncanny of the seven hells. Your life is mine."

The demon tore back and rose into the sky, becoming a cloud of a million storms. The pain subsided into a dull ache that turned my bones to rubber. I couldn't move. I couldn't speak. I couldn't explain a drop of what was happening.

A sudden flash of light blinded me, and I squeezed my eyes closed through a whirlpool of wind and thunder. My feet left the ground, swept up by the demon. I waited for the fall, my hands clasped to my ears, my eyes closed so tightly that they hurt. Instead of an impact, everything became still. Muffled voices and the scent of sweet root.

I opened my eyes to Fray's frantic face hovering above mine. I sat up onto my knees, my body feeling as if it were weighed down by hundred-pound stones.

"Izzy!" Olio cried from the open doorway where Kester stood. Branch had since gone. "Izzy, they're coming. We have to go!"

Fray took me under my arms and lifted me to my feet. Immediately, Rixon's voice echoed in my mind. *It's surprising what a little lust can do to a young heart. My son did quite well.*

I took a step back from Fray, my breath catching in my throat. His eyes flashed with questions, but I had no answers to give. Right now, I refused to think more of it. There wasn't time.

"I'm all right," I told him. "I promise."

"Let's go, men!" Olio cried out, appearing in the doorway briefly and disappearing again.

I nodded to Fray. "I can walk. What happened to me?"

"Nothing. You just stood there silently with your eyes closed, and then you fell to your knees."

"I didn't say anything?"

Fray shook his head and met my eyes. His, panicked. Mine, darting away to avoid them. "Izzy, where did you go?"

I wanted to sob, but there were no tears to conjure. I felt no different, except for something deep down inside of me that churned in the empty spaces. I'd let something in. Something dark.

"I can't really tell you about it right now," I told Fray.

He pulled me close. "Tell me you're all right. Tell me something. Anything."

I grasped his waist and held him there. I waited until his breaths slowed to answer. "I'm all right. Everything is all right. We're not going to lose today." Saying those blasted a surge of adrenaline up through body. "We will win this battle."

I paused, recalling Abiyaya's words when I'd asked what she saw in my blood. *It means something terrifying will happen to your heart. It means that there is a darkness that will try to consume you. I see so much pain that it almost kills you.*

But it wouldn't kill me. She'd said as such.

Fray remained still, his mouth set tight in a straight line. I didn't know why I lied to him, why I said it would be all right. I'd planned to spend eternity and the after-life with him—I'd promised him I could— bud I'd let it all slip away with a few simple words.

It would have been nice to have him with me even in death. It would have been really, really nice.

A moment passed before the screaming began—shouts of war and of the afraid, and a heartbeat later, Fray and I sprinted from the room. Before leaving, I stopped and faced Kester.

"I know what you did," she said softly.

Her eyes gleamed with something feral. But it was no match for what she suddenly saw in my own.

A gasp escaped her lips as she attempted to pull away. "You are the darkness," she suddenly shrieked.

I tugged her close enough that our breath mingled.

"You need a new queen," I whispered.

CHAPTER THIRTY-FOUR

The sound of Branch's voice rose into the darkening sky like cinders from a fire. "Stand up! Stand up! Fight! Fight!"

Every torch was lit along the wall surrounding the Den, stirred by the winter winds, brightening the oncoming night sky, and brave warriors manned the watchtowers and signaled to the enemy: we are here, and we are not leaving.

I looked down from the watchtower at the main gate, my cloak whipping in the wind, my breath coming out in gusts that join with Fray and Olio's. *I won't let them die*, I vowed wordlessly. *I won't let these walls come down.*

"What's that noise?" Olio asked.

I trained my ears to the familiar sound. "Trumpets," I said. "They're announcing their arrival in grand fashion."

Behind me, the sun dipped behind the mountains, leaving the sky an ocean of darkness. I could smell them as they neared, a disgusting scent that churned my stomach. When did humans begin to repulse me so?

The dense, untamed forest stretched out in front of me, just barely forming the road where the other Gwylis waited under cover of night. There were more than I thought—more than Kester told us had abandoned the Den. How could that be? I could see their magic in bursts of light and in the way the clouds crashed overhead. Fray pressed his body into mine, and I recoiled enough for him to take notice. The dark, heaving sky seemed to press down, threatening to collapse on top of me.

Images flashed before my eyes: The first time I'd seen Fray and the last time we kissed. Memories and moments, things I could not possibly give up. But I'd given them up. I would never kiss him again. I'd destroyed everything.

My body grew numb to the point where I did not feel Fray's hand on my shoulder. I couldn't meet his eyes, not even as he watched my body tremor with a sob that yearned to escape. I had to tell him, because if I didn't, I'd be no better than our enemies.

Traitor. Liar. Monster.

I swallowed down my cowardice and my despair, turned to him as the sky churned and roiled, and spoke into a crack of thunder. "I killed your mother."

I stepped back as far as the platform would allow. Everyone began to shout and move below us. Everyone except Fray. He stood looking at me, yet somehow past me. I could see the physical weight of my words as they began to break him.

"I'm sorry," I said.

"You killed her," he echoed. He looked at me like he didn't recognize me. I could see our life together fading, like breath on a mirror melting away. Tears began to swell in my eyes. He turned away in time for the first drop to fall.

From the watchtower on the other end of the gate came Branch's voice. "Arrows on my command!"

Archers pulled back and nocked their arrows, the tips flickering with fire all along the Den's wall. The sight of it stirred my blood and the threads of magic weaving beneath my skin. I drew my arm across my eyes and wiped the tears away furiously.

The night took on an eerie silence, and for a moment all I heard were the torch flames stirring in the wind.

"Now!"

At Branch's word, the issuing command passed along the wall until the sky lit with deadly arrows. They rained upon the advancing soldiers, striking them down one by one. The ones that missed their targets created a barrier at the gate and along the mountain pass.

"Arrows!" Branch bellowed, and the arrows came and went again. Shrieks and screams from below told me that we were winning. So far.

I leaned over the watchtower, focusing my eyes down below. Drums from behind the wall and trumpets from the outside mingled in a battle of their own. And the men kept coming. How many were there? We'd seen hundreds of prints. What if there were thousands?

"I have to go to the ground," I said.

"She's right," said Olio. "We can't change up here."

I nodded, unable to tell him that wasn't what I meant by abandoning the watchtower.

"The gate is not made of steel or stone," Olio said, as we descended the ladders. "It will come down if they want it to."

"What do you propose?" I asked.

I looked around us, recognizing the dozens of Gwylis who had crept to join us in the main square, their paws padding softly on the stone, their breath like smoke.

"I propose we rip out their throats," said one. A burly black wolf with white-tipped ears.

"I will die standing up," said another. A dappled female.

"With the taste of blood on my lips."

I rounded on them. "I'd rather you not die at all."

But I felt the despair. Every one of them planned on dying that night.

They may kill us, but they would not break us.

Above my head, arrows hissed, streaking the night sky. The gate behind me began to tremble. At first it sounded merely as if someone were knocking to come in. Knocking, but with the trunk of a tree.

"They're trying to tear down the gate!" came a shout. Branch, maybe.

"Let them come," growled Olio, now in his Gwylis form. "Let them see what real terror looks like." They were empty words delivered with empty hope. "We are the beasts. Let's show them what we are." He strode out past me toward the gate. "We're not scared, are we?"

"No!" came the resounding reply.

"Don't show them your bellies!"

"We didn't start the war, but we will finish it," I said to the Gwylis gathered around me. The Gwylis advanced toward the gate as it rattled and splintered with barks and growls and roars.

I sprinted away, summoning my wolf form as I entered the center of the square. There stood Gwylis—in wolf form or other—bracing themselves in resolute silence. I turned until I was facing the gate, some fifty feet or so in front of me. The world around me seemed to break and shudder, just as a part of the wood split. The dead and dying's screams echoed in my ears.

"Don't let the monsters in," I growled and took a defensive stance. With each thud of the battering ram, my heart leaped from my chest. Arrows zoomed overhead. Their smell grew closer and more rancid.

Lulu. Henry. Stay by my side. I'm so afraid.

Then silence. Through the hole in the gate came a glimmer of light, and for a moment, nobody seemed to know what to do—until that light plunged through like a shooting star embedding itself into one of the pack. The sound of the wolf yelping sent my body into a panic.

Now.

Sudden rage flowed through me, mixed with fear and panic.

We had a deal, demons. Protect them.

The world stopped moving.

I closed my eyes as tightly as I could, praying that the power I felt flowing inside me was working somehow. I couldn't move, or else I was afraid to. This magic I had, that the Uncanny had given me: I didn't know it's limits. I didn't know who I'd destroy unwillingly in using it. "You said you'd help me," I said, agonizingly as my body weakened.

The voice that followed came from my mind. "We are."

I forced my eyes open to discover the same strange barrier I had set around Fray back at Stormwall. This time it surrounded the entire city. I'd multiplied the size by a thousand.

I hadn't felt a thing. The magic came as easily as breathing.

The soldiers who touched the magic barrier dissolved into dust, and the Gwylis began stepping through it unperturbed, dragging their enemies back with them. The wind brought the scent of the men's ashes to my nose, and I shuddered against it.

My magic was intoxicating. If I could do this, what could stop me from taking care of Dal Paratheon on my own? Ashe wouldn't need to risk his life. I could march right up to Stormwall's steps.

"Izzy!"

Sonia appeared, a great black wolf in my blurred vision. I tipped against her as what little strength I had left began failing before forcing myself to straighten back up. "Protect them," I told her.

Sonia smashed her muzzle into my neck. "And just where do you think you're going?"

"I have to go save someone, Sonia. I know you understand. You risk things for the people you love, don't you?"

Sonia looked at me, her eyes wide and startled. Then she nodded and stepped away. "Kill him. For me."

CHAPTER THIRTY-FIVE

I left through the back gate and looked back to make sure the barrier still stood firm. Unable to determine how long it would hold, I raced along the mountain ridge, rounding the Den, keeping myself close to the wall. I ran up the side of the peak until I was standing over the action, watching the battle from above. Clouds parted to reveal a full moon. A howl ripped from the depths of my chest, and I was off again.

I followed the trail as if it were lit before me. Down into the ridge-line and into the forest until the smell was so strong that I had to sneeze it away.

Their camp was nothing more than a dozen tents and horses tied to trees. My ears picked up screams and a rustle of leaves from the darkness. I smelled him before I saw him.

"Predictable," I said. "Leaving your men without a leader. Running like a cat from a dog."

Commander Pike approached me in slow, calm steps until he stood in the light of the full moon. He wore full armor embellished with medals. The Bear of Mirosa upon his chest was outlined in gold. His dark eyes took on an insidious color. There was madness in his eyes. The kind of madness that could only be one's undoing.

He took one quick look at me, then turned away with a roll of his eyes. "Of course it's you," he muttered. "You don't always have to be the hero, you know."

I flattened my ears. "Where is he?"

Pike tilted his head. Bored. "Where is who?"

"Prince Ashe, you filth."

"Oh, him. We killed him, per the king's orders. What use was he anyhow? He only had one arm."

No.

"You're a liar."

"Am I?" Pike Ivo lifted a hand to showcase something hanging off one gloved finger. Ashe's bow and arrow cuff. The hook dangled down like a dead fish at the end of a line. "He didn't put up a fight, and it was quick. I assure you."

The words sent a burst of grief into my heart. Sharp as a knife. He killed Ashe? And for what purpose? He wasn't a threat to anyone. Not anymore. What was the point of all of this but to cause pain and death? To take us out one by one, to rid the world of the Gwylis once and for all?

To kill the innocent to prove their power?

"I'll kill you." Shadows darted across my vision. Something horrible snaked around my belly. "I will tear out your throat."

Pike Ivo smiled. "Do it."

His eyes held mine, and I couldn't refuse the invitation.

I grinned, saliva pooling in my mouth. He would taste sweeter than anybody. Killing him was my only thought. Nothing else had seeped through yet. A concoction of anxiousness and terror churned in me. An amazing orange light emanated from my body. It was so beautiful. It curled like little fingers, beckoning me to allow it to grow. Asking permission. It was everywhere. I felt it alive inside of me. As if it were in my very bones and running hot through my blood. Fire had been my primary magic before. Now, I was made of it.

I stepped forward, savoring the terror in Pike's eyes. One step, two, three . . .

"Izzy, no!"

The heat that covered me suddenly retreated as if doused in ice water. I heard someone moving through the trees and saw him through the red spots in my vision. His scent was a thrall in my nostrils. "Ghet—"

"Izzy-"

My heart seized. Ghetee, in his wolf form, leapt into the air, hoping to set himself between Pike and I, but neither of us saw the sword until the commander had it raised in the air. Ghetee didn't have time to finish what he'd tried to tell me before the sword plunged into his belly.

CHAPTER THIRTY-SIX

I first heard the sickening sound of steel-in-flesh, then the groan of surprise and the *thump* of Ghetee's body landing hard on top of the commander. For a moment I saw everything in a haze before I realized what had happened.

A strange ringing filled my ears. I must have been moving, because the next thing I knew, I was in human form, approaching the commander as he struggled to his feet. He'd thrown Ghetee to the ground like a sack of rice and spared him only a brief glance.

My chest heaved as if it were on fire.

I tried to say something, but Pike Ivo was suddenly on his feet in front of me, his hands around my neck.

"You stupid bitch," he growled. He reared back and smashed his head into mine. This would have incapacitated any normal woman my age. But it only woke me up and stirred the red-hot rage inside me. I stumbled back as he brandished a knife from his belt. "You dirty little traitor! I'll gut you here and now."

I laughed. I wasn't scared of him or his knife. Pinpricks of magic danced across my naked skin, but it was the sight of Ghetee lying still not far from me that finally uncaged it.

The explosion was ear-splitting, a deafening crack coupled by a flash of red flame that sent slivers of fire through the air, straight into Pike Ivo's body. He screamed as his skin blackened, burning from the inside out. His eyes sunk away, leaving nothing but gaping holes in his skull. His skin burned and melted. The fabric of his uniform sizzled. He collapsed as his body dissolved into ash and smoke.

Blood, warm and sticky, flowed from my nostrils. Shadows cackled and swam around me.

I coughed and blinked away tears. My legs threatened to give way, but a whimper snapped me from it.

"Ghetee . . ." My throat felt scratchy and raw.

The young wolf shifted back into human-form before my eyes. I knew he needed to stay a wolf if he wanted to heal, but he had to have been too weak to shift back. He curled in a fetal position, clutching his abdomen where the blood began to pool in black puddles around his body. I crouched beside him, trying to access the wound, but he kept his hands pressed firmly there.

"We have to get you back to the Den." I pressed my hand on Ghetee's. A feeble attempt to stop him from bleeding out. I summoned my fire; it tickled my skin from the tips of my human hands to my toes. "Move your hands, Ghetee. Maybe I can cauterize it."

"I don't think anyone can help me now," he whispered.

"We have to try." I heard nothing but the sound of the wind in response. "Ghetee?"

His chest heaved rapidly. The amount of blood coming from his little body was dizzying. The ground beneath him began to drown in it.

Gods, why did he look so small?

"He lied to you." He rolled onto his back, blood seeping through the cracks of his fingers. He coughed, and his lips became sticky with red. "The prince isn't dead."

There wasn't time for relief. "That doesn't matter now, Ghetee." I leapt to my feet, giving him a gentle touch to his shoulder. If I could get him to move, we could make it. If he was talking, it couldn't be that bad. "Come on, let's get you up."

A horrible silence followed, and with each passing beat, the keening I felt building up in my chest rose higher in my throat.

I was struck by a sudden memory of the young wolves and me

howling into the wind and of Ghetee's wide, easy-going smile. But then, everything began to careen out of focus.

Ghetee let out another whimper. "I'm going to die, Izzy."

"No, you're not. Nobody is going to die because that wasn't the deal, Ghetee. I have to get you up."

I barely had the strength to breathe, never mind carry the young boy, but I lifted him, cradling him in my arms. His life drained, and panic ebbed and flowed through me. *No,* I thought, a sob choked my throat. Ghetee's breathing was too slow. His eyes closed and did not flutter. This was too familiar. The image of Lulu dying burst into my mind.

Everything went still. Even the wind ceased blowing, and the very first thought that came to mind was why I hadn't I been given the power to save people when they most needed it. The light in his eyes had dimmed, threatening to blow out completely. Ghetee's light had always been so blinding. Now there was nothing but darkness.

He wasn't going to make it.

Give me the pain, I thought as I sunk down to the ground. *Let me take it from you.*

I counted the rise and falls of his chest as he struggled with each inhale slowed. Finally, they stopped.

A scream burst out of me and broke the quiet of the world. "No!" I choked out, and I buried my face into the young wolf's chest. He was too young, just a child. Life had not truly begun for him. It could not be over!

I drew back and gasped. I felt as though someone had ripped the air from my lungs, leaving nothing but emptiness between my ribs. This void was stretching, as it had ten years ago at Henry's death, a hurt that only gaped wider after I lost Lulu. The pain was unbearable. It threatened to break me apart. I tore at the snow beneath Ghetee. I slammed my fists into the frozen ground, screaming until my throat burned. I felt such agony. Such fury.

Nothing will bring her back, Pedoma had said after Lulu's death. *Nothing. All you can do now is live.*

But I'd carried too much grief to find the will to keep on going.

I went back to Ghetee, my hands quivering, and brushed away the hair from his eyes. He wore a faint smile. I tricked myself into believing that the last thing he'd seen had been beautiful. I waited for his eyes to open again. I waited for him to tell me how much it hurt so I knew how make it better. To wake us both up from this nightmare.

I drew in a staggering breath. The moon was blotted out by shifting clouds, leaving me encased in a darkness that swallowed me whole.

Only then could I see them, slithering against the veil, darker than darkness itself. Not human. Not of this world. I didn't move from Ghetee's side. I would die defending him. I heard something speak to me, saying, *Kill them. You have the magic inside of you.*

Something pounded at some internal door that never should have been opened, and I searched my mind for a memory, something placating that I'd been told once that might help me stay my body. But there was nothing. My throat filled with ash.

I stayed there for what felt like hours until I finally stood on shaky legs and steeled myself. Ghetee was dead. I could not change that. It took great resolve to remove the remainder of Commander Pike Ivo's cloak and wrap it around my friend's body. I heaved him into my arms, cradling him like a mother would a child, and began the trek back to the Den.

A single hot tear ran down my cheek.

I am in no one's shadow. I will be the darkness.

CHAPTER THIRTY-SEVEN

I recognized nothing.

I couldn't remember how I'd even gotten back to the Den and through the back gate. My barrier had come down, and its effect had long ended. There was a serene sort of quiet in the place that only came after the adrenaline of fighting wore away. Tired faces passed me by, glancing my way, asking if I needed help. I could do nothing but keep walking forward. Calls for healers and the pounding of hammers rebuilding the gate were louder than the demon's voice in my head.

I saw you in a dream once, Ghetee had said. *Standing atop a mountain against a pale summer sky.*

The hammers pounding, pounding in my ears.

I stalked into the square where the injured had gathered, followed by those who had hidden like rabbits in their holes during the battle, who were coming out to help once the need had expired. They shouted all around, some looking my way as rain began to fall, first as small pitter-patters on the roofs, then drenching us in bucket-loads. After accessing whether or not Fray, Branch, Sonia, or Olio were in the pile of the dead, I continued on, my hair wet against my forehead, mixing with tears.

But you were alone, and you looked sad, as if there was nobody left in the world but you.

A voice called through the rain. Rini appeared, her human face spattered with blood, but no worse for wear. She tugged at the cloak I'd tucked Ghetee in. I held him out, unable to meet her eyes. I left his head uncovered and it lolled against Rini's chest. It looked like he was sleeping. "Isabelle," she cried out. "I thought I'd lost him!"

Her words beat in my ears like a pounding drum. Gods. She didn't know he was dead.

"He's not lost anymore," I said. "I'm so sorry." I turned away and didn't look back, even when a choked sob escaped her throat. I didn't turn because I couldn't bear to see it, to witness the agony in her eyes.

Going as fast as my feet would carry me, I made my way across the city and up the watchtower by the main gate, where I watched the retreating soldiers and their fires winding across the ridge like a burning snake.

"They'll be back."

Branch stepped across the platform from the darkness. He sniffed the air, smelling what I smelled: steel, leather, ash and fire and many, many dead men burning in a pile in the city square. He stared out at where the stars were gobbled up by smoke.

"Thank you," I said to him.

"They needed a leader," he replied, blinking the rain from his eyelashes.

"You're a good one."

Branch turned to me, and I saw then the many gashes along his face. One traversed the entire length of his cheekbone, cutting across his eye. I felt the pounding again, and I blinked, teetering on the edge of a distant memory. I said, "Ghetee is dead."

Branch didn't reply. I didn't give him a chance to. I pulled myself up onto the very top of the wall, positioning my feet so that I could crouch. I balanced there and stripped myself of my clothing until I stood naked against the night. I said my chant and leapt into the darkness below.

~

THE WINDS CARRIED RAIN THAT SENT ICE THROUGH MY BONES. I sprinted through the trees, following the trail of man-scent, slipping deeper and deeper in the darkness. The sound of my heavy breathing was the only thing keeping me level-headed. My paws digging into the snow, never all at once.

At the sudden sound of a howl, I skidded to a halt. I sniffed the air, darting my eyes from tree to tree. Not a wolf. Just the wind trying to compete.

So I howled back in response, giving it nothing to compete with.

I picked up my pace. I remembered the anger I felt when I came face to face with my father. I'd never forget the way he'd made me feel weak. That had been months ago. I was a different person now.

I was not weak.

I followed the trail until the sounds of soldiers grew nearer. I kept hidden in the shadows of the trees, keeping low to the ground. A man came close, not seeing me, pressing one hand against a tree for balance as he relieved himself. The smell of his piss assaulted my nostrils.

"Make a sound, and I'll gut you slowly," I snarled.

The man dropped his hand, going for his sword, but he thought better of it. He was young, with dark hair slicked against his head. He made a move to wipe the rain from his eyes and stared with a slack jaw.

I stepped forward, just enough for him to catch sight of me. "Where's the prince?"

The soldier shook his head. "I don't know what you're talking about."

I moved forward, an eager rumble rising from my chest, tail high, ruff standing on-end, head low. "I'll ask you once more," I said to the cowering man. "Where is the prince?"

"Hey, you won, all right?" he said. "You won. Just let me live."

A voice called, "Joel!"

I lunged, biting the man on his leg and forcing him to the ground. I took one paw and pressed it over his mouth. I stood over him, saliva dripping and mixing with the rain. "I'm going to lift my hand, and you're going to tell me in one word where he is. Is that understood?"

I lifted my paw, and the soldier cried out, "Gwylis!"

I sunk my claws into his neck and kicked his body aside as I used it as a jumping-off point. It wasn't long until the soldiers reacted, drawing their swords as I broke through the trees. Many of them hesitated, even turning their backs and attempting to run against a wall of their own comrades.

I was one against hundreds, yet they still feared me.

Some taunted me to come closer, the steel of their blades flashing against the light of the moon. One man dropped his sword into the wet earth and sank to his knees.

"A demon!" he cried out. "The darkness!"

"More than that," I growled. "Much more."

I parted my feet, my mouth suddenly going dry, and summoned the power building inside me.

My body burned from the inside out, and with a soul-shaking roar, I let the fire explode, cutting like an arrow through the men, from the very first to the very last. Their screams only made the fire stretch further and higher until the ash of the burning bodies blocked out the stars from the sky.

Somewhere, a cawing crow took flight.

On a path of fire, you will walk. And out of the flames, a beast will rule.

Howl after agonizing howl ripped from my throat. I stood back as the flames jumped from body to body, snaking through the land. It caught the dead trees and set them ablaze. Smoke grabbed the sky. Flames clawed at anything and everything except for me. I stood unharmed as my power fed on the earth, beginning to devour it whole. Maybe it would. Maybe I didn't care.

I roared alongside the thunder. I cried alongside the dead. I fell to my belly in anguish of a life that died, and shifted back into my human form. Like that, I lay naked within the ash, the rain, and the shadows.

CHAPTER THIRTY-EIGHT

My dreamless sleep ebbed away as I slowly regained consciousness.

I took in the sounds and scents that told me that I was no longer outside, but rather back home in the Den. Aware of a presence in the room, I kept my eyes shut, steadying my breathing and listening to the muffled voices outside the window above my bed.

"Nothing but charred bones . . . Every one of them dead . . .Found her . . . How do we explain this?"

I gasped and breathed in the scent of sweet root. The bed beneath was as soft as the voice telling me to take it easy. My joints ached. The pounding in my head returned when I opened my eyes.

The sun was high and casted beams of light through the open window. It was daytime, whatever day it was.

Fray sat in a chair he'd pulled to my bedside. He leaned down and brushed my hair from my forehead. I skittered back at his touch. I didn't deserve it. He shouldn't be here at all. He should hate me. He should want to kill me too.

"Are we safe?" I asked.

Fray pursed his lips. "Yeah, we're safe."

I didn't ask what had happened; I remembered it minute for minute.

The Den had been attacked. Ghetee had died. I killed Commander Pike Ivo. I killed Rixon. I killed . . .

I obliterated the entire army with my fire.

Fray handed me a cup of water along with a small cup of a thicker liquid he said would help the pain. I took it without question and sat with my back against the wall. I felt numb to the point where I could not feel my own heartbeat. My throat felt raw. My lungs weren't drawing air as they should. My eyes were dry as sand, depleted from crying.

Fray shouldn't be here. I was a monster.

I covered my face with my hands. "You shouldn't be here," I echoed my thoughts. "Not after what I did."

"Izzy," he said. "Whatever you did, I'm sure you had a reason—"

"Don't do that," I said. I shook my head. "Don't give justification for it. Don't try to understand. This is not something I want you to understand." It was too much to hold in, and I began to yell. "I want you to walk away. I want you to hate me!"

"I don't hate you," he said softly. "I don't want to walk away."

I don't want to walk away. Wouldn't it be easier if he did? I didn't trust that he wouldn't hold onto even just a little resentment. Would that feeling grow over time to eventually tear us apart?

I'd already torn us apart.

I blinked away an onslaught of tears and wiped at my eyes. "How long was I out?"

"A day."

An entire day. "Who is that talking outside?" I asked.

"Olio and Branch."

"Invite them in?"

Fray hesitated at first. He knew as well as I did that this discussion was not over. Regardless, he nodded and leaned over the bed, tapping on the window pane to get their attention. They both entered seconds later. Both looked exhausted. Both looked wary. Both kept their distance from me.

Branch spoke first, leaning against the sink, casting a narrow-eyed look at me. "Nobody has to know about it."

My mind rushed. Did they know what I'd done? How could I bear to look at Fray again? He'd leave. Why would anyone stay with someone marked for an eternity in the underworld?

I guessed my panic was evident because Olio shook his head, taking up the chair beside Fray. "You saved everyone. If anything, they want to promote you."

I relaxed my shoulders. They figured it was all Aquarius's magic. They didn't know—

Wait. "Promote me?"

Branch shifted. "Kester is gone, and—" He stopped and bit his inner lip. Never had I seen Branch at a loss for words. His gaze was so intense, I had to look away. During training, I'd never used my magic anyway close to how I had during the battle. Did Branch suspect what I'd done?

"It doesn't matter," said Olio. "She's gone, and Kester gave up her place with the elders, so that leaves us—"

"Leaderless," I said. I looked to Fray, but his usual scowling face gave nothing away. Would he take over the pack, being Rixon's son and all? Or would they have a vote?

There was a knock on the door. Sonia stuck her head in, first nodding to me, then addressing Branch. "We're doing it now."

Branch pushed off the sink, folding his big arms across his chest. "There's time yet to talk of this," he said. "Now we must judge a traitor."

THE PACK WAS ALREADY GATHERED WHEN WE ARRIVED AT THE meeting hall. We shouldered our way through, using our elbows liberally. Every Gwylis was here, and there was little room to breathe, never mind move. We managed to get toward the front where Kester stood in the center of the room, alone.

The pack leaders approach. Branch, Olio, Sonia, and six others I did not know by name. Two older women emerged, both gray and withering. They took seats behind Kester and the pack leaders. These were the elders I'd heard about. Like their now-dead queen, they sequestered themselves except in time of turmoil. I wondered if they had fought at the battle yesterday.

"We are here to judge one of our own," the smallest of the elders said. "In working with Rixon, you withheld vital information from the pack which could have aided in securing our future. What do you say, Kester?"

Kester stood tall despite the accusation. "I say that is all true," she said.

"It is true that you would allowed the Den to fall?" another elder asked. She did not wait for an answer. "The queen entrusted you to us, and you both failed. The queen is dead, so that leaves you alone to face a judgment of death."

I could tell by the clamor in the room that the sentence would be carried out with enthusiasm. But was that truly what we needed—more death?

Olio was closer to where I stood than Branch and Sonia, so I stepped out of the crowd to get his attention. When he saw me, he leaned closer.

"We cannot kill her," I said. He cast me a side-long look but listened. "We cannot start a new age with blood on our hands."

"I agree," Sonia said, having heard me. She tipped her chin to Branch and said something into his ear. The words were then passed on to the other pack leaders.

"Something to add?" the elders asked when they became aware of the commotion.

Branch took the lead. "We would like to suggest banishment."

All conversation in the room stopped. Heavier was the silence of the elders.

"Our war with the usurper king is not over," Branch said. "We need strong leadership, and we need to show them we are not savages. We do not kill our own. But we cannot allow Kester to stay within our walls. Maybe in time, she will be allowed back, but for now: banishment."

Branch spoke so clearly, so concisely, that it was a wonder he'd not been a king somewhere in a former life. Maybe even of the Den. I know I'd vote him in. But I wasn't sure that was how it worked.

In a matter of moments, the vote was over. The elders stood and declared Kester's sentence be carried out by the day's end. She'd pack what she needed and would be escorted from the Den into the wilderness. Alone.

The din of the hall grew so loud that I had to shout over to the elders to get their attention. They'd been leading Kester away, probably to her room to gather her things. They gazed at me as I approached.

"May I speak to Kester privately?" I knew the request was far-fetched, but I had to try.

The elders regarded me briefly, as most everyone did. Then they nodded. Without a word between us, Kester and I walked down the hall to the room with the fireplace. It was unlit for now and would stay that way. Without it, the room felt naked.

"Did you really think it would be that easy?" She strode across the room, her robe fluttering behind her. "To kill the queen?"

I swallowed. "I don't know what—"

"She let you kill her. She wanted you to. It was the only way for her to be free of the Uncanny and for you to rise."

"That's impossible. I saw in my vision, the two of you talking."

"You saw what Rixon let you see."

I reeled against her words. "She could have just killed herself if she wanted death that badly."

Kester scoffed. "No, no, she couldn't. That dagger—let me see it."

At first, I blinked, unsure of what she meant, but then I felt it, heavy on my hip. I unsheathed it and held in both hands. "This was my brother's."

"It wasn't at first," she said. "This dagger was created in the Old Kingdom with steel imbued with blessings from the gods."

"The gods who abandoned you."

"Before that."

I thought back to months ago when Olio had taken me around the Den, showing me the city. When asked about the blacksmith, he'd told me how his people had channeled some of their magic into the blades. There were swords of ice and fire. Had this really been where Henry had acquired the dagger?

She handed it back to me and smiled gently. "This is a demon killer. One of only a few."

With a laugh, I thought back to the wolf I'd stabbed in the forest in Stormwall. How foolish I was to think I'd scared it off with such a little blade. Not a monster that large. It could have turned and torn me to bits.

It had been the dagger that made the beast retreat. It hadn't been me at all.

"All right," I said. "Say I played into your prophecies. What's next for me?"

"Aquarius. Rixon cast a protection over Aquarius so the Uncanny could not find him, but now that protection is gone."

Why would Rixon want to protect Aquarius? They'd become enemies. None of that made sense. There was a piece . . . something I was missing. Something overlooked.

"What would I need from Aquarius?" The old wolf was useless. He could stay in Wargrave's cellar for all I cared. He was not the leader we wanted. Not ever.

The plan for myself had not changed. Ashe was still a prisoner and would play his part for a long time before I arrived. After, I would go to Hassara and retrieve the celestine. All of this did not include the exiled king.

"You saw the many Gwylis, yes? Dal Paratheon is making an army. Forcing the existing Gwylis to change others, willing or not."

I held up my hand. "You're laying too much down right now, Kester." I needed a moment to process it all.

I had seen the Gwylis, and I had questioned it then; Kester was only confirming my suspicions. But to change humans into wolves without the pack's consent: that was treasonous and vile. This was something the Uncanny savored. Had this been what the demons were waiting for?

I choked back my fear and the feeling of weight pressing on my chest. The Uncanny would take over the very bodies of the Gwylis; that was the deal Aquarius had made. If Dal Paratheon created thousands more . . . I could not fathom the chaos and destruction it would create. It would truly be the end of humanity as we knew it.

But this had been my lot all along. The dagger, the necklace, meeting Fray . . . It had all been planned long ago. An unknown force steering me before I even knew where I was going. Had the gods used Henry as a stepping stone for me?

"Aquarius is the king," Kester said. "Do you understand me? Only he has the power to reunite the Gwylis, and only you and the boy have the power to bring down the Paratheon king."

The boy. Ashe.

I shook my head. This was absurd. "They would never trust Aquarius again."

"They do not need to trust him. They only need to fear him." She approached me carefully and touched a finger to my cheek. "There is a darkness that will try to consume you."

So they said.

"The time for warnings has come and gone," she said. "I wish you well, Isabelle Rowan, but from here on out, there will be no prophecies. No more visions. There will only be you, and in the end, you will be alone."

"You call the gods back down to earth. Humans and Gwylis cannot defeat the Uncanny. Only the gods can do that."

"So why don't they do it now?"

But I knew the answer. "The gods hold grudges," I realized aloud.

"We must prove ourselves worthy of their power again," Kester said. "But your journey will not be easy. The deal you made with the Uncanny . . . They will not let you go, and every day you live and breathe, you will feel their presence grow heavier."

She knew. Of course she knew. "You don't envy me, do you?"

She shook her head. "No."

"Will I become one of them?" *Will I become evil?*

"Soon. Over time. It is vital that you trust in those who love you. They will steer you toward the light when things get dim."

"Steer me but not save me."

Kester clucked her tongue. "Nothing in this world is beyond saving."

"But you said I would be alone."

"In the end, yes."

I wrapped my arms around myself for comfort. I swore then that I would not be afraid of what was to come, and that if I did die, at least I would forge a new path for Mirosa in the process. Maybe evil could be vanquished. Someday.

CHAPTER THIRTY-NINE

I'd never seen a real funeral. Henry had been buried where he lay, and I'd gone before I could see Lulu put into the ground. I'd known a great deal of death and said my fair share of goodbyes. But never like this.

Four Gwylis died during the battle. All of them were prepared and brought to the pyre in the center of the city the following day after I last spoke with Kester. The flames were already high enough to block out what little sun the day allowed. One by one the bodies came out, carried by family members and pack members alike, wrapped in the best blankets and set down at base of the flames.

A sudden chill ran through me, penetrating my very bones. I turned just as the wails came. Rini. At her feet was a small body wrapped in reds and yellows being lifted into the air. She reached for him, grabbed for him, begged for them to put him back down. Not to burn him.

To let him be.

"Stop," I said, jogging toward them. "Let him down."

Rini threw herself at me, her face wet with tears and red with grief. "Don't let them take him," she cried. "Don't let them take my baby. I beg of you."

Olio, who'd been nearby, met my eyes. "It's winter," he told me. "We won't be able bury him until spring."

"So be it," said Rini. A flash of hope spread across her face, staying the tears if only for a second. "Let him stay until the frozen ground melts away. I will do it myself. Please."

I backed away, "Why is she begging to me—"

"Let her," said Branch, nearing us. He stepped up and took Ghetee's body into his arms, cradling it. "I will build a box for him and set him on the edge of the city, and we will wait, and when the first day of spring comes, we will make a spot here in the city where he will rest forever."

Rini agreed to this. I watched Branch take Ghetee's body away, his powerful form beside Rini's fragile one, and thought if the Den ever did choose a leader, I hoped it would be him. Branch was born to do nothing less.

That evening, I ate in the mess hall with the rest of the pack. The usual chatter was nonexistent in favor of the Gwylis paying a silent homage to their fallen friends. Four seats were left empty with full plates set before them. Ghosts were everywhere and made the air heavy and chilled.

I only stayed long enough to eat before leaving. I roamed the city, my cloak pulled tight against me, my hair stiff in the night's chill.

I was a Gwylis, the product of my ancestor's hatred. We had other names. Voiceless. Wolves. The Cursed. Soulless. All given by the very people who sought to murder us. They painted us as evil, equal to the demons of the underworld. But we'd fought back, and because of that, we would always be hunted. We would never be safe until every one of us were dead. There was a king on the throne in Stormwall, and he was no better than the one before. And he would hear of what'd happened here.

A weight pressed against my chest as I stopped walking long enough to look around. The torches were lit against the oncoming night. I could see bodies moving in the watchtowers, and I wondered how long we'd have to do this. How long would we have to fear for our lives? How long until we no longer had to sleep with one eye open?

I began walking in the opposite direction until I came to Sonia's home. I knocked lightly. She answered right away, as if she were expecting me.

"Isabelle," she said dryly.

I pursed my lips. "Can I come in?"

"My brother is not with you?"

"No," I said. "Just me, if that's all right."

I removed my boots and set them on the small front porch. She waited until I was inside to close the door, leaving us bathed in candle light.

Her home was by far the coziest I'd been to in all the Den. It was built against a small outcropping of trees so I could hear insects through the open windows. The floor was covered in patterned rugs, overlapping with no real sense of order. They were soft beneath my feet. Thick curtains clung to the doorways and windows. A small desk in the far corner held what appeared to be a miniature tree, its branches weighted by several pieces of jewelry—some of them incomplete—hanging like ornaments. The kitchen held only a small table with two chairs, and it was where Sonia led me.

Her dark eyes flashed to me from beneath thick eyelashes, and I noticed that she was still dressed in the gray of mourning. Her mouth was pulled tight. I felt like I'd interrupted something private—something incredibly painful. "What is it I can do for you?" she asked.

I took her in, wanting to hug her. "I'm sorry about Ghetee," I said. "You knew him longer than I did. I can't imagine—"

She held out her hand to stop me from talking. "Did you know that I was the one who found him?"

"He didn't tell me."

She shook her head. "No—" She took a deep breath, her voice charged be something deep and sorrowful as she pulled memories from the depths. "Your brother. Henry." She didn't wait for a reaction. "He was dying. I thought he'd left or been exiled. He was clearly a soldier. His armor and sword gave it away." She smiled slightly. "He wanted me to kill him, but I couldn't do it. I should have done it, you see. I should have, because he was the enemy and in my territory. He'd come through the Archway into my land. We had orders, and I'd gone against them. But I was sixteen years old and prone to rebellion."

Tears watered her eyes, but she continued with a clear voice. "I kept him alive until he regained his strength and wit, and even though he knew what I was—he had the opportunities, you know—he never made a move to hurt me. When he told me who he was, I knew then that I'd made a mistake. We had not choice but to assume the old ways. I had to see him as my enemy from the other side of the mountains."

There were certain moments that tied the fragments of my life together. Several of them involved Lulu, but most of them centered on Henry. Our shared moments were hammered into me, forever nailing his place in my heart. But the ones I'd missed were the ones that left me feeling broken. Hearing Sonia speak of him now, in those moments I'd missed, pieced a part of me together I hadn't realized was still so fractured. In her words, my brother continued to live.

I choked back a sob.

Sonia leaned forward, like she wanted to embrace me but thought better of it.

"When he asked me to change him, I did. It was against the laws to do such a thing without approval from Rixon. I'd broken more laws than I could count by that point, so I did the only thing I could think to do. We left together through the mountains and fled into the Old Kingdom to find somewhere new that hadn't been ravished by war, but he couldn't shake your father. He just couldn't. He was forever in his shadow, and it took the sleep from the night and the light in his eyes. I knew what he had to do. He found your father and tried to make it right." She closed her eyes. "You know the rest."

The two might have found something in each other, but did Henry think of the girl he'd left behind at Stormwall? The one he'd planned to marry . . . the one who flung herself from the highest tower after learning of his death? Heat clawed up my neck and flushed my cheeks. How could my brother have done such a thing?

I bit my lip to keep the questions from pouring out. Sonia answered them anyway.

"Your brother was not perfect, Isabelle," she said. "Nor am I. I knew about the woman back home. But I did not care."

"You didn't want him to leave, did you?" I asked.

Sonia shook her head. "I begged him not to. He wouldn't listen. You Rowans never do."

Because he was brave, I thought. He still tried to mend the world, even when he was free of my father. Free, but not entirely.

I understood, but I did not forgive him for leaving me behind. Not yet.

"Well, that's that." Sonia dusted off her hands, as if putting the whole conversation into a locked box and throwing away the key. She strode over to her desk and plucked the necklaces I'd seen hanging from the jewelry tree.

"I like that we loved the same person," I told her. "We knew him in different ways, yet we loved."

She came back and held out three necklaces, silver chains with tiny drops of jewels that shone like rainbows. "It's funny. I lost someone who wasn't never truly mine to begin with," she said. "But the pain still lingers after all of these years, and that has to count for something. Right?"

I nodded, trying my hardest to keep my emotions at bay. "Are you giving these to me?"

"I don't know you well, Isabelle Rowan, but I knew your brother, and you are exactly like him." She held them closer. "These will help you where you need to go. Take them."

"He tried to set things right," I said, taking the gift. "He tried and failed."

"But you won't. Right?"

She looked at me as if I were the sun in the sky. The hope that brought light in the darkness each day. Her sun had been dimmed the day Henry died. I wanted to be a new sun. I wanted to bring the light back to her. It was a yearning as strong as the beating of my own heart.

Sonia reached forward and tucked a stray piece of raven black hair behind my ear. "I'm glad the Scarred King is dead," she said, unabashed. "I'm glad he is gone."

"Me too, Sonia. Me too."

CHAPTER FORTY

Branch shut the door to the meeting hall after I entered. He slid the lock closed and walked ahead, his footsteps echoing in the large, empty room. He stopped in the center and crossed his arms over his chest. His eyebrows pushed together. His chapped lips pulled tightly. If there was a point beyond utter exhaustion, that was how he looked.

"A nap would do you good," I quipped. Only two days had passed now, but it felt like months. I smiled even though I knew why I was there. With him. For his actions during the battle, he'd been appointed steward of the Den, thus giving the pack time to mull over what there was to be done about a ruler.

Branch notched a finger under his belt. He looked almost normal, like he were about to chide me for some offensive move I'd done wrong. For a moment, I felt things could be like that again. But that wasn't life. Nothing was normal anymore, and he was too smart to think otherwise.

"I've done a soft vote, and most of the pack agrees that you should be officially be part of it." Branch's words came with a frown. Probably to match my own.

"What do you want me to say, Branch?" I said. "I didn't plan any of this."

"I know."

I narrowed my eyes.

"So what is this? Have you summoned me to convince me to stay? To move past what happened?"

Branch's eyes roved over my face. "Moving past it doesn't mean forgetting." He gave a weak attempt at a smile. "But I am not here for poetic wisdom.

I snorted. "Is this a goodbye?"

Branch closed his eyes briefly and bit the inside of his cheek. A gesture unlike him. "How about a farewell, instead?"

I nodded solemnly. "If they bestow you the king of this pack, know that you will do a much better job with the title than your successors."

Branch smiled at my attempt at lifting the mood. "When life gives you something good, is not wise to deny it. But, I am too old to start changing the world."

"No, you're not." I tapped my finger on my upper lip, thinking of Fray. *I love him and I've done him wrong.* "Take care of him, Branch. Please."

He nodded without question. "This isn't your fault, you know."

But he's wrong. My actions had consequences, even the tiniest ones. With those actions, I've changed the course of so many lives. Was Pyrus truly correct? Have I swayed the cosmos? Have I moved the stars?

The urge to hug the old man tore at me, but instead, we stood there, some unspoken sentiment passing between us.

I turned to leave. "You shouldn't have gotten attached," I joked.

"Izzy."

I turned and saw the old, scowling man, my greatest teacher, his hand up in a silent farewell. I bowed my head without raising my hand in response as a shiver and a roll of nausea ran through me. As I looked at Branch, I realized that if I were to call anyone here my closest friend, it would be him.

As soon as the door closed behind me, I set a path for home, letting the stars guide me when my eyes became too cloudy with tears.

I was as sure as anything that Branch understood I would never become part of their pack. The tears slid down my cheeks, like torrents from a waterfall. I finally knew what part I had to play, and the realization was a lightning strike from the heavens. Like a beast, finally uncaged.

CHAPTER FORTY-ONE

I stood outside the door of my home for a few seconds before entering. The echoes of footsteps approached before I had the door closed.

Fray came into view from the washroom, dressed in nothing but his pants with the belt undone as if he were about to bathe. He saw me and tugged his waistband up so his pants weren't falling beneath his hipbones.

Such a sight would normally have excited me, but now I felt nothing but sadness.

"Are you back?" I asked hesitantly. It'd been three days since I'd killed his mother, and Fray had not come back to the home we shared together. I slept alone. I battled my nightmares alone. I fell into despair alone.

He didn't answer, which was worse than him not being there in the first place.

"Do you want me to go?" I asked. My heels squeaked on the floor as I prepared to pivot and leave.

"No."

His entire body said differently, as though he were forcing himself to be here. He sunk down into a chair and rested his head in his hands. His shoulders shook, convulsed so violently that I feared something horrible was happening to him. But then I heard the sobs, and the force of them drew me to him.

"Fray," I said. I crouched in front of him, inwardly screaming at him to look at me. Tears pricked my own eyes. I placed a tentative hand to his knee. With a heaving breath, he stood and took me into his arms. I held on tight, trying to siphon the sorrow from his body. But I couldn't help. Years and years of pain held inside for so long, it had to be released. I could only be there for him and hope for it to end. For things to get better.

I watched the moon from the little window above our bed. Fray laid down to rest and fell asleep as though he had not closed his eyes in years. I watched him from across the room, seated at the very table where I saw our life together fall away. I waited until his breathing grew steady and for his body to relax to slip into a change of clothes.

I wouldn't let him risk his life for me. Ever.

I pulled on my cloak and packed my bag: Henry's dagger, the vials, my necklace, Henry's sword and diary, and some food. I laced up my boots and looked around the home. *It's a good home*, I thought. A good place with good memories. There weren't many of those around.

I paused at the open door and looked back to Fray's sleeping form. I resisted the urge to brush away a stray piece of hair from his eyes, but I couldn't risk waking him. It was easier this way.

Stay, he'd once said. I broke my promise that I would, and I hoped he'd forgive me.

"I love you," I said softly. "Don't come after me."

I closed the door and vanished into the night.

It was time to take back what was mine.

CHAPTER FORTY-TWO

There was a rundown inn just five miles outside of Stormwall, run by a frail old man and his equally frail wife. They greeted me as I entered, gifting me sincere smiles and fetching me a towel to dry off the day's rainfall. Along the way, I'd sold the silver chains from Sonia and received more than enough to get me where I was going. I shook the money out of my pouch onto the counter and let them take what I owed. After, they walked me up a set of creaky stairs to a room on the second floor.

"Do you have many guests tonight?" I asked before entering the room.

"You're it," said the man, handing me my key. I thanked him, closed the door, and clicked the lock into place.

I'd been riding for days and when those days turned into weeks, I began to wonder if it would be easier changing into a wolf. But I had my necklaces and I had my pack. Plus, finding clothes when I emerged past the Archway would be precarious, especially of the way was guarded. I'd found sprouts of grass; a sign that spring was coming. I saw the spots where I'd once rested alongside Fray and felt a pang of sadness as I remembered the journey so many months ago.

Fray, I thought one lonely night where the cloudy sky felt moonless.

I'd loved him, and I left him when I begged him not to do the same. He'll never forgive me. Ever. I wrapped my arms around myself that night and pushed the thought of him away. If I were to get through this, I'd have to forget him.

I took the candle that was already lit and used it to light the others around the room. Lowering my hood, I brushed my dirty, wet hair back and dropped my pack to the floor. The entire journey past the Archway and back into the New Kingdom had been long, and the solitude of sleeping beneath the sky with nothing but the trees to protect me was far worse than this room. There were too many walls. It was too contained. There was no space for my grief to fly.

I trusted Branch would know where I'd gone and would do his best to keep Fray in the Den, but there were some moments at night where I swore I could smell him. Fray. A small part of me wished he would come so I would not be alone. The other part, the more dominant part, knew he wouldn't.

"I left some extra towels by your door, dear," said the innkeeper's wife from the hallway. "Also some warm water for a bath."

"Thank you," I replied, pressing my ear to the door to make sure she'd left. Her retreating footsteps down the creaky stairs solidified this. I dragged the basin of water and towels into the washroom.

Time to get things in order.

I went into the washroom and looked at myself in the mirror. I splashed some warm water onto my face before retrieving Henry's dagger and held it to the tied end of my hair. I told myself that I'd have to be unrecognizable if I wanted to slip through the city unnoticed. This was the first—and probably hardest—step. What other choice did I have?

I closed my eyes and ran my ponytail along the blade. Stray black strands fell into the sink, but I held the longest pieces in my hand as I watched my hair come loose around my head, stopping just below my ears.

Not done yet.

I kept on chopping. With the worst part over, evening it out became an easy task, even without being able to see the back. I'd have to have someone clean it up sometime soon, but for now I was content with who I saw staring back at me.

My hair was gone, shorter than a boy's cropped cut. I'd left some pieces longer around my ears and forehead. They stuck up every which way rebelliously. The lack of hair seemed to bring out the features of my face. My forehead, my eyes, my chin and neck even. I looked different, which was exactly what I wanted to be.

After, I stripped down and changed into a dry pair of pants and a tunic, and when I was done, I stood at the only window in my room, which so happened to be facing the direction of the well-lit crown city of Stormwall.

I went back into the bathroom, took the dagger from atop the sink, and sliced a clean line across my face, forehead to chin. My mouth filled with blood as I held back my cries of pain. With the second cut, I let out a squeal and let the tears flow to mix with the blood. Soon enough, my face looked as though I'd been in the cruelest knife fight of my life. I waited a little while for the blood to clot, which had only been seconds, before gathering my things and leaving the room.

I descended the stairs with my face buried deep in my hood. As I passed the front desk, I set my room key upon the desk and thanked the old couple.

"No refunds," said the woman. I'd only been in the room for less than an hour. If they found this suspect, they didn't show it.

"That's all right," I replied. I winced with every word. "May I ask if you have a crow?"

"We do. If you whistle outside—"

"Does he know the Old Kingdom?"

The couple stared at me as if I had fourteen eyes. I was sure they finally noticed the cuts across my face and the quickness of my stay. I could be anything-a thief, a murderer-that posed a threat to them. The candles danced, rising in their intensity, by my own will or not.

My mouth tugged into a grin. "No bother," I said. "I'll ask the bird myself."

Once outside, I whistled for the crow, who came almost immediately, landing on the railing of the porch. I stroked her head with a finger and asked it softly. "Do you know the land beyond the Archway?" The crow kicked out her foot in reply. I took a letter from my pocket and tied it tightly around the bird's spindly leg. "Don't rush."

Once the bird faded from view, I turned in the direction of Stormwall.

We all want to save the world at some point in our lives, I thought. *It takes a brave person to think they can, but an even braver one to realize they can't. But just saving one person can make all the difference. One life.*

I could sway the cosmos and move even the stars.

I wanted so badly to do right, but I knew uncertainty and fear would only drive me from my goals. Thoughts of Fray came in waves, and tonight I was drowning. I missed him like crazy, but this was not about him. I hoped he would understand. I hoped he'd forgive me.

CHAPTER FORTY-THREE

The city smelled of death.

Soldiers drifted all around like packs of wolves, confident in their ability to scare off most anyone who came near. I knew without even having to look at the insignia on their armor that they were Peek Island soldiers, while the ones with the timid walk were my father's men. They all bore the silver scaled fish on their breast. *Dal Paratheon really did take over*, I thought. *Down to the very last detail.*

I swallowed the great lump rising in my throat.

I turned toward the main square at the exact location where I'd saved Fray from death. The stage was still there and looked to have been used recently. The rain had done a good job of washing the evidence away for the most part, but the scent of blood was still strong.

A flash of crimson in front of my eyes. Gods, what happened here?

A voice called out, but not to me. I drew away anyhow, slithering in the shadows between two buildings. I pressed myself against the stone, taking breaths in deep gulps.

Be brave, I reminded myself. *And stay composed.* One day I would walk without fear. Until that day, I needed to stay strong.

I counted to three and stepped out from between the buildings. I hunched over, concealing my face within my hood, willing myself to become as invisible as any other shadow in the night seeking shelter from the rain.

I crossed the streets and walked on toward the Barge, eliciting not a glance from townsfolk or soldiers alike. Every now and then, I'd see someone I recognized, and I'd quicken my step. That was before I saw my face plastered on a storefront door.

It was poorly drawn and stated I was wanted for treason. The reward was astronomical, something Dal would never pay, if I had to guess. He'd kill the person who turned me in just as fast as he'd kill me.

A wisp of a memory crawled into my mind, overlaid with the faces of those long dead, and I quickly shook it away.

I hurried along, confident that each and every person sensed my presence. Ashe must have been bound in a dank prison cell by now, starved and beaten, the city likewise torn and hungry. The promise of a monetary reward would bring out the demons within. I was sure even the closest of my friends would turn me in.

Two steps into the dark, rain-sodden streets of the Barge, and I felt like I was two steps into hell.

The entrance was void of any soldiers. The smell of death was stronger here, as if it'd been where the bodies of executed prisoners were dropped. A shudder ran down my spine at the real possibility. Things had changed a lot. Even my father had never been this cruel.

When I approached Wargrave's Wears, I encountered the same mangy cat who always stood outside, only this time it darted away upon seeing me. *Must be scared of dogs*, I thought with a chuckle.

I knocked.

A light lit up from within, and seconds later the door inched open. "Visits at this hour are for the sneaky, if I knew better," a voice grumbled.

"You'd know better than anyone," I said, speaking loudly over the beating of the rain.

Wargrave creaked the door open enough for his face to fit through. "Remove your hood," he said. "I—"

He stopped and pulled the door open the rest of the way. He stepped over the threshold, one bony hand reaching to pull back my hood. I drew back, and he straightened, a grin spreading across his face.

"A lot has changed, Wargrave," I said. The door was open just enough for me to wedge my boot in it. I wouldn't put it past the shopkeeper to hand me over to Dal Paratheon. He did swindle me out of more jewelry than I cared to give. But obtaining the Voiceless cure had been worth it, and so was risking standing at his doorstep now. "The reward to help me may be worth less to you than it would be to turn me in."

The old man's eyes brightened for a moment, recalling the reward poster he'd clearly seen in the city at some point. I could practically see the gold coin dancing across his vision.

"And you risk soldiers coming into your shop," I added. I watched his grin fall. "Nobody wants that, do they?"

Wargrave raised his eyebrows. "So it seems." Sudden dismay slacked his face. "What have you done?"

"Not what I've done, but what you've done."

Wargrave's lips twisted in a forced smile full of teeth, jagged like broken rocks. He inched back as if allowing me to enter, but before I took a step, he swung out a hand, pushing the door in my face. I stopped it before it could close, palm flat against the wood, and summoned only a fraction of my strength to push back. The door flew open, breaking off one of the hinges.

I stepped inside.

The place was just as it had been before. Cluttered and smelling of rot that may had been more from the old man than the shop itself. I approached the counter where I'd once spilled out my mother's jewelry to pay for the sabrecat tooth. It seemed so long ago. Like an entire lifetime had passed since then.

Wargrave laughed, an attempt to hide the sudden fear. "What are you going to do to me?"

I gifted him a smile before replacing the door, crooked, but still good. I then surveyed the shop and its usual ware of useless junk.

"I wish to make a deal," I said, facing the shop owner. Water dripped from the edges of my cloak and puddled at my feet.

Wargrave made one last attempt at courage. "I don't do dealings—"

I held up my hand and removed my hood. "Don't do dealings with shadows. I know."

I waited for him to take in my face that had since healed of the knife wounds. I turned to the candle on the front counter. With a blink of my eyes, I turned its flickering flame to a sudden burst that scorched the ceiling in a splash of black.

"I know," I continued, allowing the flame to dissolve. "But I am no shadow."

ABOUT THE AUTHOR

Celia Mcmahon is a devourer of books and coffee. If she's not busy buying more books than she can read or discovering new ways of being tired, you can find her scouring the world army-wife style for book ideas.